Praise for Gre

MW01168544

An eye for detail and a knack for story-telling distinguish this unflinching novel of rural America.

— *PUBLISHERS WEEKLY*

East of Denver is painstakingly funny—the novel offers a deep, dark look into the real life issues that make society uncomfortable.

— *THE WEEKENDER*

A breezily readable summer novel that not only entertains but also surprises. It explores the dynamics of family relationships without ever stooping to sentimentality, and it's one of this summer's most pleasant surprises.

— *AUSTIN AMERICAN-STATESMAN*

There is pathos. Sadness. Dark glimmers of hope. The entire book reveals this balance and shift and makes it absolutely worthwhile.

— *CURLED UP WITH A GOOD BOOK*

This is writing on a par with that of top-flight black-comic novelists like Sam Lipsyte and Jess Walter, and it deserves to be read.

— LEV GROSSMAN, AUTHOR OF THE *MAGICIANS TRILOGY*

A witty, snarky, and thoroughly enjoyable read.

— *Portland Book Review*

What makes [East of Denver] special, and especially powerful, is that Hill, like his damaged characters, has a real talent for fucking everything up.

— *Tropmag*

An agreeable, off beat debut novel with an ending as quirkily satisfying as the rest of the book.

— *Kirkus*

Vol 2: The Lonesome Trials of Johnny Riles

A stunning read.

— *The Writing Bug*

Impressively well written from beginning to end.

— *Midwest Book Review*

The Lonesome Trials of Johnny Riles is a damn fine country noir.

— *Booklist*

The Lonesome Trials of Johnny Riles is a wild, weird, fun ride.

— *Yuma Pioneer*

An unapologetic triumph of contemporary Rural American Realism.

— ZACH BODDICKER, AUTHOR OF *THE ESSENTIAL CARL MAHOGANY*

VOL 3: ZEBRA SKIN SHIRT

A funhouse-mirror holograph of a novel.

— JOHN VERNON, AUTHOR OF *LUCKY BILLY*

Zebra Skin Shirt is a cosmic ordeal, Greg Hill's third excellent novel in a row, and a trip well worth taking.

— MIKE MOLNAR, *MASTER OF GUITAR AND PHILOSOPHY*

Three cheers for the unforgettable former amateur basketball referee, Narwhal W. Slotterfield, and his creator, the wildly imaginative Gregory Hill.

— MIKE KEEFE, POLITICAL CARTOONIST

An excellent novel from an author that clearly understands the stupidity, chaos and madness of existence, and isn't afraid to embrace it all and put it on the page.

— *SUSPECT PRESS*

SISTER
LIBERTY

GREGORY HILL
DAISY DOG PRESS

The characters in this novel are imaginary.

Published in 2022 by Daisy Dog Press, a member of the Sparky the Dog Entertainment Empire

Designed by Gregory Hill

ISBN (print edition): 979-8-218-08169-0

ISBN (e-book edition): 979-8-218-08170-6

vtff: ts

mdr: slb 301-167

Books by Gregory Hill

SISTER LIBERTY

Stables Family Chronicles: Vol I

EAST OF DENVER

Strattford County: Vol I

COLORADO BOOK AWARD FOR LITERARY FICTION

THE LONESOME TRIALS OF JOHNNY RILES

Strattford County Series: Vol II

ZEBRA SKIN SHIRT

Strattford County Series: Vol III

AMERICAN FICTION AWARD FOR LITERARY FICTION

FINALIST: FORWARD INDIE AWARDS

FINALIST: NATIONAL INDIE EXCELLENCE AWARDS

For my sister Rebecca

I took my first breath in the year of 1942, during the final song of a performance by the Stables Family Band at the Bijou Theatre in Cumber, Wisconsin. It was August as hell and my mother was playing fiddle.

In anticipation of my birth, Mother had worn my grandmother's wedding dress to the show that night.

Long ago, Grandmother had sewn the dress for her own wedding. She'd been pregnant at the time and, being of an era that frowned upon pre-nuptial fornication, she'd included in the garment's design numerous folds and frills and fluffy things that drew attention away from the bulging evidence of her wickedness.

Grandmother's bulging wickedness would eventually emerge as my mother, who would eventually attain several wicked bulges of her own, one of which would eventually turn into me: Caution Irrational Stables.

As of the night of my birth, the dress's white cotton had aged into the color of sunstained newsprint, and it was perforated with moth bites. Nevertheless, it looked great on Mother. Everything always looked great on Mother, pregnant or otherwise. Even in her mid-thirties, she had remained a dish, thanks to her lifelong loves of performance, moonshine, amphetamines, and rigorous fucking.

My first memory, planted that firefly and frogsong evening, is of my babyhead colliding with the Bijou's age-warped stage. The impact jiggered my soft body all the way to the soles of my wrinkled little feet.

My universe at this juncture consisted of a cotton-dress sky, a hardwood floor, and Mother's two stocky legs. But this universe was rapidly expanding, and now, from the other side of Mother's dress, came the agitation of an audience, greedy and entitled.

Vibratories of hundreds of boots stomping in merciless unison shook the wavered floorboards below me. My untouched fingers spasmed into involuntary fists.

In the dim light afforded by my birthtent, my untrained eyes followed my mother's bare foot as it lifted its blood-speckled toes and dropped them floorward, and then did so twice more. My abode fell into complete darkness. The stage curtains had closed.

Of some concern was my inability to inhale. My nostrils had become clogged with a quantity of mucous far beyond the pneumatic power of my tiny lungs. I redirected my respiration to my mouth. This endeavor should have liberated my breath, but it did not.

Bereft of air, I had by now settled into the lackluster mouth-stretching yawns of a fish tossed to the bottom of a rowboat. I found myself becoming disillusioned.

While the audience's slap-claps and stomp-bomps walloped the pink folds of my wet ears, Mother's toes massaged my chest with apologetic squeezes. My teeny diaphragm jerked up and down noncommittally. My fingers groped for my throat. There they encountered a tightly coiled rope of flesh. Oh, to be murdered by the very umbilicus that had heretofore sustained me. My first brush with irony.

Unseen by me in the midst of this unseen struggle, the curtains spread open. As was the tradition, the band approached the lip of the stage to perform one final song. This intimate moment was the conclusion of any Stables Family performance, barring those that were cut short by a slow-motion drunken slugfest between members of the band and/or the audience.

Mother followed the rest of the group to the front of the stage, dragging me along the riveted planks by my own umbilical cord. The tugging spun my body once, twice, until the cord unwound from my throat like the last inches of thread spinning off the spool. Mother's practiced hand darted under the garish dress and tucked the cord's slack into the elastic of her underdrawers, all without losing her stride or betraying the miracle that was bouncing along between her feet.

The band had by now assembled in a line, their eyebrows dripping sweat and their limbs poised to begin the encoric tune.

My first contribution to the Stables Family band was a single squawk in the midst of that brief moment of silence.

Squawk, I did, and there proceeded a longer-than-brief moment while band and audience alike attempted to reconcile what they'd just heard with the fact that there were no geese in the auditorium.

Mother, being as she was both a natural ham and unnaturally stoic, flapped her bow-arm up and down and replicated upon her fiddle, as best she could, the squawk of my first exhalation.

The noise thus explained, the recently-pregnant silence was replaced with hooting and hollering and general glee.

On that August evening of 1942, as I took my first unencumbered gulps of air, as I lay dripping upon a wooden floor under my grandmother's hoop dress, the Stables Family Band performed what is considered one of their finer versions of one of their lesser songs, *A Light in Yonder Glade*.

The show that night was being broadcast across thirty-eight states from the mighty needle of WOZI's 50,000 watt AM transmitter just up the hill. It is said that the slender, two-hundred-foot iron tower lured fireflies with its weird, crackling noises. The fireflies would spiral around this electromagnetic god until they became so saturated with ionic madness that they would splatter in small static explosions. It is further said that the accumulation of bug guts had rendered the tower luminescent, a glowing, magical wand, visible from great distances.

Those who listened to the broadcast that night will swear they heard something magical in that final song. Maybe. Or maybe it was just bug guts.

The encore concluded, the curtains closed, and the audience began mumbling its way outside.

In a deviation from standard protocol, Mother did not follow the rest of the band stage left. Rather, she veered thru a slit in the canvas backdrop, a green-grass-and-blue-sky scene that hung at the rear of the stage. There, in this dark place littered with ladders and ropes and the stuff of fizzled ideas, Mother eased herself to the dusty floor, lay her fiddle by her side, fished me out from under her dress, held my belly to her face, and, with her tobacco-stained teeth, severed my umbilical cord. I was glad to be rid of the thing, and gladder still to be held tightly against the breast of the brave woman who would be my only source of nutrition for the next dozen months.

It was my older sister, Lil' Annie Stables, who first noticed Mother's absence from the obligatory post-show meet 'n' greet with the winners of WOZI's Luckiest Fan Contest. Receiving no answer to her pleas of *Where's Mama?* Lil' Annie snuck back to the stage and followed the trail of blood-tinged amniotic fluid that led directly to Mother and me. When she found us, Lil' Annie squealed so loud that the meet 'n' greet was cut short and the rest of the band hastily relocated themselves to our back-stage maternal scene.

In certain circles, it's considered auspicious to be born during a live radio broadcast. The Stables Family Band was one of those circles. Surely this newborn would grow into a prodigy and then lead the band into the second half of the century.

All my aunts and uncles and siblings and cousins began debating which musical instrument would most suit their newest bandmate. It came down to a split between the trumpet or the accordion.

My name is Caution Irrational Stables. I am not special.

Was my *family band* special? We had a couple of non-hits in the Hit Parade in the 40's. We recorded harmonized promo spots for radio stations throughout the Midwest and the South. "Howdy!

We're the Stables Family Band. *Doink, doink!* You're listening to WHIF!"

In spite of our achievements, I'm confident that you've never heard of us. I may or may not address this paradox in the coming pages. For now, let me state clearly, the Stables Family Band was not special, not in any historical sense. Not in any sense at all.

Was my *family* special? We came to America from across a great ocean. And your family didn't? Of course they did. Unless they didn't. But they probably did. My family owns piles of scrapbooks stacked with tintypes, postcards, and unorganized, redundant photos. And your family doesn't? Of course they do.

You and I are exactly the same, but for one thing. I was born onstage.

NOTE OF CONTEXTUALIZATION FROM GHOSTWRITER, GREGORY HILL
(Included in direct violation of contractual stipulation)

Several years ago, I received in the mail a letter from Janet Pastorville, CEO and sole employee of the Showboat Express Talent Agency, based in Nashville, Tennessee. In shaky handwriting, she asked in plain terms if I'd be interested in guiding her client Caution Stables thru the thickets of his memoirs. Ms. Pastorville assured me that these memoirs would be "a true accounting of the passion, perseverance, and adventure behind The Stables Family Band." In the event that I had never heard of the Stables Family Band, Agent Pastorville assured me that "this is only because their story has never been told" and that "Mr. Stables' memoirs hold the key to unlocking a quintessentially American success story."

Further, Agent Pastorville allowed that Mr. Stables had requested me, not because of my experience as a spectacularly unfamous author of three middling novels, but because, several years earlier, I'd been invited to ghostwrite the memoirs of a dying man who'd spent forty years in prison for petty crimes. That project did not make it past the first interview.

Caution Stables, I guess, had known the guy's wife, and she had told him that, during the sole hour I'd spent with her husband, I had been both non-confrontational and affordable. Being timid and cheap apparently ticked all the important boxes on Caution's must-have list, and so, in spite of the complete failure of my first gig as a ghostwriter, Mr. Stables had insisted that Agent Pastorville contact me immediately.

Of course I took the job.

It was on February 18, 2019, a cold and bitter day, that Caution Stables welcomed me into his home, a decrepit trailer in a ghost town called Last Chance, on Highway 36, upon the Serengeti prairie of eastern Colorado. "Last Chance" was clearly a reference to a bygone era, the titular *chance* having expired some time ago, along with the bulk of the town's inhabitants.

The town was a cluster of broken-windowed buildings huddled together at the bottom of a long, sloping dip in the highway's otherwise dead-flatness. It was as if the land had been flat when the buildings had been constructed, but then the earth had sunk and the entire town had slid down the sides of this pit to congregate at the low point. Birds chittered in cottonwood trees. The ground was littered with faded tin cans.

Inside Caution Stables' trailer house, winter flies buzzed upsidedown upon countertops. A pack of cigarettes was perched upon the arm of a cracked-pleather recliner. Scattered about the carpet were several coffee cups overflowing with cigarette ash.

Although the day was bitter cold, the sun was bright, and so Mr. Stables insisted we sit on the front porch. Stables, a thin, older man with a grizzled wattle and a stoop in one shoulder, led me out. He wore a bathrobe, tied around the waist by a leather belt. The tarnished belt buckle resembled a miniature 45-rpm record.

The front porch was an upsidedown stock tank whose unreinforced bottomtop sank and popped at the slightest motion. Upon the tank sat two black beanbags that exhaled white pellets from their seams as we shifted ourselves into comfort. There were no signs of any other inhabitants in any of the other broken-windowed buildings at this town nestled in the bottom of a dip in the road. Beyond the town's humble perimeter lay a world of rolling prairie dusted with a recent snow. Under the glare of an open sky, this snow was sublimating into refractory and otherwise invisible steam.

Mr. Stables lit a cigarette. A pair of extraordinarily loud motorcycles crested the hill at the east end of town and deafened past us on Highway 36 and disappeared over the hill at the west end of town.

Across the road, at the edge of shouting distance, a door

opened on a barn that looked as if it lilted according to the direction of the latest breeze. A woman dressed in denim coveralls emerged leading a full-grown tiger on a leash.

Mr. Stables said, "That's Mrs. Stables."

She waved at us as if she weren't casually taking a full-grown tiger for a walk. I waved back. She pointed the tiger away from us, instructed it to sit, and then unfastened its leash. She removed a Frisbee from her knit handbag and expertly flung it far, fast, and high away from us and toward the southern sun. The creature sprang, soaring over a barbed wire fence and bounding thru the grass and over the hill.

I said, "Where'd you get the cat?"

"She was on the side of the road."

"This road?" Highway 36 was a lesser cousin to Route 66. Two lanes, linking the Rocky Mountains to Ulrich Ohio, the clay capital of the world.

Caution said, "We're pretty sure she fell off a truck."

"Like a traveling circus truck?"

"Something more clandestine, I suspect."

I said, "It seems well-behaved, considering."

Mr. Stables continued, "There are organizations which are known to train tigers to do unspeakable things."

He offered me a sip from a two-liter bottle of Neon Green, a caffeinated soda whose logo was regularly featured on the hoods of racecars. I took a gulp and handed it back to him.

He said, "When I die, it is my wish that she shall eat my corpse."

I reached into my satchel and removed a notebook and a pen and a fantastically small electronic recording device. The interview began.

Caution Irrational Stables recited his story in the avant-garde fashion typical of the American Midwest. Never use a proper noun when a pronoun would make things more incomprehensible. Recite events out of order, provide no context, let the audience sort it out.

When interrupted by a clarifying question, he would pause his non-narrative just long enough to glare at me as if I were a complete ignoramus. Because, what kind of dumbshit can't deduce the antecedents in sentences like this marvel: "When he got there, they said that he'd have to bring the baby home, but then they changed their mind and she said they wouldn't take the shortcut."

Mr. Stables' unreliable narration was augmented by a stack of clippings and showbills and photos, and a half-dozen wooden boxes overflowing with sheet music and every imaginable format of recording media: 78-rpm records, homemade cassettes, reel-to-reel tapes, 45s, LPs, even some wax cylinders. He gave me permission to borrow, scan, transcribe, copy anything I wanted.

Thus began my second gig as a ghostwriter.

After 196 hours of interviews conducted upon that same south-facing porch, I hired an army of underpaid Filipinos to transcribe the whole mess. And then I re-transcribed it myself because it turns out underpaid Filipinos aren't necessary qualified to interpret the utterances of such a man as Caution Irrational Stables. After months of cross-checking, misery, depression, and a brief addiction to a substance I'd rather not publicize, I've discovered that I'm only marginally more suited to this task than the underpaid Filipinos.

I beg your patience. Although this tale concerns a family of musicians, this first volume of the *Stables Family Chronicles* contains very little musical commentary. I'm compelled to warn you: the words "Stables Family Band" will not appear again, not until the second volume, at earliest. In fact, the name *Stables* will appear only once more, as the events recounted herein take place while the family name was still *Lestables*, a rare and awkward French appellation that means "the tables."

Within the following pages, you'll find zero inspirational recording sessions, no messianic births (the account of Caution's on-stage birth does not qualify), and neither drug addiction nor miraculous recovery. I'm saving those bits for later.

It's often said that the man who knows he has a small anus does not swallow coconuts. As I continue to wrestle with this project, I'm beginning to suspect that, in answering Mr. Stable's call, I've swallowed the whole fucking deserted island.

Come with me now to a remote village in the south of France, in May of 1885, where we shall catch our first scent of Arthur Lestables, the last patriarch to *la famille Lestables*.

NOTE: This book includes a brief appendix to aid the reader in the pronunciation of some of the French names that he or she is about to encounter.

SISTER LIBERTY
Stables Family Chronicles, Volume 1

Part One

But if you would laugh when others laugh and weep when they weep then you must be prepared to die as they die and live as they live.

— Henry Miller *Tropic of Capricorn*

Chapter One

IN 1885, AT THE AGE OF FIFTY-THREE, ARTHUR PASCAL LESTABLES drowned his neighbor Henri Deplouc in a pond. The pond was fed by a clear, stony brook that descended from the mountains just to the north. To the south lay a clearing dotted with chestnut trees, vineyards, stone houses, thatch-roofed barns, stacks of hay, and napping cats.

The pond was well-lit—it was midday, early May—and it was scaled with bright algae. Into this pond did Arthur Lestables throw Henri Deplouc, who made a large splash followed by numerous bubbles followed by silence interrupted by the occasional *tweetle tweet* of a nearby family of swallows.

Arthur remained at the edge of the pond until Deplouc and his water-ballooned tunic sank below the surface. Then he rolled a cigarette and walked to the nearby village of Sanvisa, where he turned himself in to the constable.

Days later, after a brief trial, the Honorable Magistrate Eugène Fermenté sentenced Arthur to hang to death, as was the accepted fashion of dispatching murderers in the village of Sanvisa.

Arthur Lestables' final act would arrive on the drizzling afternoon of May 14th, 1885 while he was standing atop the shoulders of Junior Deplouc, the aggrieved son of the deceased Henri Deplouc.

Arthur Lestables was standing atop the shoulders of Junior Deplouc because, in an attempt to forestall her husband's death, Arthur's wife Annie Lestables had burned down the village gallows the week before. The act had earned her a two-month sentence in the Sanvisa jail, the first week of which she'd served in the same cell as her condemned husband, Arthur.

That week had been bittersweet, made less sweet by the fact that the doomed couple shared the jail's cell with a constant parade of the town's tipplers, gamblers, and depressed symbolist poets.

In the rare moments when one of their cellmates was not weeping, vomiting, reciting, or otherwise rendering it impossible to converse, the couple collaborated to compose the Final Statement of Arthur Lestables. Speaking in his clusterbomb of a voice, Arthur would pace the cell's hardpacked floor while Annie tidied his grammar and rendered sensible the overall rhetorical shape of what would be his last words. These were the happiest moments of a marriage that had endured twelve years of famine, had produced one child, and which was very nearly at its end.

Shortly before noon on the day of Arthur's execution, a husky bailiff swung open the cell door. With breath that suggested a fondness for apple wine, and in a voice that teetered between apology and bravado, he said, "Monsieur Lestables, it's time."

"Let us not dally," said Arthur, unaccountably cheerful. He smiled toward Annie. "How do I look?"

With maternal focus, Annie licked her fingers and flattened a cowlick that rose out of Arthur's coif. Hands on his shoulders, she held him at arm's length and tilted her head.

Reconsidering, she returned his hair into its earlier state, a state that befitted this man who had always looked as if he'd just awoken from a nap in the wilderness.

"There," she said. "Perfect."

She reached for her hat, which hung from a wooden post on the wall.

The bailiff said, "You'll stay here, Madame. Per local statues, 'Anyone who attempts or succeeds at the desecration of the village gallows shall be forever banned from attending public executions.'"

"Yes, but—"

"It's okay darling," said Arthur.

In a low voice, the bailiff said, "Madame, Monsieur, between you and me, nobody will mourn the loss of the scoundrel Henri Deplouc. But Arthur has committed a crime, and so justice shall prevail. Come now, Arthur."

The bailiff led the condemned away.

Annie retreated to the wooden stool in the corner of the cell. There she remained, idly caressing the thin strands of Arthur's hair that had become stuck to her fingers.

*   *   *   *

The entire county had gathered in the muddy field facing the charred remains of the gallows. These gallows, built of unnecessarily massive timbers, had been the tallest structure in the village, a designation that, thanks to Annie's arson, had reverted back to the steeple atop the village chapel.

Directly behind the charred remains of the gallows stood a chestnut tree with a symmetrical, bellshaped canopy whose height far exceeded that of any man-made structure within two hundred miles. The tree was sufficiently ancient to have been used many hundreds of years prior as a meeting-place for sexually curious Roman adolescents.

Just beyond the tree lay the entrance to the village cemetery, seven hectares decorated with a variety of tombstones, crypts, wooden crosses, and one freshly dug grave.

Dangling from a branch that extended horizontally from the great tree's trunk was a rope that ended in a noose, or, as the locals called it, *la cravate infidèle*. Below the noose was a stepladder. The bailiff led Arthur to the foot of this ladder.

Here, the widow of Henri Deplouc stepped from the crowd. A tall woman with poor posture, Euphémie Deplouc declared, "I wish to exercise my right to bind the wrists of the man who drowned my husband."

The bailiff nodded his consent and Euphémie uncoiled a length of string and began wrapping it around Arthur's wrists behind his back. Arthur could not see her, but he knew that three of Euphémie's fingers were askew, having been snapped by her husband only hours before Arthur had chucked him into the pond. Euphémie grunted as she knotted the string. Arthur winced sympathetically.

Finished, the widow whispered, "There is a place for you, Arthur, always." She retreated into the crowd.

The bailiff nodded to Arthur, who expertly ascended the ladder and balanced himself neatly upon the uppermost rung. He leaned forward, dipped his head, and slipped it into the dangling noose. Rain dripped from the chestnut tree's leaves, droplets spiraled their way down the length of the rope and darkened Arthur's tunic.

Another figure emerged from the crowd, Junior Deplouc, the adolescent son of the deceased. Junior stood straight upon the muddy ground directly before the stepladder, his back to Arthur.

Arthur carefully stepped off the ladder and onto the wet shoulders of this young man who had accepted his hereditary right to fulfill the role traditionally reserved for a horse, as was the regional custom when a proper gallows was not available.

Thus did the attending audience witness the scrawny adolescent shit Junior Deplouc quivering under the hulking weight of Arthur Lestables. Arthur was doing a remarkable job of maintaining his balance considering his hands were tied behind his back and a noose was dangling around his neck.

The town vicar, clad in a woolen robe and, in spite of the gloomy weather, sweating like a glass of lemonade, dragged the stepladder thru the mud so it now faced the uncertain totem formed by Junior and Arthur.

The vicar climbed the ladder, leaned forward, and offered Arthur the customary final cigarette, which was accepted by eager lips. Before the vicar could ignite the cigarette, a drop of rain slid from the tip of Arthur's nose and landed upon the rolling paper. The water soaked thru and the cigarette broke in half, spilling tobacco into Arthur's beard.

The vicar plunged his hands into his robe and skillfully rolled another cigarette. Upon producing it, he covered it with one hand so as to keep it dry and held it out to Arthur's side-turned mouth. Here, the vicar ran out of hands, for, even with the cigarette secured in Arthur's mouth, the vicar needed one hand to block the rain, one hand to hold the matchbox, and yet another hand to strike the match. Meanwhile, Junior Deplouc's bare feet had begun to sink into the mud.

Sensing the precarious nature of the situation, the Honorable Magistrate Eugène Fermenté hustled forward, climbed the now-precarious ladder to stand just below the vicar, and withdrew a match from his own robe.

In this intimate formation, the vicar's left hand shielded Arthur's cigarette and his right hand shielded the Honorable Magistrate Fermenté's match. After several attempts, the Magistrate successfully ignited a flame and held it to the tip of the cigarette.

Arthur took one deep drag and then spat the cigarette toward the earth, shouting, "I beseech you and your murderous sticks of fire!"

The spitting of the cigarette had been pre-planned, a part of the performance as rehearsed in the jail with Annie. The performance, even in spite of the rain, was going swimmingly. It would

have continued to go swimmingly had a gust of wind not redirected the falling cigarette's trajectory in such a way that it curved
back toward the young man upon whose straining shoulders
Arthur was perched.

Junior shifted his hips in an attempt to dodge the incoming
cigarette, which dropped neatly thru the collar of his shirt where
it came to a smoldering rest in his navel. He performed several
quick hops while batting at his belly. For a moment, and only a
moment, Arthur rode the shoulders of the hot-bellied youth.

Meanwhile, the ladder began to tilt into the mud and so the
Honorable Magistrate dove off and landed in a splat. This sent the
ladder to tip over altogether, sending the vicar mudbound as well.

Junior, in a voice that was at once aggrieved and agonized,
shouted, "Accursed fuckmeister!" and lurched out from under the
boots of the man whose life he had been temporarily preserving.

As the vicar and the Honorable Magistrate pressed themselves
upward, Junior hastened to pluck the cigarette from his smoldering belly button and Arthur commenced to strangling.

He would have died there and then but for the broken fingers
of Henri Deplouc's widow Euphémie. As has been mentioned, it
was Henri who had crushed those fingers. Immediately before
Arthur had pushed him into the pond, Henri had claimed the
injuries had occurred while he was demonstrating to Euphémie
how to churn butter. As with most things Henri Deplouc has said
during his life, this had been a lie.

In any case, Euphémie had been unable to cinch the string
securely with her damaged fingers. And so, as Arthur dangled on
the noose with his legs flailing, he was able to liberate his hands
from their bondage and, using his legendary upper body strength,
reach to the rope above his head and haul himself upward until
the noose slacked against his neck. Here, with a face as red as a
pustule, Arthur gasped several times and twisted hypnotic circles
on the wet, creaking rope.

The townsfolk accepted his stare in mute idiocy, vaguely
aware of the injustice that was playing out before their rheumy

eyes. Everyone knew Henri Deplouc had been a lousy *salaud*, but everyone—except Arthur Lestables—had been entirely uninspired to do a goddamned thing about it.

Junior, with his shirt rolled up over his scrawny, smoldering gut, held the remains of Arthur's discarded cigarette between two fingers.

The Honorable Magistrate Eugène Fermenté had endured quite enough of this horseplay. "Junior," he said, "Get yourself back underneath that son of an ox or I'll see that you hang with him." In a slightly less contemptuous tone, he added, "If this execution is not conducted with the grace it deserves, these people"—he gestured to the assembled crowd—"will be mightily dissatisfied."

As Junior took a reluctant step toward the dangling feet, Arthur said, hoarsely, "This guppy will not serve as my final toehold on this world." He kicked Junior in the ear, sending the youth to splat upon the mud and sending Arthur spinning round and round.

Compelled now to prove his manhood, as was the custom in those parts after one had been publicly humiliated, Junior pushed himself upright, shook the water out of his lengthy hair, and took a swing at one of Arthur's spinning ankles. He missed. But trying is half the battle, and having won that half, Junior retreated safely out of kicking range, where he raised his chin and feigned dignity.

The townsfolk had begun to mutter amongst themselves.

Here, Arthur began to hand-over-hand his way up the rope until he was grasping a stubby branch that grew out of the great limb above. He dangled this way for several moments, the branch bending perilously. His eyes darted here and there as he considered his future.

The Honorable Magistrate Eugène Fermenté reached into his mudded robe and withdrew a revolver. He aimed it at the condemned man's torso.

Arthur's meticulous plan had been going haywire ever since the cigarette had blown down Junior's shirt. Nevertheless, he remained alive, and, with the noose slackened, he had a voice.

Dangling from the limb of the ancient chestnut tree, he looked into the face of every person in attendance, twisting himself left and right. None held his gaze except the Honorable Magistrate Eugène Fermenté, who pulled back the hammer on his revolver and offered forth, "This execution shall conclude with no further nincompoopery. Arthur Lestables, for the drowning murder of Henri Deplouc Senior, and, furthermore, for being a troublesome pain in the groin at this very moment, you shall die by whatever goddamned means is most convenient to me. But first, as a man of honor, I recognize your right to a final proclamation. I suggest you curtail your proclivity for longwindedness. The annual Festival of Strawberries shall commence in one hour and nobody here wants to miss the crowning of this year's Strawberry Queen." He gestured to the onlookers. "These folks came here to see a man die, not to see him climbing ropes like some sort of a nitwit."

The townsfolk murmured their approval. Indeed, the opening ceremony of the Strawberry Festival was a thing not to be missed.

Arthur, whose face was returning to its normal shade of sun-battered beige, declared, wheezily, "Fellow townsfolk, remember and reflect upon these words, though they represent a truth beyond the capacity of your tiny minds."

The Magistrate said, "Say the damned words, Arthur."

Arthur nodded gravely. "Do any of you understand human goodness?"

The Magistrate said, "I'll have no rhetorical questions out of you, Lestables."

Arthur continued. "Human goodness is a concept for which I, today, will die gladly. I, Arthur Pascal Lestables, represent only the tip of the eagle's beak in the army of positive progression. I assure you that the wisdom engendered by scientific progress will bring a day—not distant, but soon—whenupon your faulty morals and misguided religions will be replaced by decency and well-measured wisdom. As my mentor, Monsieur Isidore Marie Auguste François Xavier Comte, was wont to say, '*Science, d'où prévoyance; prévoyance, d'où action.*' As I say, you can stop me, but you cannot erase me. Nor can you hinder the inevitable mechanisms that will render your laws and superstitions into relics of a shameful and savage past."

The audience was making no sense of this.

"Penultimately, to my loving wife, who cannot hear me because she languishes in a cell, I say, love is the principle, order is the foundation, and progress is the goal. Ever onward!"

The Magistrate removed a fob watch from his pocket. "Wrap it up."

With his neck tendons taught as cello strings, Arthur Lestables bellowed, "Henri Deplouc was a reprehensible creature. Cruel to his wife, a devil to his livestock, and a stain upon the very concept of table manners. We all know this, and yet only I, Arthur Lestables, was willing to intervene. I bear no ill will. But I ask that you remember, honorable townsfolk, 'twas not I that killed the deceased. 'Twas his inability to swim."

This elicited much laughter.

Satisfied that he'd landed his punch line, Arthur Lestables released his hands from the branch. His fall was arrested by the noose, which snapped his neck and clamped his teeth against his tongue, the tip of which landed with a moist *thwap* upon the muddy ground at the feet of Junior Deplouc.

Arthur Pascal Lestables swung for several minutes, chest pumping, arms twitching, legs dancing a frantic jig accompanied stage left by the customary accordionist. This continued in a diminishing fashion for a full quarter of an hour, until Arthur arched backward grotesquely so his heels touched the back of his head. After a moment, the muscles released and his body hung limp, urine mingling with the rain that ran from his pantlegs. By this point, the townsfolk had grown weary, and, led by the sweating, soiled vicar, had begun the uphill trek to the village square for the coronation of the Strawberry Queen.

The Magistrate and Junior Deplouc were the second- and third-to-last people ever to see Arthur Lestables' body.

Junior wiped his hands on the front of his trousers and said, "I'd say his murdersome days are concluded."

The Magistrate put his arm on Junior's shoulder. "Son, if justice wasn't blind when you woke up this morning, it surely is now, for that was a damned ugly spectacle." He slid his pistol back into his robe. "Come along. I must attend to the judging of preserves."

The very last person to see Arthur Lestables was his eleven-year-old son, Auguste, who earlier that year had taken employment as the village gravedigger.

And so it was that young Auguste Lestables had the privilege of cutting down his father's corpse, dragging it a hundred yards thru the cemetery to the Lestables family plot, and rolling him into the muddy hole he'd dug that morning for that very purpose.

It had been a miserable, sweltering, shitty rainy day, and so it would remain.

Chapter Two

AUGUSTE PRESSED HIS SPADE INTO THE DRENCHED EARTH AND scooped a dripping viscera of mudlump. He attempted to heave the mass into his father's grave, but the mud stuck to the blade, and it made the spade heavy and so he tossed it aside. He settled upon his knees and, with two hands and numerous sighs, he started shoving the less-than-firmament over the grave's edge.

The sky had by now darkened, casting the grave into opaque shadow. This shadow would be one of the day's few mercies upon the boy; it obscured the mud as it dripped chocolate-like onto his father's swollen face. The shadow did not muffle the splattering.

Little Auguste, the miniature golem filling the hole where his father would decay.

The grave would have no stone. The Lestables family plot was in the budget section of the cemetery, where a body's only monument was the sprinkling of yellow mustard flowers that, next spring, would grow from the soil disturbed by the gravedigger's shovel.

When Auguste had filled the grave, he reclined upon the mound of his work. He stretched himself long, hands crossed on his chest, and watched the rain strike his eyeballs.

Arthur Lestables had never been much for putting food on the table—the slender frames of both Auguste and his mother attested to that. But Arthur did excel at expounding on the subject of positivistic philosophy. Throughout his life, twice a day, breakfast and bedtime, Auguste had been forced to endure the latest revisions to Arthur's work-in-perpetual-progress, *The Theory of Human Development: Past and Future: Complete With Amendments, Tangents, Redundancies, Post Scripta, and Citations, as Buttressed by— and Based Upon—Plutidinous and Heretofore Unpublicized Observations of the Sage Philosopher, Monsieur Isidore Marie Auguste François Xavier Comte, Son of Montpellier, Resident of Paris, as Witnessed Firsthand by The Humble Author Arthur Lestables of Sanvisa.*

"Reason above all things, boy."

Cold mush pushed thru the threads of Auguste's handed-down linen shirt. Tiny bugs fled under his collar to escape the rain. A beetle the size of a sesame seed climbed over his sternum and perched upon one of the tendons of his neck. It was struck by a raindrop, which encapsulated it and then slid down Auguste's throat to mingle with the mud.

Arthur Lestables had been a harmless, thick-headed man who, although he'd had no formal education, desired nothing more than to be a celebrated intellectual. To achieve this, he had engaged in laborious activities as infrequently as possible. He preferred, rather, to strike a thoughtful pose under a shade tree and await the sort of inspirational lightning that he believed was the foundation of genius.

His auto-didactical postures had eventually earned him a

degree of respect from his fellow villagers; Sanvisa had never produced a celebrated intellectual, and so the inhabitants were curious to see how it might be accomplished, and so they had tolerated Arthur's muddle-headed passions.

Auguste fell asleep atop his father's grave in this sweatshop of the dead.

Chapter Three

By the time Auguste quivered awake, the rain had slowed to a drizzle. The evening was now a gloom-clouded sky and humming frogs. To the south, the Strawberry Festival seeped afterhours glimmers of laughter and wheezing accordions.

Auguste pressed himself upward and used the edges of his hands to squeegee mud from his britches. With his shovel as a walking stick, he strode toward the cemetery's blackironed exit, passing countless vaults, crypts, mausolea, and haphazardly erected stones along the way. He hadn't brought a lantern, and now the night was complete and empty. The rain recommenced, followed shortly by the distant groans of disappointed Strawberry Festival-goers.

Auguste slowed his walk as he came to an ancient collection of primitive mausolea. Shaped of thick igneous plates, they resembled pup tents constructed in stone, nine feet tall at the peak, each with a triangular wooden door. Crosses and names carved, flowers and notes tucked into the seams between the stones.

At one of these structures, Auguste stopped. The cracks in its masonry leaked flickering light. A candle was burning within. He leaned his shovel against the outer wall, then pulled open the wooden door and entered. This was the resting place of Henri Deplouc, whom Auguste's father had thrown into a pond.

Auguste had dragged Deplouc's body to this place and installed it in the marble sarcophagus within. The sarcophagus, roughly waist-high, contained a historical assortment of Deplouc corpses, each of them wrapped in cheesecloth and lain softly upon those who had come before.

As long as there was a sufficient interval between new additions, decay would reduce the volume of the ancestral Deploucs such that there was always room for another. In this case, the interval had not been sufficient; the Deplouc family had suffered multiple tragedies in recent years, and so, before he could place Henri Deplouc into the box, Auguste had had to first smash flat the stack of corpses with a lead-headed hammer invented by some earlier gravedigger for just that purpose.

Auguste warmed his hands over the candle that was burning atop the sarcophagus' lid. So typical of the Deplouc family, wasting money on unattended candles. Auguste held the thick column of beeswax before himself, tipping it sideways so the flame melted the upper rim and dripped wax upon his hand.

From the outside came the careless barking of couples drunk on strawberry wine. Cemeteries attract lovers. One pair of voices grew louder, soppy footsteps grew closer. And then the door to the mausoleum began to swing open. Quickly, Auguste returned the candle to where he'd found it and scurried behind the sarcophagus.

The couple entered, whispering and giggling. Auguste recognized their voices. The male was Junior Deplouc. The girl, Fanny Potiron, was a *belle demoiselle*, aged sixteen-years. She had once made eye contact with Auguste as he and his father had driven their wagon past her family farm.

Drunk and virile, Junior slurred, "You saw the dog die. Now watch the puppy play."

Fanny, imperiously, "Bow to your queen."

"Bow to your king."

"You promised a cigarette."

"And I will give you a cigar."

Haughty unbuttoning. The sound of exposure.

"Well?" said Junior, seeking an opinion.

"You're only fourteen. It still has time to grow."

"You've seen others, have you?"

"Seen...and experienced."

Turning heel, "Is this *experience* how you earned your crown, Strawberry Queen?"

"I prefer to think that it were my crocheting skills what put me over the top. Do you have a cigarette or not?"

"Would you like to see a dead man?"

"I've no desire to watch worms wriggle in meat."

Striking of a match. "This is my father's meat you speak of."

"Seriously?" The hem of a dress rotating. Fanny's finger sliding over letters carved into the lid. "Put your cock away, Junior. In front of your father's tomb. Have some couth."

Junior leered, "I will gladly put it away...inside your lady-pocket."

The Strawberry Queen took this as her cue to exit.

"Wench!" cried Junior. He lurched after her out of the tomb. From the outside, shouts, slaps, *oof!* Then silence, but for rain.

The Strawberry Queen was a half-foot taller than Junior and, having handled swine for her entire life, perfectly capable of breaking him in two. Auguste did not worry on her behalf. He edged out from his hiding spot and crept outside.

On the ground lit by the blurred glow of the moon thru a low-hanging nimbus cloud, sat Junior Deplouc in celibate defeat. The splattering rain had wetted his hair against a fresh lump on his forehead—presumably as rendered by the shovel which was now impaled into the ground between his splayed legs. The slender boy might have been beautiful were it not for his bloodied nose, or his lips which writhed as if they were trying to tear their own teeth off.

No sign of Fanny.

Junior was not pleased to see the son of his father's murderer emerge from the same tomb in which he, Junior, had recently exposed his penis to the *salope* Strawberry Queen. Eager for revenge, and perfectly happy to exact it from the nearest possible victim, Junior sprang from the ground and tackled Auguste, sending them both to topple backward into the tomb.

With loathsome hate in his puckered eyes, Junior straddled Auguste's thin frame. He gathered an entire life of cruelty, self-loathing, and violence into his fist and punched downward with the intention of breaking the smaller boy's jaw.

The fist glanced off Auguste's forehead and cracked against the stone floor. As Auguste squirmed beneath, Junior lifted his hand and worked his fingers as if squeezing an invisible ball. He couldn't get his middle finger to close against the palm. Blood dripped from a split knuckle.

"You broke my hand."

Auguste, recalling his father's last words, couldn't help himself. "'Twas not *I* that broke your hand. 'Twas *your* inability to aim."

Auguste slid out from under Junior and attempted to flee the vault. Junior caught him by the hair, spun him around and landed a gut punch with his injured hand.

Auguste fell to the floor clutching his belly. Junior spat an aerosolized mist of saliva, bile, and strawberry wine toward his floorbound opponent who was gulping teaspoons of air. With evil mischief, Junior leaned a shoulder against the lid to the sarcophagus. The lid slid partially open, sufficient to release into the darkened room the full bouquet of Henri Deplouc's decomposition.

Junior pushed the lid with his unbroken hand and managed to spin it so it teetered on the lip of the sarcophagus. From there, he needed only to nudge the overhanging portion of the lid until it slid with a millstone grind to collide with the floor. There was a dull explosive thud as the lid cracked in half and sent a plume of dust into the already noxious air. Junior sneezed violently, then he leaned into the sarcophagus to stare longingly at the remains of his father. He reached his fingers toward the bloated face.

Auguste was familiar with Junior's capacity for semi-crazed behavior; he'd seen him dismantle snapping turtles by prying their shells apart, seen him tie other children by their ankles and drag them thru nettles.

As Junior stroked the hair of his putrescent father, Auguste arrived at two simultaneous revelations. First, that he had no desire to reenact with Junior the conflict that had occurred between their fathers. Second, that Junior intended to force Auguste into the sarcophagus, replace the halves of the broken lid, and leave him to sort things out on his own.

Junior shook off some hair that had become stuck to his fingers and turned to Auguste.

Auguste attempted a reconciliatory smile.

Junior responded by hissing like a consumptive goat. "I will not be no more humiliated." As he started toward Auguste, the younger boy drew himself to his hands and knees and scrambled thru the doorway into the rain-fresh air of the cemetery.

Junior followed immediately, only to be broadsided square on the nose with the flat of the gravedigger's shovel. As he fell backward into the vault, Auguste cast the shovel aside and slammed shut the wooden door and closed the clasp.

Chapter Four

Dawn had set its crimson glow to the shallow-clouded eastern sky. Steam and smoke rose from chimneys. In the woods that bordered the path, finches skipped and diddled, spiders reknitted rain-ripped webs, and snails sapped water that dripped from the leaves of saturated trees.

Auguste was nearly to home. His trousers were heavy with drizzle, his young eyes pink with exhaustion. His mother was in jail, his father under a ton of mud. And Junior's cries would soon be attracting the attention of the cemetery's caretaker who would soon be arriving for another day of sucking on his pipe and scavenging valuables from bony fingers.

Auguste entered the garden of the humble *maison Lestables* and nodded politely to the cock that had taken its customary morning perch atop the thatched roof. The boy splashed his face from the horse trough and entered the house. Inside, he lit a fire and lay before it and he slept while steam rose from his clothes.

He awoke and listened at the door. Hooves sucking mud, a clattering of tack. A voice coaxing the horse to a stop.

He cracked the door to see a horse-and-wagon bearing a

woman, drenched. She raised a hand, wiggled her thumb and forefinger as a hello. The other fingers were bandaged together by a strip of fabric.

This was Euphémie, the widow of Henri Deplouc and mother to Junior Deplouc, seated atop her deceased husband's hay wagon.

Euphémie had grown up taller than any of the boys her age and had remained taller than most of the men in the village. Years of teasing and hostility had left her with the posture of someone who's always trying to look shorter than she really is. Here, though, after witnessing yesterday the death of the man who had killed her husband, Euphémie, a woman of thirty-two years, a widow of less than three weeks, climbed down from the hay wagon, wiped the wet hair from her eyes, flicked a small green amphibian off the front of her soiled dress, and, for the first time in her life, straightened her spine.

The door to the house creaked and Euphémie saw Auguste peeking at her. She inquired with her eyes and the boy answered by opening the door wide. Euphémie hugged the boy, patting him on the back of his dirty head.

The boy said, "The cemetery was muddy."

The widow touched Auguste's cheek with her broken fingers. "You are a good boy."

"My mother is in jail."

Euphémie said, "Fetch me the prising bar."

Auguste followed her eyes to the rear of the wagon. There, next to an inconspicuous steamer trunk, sat a wooden crate whose size was entirely conspicuous.

"*Vas-y!*" said Euphémie.

Auguste ran to the barn, which was more of a lean-to, and returned with the iron prising bar, nearly as tall as he was. Euphémie lifted him by the waist and placed him upon the bed of the wagon. "Open the crate."

Auguste wedged the bar under the lid and pulled downward until the wood creaked against its nails. He moved the bar to another spot, and another, until he had loosened the lid so he could press it upward and slide it over the edge of the wagon to knife itself into the wet ground.

Annie Lestables sat up in the crate, hair decorated with straw.

Auguste gasped. "Mother! You have escaped!"

Annie's weary eyes brightened. "*Mon trésor.*" Immediately, she added, "Have you buried your father?"

Auguste tried to speak but he could not, so he nodded.

Annie held the boy. She whispered to him, "Remember that silly thing your father used to say? 'Slow your tears before you become a raisin.'"

Auguste sniffled.

Annie said, "And how would you would reply to him?"

Auguste looked up to his mother's brown eyes and said, "'I'm not a grape, Papa, I'm a little boy.'"

Annie released Auguste. "Run, now, and fetch my bag from beneath the bed."

Auguste tilted his head querulously.

"Because," said Annie, "we're leaving Sanvisa."

"But our house is *here*."

"We'll find something better. Get my bag."

"But Father's writings!"

Euphémie said, "Grab what you can carry. There's room in the steamer trunk."

Auguste hurried to the house.

The low clouds began to drizzle. The frogs modulated their conversations.

Euphémie said to Annie, "I pray I did not jostle you too much."

"Freedom is purchased in bruises," said Annie. "Speaking of, where is your son?"

"Junior was last seen with a flagon of mead in his hand and with his eyes fixed upon the bosom of the Strawberry Queen."

Hoisting herself out of the crate, Annie said, "This complicates our plans, no?"

Euphémie said, "The girl can handle herself."

Annie adjusted her eyebrows. "And Junior?"

"He will remain here, with his father."

Auguste, within the house, overheard this, and he recalled the sound of Junior's aggrieved fists upon the locked door of the tomb. It would probably be best not to speak of the incident to anyone, ever.

Delicately, Annie said, "His father is dead."

Euphémie said, less-delicately, "The boy *is* his father. He will not accompany us. I'd prefer not to speak any further on the subject."

Auguste took comfort in this thought. He exited the house carrying Annie's canvas haversack upon his shoulder and a great stack of loose papers in his hands.

Euphémie climbed onto the wagon, opened the steamer trunk, and added Annie's sack and Arthur's papers to the belongings inside and then belted it shut. Then she leaned against the wooden crate in which she had conveyed Annie and, with a mighty grunt, shoved it off the wagon to splat in the mud.

They arranged themselves upon the wagon's seat with Auguste in between and Euphémie at the reins. Speaking just loud enough to be heard over the rain, she asked the horse to drag them along. With hesitant plodding, the horse complied.

Thereby did our Sanvisians commence their escape from the only village they'd ever known.

Chapter Five

Two gloomy days later, lit by a shadowless smear of sunrise trapped behind still-raining, still-dreary clouds, the horse was dragging the wagon and its occupants thru a great maze of coastal swamp that led to the harbor town of Port-Le Final. Iridescent dragonflies hovered like pencils above puddles of rainwater, sliding aside to accommodate the mud-gummed wagon.

Miles away, on the hazy end of the great swampy meadow, a sizable cathedral loomed over Port-Le Final. As the horse drew them near, and as the morning's haze dissipated, Auguste grew confused. Why wasn't there any glass in the great windows? And shouldn't the cathedral be in the middle of town, rather than here on the outskirts?

As they approached, the cathedral was revealed to be a façade. Behind it were haphazard piles of stones. Rain-blackened buttresses flew nowhere, supported nothing. Gargoyles, half-emerged from their limestone wombs, lay tumbleabout in an overgrown sculptuary. It was as if someone had decided to stop construction before the building had reached half of its intended glory.

Which was exactly the case. The project had begun in the year 1129. For roughly seven centuries, its construction had been plagued by wars, sex scandals, proletarian revolts, and plagues. The final straw in the haystack that broke the camel's back arrived in 1791, after a Prussian subcontractor hired to design the rain gutters mistook the cathedral's blueprints for demonic scriptures and fed them to his hogs.

With the cathedral behind them, the road grew wider and soon the horse and wagon clopped into town. Thatched roofs crowded together, smoke bled from chimneys, men and women slogged chickens and infants thru mud and horseshit.

From every corner, starving street urchins tried to arouse the attention of the newcomers. Auguste clung to his mother's sleeve.

Euphémie tipped an ear, sniffed for coal smoke, and directed the horse toward the clang of hammer upon iron. Thereby did they locate the farrier, who directed them to a stable. The stable man offered them a handful of coins for the wagon but he refused to buy the old mare. So they led her to a *boucherie chevaline* and traded her to a man in a bloody apron for a smaller handful of coins.

As they left the butcher, Auguste said, "What will they do with Claire?"

Euphémie said, "They will cut her into pieces and feed her to the rich."

Led by the masts of great ships waving back and forth, the Sanvisians walked south. When they reached the docks, the widows counted their coins and bickered with travel brokers who, in lieu of cash payment, extended numerous offers of sex-for-portage.

Lost to history is the recollection of which of the widows led one of these brokers into an outdoor privy and, somewhat later, emerged, holding in her sticky hand three flimsy tickets for a ship that would, that afternoon, sail around Spain to the northern French port town of Le Havre. From Le Havre, with the grace of good chance, they would board a vessel—any vessel—and put as many miles as possible between themselves and the corpses that lay rotting in the cemetery of their hometown.

Their ship was *Le Moucheron*, a barnacled sloop, decades removed from its employment in Napoleon's navy. Honorably discharged, decommissioned, scuttled, and then repurposed, it had settled into semi-retirement as a shuttle of humans, beasts, and commerce.

The journey would last four days, during which our heroes would eat nothing and drink only rancid water. Other than deprivation—to which our heroes were no strangers—little of interest would occur on this leg of their journey. And so, as they float along, let us venture into the past and thereby gain a clearer picture of the dead man, Arthur Lestables.

INTERLUDE

Concerning the Intellectual Formation of Arthur Lestables

WITH THE EXCEPTION OF THE FINAL DAYS THAT HE AND ANNIE HAD shared in jail, Arthur Lestables had been an improvident provider, a Stegnerian dreamer, a balloon inflated by the vacuous atmosphere that followed him like a scentless perfume. Arthur planted crops that wouldn't grow, he slept overlong, and had had very little interest in procreation. This latter fact did not trouble Annie greatly, and so it was a pleasant surprise that they did manage, on a particularly romantic rainsprinkle afternoon, to successfully complete the ritual that necessarily precedes pregnancy.

With that bit out of the way, the couple explored their respective blisses as they saw fit.

In Arthur's case, bliss consisted of sporadic employment, poor money management, and a stint in the hoosegow for illicitly shearing one of the vicar's sheep. He had hobbies; amongst them was the translation of foreign literary texts into French. Arthur spoke French, obviously, and he had a functional grasp of the old dialect his grandparents had spoken. Beyond that, his linguistic talents consisted of claims to have studied Italian, Latin, German, and ancient Greek at a *lycée* he'd never attended.

But he had excellent handwriting, and he had a knack for eliciting entirely new narratives from texts he couldn't possibly have understood. His translation of Faustus, in spite of its failure to capture a single element of the plot—or any of Goethe's other intentions—was abstruse enough to seem brilliant, at least to the handful of tavern buddies to whom he'd shown it.

On a windless autumn afternoon twenty-seven years prior to the current date of 1885, young bachelor Arthur Lestables was lounging under the very same chestnut tree that would one day suspend his body.

He had in his lap an Arabic translation of Maimonides' *Treatise on Poisons and Their Antidotes*, which he'd found discarded by a caravan of gypsies who had recently trotted their horses and carts thru the village on the same nomadic schedule as the great cranes that would for several days each year leak across the sky north to south like volcanic exhalations.

Arthur, who knew nothing of Romani, rabbis, antidotes, or Arabic, believed that he was reading an Aristotelian lecture on taxonomy, and he was in the midst of proving that the peacock was the cousin of hippogriffin, when he was interrupted by a young scad whose summons would opportune the position that would serve him as compass and clock for the remainder of his life.

"What brings you?" said Arthur, laying aside his quill.

"Apologies, Monsieur Lestables. I've just come from the tavern. A philosopher has landed there, and he is in desperate need of a scribe."

"I am a translator, not a scribe."

"Begging pardon, what is the difference?"

"What is the difference between a cloud and a cup of water?" huffed Arthur.

"I've no mind for riddles, Monsieur, but I do know this: the man is well-to-do."

Arthur tilted his head. "How well?"

"Well enough to employ his own servant."

"Describe for me this philosopher's accent."

"Posh."

"Carry on," said Arthur.

"He requested you, Monsieur. For an interview."

Arthur entered the tavern with his scrivener's box wedged under his sweaty left armpit. At the familiar wooden tables sat a familiar group of daytime tipplers—the type of crowd that cycles from jocular threats to seduce each other's wives, to comforting those whose wives had been seduced, and, further, to wishing that, just once, someone would choose them as an object of seduction. Jovial, mostly, with one or two louts whose flaws were overlooked as long as their greater transgressions remained sequestered from this meeting place.

The tipplers had gathered around a man whose fine black suit stood in great contrast to their manure-stained trousers.

Seeing Arthur, the man stood from the table. "I am told that you've transcribed the works of Ben Johnson." His accent was northern, with a distinct "uh" tagged to the end of every word, definitely posh. He reached his hand toward Arthur.

Arthur approached, the tipplers parting like bobbing ducklings, and shook the offered hand. "Who is it seeks my quill?"

The suited man rubbed a kerchief upon his lower lip. "I, Auguste Comte."

"You claim to be a philosopher."

"Amongst other suggestible things."

"You seek a scrivener."

"My previous adjoint was taken yesterday by pustules and poor respiration."

"And you, do you breathe freely?"

The philosopher demonstrated his vigor with a deep breath, no rattles. "As soon as the pustules showed themselves, I left the man to die in a meadow."

Arthur nodded. "I will work for you."

Auguste Comte said, "You will accompany me to Paris. I will meet you at dawn tomorrow."

· · ·

Arthur went home and informed his mother of his fortune. She fed him large biscuits for dinner, filled his cup with wine, unable to hide her delight. Arthur took this delight for maternal pride. He was mistaken. The woman was happy to be rid of her son.

At dawn, Arthur walked to the boarding house where he was to meet the philosopher. Comte was not yet present, but his valise, a pip of a man, stood on the threshold and shared a bite of bleu cheese with Arthur.

The pip said, "The horses and asses will be delivered soon."

"So we're riding, then," said Arthur.

"You are welcome to walk if you wish."

"No, no," said Arthur. "I'm a natural horseman."

The pip tilted his head. "You'll not last."

"So say you," declared Arthur. "I could lift you over my head as easily as if you were a duck." He flexed his arms, which were still several years away from achieving the legendary strength that would allow him to hoist himself upward by his own noose.

"I'd worry less about lifting and more about letting go."

They sucked on their cheese.

Arthur said, "What do you mean by 'letting go'?"

"Best not think about it. I'm curious about your name. Lestables?"

"It means the tables."

"I guessed that," said the pip.

"One of my ancestors was a celebrated carpenter," said Arthur. He accepted another morsel of cheese.

"Then why isn't your name Charpentier?"

"He specialized in tables, obviously."

"You know what I think? I think your ancestor was not a celebrated carpenter at all. Rather, he was celebrated for his unvarying consistency. Robust, healthy, always on time."

"I know where this is headed," said Arthur.

The pip said, "In other words, he was stable. So, just as the uncivilized man would be called *Lesauvage*, your ancestor was called *Lestable*."

Arthur said, "This is not the first time a stranger has attempted to explain to me my own name."

"But then someone—perhaps a priest or a lawyer—was filling out a form—perhaps a marriage license—and he thought it would be funny to tack an *s* on the end. *Lestables*. *Les tables*. Rhymes with *baisable*."

"And now you're going to claim that my ancestor was illiterate and so he was easily duped."

"How else to explain such a ridiculous name?"

Arthur said, "The man made the finest tables in all of Europe."

The horses and asses arrived, led by a pair of stable boys who accepted coins from a purse that hung from the pip's neck and then promptly left.

The pip and Arthur loaded, balanced, and tied the philosopher's luggage upon the backs of the animals. Then they waited.

"Is the master a pleasant man?" asked Arthur.

"In the same way that a hornet is a pleasant insect, yes."

Arthur puffed his chest. "Would you believe, I've never been stung?"

"By hornets?"

"By anything. Not once. My mother can confirm this."

"Surely you've gotten into nettles."

"I'm referring strictly to the animal kingdom."

"Not even an ant?" said the pip.

"Ants bite. A sting is administered by the hindquarters."

"I suppose this leaves out spiders as well," said the pip. He then added, "What of scorpions, with their ungainly tails?"

"Never been stung."

"Unless we include nettles."

"Which have no hindquarters," said Arthur.

"I've been stung more times than I can count, and by all manner of creatures, including a jellyfish."

"My condolences."

"Jellyfish have no hindquarters. They sting with their legs."

"Fine," said Arthur.

"Believe me, those legs pack a punch."

"So I've heard."

"You ever been stung by a jellyfish?"

"I've never been stung by anything."

"I shall tell people about this someday," said the pip, "and do you know what they'll say to me?"

"I wouldn't dare to guess."

"They'll accuse me of lying."

Arthur said, "I stand by my word."

"I stand by my earlier statement," said the pip. "You'll not last."

The horses and asses twitched under the sun.

It was not until mid-afternoon that Comte finally appeared, limping on his cane. His moustache was decorated with bread-crumbs, stuck fast by honey.

Comte growled, "The innkeeper swore that the mattress would be plump with feathers. The cad did not mention that the feathers were still attached to the geese." Comte climbed atop his horse. "Move. We are late."

They proceeded toward Montpellier, a half-day's ride. Comte at the head, with Arthur next, slouching proudly in the hired saddle, and the pip at the rear, leading the asses.

Comte's horse was familiar with the journey and needed little guidance. Soon, the philosopher's head began lolling back and forth, propped up by the starched collar that rose from his coat all the way to the bottoms of his ears.

Arthur watched with fascination as his master teetered upon his saddle underneath the crisp shadows of the forest. The philosopher would occasionally wake himself with a violent snort. He would look about, recollect his purpose, return to slumber.

Whenever this happened, Arthur would turn querulously to the pip riding behind him. The pip would shrug. The journey would continue.

Eventually, Comte settled into a steady, if noisy, sleep, upright though he was. He began muttering, as one might when trying to remember the grocery list one had forgotten to bring to the market.

Mid-afternoon, the path brought them to a clearing where a peasant woman stood before a cast-iron cauldron, stirring a steaming liquid.

Seeing the trio of travelers led by the muttering dandy upon his horse, the woman cried, "*Ragoût de mouton!*"

Comte snapped awake, nearly falling out of his saddle. He said, "Woman, it is unwise to shout at a man on a horse."

She lifted the spoon out of the cauldron, blew across it to send a waft of broth toward Comte's nostrils.

Comte raised his haughty chin. "Good day, witch." He spread his boots, ready to spur his horse forward.

Arthur gazed longingly at the cauldron, sniffed the larded air, and asserted himself. "Master," he said, "Let us rest here a moment. A well-fed beast is more kind to one's posterior than a hard-rode beast."

The woman added, "There's a brook, yonder where the animals can drink their bellies full and chew the supple grass while you good gentlemen sup."

Comte growled, "Who will pay for this supper?"

Arthur, with saliva dripping from the corners of his mouth, said, "I've a few sous."

"He's hungry, this one," said the woman.

Comte conceded by crawling off his horse. "Have you any wine, witch?"

. . .

The men reclined upon the soft grass. Arthur and the pip slurped stew from wooden bowls. Complaining of an upset stomach, Comte declined to eat, choosing instead to drink greedily from the woman's flagon of wine.

He turned to Arthur, "Did you get everything, then?"

Arthur said, "I'd have preferred fewer onions and more mutton."

Comte said, "Read it back to me."

Arthur's eyes crossed. "Read it—?"

The pip, who had seen this sort of thing play out more than once, shook his head just enough to gain Arthur's attention.

In a flash, Arthur understood what the score was, and it was not in his favor. Comte had expected him to transcribe his every word, including his nonsensical sleep-mutterings. Arthur had transcribed nothing.

Arthur scrambled toward his horse. From his scrivener's box, he extracted a sheaf of papers and a quill and inkpot. "At your service, Master Comte."

A leaf of paper floated from the stack in his hand and alighted itself on the ground near Comte's knee. The paper was decorated with a translation of what was either a Shakespearian sonnet or a recipe for borscht.

Comte held it to his nose.

Arthur reached forth to unburden his master of this sheet of paper. "I shall make amends."

Comte ignored his scribe. He inspected the paper, running his finger over the words.

The fire below the cauldron was growing weak; the woman fed it a handful of twigs.

Comte said, "Perfectly adequate." He returned the sheet to Arthur.

"Thank you, master."

The philosopher stood, brushed grass from his bottom, and said, "Let us resume."

As they mounted their horses, Arthur whispered to the pip, "You're a helpful one."

The pip said, "Now you know."

"Know what?"

"This great man, he can't read."

For the remainder of the day, Arthur rode alongside Comte, who was by now wide awake and speaking in loud, dense sentences. Arthur leaned toward the man, scribbling furiously with ink-stained fingers.

"...it is therefore inevitable, as discussed prior, that the future is the predicate of the past. Is this any less applicable in the arts, the social arts, than it is in the sciences? Does the causation of a thing cause the history of a thing? Is a thing greater than its parts? These are some of the..."

It was a difficult task under any circumstance, virtually impossible on a horse. In order to conserve his limited stock of paper, Arthur's script became smaller and smaller.

The sun had nearly set by the time they arrived in Montpellier, rendering the entire city in shadow except for the orange-lit towers of the cathedral that rose from the center of town.

Arthur's hands were cramped, his ink reduced to a few drops, his final sheet of paper stuffed full of Comte's baffling positivism.

The pip led the way into town, the animals' hooves clattering upon the cobblestones. Vendors splashed water upon the viscera and dog shit that had accumulated in front of their shops and swept it all into the gutter in the center of the street.

A clock tower rang.

"Scribe, what do you know of the wine in this country? Much has changed since I was born here."

Although he held no quill, Arthur's hands reflexively began to write. He gathered himself and said, "Not much, sir, except that there's very little of it. The vineyards have suffered the blight these past years."

Comte said, "Then we'll have to drink of an earlier vintage." To the pip he said, "When am I due?"

"Half an hour."

"Mind the beasts, find our lodging, and see that I arrive on time."

Thirty minutes later, in a hall bounded by rotting tapestries and flickering lamps, Comte lectured a small group of provincial philosophers.

As soon as the lecture began, the pip had retired to the inn, leaving Arthur to deal with Comte on his own. Arthur was seated at the back of the mostly-empty hall, and, having acquired a dozen sheets of paper from a timid cleaning lady who had access to the supply grotto, he resumed his transcriptions. His fingers were stiff, the lighting poor, and the subject of the lecture nearly incomprehensible.

"...the senses are to be trusted insofar as they impart no emotional coloration upon the object being observed...the vanity of man is founded in his insistence that his intellect alone will unveil the fabric of truth...the emotional prowess of the woman must be included in our equation...the destiny of humankind is hermaphroditic, a mingling..."

Four hours later, at the conclusion of the lecture, the meager audience had fallen asleep.

When Comte and Arthur returned to the hostel, the pip was snoring in the bed, an empty wine bottle in his limp hand.

Comte shoved the pip aside and sat upon the mattress. Arthur stood before him, candle in hand, ready for instruction.

Comte said, "The people of the south have always been simple."

"What brings you here?"

"A trajectory; *here* lies between Italy, where I've been, and Paris, where I wish to be. Read back to me what I said today."

Arthur squinted and recited words he could not clearly see.

***

Several more days. Ride to the next town. Lecture, put the audience to sleep, transcribe, repeat.

In Bordeaux, Arthur, who hadn't slept properly in a week, allowed his eyes to briefly close during Comte's lecture and only awoke when the master struck him in the head with a well-aimed apple core tossed from across the room.

He was fired the next morning.

"Very well, master. What salary am I due?"

"I've provided food and lodgings. That is your due." Comte snapped his fingers. "Now give me what is mine."

Arthur reached into his satchel and surrendered to Comte a great stack of papers.

The pip shrugged. "Don't feel too badly. The next one won't last either."

***

It took Arthur nearly a month to walk back to Sanvisa. He arrived to discover that no one in town recognized him. His beard had grown shaggy, his frame skeletal, and his clothes rags.

When the villagers did sort out who he was, they informed him that, in his absence, a plague had dispatched a third of the townsfolk, including his own mother.

And so Arthur settled into his home and began to study his transcriptions of Comte. For he had absconded with every word he'd taken down. To Comte, he had given an Aristotelian lecture on taxonomy.

As years progressed, and as Arthur Lestables proceeded from dreams to drams to his eventual marriage to Annie, any lingering enmity toward his dickish employer was replaced by a reverence toward those brief days of employment. Arthur re-shaped his baffling encounter with the inventor of Logical Positivism into a personal origin story. He studied the transcriptions until they became his credo, and, when the time came, he insisted on naming his only son Auguste.

In short, he turned his greatest failure into his greatest strength.

Chapter Six

In 1885, on the thirtieth of May, *Le Moucheron* dropped anchor just off the upper left corner of France, in the port town of Le Havre.

The widows hefted the trunk off the gangplank and trundled it out of the shipyards. Auguste followed, kicking his bare feet against the cobbled street.

"Mother," called the boy, "is this the richest place?"

"If so, we are the poorest people."

The boy said, "The streets are made with bricks!"

"*Oui*," said Annie, "and our house was made of mud."

On a street corner, a man cranked a hurdy gurdy while a dog danced upon its hind legs. From the shadows came the moans of beggars, dressed similarly to our heroes, with similarly sunken cheeks, clumpy hair, and unshod feet.

Euphémie said, "Sit for a moment. I'll find something to eat."

She and Annie lowered the trunk to the cobblestones and Auguste climbed atop and sat. Euphémie strode away, her nose on the alert for a bakery.

"Mother, why did Papa kill Euphémie's husband?"

"Because Monsieur Deplouc broke her fingers."

"Yes, but why did he *kill* Monsieur Deplouc? He could have made justice some other way. For instance, why didn't Papa just break Deplouc's fingers?"

The temperature of Annie's voice raised several degrees. "In addition to breaking her fingers, Monsieur Deplouc liked to drag Euphémie across the meadow by the hair. If he was unhappy, he would strike her with his fists until her torso turned purple. He tried to destroy her. He hated *everything*. He captured dogs and fed them to his swine. He stole flour from his neighbors and impregnated their daughters. He was a monster."

"So father did right?"

Annie put her arm around Auguste's shoulder. "He fancied himself a man of vision. He was not. But, yes, he was a good man, insofar as he wanted the world to be a good place."

Auguste said, "Still, I would prefer that he were alive."

Euphémie returned with a loaf of black bread, which she handed to Auguste. The boy looked to his mother, who nodded. He tore off a chunk and chewed happily.

Annie said, "How many *sous* remain in the purse?"

"Same as before."

Annie said, "This bread is stolen?"

Euphémie shook her head. "A gift. I found a group of women who will feed anyone who can remember a sentence from the Bible. I gave them three, one for each of us. *Then the Lord rained upon Sodom and Gomorrah brimstone and fire from out of heaven. He overthrew those cities and all the inhabitants. But Lot's wife looked back from behind him, and she became a pillar of salt.*"

The boy said to Euphémie, "Are you sad that my father murdered your husband?"

Euphémie stayed Annie's arm, saying, "The question deserves an answer." To Auguste she said, "I was sad only in that I didn't get to do it myself."

"Enough," said Annie. "We need to find a hostel."

Euphémie and Annie heaved the trunk and they traveled deeper into Le Havre.

Chapter Seven

NIGHT SETTLED. THE SOUND OF GULLS, THE WIND OF THE SEA, LAMB fat bubbling above coal fires.

After counting their coins, the Sanvisians allowed that they could not justify renting a room in even the lowliest of Le Havre's hostels, not at these port-town prices, and certainly not if they hoped to afford passage on a ship that would take them...somewhere else.

At the recommendation of a beggar woman, they brought themselves to a decrepit barracks at the seaward edge of town.

"It's a squat," the beggar woman had said. "It's not clean, and you're unlikely to make friends, but it's a sight better than you three sleeping on the street. Handsome women like yourselfs, oof."

The squat had originally served as a holding pen for kidnapped Africans as they were sorted and packed into ships destined for America. Though it had been abandoned forty years prior, the structure, with its low ceilings and iron-barred windows, was still successfully separating humans from their humanity.

In the center of the sizeable gathering room, a vacant-eyed man tended a fire of wood torn from the building's architecture. The floor around the fire was littered with tired, poor, huddled masses. The Sanvisians carried their trunk to the outer edge of this circle and sat it down and leaned on it and listened to their empty stomachs.

Flamelight glinted off blinking eyes. Hunger, fear, the concavity of despair. Misty wind pierced the walls. Teeth chattered. A grandmother whispered a song to a bundle of rags.

Auguste placed his head upon Annie's lap and fell asleep.

The women conversed quietly.

"We cannot survive here."

"Soon, we'll sail west."

"What ship will carry us? We have no money."

"We'll do what we must."

They fell into disjointed dreams.

They were awoken before dawn by a violent clanging, followed by the frightened cries of their fellow squatters. The room emptied, with the exception of the Sanvisians, who had no idea what was happening. What was happening was a mob of thickset vigilantes had chosen that night to visit destruction upon the town's growing population of tramps, beggars, and other unfortunate souls.

The mob burst into the barracks, armed with torches and sticks that they banged against the walls and clattered against the window bars. They formed a circle around our heroes.

Auguste spoke sleepily, "We are only sleeping, sirs."

"Fuck off, fish," said a mustachioed man whose breath was so ripe with liquor that Auguste feared it would ignite in the flames of the torch he was waving about. The man kicked at the embers of the fire. "Trying to burn another block, eh?"

The circle of torches tightened, sticks poked at our heroes, who were by now standing upright. Soon, Annie and Euphémie and

Auguste were being prodded out the barracks' front door into a mist that wetted their garments. The cobbled street was cold and slick.

The mob surrounded them.

Annie said, "Our trunk."

One of the torch-bearers said, "Not yours no more."

He pressed Annie's shoulder. "To the sea, little fishy. If you don't like to swim, *mon cher minou*, I'll show you how to purr."

Euphémie said, "Touch us, and I'll fillet you like a haddock." She reached into her blouse and withdrew a dagger, a polished silver blade affixed to a bone handle.

A torch came down upon her wrist and the knife collided with the brick road. A large-knuckled hand snatched it up. "Kindly motivate yourselves in the direction of the docks," said the mouth associated with the hairy arm.

Euphémie bared her teeth and growled. Annie held Auguste against her legs.

There now appeared a new noise, a distant, swirling whistling that echoed against the alley's stone labyrinth. The whistling grew closer. The torches wavered a moment and then the mob fled into the night. At the very rear, one of their number, a tiny fellow struggled to keep up, listing left and right as he balanced Annie's trunk upon his back.

"Father's papers!" cried Auguste. He looked to Annie, seeking permission to pursue the tiny fellow. Instead, Annie held him fast.

"They're all that's left!" said Auguste, struggling.

Annie turned him around to face her, shook him by his shoulders. "Auguste, *you* are all I have left." Anger flashed in her eyes, reflected in Auguste's as fear. Annie squeezed him tightly to her chest. "It's bad luck, son, that's all."

Euphémie said, "And there's more luck coming."

From the opposite end of the alley, three whistling silhouettes approached. As they drew closer, the dim blue light of the stars revealed them to be women, clad in long skirts and puffy-shouldered blouses, lips puckered, proper posture.

The trio of women encircled our heroes. The whistling ceased. Euphémie said, "You're the ones who gave me bread."

Chapter Eight

ONE OF THE BREAD-GIVERS, A PETITE YOUNG WOMAN WHOSE FACE WAS decorated with freckles, curtsied and said, "We should have warned you about the hooligans. I am called Sister Temperance."

She had a strange accent.

"They fear you," said Auguste, impressed.

Another of the bread-givers said, "They're afraid of everything." This one also had the strange accent. She was older, with greying hair and a round nose. "Why else would they prey on the weak? I am Sister Gravity." Another curtsy.

The third bread-giver stepped forward, a stout woman with her dark hair pulled back to frame her oval face. She was clearly the chief of the trio. Solemnly, in the same accent, she said, "I am Sister Honora. And you are safe now." She did not curtsy.

Auguste said, "They stole our trunk."

Sister Gravity said, "It's gone now. No use chasing for it."

Auguste said, "Bu—"

The chief, Sister Honora, said, "We must move on."

Euphémie said, "Who are you, who feed strangers during the day and rescue them in the middle of the night?" She crossed her arms over her chest.

"We are the Solemnites," said Sister Honora, "and we offer sanctuary. Do you accept?"

Without hesitation, Annie said, "Yes, yes we do." Turning to Euphémie and Auguste, she repeated, "We do."

Euphémie nodded warily.

Auguste nodded vigorously.

Whistling all the while, the Solemnites led the quivering refugees inland along the dormant streets and alleys of Le Havre, to the outer edge of town and beyond. They passed the septic wafting of the middenfields and into a forest of beech and oak.

Within the forest was a clearing, and within that clearing was a long low tent cast grey in the moonlight, and within that tent was a pulpit. Next to the pulpit, a cauldron of stew simmered over a charcoal fire. Wooden chairs were folded and stacked and the floor was covered with blankets upon which all present seated themselves, with the exception of the chief, Sister Honora. She stood adjacent to the cauldron with a ladle in one hand and a wooden bowl in the other.

"The Lord has called us to do his bidding, and his bidding is to be just and right and to allow his light to shine upon all his children. To this we solemnly vow, for we are Solemnites. Do you welcome the Lord into your lives?"

Euphémie tilted her head. "Might we welcome the Lord on a provisional basis?"

Sister Honora tapped the ladle on the edge of the cauldron, from whence the scent of rabbit and cabbage drifted. "You want to test the waters, do you?"

Euphémie said, "Yes, if you don't mind. You have been kind and solemn, having recently saved us from both hunger and abuse. But I'd require more information before I could commit to a full submergence."

Sister Honora's eyes flashed with something that implied excitement.

Euphémie added, "I'm speaking with utmost respect, of course."

Annie was stroking Auguste's hair. The boy was fixated upon the cauldron. He said, "May we please have some soup?"

Sister Honora smiled grimly. "The Family of Solemn is not a fortress. Nor is the Family a prison. All are welcome. Any may leave at any time. We are not a building, not of stone nor brick nor wood nor mud. We are the fingers of the sun as it sweeps daily across the land. Exit your dreary prison, flee your nervous fortress and feel the Lord's light upon your skin. The light sustains the spirit, but it is you who must choose to remain in its glow. We offer you to partake in our meager bounty until you are ready to make that choice. Whichever choice that may be." The final sentence was colored by a veneer of resignation, as if this same offer had been declined by countless others.

Euphémie said, "The terms are reasonable."

Sister Honora's face became slightly less grim. She filled the bowls and passed them to Sister Temperance, who solemnly presented them to the widows and the boy.

As Auguste slurped his soup, his eyes strayed to the far corner of the tent where a small mound of blankets was gently snoring.

Sister Honora said, "That is Pansy. She is my daughter."

"And a very good sleeper," said Sister Gravity.

After soup, the Sisters arranged more blankets and the Sanvisians slept.

Chapter Nine

AUGUSTE AND THE GIRL PANSY SPENT MUCH OF THE NEXT DAY walking the paths in the forest. Pansy explained that she and the other Solemnites were from America, from a place called Indiana.

She led Auguste to the edge of a brook where they sat upon grass and tossed stones at small fishes that glittered about the water. "We have been in France for a year."

Auguste said, "I have been in France my whole life. This is my first time north."

"It was my mother who convinced the village council to send us to France," said Pansy.

Green-flecked sunlight passed thru the leaves above.

Pansy said, "You have a funny accent."

Auguste said, "Your accent is also funny. But you're easier to understand than your grownups."

Pansy said, "They have heavy tongues. I speak French in the proper fashion. My mother had lessons as a girl and it was she who taught the rest of us. So that's why we came to France instead of one of the other countries. That, and because France is notoriously immoral." Pansy regarded Auguste as if seeing him for the first time. "You are a *plouc*. Do you know that word?"

The boy shrugged.

The girl said, "It means you are uncivilized."

"You are very wise."

"I will change the subject now. Do you know the meaning of my name?"

Auguste considered for a moment. "Pansy sounds like *pensée*. And *pensée* can refer to either a flower or to a thought. I think both would be appropriate for you. I shall combine the two. Your name indicates that you are a thoughtful flower."

"Thoughtful flower," said Pansy. "That is an acceptable answer. I won't be called Pansy forever. When I'm sixteen, I'll receive my Solemn name, which will be chosen by Reverend Steadfast."

Auguste said, "Would you like to guess what my name means?"

"No need to guess. Augustus was the lesser of the Caesars."

"You guess incorrectly. I am named after Auguste Comte, the great philosopher. My father was his scribe, briefly." Auguste considered for a moment, then added, "My father drowned a man and was hanged for it."

"Then your father was a bad man."

"The man he drowned was worse."

"Sister Gravity's husband was recently killed."

"Did he do something evil?"

"Uncertain. We learnt of the tragedy in our most recent correspondence from Reverend Steadfast. The letter made no mention of evil. He said only that Brother Gravity had fallen ill with the croup, and had begun to recover. But then his pulmonaries were attacked by the white thrush."

"What are croup and white thrush?"

"Illnesses, like *la grippe* or *la pneumonie*."

Auguste said, "Do you miss your father?"

"My father is dead."

"Oh," said Auguste. "By what means?"

"I've no idea. I was very small."

"Perhaps you are lucky in this. Do you miss him?"

"It's been very long since I saw him. I have no memories. When we first arrived in France, I did miss *other* things. Food, friends, the quotidian routines, the hebdomadarian routines, routines of all kinds. It took some time, but I'm very adaptable."

"I'm eleven years old."

"I'm eleven-and-a-half."

Auguste said, "Do you wish you still had a father?"

Pansy filled her cheeks with air, which she released noisily. "I don't like to wish for things that already haven't happened."

Auguste did not care for this answer. "You miss your father."

"I never knew him, so, no. But if I did still have a father, he'd be missing me very much, and I'd miss him very much and that would be awful. Anyway, Mother is perfectly good to me. Do you miss your father?"

"Intensely." Auguste introspected. "But also vaguely, as if he were a shape disappearing into the fog."

Pansy took Auguste's hand. "We will be friends, you and I."

They walked the soft bank of the gurgling brook.

Auguste said, "I'm hungry."

"I know of a blackberry patch. Come."

Pansy led him thru the forest, whistling a single thread of a tune.

Speaking thru a mouthful of blackberries, Auguste said, "What is your church?"

Pansy said, "We are solemn, always. No one laughs. We are kind without joy. Joy is indulgent. Would you like to whistle with me?"

Auguste said, "I would like it very much. But I do not know how."

Auguste braced for her to tell him how easy it is to whistle if he would just do such-and-such, as happened any time he confessed this weakness.

He was much pleased when Pansy said only, "A pity."

. . .

They returned to the camp around noon, faces and fingers stained with berry juice. The Sisters and the widows were outside picnicking, seated on their skirts, sharing bread and broth. Blue and red and yellow birds crept forward for crumbs.

The children joined the adults on the warm grass. Pansy squirmed as her mother, Sister Honora, licked her thumb and tried to wipe the blackberry stains from the girl's cheeks.

Annie said, "Son, we have been speaking with the Sisters."

The boy sucked broth from a chunk of bread.

Annie continued. "One of the Sisters"—she gestured toward the kind-faced one, Sister Gravity—"has recently experienced a tragedy not unlike our own."

Auguste said, "Yes. Pansy told me so. I'm sorry, Sister Gravity."

Sister Gravity said, "Your mother and Euphémie have told me of the horrors that have befallen you as well." Her expression fell dark, but then brightened immediately. "We shall carry on."

Auguste said, again, "I'm sorry, Sister Gravity."

Young Sister Temperance, fresh-faced and freckled, said, "The Lord delights to remind us of the seriousness of all things."

Sister Honora said, "In light of Sister Gravity's loss, we have decided to conclude our mission. It is time to return to America."

Pansy gasped. "Mother, this news is not surprising. And yet I'm not altogether pleased by it."

Sister Honora said, "There is no need for displeasure."

Pansy said, "I've only just now made a friend."

Auguste stuffed the last of his bread into his mouth and chewed it within reddening cheeks.

Sister Temperance said, "It's the wisest choice."

Sister Gravity looked up from her bowl. "I was not in favor of it, not until."

Sister Temperance said, "Not until we met you. The past year has been filled with adventure and hardship, joy and despair. But, prior to yesterday, we had not persuaded anyone to join us in the solemn worship of God."

Sister Honora said, "But now, we have. And so our mission is concluded."

Temperance said, "Sister Honora has found a ship. It sails tomorrow for New York."

Pansy and Auguste looked to one another. Must it end so quickly?

"Furthermore," said Sister Gravity, "and I think this will please you, Pansy, we have secured passage for our three guests."

Pansy clapped her berry-stained hands. "They are coming with us!"

Sister Gravity said, "Yes, mostly. We'll be on the same ship. But they'll be traveling in an unofficial capacity."

Auguste said, "What does 'unofficial capacity' mean?"

Euphémie, who had been studiously tossing bread crumbs to the birds, said, "We'll be stowaways."

Pansy said, "Is such a thing moral?"

Honora said, "It would be immoral to do otherwise."

Sister Temperance said, "You have suffered enough."

Sister Gravity said, "We don't build fortresses, we don't build prisons. We offer freedom to those who would take it."

Euphémie, sensing a need for gratitude, said, quite convincingly, "You have cast your light upon us. We pledge to repay your generosity by reflecting this light unto those who suffer greater poverty than we."

Sister Gravity placed her right hand on her heart. "A pledge is a serious proposition. Are you certain?"

Annie and Euphémie nodded.

Sister Temperance placed her left hand on her belly. "You promise?"

Auguste joined the widows in nodding.

Sister Honora covered her forehead with both hands. "Do you vow, solemnly?"

Annie placed her right hand on her heart. "We pledge, promise, and solemnly vow to act as reflective vessels to the Lord's light."

Euphémie placed her left hand upon her belly, and said, "You are our Sisters, and we would be yours."

Auguste placed both hands on his forehead, "I shall be your friend."

The three Solemn Sisters plus Pansy encircled the Sanvisians and held hands and closed their eyes and began to pray, silently and solemnly. As the prayer went on, and on, Euphémie watched a line of ants crawl over her foot. The ants disappeared into a bush, and then re-emerged bearing upon their collective mass a very young, dead bird. The prayer continued as the ants carried the bird back the way they had come, this time routing around Euphémie's foot. Euphémie winked at Annie several times in hopes that she'd witness this marvel of nature, but Annie was studiously pretending to pray. Auguste's eyes were downcast in imitation of the others, and his tongue was licking berry juice off his upper lip.

Observed by no one but Euphémie—who found this all painfully funny—a raccoon's arm emerged from a bush and snatched the bird away from the ants and then retracted.

By the time Sister Gravity finally said, "Amen," tears were oozing down Euphémie's cheeks, a display of solemnity courtesy of suppressed hilarity.

Sister Honora said, "A great ship awaits us."

The Sisters set to dismantling the tent. They refused help from their guests saying, "Take this moment to reflect. You are about to undertake a great journey."

Auguste led the widows to the brook where he and Pansy had spoken earlier that day. The widows spread their skirts and sat on the swampy grass.

Auguste said, "They are very kind to us."

Euphémie said, "Only because they think they're saving our souls."

Annie said, "Don't be cynical. They are kind to us because they are kind."

Auguste said, "Do people in America break fingers or drown people or hang them from trees or steal their trunks?"

Annie said, "No, son, they do not."

That night, in the tent, Auguste dreamt of white-wigged philosophers and feather-frocked Indians. Meanwhile, the widows whispered between themselves.

"They're good people."

"Considering."

"They do not delight in lacing a man to a tree. Their husbands do not bruise their faces. We will accept their kindness with grace."

"And your boy will flirt with the girl, and we will learn a new language, and we will emerge on the other side of the horizon and we will never come to this place again."

"He believes there are six legged-oxen in America."

"Is this true?"

"I know nothing about the place."

Chapter Ten

THE NEXT EVENING, WITH THEIR STRATEGY LAID OUT AND THEIR luggage tidily packed, the entire group ventured to the shoreline, boarded a rowboat, and pushed off into the bay. Sister Gravity cranked at the oars, drawing the little boat thru a floating maze of creaking, barnacled ships.

Pansy said, "America is a three-week trip. Only, sometimes ships sink. But that's rare so you needn't worry. After we get to New York, we will ride a train across three states and we'll then arrive in Indiana and then we'll switch trains and then we'll be in Restive and then we'll walk to our home in Solemn."

Sister Honora said, "Quiet now."

A quarter mile off the dock, creaking under a sky of stars lay a line of ships that were too large to approach the shallow bay. Steam power had by now entered the shipping world and many of these vessels were hissing and spitting and whistling.

Sister Gravity paused in her rowing and said, "Which one?"

Sister Honora peered into the night. "To the left."

Sister Gravity resumed her oarwork.

Euphémie said, "That's not a passenger ship."

"Oh, no," said Sister Honora. "That is the *Isère*. She's a freighter."

"I hope the *Isère* is freighting cases of wine," said Euphémie, to no reaction.

"Boxes," said Sister Gravity, grunting against the oars. "The hold contains great boxes, some as large as a house. We're told they contain gifts for the mayor of New York."

"And we shall be the greatest of those gifts!" said Auguste.

Sister Gravity gave the oars a mighty tug, then said, "Sister Temperance, would you do me a kindness and offer that handsome lad's hair a playful tussle?"

Sister Temperance complied. Auguste smiled broadly.

With ill intent in her eye, Temperance said, "Wouldst Sister Gravity have me pinch the handsome lad's cheeks?"

Sister Gravity nodded her assent.

This time, Pansy joined in. She went for the ears while Temperance pinched the delighted boy's cheeks.

Annie rested her arm around Euphémie. They were floating between ships in the middle of the night to board a freighter that would cross an ocean, and women with strange names were making Auguste giggle.

Sister Honora said, gently, "Solemn, Sisters, solemn."

Temperance and Pansy ceased their frolic and said, in unison, "Sorry, Sister Honora."

"Me, too," said Auguste.

"Me, too, but slightly less so," said Sister Gravity with a wink for Auguste.

Sister Honora said, "A bit further." To the Sanvisians, she said, "As unofficial passengers, you will be confined to the cargo hold for the duration."

Annie said, "Just so long as we have something to drink."

Sister Gravity said, "We'll see that you have water and food. And don't worry. We took a similar freighter on our journey from America. The men on these ships aren't as naughty as their reputation. Some of them are kind. It is one of these kind men who will meet you tonight and show you to your quarters."

The rowboat came to the port side of the ship, near the sloop.

Sister Gravity gave a whistle. Far above, a shadow leaned over the top deck. The end of a rope ladder fell toward them and splashed in the water.

Sister Honora said, "Can you all swim?"

Auguste said, "I swim very well, Sister."

"And your mother? And her friend?"

"They are silent," said Auguste, "because they cannot."

Sister Gravity guided the boat adjacent to the ladder. She loosed the oars and stood, shifting her hips to steady the wobbling boat. "Climb quick and careful. Three limbs touch the ladder at all times. If you fall, you're on your own. The moment the last of you steps off this boat, we're around to the other end of the ship, where we'll receive a proper welcome."

Sister Honora said, "Climb, now. A man, our ally, awaits at the top of the ladder. He will lead you to the cargo hold. Remain there until we find you."

"Thank you, Sisters," said Annie. She mounted the uncertain ladder and began her ascent, followed shortly by Auguste.

Euphémie watched unhappily as Annie and the boy scrambled upward. Sister Gravity squeezed her hand. "Make haste."

A moment later, Euphémie was clinging to the ladder, listening to the splash of Gravity's oars propelling the boat away.

Chapter Eleven

EUPHÉMIE HAD SPENT HER LIFE SCRAPING PIGSKINS, FARMING potatoes, and carrying water. She had survived twelve years with her monstrous husband. She feared nothing, no man, no obstacle. But that ascension, with three broken fingers, up twenty feet of an uncertain rope ladder, it was a trial.

She pulled her long body upward. The mist and spray of water wetted her skirt to her legs. As she hooked her elbows on the slick wooden rungs, her feet struggled to find purchase.

She hung for a moment, swaying. If she didn't climb this ladder right now, she would never again enjoy the calm heat of Annie who awaited her those two-dozen feet above.

Euphémie gripped her naked toes around the ladder's pegged rungs. Her limbs were as cold as lead and twice as heavy, as if something were trying to drag her into the sea. She cast a superstitious eye downward, and there it was, the bloated, naked husk of Henri Deplouc floating just beneath the starlit reflections, his bulging eyes, tendrils of his unruly hair shifting in liquid motion, mimicked in miniature by his slender penis.

Euphémie shivered in the wet misery.

Henri's mouth fell open and an eel slid out and encircled his throat. Another eel, and another, dozens of them, spilled out, from eyes, ears, asshole, every orifice, and they swarmed over his body.

Euphémie's good hand slipped, one of her feet slipped, and she was left dangling with a knee over one rung and her broken fingers curled around another.

In the black sea, the mass of eels writhed in a vaguely human shape. The mass flashed a burst of phosphorescence, and then the eels unwound and cast off in a hundred different directions, slick arrows in the water. Henri Deplouc's body had disappeared.

From above, unseen fingers jerked the ladder impatiently. Euphémie swung her good hand upward and grappled a rung. She squirmed until her left foot found a rung. The ladder jerked again, pulling her further away from the sea below. She was being drawn out of this death a few inches at a time.

A large, square hand reached over the rail and clasped her wrist and dragged her upward, grinding her ribs and hip against wet iron, and then she slid to the deck, and above her the sky was a nighttime cloud of smoke and steam. A face, then another, then another bent toward her. The boy, delighted; Annie, relieved; and a bearded sailor, irritated.

Speaking French with a foreign accent, the sailor said, "Welcome aboard. Now move."

He lit an oil lamp and led them down iron ladders and into the cargo hold. As advertised, the great room was packed with enormous wooden crates. Dripping and shivering, they followed the man and his lamp along a narrow alley within this city of containers. He stopped before a wooden crate whose face extended upward beyond the reach of the lamp, and whose wood was overlain with stencils reading *la tête* and black arrows overlain with *ce côté vers le haut*.

The sailor reached his fingers under one of the great, roughcut planks that made up the crate. He gave a mighty heave, the wood flexed, nails squeaked, and the plank peeled back far enough to allow entry.

"There's a bucket inside. The Solemn ladies will bring you food and water."

"How about bedding?" said Euphémie.

"The ladies will take care of you. You must be quiet." Sensing their dismay, he said, "But not altogether silent. There is little activity in the hold."

Auguste said, "What is inside the box?"

The man said, "Can you read? It's a head."

"Just one?"

"You are lucky to know those women. I don't want to see you again. You understand?"

He left them in the dark.

Feeling their way, they found the bottom of the crate covered with several inches of straw, apparently intended as a cushion for the cold metal object that took up most of the crate's interior.

Auguste whispered, "If this is a head, it is the biggest head of all."

"Shhh," said Annie.

By crawling blindly, they discovered in a corner a gap large enough for the three of them to sit upright, sufficient even for Euphémie to fully stretch out on her back. And yes, there was a bucket.

"What's this for?" said Auguste's small voice.

"Shit and piss," said Euphémie.

"I must use it," said Auguste.

"Aim well," said Annie.

They took turns on the bucket, and then, exhausted, the widows lay upon the straw with Auguste curled between them. They fell asleep to the sway of the ship.

Auguste squeezed out from between the women. Curious and

alert, he crept within the box. The walls were splintery wood, the alleged head had a skin of cold, curved metal. Squirming along the bottom edge of the crate, Auguste followed this curve until, halfway around, he found an opening—the throat, he presumed—large enough to climb inside. He remained there a while, the sound of his breath reflecting against the skin. I am a brain, he thought.

He returned to the widows and slept.

They awoke. They slept. They grew thirsty. The boat swayed. The bucket grew distressingly full.

"They have abandoned us."

"They will return."

They slept, woke, waited.

Tap, tap, tap.

Euphémie whispered, "We are discovered."

Sisters Gravity and Temperance pried back the plank and greeted the refugees with the light of an oil lantern and the sound of a cheerful tune, whistled softly.

Gravity and Temperance presented them with a sack of stale bread and salted pig meat as well as a gut bag of sour water, all of which were eagerly consumed.

After the final crumb had been licked off the final finger, Annie said, "How far have we come?"

Sister Temperance said, "We have not left the port. The weather is uncooperative. We're to sail soon."

Sister Gravity said, "We would have come earlier except we're stationed near the forequarters where the officers can see us. The crew is currently gathered at the fo'c'scle staring at the clouds and shouting at gulls."

"What time is it?"

"Mid-day, tomorrow," said Temperance.

Sister Gravity said, "We apologize for the quality of the food."

Euphémie said, "It's only three weeks."

"Not counting the weather delay," said Temperance.

Sister Gravity said, "We'll return tomorrow. You may keep this lantern. Here is a box of matches. You may exit the crate, walk around the hold if you wish. Keep an ear for visitors. Now fetch us your waste bucket. We've left another one just outside, along with a sack of sawdust. Pour it over your excretions. It covers the aroma." As if remembering, she said, "Auguste, do you read?"

Annie answered for her son. "In French, yes."

Sister Gravity placed a thin booklet in Auguste's hand. "This is a story of a great man."

Auguste said, "Is he wise?"

"Yes."

"Does he believe that humanity will one day replace superstition with reason?"

Annie said, "Auguste's father fancied himself a philosopher. He idolized a man named Auguste Comte, hence the name."

"Oh," said Sister Gravity, "And who is Monsieur Comte?"

Annie spoke before the boy could, "A radical. A dangerous, misguided radical." She put a firm hand upon Auguste's shoulder, a sign that he should not speak.

Auguste accepted the pamphlet.

Sister Gravity said, "We'll bring blankets tomorrow. And we shall start our English lessons." She pinched Auguste's cheeks and then she and Temperance bade the stowaways good day.

Outside the crate, Annie was seated next to Auguste, who was studying Sister Gravity's gift in the lantern light.

L'argument pour la solennité chrétienne:

une petite bible pour les petits

"Let's have a look, son." Annie flipped the pages of the typeset work. She handed it back. "Keep in mind that this is a work of fiction."

The next day, Sisters Gravity and Temperance returned with a fresh bucket, more food, and three woolen blankets.

Auguste greeted them with perfect solemnity. "I thank you for your kind gift, Sisters." He gestured for them to join him where he sat on the hold's iron floor with his back against the crate.

Sister Gravity said, "I hope the words were spelled correctly."

"Are you the author?"

"I was assisted by my Sisters."

Sister Temperance said, "And from God himself, who is the conception of all ideas."

"Of course," said Sister Gravity.

Auguste said, "I appreciate the fact that you write in the vernacular rather than the literary style."

"Did you find the story spiritually fulfilling?" said Sister Temperance, always eager to guide a conversation heavenward.

"I am familiar with the tales of the messiah. It is common to my village. My father considered it hogwash. He was a positivist, taught by the great Auguste Comte. Nonetheless, aside from some minor issues, I found it satisfying."

"Issues?" said Temperance.

"For instance," said Auguste, "if a supernatural creator-of-all-things were to cleave himself in two, and then deliver the lesser product of this cleavage to the surface of Earth with the understanding that this lesser product, known as the Christ, would eventually be attached to a wooden cross via spikes thru his hands and feet." Auguste took a breath, having forgotten to breathe. "Clearly this supernatural being is not joking around. This was the part I really liked, actually."

"And what of the resurrection?" said Sister Gravity.

"Pardon?" said Auguste.

"The revivification of Christ."

Auguste said, "That part was unnecessary."

Sister Temperance remained solemn in the face of this blasphemy.

Auguste said, "It compromised the theme."

Sister Temperance said, "That *is* the theme. From death comes life."

"I disagree. The theme is *love demands sacrifice*. But, by bringing the Christ back to life, the sacrifice is nullified. If, as is implied, the god character possessed precognition, then he *knew* his son would arise from the dead. So he knew he wasn't making a sacrifice. It's more of a trick. Like testing a dog's loyalty by leaving it in a room with a cake. Of course the dog will eat the cake. Dogs can't help themselves eating cake, just as people can't help but kill one another. As it's written, the story merely confirms for me what I already know, which is that certain circumstances have predictable outcomes."

Sister Temperance said, "I don't understand."

"It's quite simple. A dog is inferior to a human and so it is unfair to expect—"

Sister Gravity said, "Is your mother around, sweetheart?"

Auguste poked his head inside the crate. "Mother, we have guests." To Sister Gravity he said, "Do you have something more grown-up I could read?"

"Yes," said Sister Temperance. "We have a book that focuses entirely on solemnity, which, as you know, is absolutely integral to our faith. But it's a book for adults, not little boys."

"I am a little boy who has read Goethe, Plato, and the Egyptian Book of the Dead."

Annie stepped out of the box blinking against the dim lamp-light. "He read those in French, of course."

"Translated by my father."

Sister Gravity nodded gently. "I'm sure we have something."

Annie said, "Perhaps in English? He needs to learn. We all do."

"Brilliant. I'll bring the English version of *La petite bible pour les petits*! It's called *The Little Bible for Little People*."

Auguste brightened, tried these new words. "Suh liddle beebluh fuh liddle peepluh."

Sister Gravity tapped the side of her nose. *"Formidable!"*

Euphémie climbed out of the crate, groaning as she stretched herself to her full height, running her fingers thru her loose hair.

Sisters Gravity and Temperance bowed slightly and said together, "Good afternoon, Sister."

Euphémie smeared some sleep from the corner of her eye. "Oh, for a drop of sunlight."

From the other end of the great, dark room, footsteps clapped against the floor. They grew louder, quicker, and then young Pansy appeared in the lamplight, breathlessly failing to be solemn.

"The weather has cleared! We lift anchor tomorrow."

Auguste and Annie and Euphémie were much relieved by this news. Sisters Gravity and Temperance covered their faces to hide their satisfaction. Pansy, in a gleeful disregard for the seriousness of life, bounced up and down.

As if from nowhere, Pansy's mother, Sister Honora, stepped into the light. She whistled sharply and clapped her hands.

All enthusiasm was immediately internalized. Pansy turned her eyes floorward, the widows flattened their lips, Gravity and Temperance loosened the muscles of their faces so it looked as if they might have just woken up, and Auguste stuffed his right fist into his mouth.

"Pansy has shared the news, then," said Honora.

Everyone nodded.

Sister Honora winked. "Carry on." She walked away into the dark, leaving them to giggle into their palms.

· · ·

Auguste took Pansy by the hand. "Our crate contains a head. Come!" He led her into the great box.

Temperance said to Annie, "The boy is educated."

Annie said, "It's his father's influence. I'm sorry."

Sister Gravity said, "They say it's better to be open to debate than to be closed for business."

Sister Temperance said, "Let's learn some English."

"*Oui*," said Euphémie.

Later that night, Annie and Euphémie and Auguste were awakened from their blanketed nest by the chain-and-pulley rumble of a hoisting anchor. In the darkness, the three refugees, hidden in a crate which they shared with a giant head, weak and hungry, with parasites wiggling in their intestines, and the memory of their little village in the south of France already giving way to a new and vague American utopia, shared a silent optimism.

Chapter Twelve

AFTERNOONS, SISTERS GRAVITY AND TEMPERANCE WOULD DESCEND to the hold where they'd sit with Annie and Euphémie and tutor them in English. Gravity and Temperance were excellent teachers. Annie and Euphémie were eager students, and their acquisition of English went as smoothly as one could hope from a pair of poorly-educated women in their early thirties.

Pansy became Auguste's teacher, naturally. Also naturally, her approach was less formal than that of Gravity and Temperance. Rather than focusing on formalities, she preferred to simply speak English until Auguste understood her.

Whereas Auguste would soon adopt English as his primary language, the widows would always remain French, at least internally. For the rest of their lives, they would conduct their private conversations (and their private thoughts) in their *langue maternelle*.

As a general rule, the reader can assume that, as this account unfolds, the Sanvisians are speaking a gradually-improving—and eventually fluent—version of English.

One day, Pansy came to the crate and said, "Auguste, come wander with me."

The boy closed the book he was studying—he spent hours each day comparing the English and French editions of Sister Gravity's texts—and said, "Wander where?"

"Anywhere," said Pansy, "as long as it's not this dreary pit. Come!"

"I remind you that I am a stowaway."

"*Bof!*" said Pansy. "I wander all the time. I know everything about this tub. You won't catch a whiff of trouble. I am known and adored by all."

Pansy was amiably tolerated by the entire crew of the *Isère*, from Captain de Saune to Ensign Lutkefisk. She was not, however, permitted to roam the ship at will. And she certainly wasn't allowed to harbor stowaways.

Auguste said, "If my mother finds out—"

Pansy brought her wary friend out of the hold. They scampered the narrow hallway that ran along the outer hull of the ship, against which they could press their ears and hear the whoosh and tick of the passing ocean, and then Pansy led Auguste down another passageway, to a thick iron door at the lower deck of the stern.

"You'll like this." She leaned hard against the door and pushed it open, releasing an aroma of rotting grease. She skipped across the threshold. "Come along. There's no one here."

This was the engine room, and Auguste very much did like it. The *Isère's* steam engine was a monster of modern engineering, with flywheels taller than a horse, glass-faced pressure gauges, and two-handed valve wheels, and it was all tied together within a circulatory system of shiny brass.

"Why does the machine not move?" said Auguste.

"Because wind is cheaper than coal," said Pansy. "They'll fire up the engine when the wind lets up. Usually about halfway across."

Auguste slid his fingers over rivets, puzzled over the three brass balls at the top of the centrifugal governor, and gaped at the enormity of it all.

Footsteps. Pansy's eyes widened and she took Auguste by the shoulders and stuffed him out of sight behind the opened door. She cried, "*Au secours! Je suis perdue!* Help! I am lost!"

The footsteps grew closer and soon two crewmen appeared in the doorway. The sailors were just as surprised to see Pansy here as she was to see them, but they offered her no suspicion. Rather, they politely gave her directions to the topside and wished her a good day.

Pansy curtsied, and the crewmen continued to their business at the very rear of the engine room. Once the men were out of sight, Pansy pulled Auguste from behind the door and rushed him along the hallway and back into the hold.

Safe now within the perpetual midnight of the wooden labyrinth, they slowly made their way back to the crate with the head in it.

Auguste said, "We were foolish to leave the hold, yes?" His chest was still heaving from the adventure.

"Yes," said Pansy.

"I was very nearly discovered as a stowaway."

"Yes."

"But I was not discovered."

"Also, yes."

After a moment, Auguste said, "Is it okay, Pansy, that I liked being nearly discovered?"

"Of course," said Pansy. "As long as you're solemn about it."

"I would like to be nearly discovered again," said Auguste, solemnly.

. . .

Two days later, Pansy led Auguste to the mess hall, a short-ceilinged room of benches and tables.

"Look," said Pansy. "Windows."

She slid a chair underneath a porthole and stood upon it and drew Auguste to join her. Standing close, they pressed their faces against the glass, squinted against the mid-Atlantic sun, and watched the spray of waves.

Pansy leapt down and skipped to the rear of the hall, where she took a seat at a strange piano that was secured to the floor with ropes and eyehooks. The piano was an upright, with numerous ebony and ivory knobs above the keys.

In a tone that suggested she was introducing to Auguste a new and dangerous variety of sin, Pansy whispered, "This is a *musical instrument*."

She instructed him to sit next to her and press his feet upon a pair of wooden pedals. As Auguste operated the pedals, Pansy laid her fingers upon a cluster of keys. A wheezing, desperate, fantastically unpleasant sound emerged. At this, Auguste leapt away from the organ.

Pansy giggled. "You've never seen a piano?"

Auguste glared at her. "Of course I have." The year prior, a crew of rowdies had waggoned into Sanvisa and set up a makeshift stage, as well as a collection box. Not having ever seen money, much less having owned any, Auguste hadn't a chance of attending the performance. But, as the rowdies were rehearsing one chirpy afternoon, he had climbed a sycamore and observed them from afar, until a bee had settled upon his nose and sent him away in terror.

Auguste said, "But I've never heard one sound so awful."

"Solemnites are not allowed to make music, or sing. But we can still make noises. As long as my performance is unmusical, I still get to go to heaven. Here, try."

Auguste pressed upon several keys, accidentally producing a G-sharp minor triad. Pleased with this, he shifted two fingers and accidentally played a C-sharp-seven, which he then accidentally resolved into an F-sharp major seven. In his first try, he'd happened upon a foundation of western harmonic movement.

The girl pushed his hands out of the way. "Not like that!"

She made a show of stretching her fingers and then crushed out a litter of notes, in a precisely non-musical fashion.

Auguste said, "I prefer mine to yours."

Pansy said, "God thinks otherwise."

"Maybe God is wrong."

Pansy was deciding how to dismantle this argument when the mess hall's door squealed open and a bearded sailor strode into the room.

Auguste dove off the bench and slid under one of the long wooden tables, hands around his knees.

The bearded sailor said, "The little girl is practicing again."

Pansy said, "The old man is eavesdropping again."

These two knew each other. Auguste's terror slackened.

"Have you suddenly overcome your fear of damnation?" said the sailor. "Have you overcome your fear of *me*?"

"I don't know what you're talking about."

"My dear girl. Your mother agreed you'd keep them out of sight."

Auguste now recognized this as the crewman who'd supplied the rope ladder that he and Annie and Euphémie had scaled to board the *Isère* and who had first led them to their great wooden box.

The sailor's feet took a step closer to Pansy's feet, which then backed away.

Pansy said, "Pleasant notes played in error are evidence that I've betrayed you?"

"*Au contraire*; the pleasant notes were a relief for my tortured ears. The evidence of betrayal is the skinny boy hiding under the table."

Pansy said, "Auguste, you can come out."

"Stay where you are," said the sailor. "I'm going to leave now. You will immediately stop with your excursions. You'll have plenty of time to act like fools once you're off this boat. Do you hear?"

"I hear, and I understand, and I apologize," said Pansy, somehow producing a pair of dimples in her unsmiling cheeks.

"You'll either be discrete, or you'll be shark food. And if you're caught, I'll be the one to pitch you overboard."

The man stomped out of the room.

Crawling out from under the table, Auguste whispered, "We were foolish again."

Pansy whispered, "And yet you remain undiscovered." Sensing Auguste's skepticism, she added, "Khalid is grumpy, but he's also discrete."

Auguste said, "I think we should not wander any more, for a few days at least."

Chapter Thirteen

ON THE EVENING OF THE THIRTEENTH DAY OF THE VOYAGE, PANSY came to the cargo hold and found Auguste seated outside the crate, reading by lantern light.

"Let's go," said Pansy. "Now."

"More information, please."

Pansy spoke hurriedly. "The entire crew is in the mess hall getting drunk to celebrate the midway. Midway means we're halfway there. It also means we're in the doldrums. Doldrums means there's no wind."

Auguste shrugged, as if to say, "So...?"

"So," said Pansy, "they've left the topside completely, utterly, fantastically unattended."

Auguste snapped his book shut.

⁂

Stars above, water below, half-moon casting the scene in a pale, ghostly gauze.

Pansy said, "You are aware that you are, once again, at risk of being nearly discovered."

Auguste drew fresh salty air into his young lungs. "At this moment, I am aware only of joy."

August's legs braced themselves against the complete stillness of the ship. He said, "Why are the sails tied up?"

Pansy said, "Because there's no wind in the doldrums. As soon as the crew finishes their rum party, they'll stoke the engine and we'll be on our way."

They were at rear of the ship. Pansy stood behind as Auguste leaned against the rail. Far below, phosphorescent swirls of water lapped against the *Isére's* hull. In the distance, miles away, silent lightning strobed within the silhouette of a bubbling mass of clouds.

Auguste said, "Are there storms in the doldrums?"

Pansy said, "By definition, no."

Auguste's brow furrowed.

Pansy said, "Obviously, that—" she nodded toward the mass of clouds "—is a storm. But it's very far away."

The air was rent by thunder. The waves lapped the boat more aggressively. The boat shifted less gently.

Pansy said, "Then again, the ocean is a fickle beast. Not every ship finds its port."

Auguste said, "You're morbid."

"Says the grave-digger who thinks God made a plotting error when he resurrected his son. Come. Let's lie down and marvel at the stars."

Auguste followed Pansy to a column of thick rope that had been coiled at the bottom of the sternmost mast. The rope was wound in such a way that the children could climb the outer edge and then drop into the center and lay comfortably upon their backs.

The tip of the mast wobbled against the brilliant display above them. Stars plunged from constellations, leaving green trails in their wake. The children's hands met, their fingers interlaced, and their eyes closed to the sounds of languid rigging and distant thunder.

They awoke to raindrops bouncing off their faces. The sky was crisscrossed with jagged lightning, overlain in bluewhite arcs that jerked their shadows in a spastic dance. Wind poured an endless rumble of thunder into their cavity within the rope coil. In a moment, they were drecked with rain, which came in increasingly violent waves. A sail became unfurled from the mast and began to flap sharply in the torrent.

The ship tacked leeward, sending Pansy to slide on top of Auguste. A pool of water was accumulating at the bottom of their hiding space.

The ship leveled out and Auguste stood to peek over the edge of the coil of rope. A greenflecked wave rose over the hull, crashed forward onto the deck, into the hiding place. The children were instantly chilled, and the rope coil was now waist deep with saltwater.

Auguste muttered, *"Fichtre."*

Pansy said, "Swearing will not help things."

Within the groaning wind and the creaking of the ship, the children detected slurred shouts from drunken sailors as they spilled out upon the deck and raced to secure various unsecured items. According to the loudest of these voices, these things should have been done long ago and someone would hang for this half-assery.

The shelter shifted; the rope was unraveling.

Pansy sprang out of the coil, followed immediately by Auguste. As they scurried in search of a downladder, they passed a dozen crewmen hurrying to salvage the sails before the wind could tear them from the masts.

"There!" cried Pansy. "The lifeboats!"

Chapter Fourteen

THE SHIP TILTED FORWARD AND THE GREAT HEAD CLUNKED AGAINST the wood of the Sanvisians' crate.

"It's only a storm," said Honora.

Euphémie said, "It seems very bad."

The English lesson had become impossible, what with the groaning of the colossus' dismembered limbs as they rocked back and forth in their crates.

"I'm sure we're safe," said Temperance. "The *Isère* is made of iron. Bless the Lord."

Annie said, "I'd feel safer if we weren't sharing our room with a head."

Honora said, "Let us exit, then."

The four women climbed out of the sanctuary and kept bent-kneed-balance against the listing of the ship. Annie held the lantern next to her ear and peered about. The hold's two hundred and twelve boxes were secured by a crisscrossed network of ropes; ropes that were practically vibrating with the strain of preventing calamity.

Sister Honora said, "Has anyone seen the children?"

"There they are," said Euphémie. She pointed toward the flickering of a lantern that was approaching from the alleyway that led away from their crate.

"Auguste?" cried Annie. "Pansy?"

The lantern hastened toward them with a great huffing and puffing. It was held by Sister Gravity. She was breathless and her dress was soaked and clinging to her body. "Where are the children?"

Annie cast an eye toward Euphémie, who raised her shoulders.

Honora said, "You've been on deck, Sister Gravity?"

Gravity grabbed a handful of her skirt and wrung out a slosh of water. "It's a tempest. And we have to meet it, and we have to find the children."

In a diminished voice, Temperance said, "But the children would never go up."

Honora said, "Obviously. I'm sure they're safe."

"What's safe in a storm?" said Annie. Thus far, she had been calm, but this calmness was nearing its end.

Sister Gravity said, "Aye, the question is, what's the *least*-safe place?"

Blank looks.

"Because," said Sister Gravity, patiently, "our goal is not merely to *find* them, but to *save* them."

More blank looks.

Gravity, less patient, "If, God forbid, they somehow ended up on deck, then they would need our help moreso than if they were instead messing about in some broom closet."

Sister Honora scoffed. "My daughter is no fool."

"Auguste, neither," added Euphémie.

"But they are children," said Sister Gravity, "and children do foolish things. If they've gone topside, they're in the worst possible danger; and so that's precisely where we should look."

The women emerged from the hatch one by one, the previous helping to draw out the next until they were all on deck. Sister Gravity brought them together into a scrum, arms on shoulders, weaving as one to counter the lurching of the ship.

Wind-flung rain and saltwater; drunken sailors in yellow slickers dashing from one place to the next, dodging the sea creatures heaved to the deck by the white foam of the waves.

Gravity grinned at Euphémie and Annie in their drenched dresses. In full voice, she cried, "Sister Honora, to the bow. Sister Temperance, starboard. I'll take port. Widows, to the stern—that's the rear. If you find the children, get them below decks. If you don't find them, keep looking."

The storm flung a giant octopus onto the deck. It clacked its beak, slapped its arms, and spilled black ink in all directions.

"Go!" cried Sister Gravity.

The women divided and dodged and shouted for Auguste and Pansy against a meteorological violence that swallowed every syllable.

Chapter Fifteen

THE CAPTAIN AND THE FIRST MATE WERE STRUGGLING AT THE WHEEL. Steering the ship was out of the question; their only concern was to anticipate the next wave, and the next. With luck, they might save the rudder. As for saving the masts, that would require something far more substantial than luck.

The mid-mast was in the greatest danger. Its unfurled sails were flapping wildly, threatening to snap the great length of timber. Sailors scurried upward, ignored the cracking of wood, refused to descend to safety, and frantically sawed their knives against the wet ropes that held the sails. And they succeeded. With the last of the moorings severed, the canvas flew madly into the churling darkness.

In drunken relief, and with knives clamped between teeth, the crewmen scrambled downward, swinging from wayward ropes, leaping the final two fathoms.

On the right side of the ship, Sister Gravity squinted against the rain and watched the lifeboat swing helplessly from its two davit arms. Surely this was the safest unsafe place.

Maybe not so safe; for the past two decades, the cast-iron eyelet that connected the lifeboat's stern to its davit had been slowly failing. An invisible crack, brittle metal, saltwater. And now a roiling storm.

The eyelet shattered and Sister Gravity gaped as the lifeboat swung to dangle vertically from the mainhold, where it banged repeatedly upon the iron side of the great ship. The canvas top was flung off by the wind and there, *there* they were, hanging onto the plank benches, their little legs swinging, their screams silenced by the tempest.

Sister Gravity let loose with a Solemnitic whistle that pierced the wind.

Within moments, Captain De Saune, the sailors, the Solemnites, and the two widows had formed a human chain that dangled from the lip of the ship down to the banging lifeboat. Arms reached and held the lifeboat still, other arms beckoned for the children.

Under assault from waves and wind and airborne sea creatures, Auguste and Pansy scrambled up the bodies and into the arms of their mothers.

Then the human chain climbed itself upward, with the adults accumulating upon the deck in a huddle that formed around the terrified children. The smell of rum was strong inside this huddle.

The weather relented. The boat stilled, the clouds gave way to the stars. Swaying legs righted themselves. Waves lapped and block-and-tackles clacked and dozens of lungs wheezed in sweet relief. And then, Sister Temperance screamed, "Sister Gravity!" She pushed her way to the edge of the ship. There hung the lifeboat, lazily twisting back and forth. Dangling just below the lifeboat was Sister Gravity. During the rescue of the children, one of her wrists had caught in one of the wayward mooring ropes.

Upon seeing Temperance, Gravity made a little smile to suggest that she was perfectly fine, no need for concern.

And then the ocean sent forth a final, mighty wave.

Leaning over the rail, Sister Temperance stared deep into Sister Gravity's contracted irises. Gravity offered a little flick of her fingers, a willingness to part, having saved the children, having achieved something worthwhile.

The wave consumed the lifeboat, rose over the ship, and then broke into a mist, a fog that floated away from the ship with the warm breath of malice.

The lifeboat had disappeared.

A miracle, a timid, whistling cry. There, under the light of fading stars and a half-moon, Sister Gravity calmly paddled in the still water. She leaned back and closed her eyes. Her dress floated up to encircle her head like the petals of a flower.

Off the stern, the sun peeked over the watery horizon, rosy light racing across the sea toward the *Isère*.

Behind Sister Gravity, there appeared ripples, belching bubbles, and the tip of a massive bone spear rose from the water. The spear was as long as a pine tree is tall, a twisted horn followed by the spotted round face and featureless eyes and body of a narwhal. A narwhal is a porpoise, and porpoises are not the size of whales. But this narwhal was as large as a sperm whale, and it breeched the water and then clamped its jaws over the awestruck lillyflower of Sister Gravity.

There was a moment of calm as the great narwhal became still. It floated for a moment, as if it were relaxing. Then a flap of the tail and a wave of the arms, and the beast propelled itself backward into the sea.

The tip of the horn disappeared with tiny *ploop* and the *Isère's* seventy-four remaining souls were left to stare awestricken at a patch of purple water.

. . .

By the time officers and crew regained their wits, the stowaways had disappeared.

Chapter Sixteen

IN THE HOLD, THE ROPES HAD REMAINED SECURE AND THE FAMILIAR alleys had remained intact. Still, the darkened shapes of the two-hundred and fourteen giant wooden boxes seemed to loom differently from before.

With quick steps, Sister Honora led the Sanvisians to their head-crate, ushered them inside, and lit their lamp. Then she was gone, and they were alone to shiver together in wordless ruminations of mournful exhaustion.

Several wordless hours later, Honora returned.

"I've spoken to the Captain."

Eyes blinked at her.

"He has not yet settled upon your fate."

Auguste mumbled, "Whatever punishment he deems, I shall deserve it."

"For now," said Honora, "he deems that you join us for Sister Gravity's funeral."

The sun was frozen directly overhead, the sea remained tauntingly calm, and water dripped from the remnants of the sails.

The crew had assembled midship, facing upward to the wheel-house deck from whence Captain De Saune would soon deliver Sister Gravity's eulogy. At the fore of the crew stood Sister Temperance and Pansy, clad in their blackest dresses.

On the deck behind the gathered crew, a hatch lifted open and Sister Honora and the three French stowaways emerged. The stowaways followed Honora to stand at the rear of the group, their faces downcast in fear and shame—as tempered by a touch of raging optimism; for they could not help but quietly revel in this rare exposure to daylight.

Honora whispered to them encouraging words and then she hurried away to ascend the stairs to the wheelhouse. A few moments later, she and Captain De Saune appeared at the deck at the fore of the wheelhouse. Honora remained a step back as the Captain approached the handrail and prepared to address those gathered. Chitchat ceased.

Speaking in French with the resounding sadness of one who has previously addressed groups of traumatized seafarers, he bellowed, "Gentlemen, in the face of the gale, in the blackness of night, with the charge of bravery where cowardice leads to death, and with all these obstacles further complicated by extreme drunkenness, you have made me proud to be your Captain.

"And yet, in spite of all courage, one of our number has been—"

He removed a kerchief from his trouser pocket, wiped his brow, blew his nose.

"—lost. A woman, a righteous powerful woman. And a formidable cook."

General agreement from the crew, for whom Gravity had ladled many bowls of soup in the mess hall.

The Captain extended an index finger downward toward Pansy, who stood small next to Sister Temperance. He pointed his other index finger toward the stowaways standing at the rear of those congregated. The crewmen turned their stone faces to examine the widows and the young boy trying to hide behind his mother.

The Captain continued. "We lost one, we saved two. To the children who were rescued by Sister Gravity's sacrifice, I offer a piece of advice born of personal experience. Try not to dwell on the guilt. It will eat you up." Here, the captain squeezed his eyes shut, then opened them, now moist. "That's all I've got."

The Captain withdrew and Sister Honora stepped forth. She opened her Bible and leaned into the railing. Speaking English in a voice devoid of emotion, she recited:

> The Lord sent a great wind on the sea and the sailors said to one another, "Come, let us cast lots to find out who is responsible for this calamity." They cast lots and the lot fell on Jonah. The sea was getting rougher and rougher. So they asked him, "What should we do?"
>
> "Throw me into the sea," Jonah replied, "and it will become calm."
>
> The men refused to do this, as they admired Jonah greatly. "Let us instead row back to land," they said.
>
> But they could not row, for the sea grew even wilder than before. So they threw Jonah overboard, and the raging sea grew solemn.
>
> Now the Lord provided a huge fish to swallow Jonah. From inside the fish Jonah prayed. "God, you have hurled me into very heart of the seas, and the currents swirled about me; all your waves and breakers swept over me. The engulfing waters threatened me, seaweed wrapped around my head. When my life was ebbing away, I remembered you, Lord, and my solemn prayer rose to you, to your holy temple."
>
> And the Lord was satisfied. He commanded the fish, and it vomited Jonah onto dry land.

Sister Honora closed the Bible and folded her hands atop one another. "Blessed be the word of God." A few of the crew murmured their approval. Honora continued. "I know not whether, three days hence, the horned monster will vomit Sister Gravity unto dry land, or whether she will be brought instead to the Kingdom of Heaven. Whatever be the case, we shall remember her sacrifice and honor the two children for whose lives she gave her own."

She bent her head and whistled softly. In spite of their hangovers, and the fact that most of them did not speak English, the crewmen were moved to join her. Their unpracticed harmonies lent a distinctly amateurish air to the proceedings. Honora tolerated this for a few moments, and then raised her hands and brought the clamor to a stop.

The Captain stepped forth once again, to mutter a few words about maritime duty and the honor of conveying this great colossus to a country as bold as America. He closed a with roar, "Mend the sails and fire the boiler, lads! We shall split the sea asunder!"

The crew cried "Huzzah!" and scattered to meet the multitude of repairs that awaited.

Honora intercepted the stowaways before they reached the downhatch. "The Captain has decided to confine you to the brig for the rest of the voyage."

Auguste said, "Is this news good or bad?"

Euphémie said, "It is better than drowning."

Honora allowed her eyes to brighten, "It's much better than drowning. Come, I'll lead you."

Chapter Seventeen

As accommodations went, the brig was a significant step up from their crate. It had three cots, and one of them was long enough to accommodate Euphémie. In the corner, hidden behind a privacy sheet, was a latrine bucket with a removable tin lid. The brig even had a portal. The glass was painted black, but it passed enough light to tell day from night.

The widows did not suffer greatly from this new confinement. They might have *enjoyed* it, were it not for Auguste. As far as he was concerned, he was practically a murderer and he deserved nothing less than to be tied to a rope and dragged behind the ship until the sea had picked his bones clean. The brig was far too comfortable for one so vile as he. He brooded, spoke only in short spurts. And Pansy paid him no visits.

When Annie attempted to lift his spirits by inviting him to imagine the glories of America, Auguste demurred, "Leave me to my solemnity. It's all I have left."

A week passed. The floor of the brig accumulated a carpet of crescent-shaped fingernail fragments. The room stank. Annie suffered coughing fits. Tiny insects sought refuge in the follicles of their scalps.

One evening, as Auguste slept, Euphémie said to Annie, "They'll send us back to Sanvisa."

Annie said, "The Sisters will not allow it."

Euphémie said, "You're quick to trust our lives to believers. I would remind you that your husband was hanged by his own vicar."

In the midst of a dream, Auguste murmured, in English, "I am much sorry, Sister Gravity. You are kind to me. Please make me the pardon."

"What does he say?" whispered Annie, who was less certain with the new language than Euphémie.

"The usual. Oh, poor boy."

The next day, Sister Honora spoke thru the iron bars of the door's window. "We make landfall tomorrow. A caravan of ships has begun to escort us to New York! The *Isère*'s cargo is a celebrity."

Euphémie and Annie perked up at this news, even in spite of their uncertain fate. To walk on solid land, to see one another in the sunlight, to *be* somewhere.

Honora said, "There will be a great deal of activity once we dock. Cranes will unload the crates. The Captain and his mates will have to endure various ceremonies. Manifests will have to be confirmed. The newspapermen will demand to see portions of the colossus. It will be a spectacle. All of this means that you will remain in the brig for at least two more days. Once you do step off the ship, there will be an inquest and then you will most likely be sent back to France.

. . .

Early the next morning, the ship became still, the swish of the water stopped, the engine ceased its hissing and clanking. And then, from the assembled crew, a chorus of *huzzahs* and stomping boots.

Auguste asked, "Are we in America, Mother?"

"We are adjacent to it, son."

"Then we have made it."

It was June 17, 1885.

Chapter Eighteen

OUTSIDE, CHAINS CLANKED AND SAILORS HEAVED. IN THE BRIG, THE stowaways awaited their fate.

Auguste began to question the widows. *"Quelle sorte de nourriture mangent les Américains?"*

"English, please," said Annie.

"What food do America eat?"

Annie said, "Same as us, I expect. Bread, water, cheese, chickens."

Euphémie said, "I hear they eat tobacco and spill the juice over their furry chins."

"Do they drink wine?" said Auguste.

"What do you know of wine?" said Annie.

"I drinked it from a bowl. When I was young. It made me piss. Mother, are you anxious?"

Euphémie said, "Don't ask such questions."

"Don't be anxious," said Auguste, "the Solemnites will protect us."

That afternoon, Sister Temperance brought them food, water, and news. "We are at anchor. The cranes and derricks are steaming up.

A great crowd has gathered at the dock. The *Isère*'s cargo is precious." With a wink she added, "Even more precious than they know."

"Any news of the Captain's intentions with respect to our freedom?" said Euphémie.

"He has been very occupied. But Sister Honora whispers into his ear at every opportunity."

"What does she whisper?" said Annie.

"'Do not send them to jail. Do not send them back to France.'"

Euphémie said, "What is it like out there? The sky? The air? The people?"

"The people are a great crowd," said Temperance. "Spitting brown juice as if they were grasshoppers."

"It is tobacco," said Auguste, grinning at Euphémie. "You were right."

"The air is dense," said Temperance. "Clouds reach all the way to the ground. You feel it, yes? New York is eager for its colossus."

She swapped them a new latrine bucket and then rushed away.

Temperance returned the next day, this time with a sack of fresh apples that had been ushered onto the ship from the dock.

"The Captain has not forgotten you. Keep hope."

She swapped out the latrine bucket and then left.

Chapter Nineteen

A CLATTER OF KEYS. THE DOOR SWUNG OPEN. BEFORE THEM STOOD Captain De Saune, weary, glaring at their sorry mass of desperation and poverty.

"*Mesdames, mon petit.* I have ushered a great big lady to stand sentinel over this land. I have heard speeches in her honor. My hand is sore from congratulations. The statue is copper and iron. You are flesh and spirit. You are parasites on my vessel. I would leave you here to rot. I would bring you to an inquest. But I'll soon have an empty cargo hold that I must fill with wheat. I need to assemble a crew for the return to France and, frankly, I can't bear much more of Sister Honora's pleading. It was her kin, after all, who was eaten by the whale. She deserves a say. She is relentless with her mercy. So, tonight, you leave my ship."

Auguste said, "*Monsieur le capitaine,* we will not be sent back to France?"

"Not on the *Isère.*"

"And we will not go to prison?"

"There is one last crate to be unloaded. It is the same one in which you stowed-away. It's currently in the hold, unobserved."

He tapped the door to the brig. "Unlocked. As soon as I part, you shall go directly to your crate and remain there until it is lifted off the ship. The Sisters will remove you later this evening. And then we will never see one another again."

"Sir, your charity—"

"My charity has its bounds. *Adieu*."

Within a head, within a crate, within the hold of a freighter anchored to the shores of the New World, Auguste and Annie and Euphémie gripped tightly to the latticework of their escape pod, awaiting final deliverance from their age of mud, of being stomped into the mud.

The crate lurched. The head rocked back and forth in the rotting straw. Annie was greatly pleased to hear Auguste giggle. She clamped her hand over his mouth in order that no one else might hear.

Upward, swing sideways, then jitter downward.

The crate alighted gently. The chain was unhooked. Footsteps faded.

The stowaways sat in the dark, the stillness broken only by crickets.

"Mother?"

"Yes?"

"Are those American crickets?"

"Everything is American now."

"Mother?"

"Yes?"

"I knew the Sisters would save us."

Footsteps atop their vessel, nails prised, and then three sets of hands reached them and they were lifted out onto a great stack of crates and the stars were above and the sky was lightening over the ocean, and the thin straight silhouettes of Sister Temperance,

Sister Honora, and Pansy rushed to embrace them and brush straw out of their hair.

Pansy held Auguste by the shoulders and rotated him until he faced the electric glory of New York City, Edison's lights and steam and smoke and concrete and marble.

Auguste could not speak. Euphémie gasped. Annie leaned tightly against Euphémie.

The missionaries offered them a bladder of water. The refugees drank. The stifling summer air was paradise.

This was not Sanvisa.

The city's breath was a dull rumble, indistinct. It reminded Auguste of Pansy's misplaced chords played on the ship's organ. A rat peeked its nose over the edge of the crate. Pansy shooed it away. Annie walked slow circles, gazing at the sky, the dim stars.

Euphémie tried, and failed, to run her fingers thru her tangled hair. "Might we have the chance to bathe?"

Sister Honora said, "Not yet. We have a train to catch."

Part Two

"But you are American, so you don't believe."

"Ho!" hooted the doctor, "because I'm American I believe anything, so I say beware!"

— Djuna Barnes, *Nightwood*

Chapter Twenty

In the darkness, their bare feet told them more than their eyes or ears. Climb down the stack of enormous playblocks, all the way to the salted, smoothed planks of the dock itself, crossing onto dirt, onto cobblestones, toward the glowing city, across soft sand paths, past warehouses and idle taverns and, now, more cobbles, into the canyons of New York, walled-in by brick buildings as tall as a cathedral.

Now, the sun began to rise, sending stray light between the gaps in these canyons. The city's indistinct rumble began to divide itself into hooves, voices, bells, steam whistles. Dogs barking, milkmen on horse carts, merchants sweeping the sidewalks in front of their bakeries, or cobblehouses, or butchershops.

The sun climbed, and the world awoke, shops opening and sidewalks swept. Straight boulevards, coal smoke, strange faces, ornate footwear. The clinking of streetcars and the whistle of a traffic cop. Charcoal, food, and grease, Hebrew newspapers wrapped around warm bread.

The Sisters implored Auguste to stay to the walkways, but the masses of bowler-headed pedestrians repeatedly edged him into the street where he was obliged to dodge trolleys and horse carts and rickshaws. In avoiding a man who straddled a slender, tall, spoked wheel, Auguste stepped a bare foot into a fresh mound of horseshit and found comfort in its familiarity.

"Velocipede," whispered Pansy.

Pedestrian eyes followed Euphémie, standing a head above virtually anyone else. These past weeks, her spine had grown straighter even as her once-broken fingers remained crooked.

Annie was dumbstruck, and self-conscious about her disintegrating dress. She avoided the eyes of strangers. Euphémie met eyes eagerly.

Sisters Honora and Temperance were not so impressed as the Sanvisians; they'd already seen New York, they were tired, they wished to be home, and they desperately missed Sister Gravity and her irrepressible goodness.

Pansy was managing well enough. She pointed out novelties to Auguste, using English only, and Auguste understood little of what he heard, except when they passed a family of French beggars whose children were complaining of hunger.

The train depot was cavernous, the ceilings dripped with condensed steam, the walls were blackened with coal smoke, pigeons coasted from one impossible windowsill to another, and the whole place reverberated with American accents.

The Sisters led them to a relatively uncrowded area at the base of a great slab of a wall. There, they set their trunks on the marble floor. Sister Honora said, "You may rest for a moment. Sister Temperance will purchase our tickets. I will send a telegram to alert Solemn of our arrival, and to explain why Sister Gravity will not be present."

Honora entrusted Pansy with some coins for food and instructed her to show their exhausted and unbathed friends to the bathrooms. As soon as Honora and Temperance had parted, the girl disappeared into the crowd, to return shortly with a paper sack filled with fried oysters.

She and the Sanvisians gnawed the briny meat, licked the breading from their fingers, savored the grease. Pansy led them to a water fountain and they drank. She introduced them to American bathrooms, explained indoor plumbing.

Auguste entered the men's room. He followed Pansy's instructions and turned the lever that made water come out of the faucet. He rinsed a month of grime from his face, his hair, hands, and forearms. Then into the stall, where he washed his feet in the toilet and then squatted on the seat and used the fixture for its intended purpose. As he emerged from the bathroom, he said hello—in English—to a man in a pinstriped suit, and the man said, "Good day."

Returning, he found Annie and Euphémie and Pansy sitting on the trunks, their hair wet, their faces and hands clean, and their moods steadily rising under the influence of the New World.

Presently, Temperance returned with train tickets. She was followed shortly by Honora.

"We depart in twenty minutes. Come, let us advance to the platform."

A man in a silly hat examined their tickets and pointed them toward a chuffing locomotive. Third class, yes, they entered the car and sat together and stowed their trunks in great shelves above their heads. Other passengers filed in, occupied the remaining seats, paid no heed to our heroes. Men smoked pipes and snuffed tobacco that they'd rubbed upon their hands.

Auguste and Pansy sat across from each other, a small table between them, their noses pressed to the windows.

Pansy said, "You've never traveled so fast as you will today."

"I am on a chair. No crate. No head."

"You are in America, and you are welcome here."

Auguste said, "Are we Americans now?"

"I don't know the rules, exactly," said Pansy, "But I'd say that the further west we go, the more American you'll be."

. . .

A whistle and a jerk and they were off. The other riders stared at newspapers or books, unimpressed with the majesty of locomotion. The pressure of steam, heat, water, iron plugging and creeping, and now they exited the station into sunlight, clanking thru the city and past starving dogs and brick apartments and smoke everywhere and a steam shovel chews at the ground, and a steam roller flattens a path for new cobbles. The great clock with arms as long as men, and men everywhere fiddling with their fob watches.

The train stops and starts and gains speed and an hour passes with the boy staring out the window the entire time, and his mother and Euphémie are also staring, and now they are not so afraid to be noticed, and so the widows speak in French, pointing out American things: electrical lines, the gothic mass of the Brooklyn Bridge, a Siamese cat chasing a drunkard.

The buildings grow shorter, the space between them expands. Houses appear now, with clotheslines, and here, a field of amber grain, ready for harvest, and orchards now, grids of trees, so many trees, and they cross rivers on great bridges, and they are in the country, and Auguste has fallen asleep, and his mother is stroking his hair, and Euphémie is stroking his mother's hair, and the Sisters of Solemn are aglow with the homeward draw.

The clouds thin and the sun reaches forth, the American sun. A man in a silly hat asks for tickets and Pansy kicks under the table to awake Auguste, who rubs his face as if everything that's ever happened to him up to this very moment has been a dream, and Pansy brings him to the toilet where he pees into a hole that opens directly to the railroad ties which speed by and he peers into that hole until Pansy pounds on the door and he unlatches it and they walk up and down the cars. They enter a dining car—all that uneaten food on all those plates—and are glared at so they leave.

The train enters the countryside and stops less frequently. Cattle, water tanks, whistle stops, mailbags. Smoke and steam and flecks of ash enter the windows. The passengers unbutton their collars.

Auguste sees black people in fields, following oxen, cutting alfalfa. "Who are those?"

Sister Temperance says, "Those are Negroes. They are a strong race, from Africa. When my father was a boy, Negroes were owned by white people. But that's all over now, and they are equal to all, for this is America. You'll see, very soon, you'll see. Look at those plows. They're made of iron."

At night it seems as if they are making no progress at all, but by sunrise the grazing pastures have been replaced by deciduous forests whose encroaching growth tickles the passing train. The locomotive curls around small mountains, twisting sunlight into shade.

As the towns grow farther apart, the passengers thin, each stop disgorging more people than climb aboard.

The conductor announces the crossing into Indiana. Indiana looks no different from Ohio, the same trees and hills and cloud-specked skies.

Night, the refugees are jiggered awake by Pansy.

"We change trains at the next depot."

A nameless depot in a nameless place where nameless birds chitter. Tow the trunks to the platform, watch the train chug away, await the sunrise, crows howling at ravens, cup hands and drink from a puddle beneath a dripping watertower.

Squeal of iron, hiss of the whistle, all aboard. This new train is slower and smaller. Pansy and Auguste run unhindered thru the cars.

Chapter Twenty-One

SEVERAL HOURS LATER, THE TRAIN COASTED TO A STOP AT AN unremarkable town called Restive and they disembarked into the heat and humidity of Southern Indiana in mid-June. A lumber mill whirred in the distance. It was after noon. No one had come to meet them.

"It is a further two miles to Solemn," said Sister Honora. "We shall have to walk."

They formed a line: woman, trunk, woman, woman, trunk, woman, child, child; a train of their own, following one track of a wagon wheel road. With legs stiff and uncertain of the steady ground, they marched toward Solemn. The woodsy air was paradise, the world was green with untamed flora, humming with unknown fauna.

The road under the trees was littered with nuts. Pansy showed Auguste how to crack the shells of hickories and buckeyes, and they ate until Sister Honora told them to knock it off or suffer a tummy-ache.

A cicada sang, joined immediately by thousands more, and the air was filled with their throbbing whir. Sister Temperance accompanied the insects with a whistling drone, swelling and retreating. Honora and Pansy joined in, rising and falling. The sound became a convection current, an endless climb and descent, with no center to itself.

They didn't hear the wagon until it had nearly overtaken them. It was piloted by a man in a white straw hat, and it was loaded with planks of fresh-milled, fragrant hickory. The driver slowed the horse to match the pace of the walkers, who ceased their whistling. He fixed his eyes upon Euphémie, tipped his hat. "Just off the train?"

Euphémie did not return his gaze.

Sister Honora said, "We are walking to Solemn."

"I'll take you. It's on my way."

"To where?"

"New Harmony," said the man.

"That's two hundred miles."

"Sadly, this is true."

"You don't have saw mills in New Harmony?" said Honora.

"I was to meet a bride here. But I've waited a week and she has not arrived. None of you would be called Bernadette, perchance?" The man expectorated a slender line of tobacco juice over the side of the wagon where it wrapped itself around a wheel spoke.

All four women, as well as Pansy and Auguste vigorously shook their heads.

"Well, then," said the man, "I expect I shall use this wood for a hogshead rather than a nursery. Do you want a lift or not?"

When Sisters Temperance and Honora did not immediately reply, Annie said, in English, "Yes, sir. We desire your aid."

"You got a sweet way of talking, miss."

Honora said, "Don't expect her to marry you."

"Don't expect *any* of us to marry you," said Pansy.

The man said, "Low expectations is my secret to happiness. Climb in."

Pansy asked her mother permission to continue on foot with Auguste. "It's only two miles. I know the way."

Sister Honora allowed that she'd earned a few moments of independence. "Walk well."

Annie and Euphémie shrugged their approval.

The women boarded the wagon. The straw hat man clicked his tongue and the horse pulled away with the widows and missionaries and their trunks sitting high upon the stacked wood, a bouquet of dresses and bonnets and cheerful waves.

Pansy led Auguste into the trees that flanked the wagon path. She stepped quickly, eager to prove her familiarity with the place. The ground was layered with deciduous decay, snails crawled upon moist plants, birds made racket in the cool air.

With Auguste hustling to keep up, Pansy said, "Look here. This is poison ivy. My grandpa was impervious to it. I am not."

She gently guided Auguste's hand to brush against the ivy. "There. We'll soon know."

They continued walking.

Although the trees were different from those in Sanvisa, they were still trees. Although the birds sang different songs, they still sang.

Pansy looked around as if she were trying to place herself. "This way."

They came to a path and they followed it. The land sloped downward. The trees opened up to reveal a sunlit river, slow-moving, wider than a tossed rock. Pansy grabbed a woody vine that dangled from one of the overhanging limbs and ran and jumped so she swung out over the stream. Pendulating, she shouted, "There's lots of streams and brooks and so forth. This here is a crick. Push, please."

Auguste placed his hands upon the middle of her back. Her spine and ribs were just under the skin under her dress. He gave a nudge, careful not to slip on the bank's loose soil. As she swung out over the water, Pansy said, "Again. Harder."

Auguste pushed Pansy into a wide arc. She squealed with unsolemn delight.

A geodesic reptile was sunning upon a log that rose and fell with the slow pulse of the water. The creature's beak was chipped, its shell peeling.

"That's a snapping turtle," said Pansy. "It'll rip your arm off."

"Crossvine creepers. Dutch horns. That's an elm. Birch. Sycamore. Oh, another poison ivy. How's your hand?"

Auguste held it up. He'd scratched it thoroughly.

"Does it hurt?"

"I can block out pain. Have we much further to go?"

"Are you tired?"

"Not a bit. I like this." He waved his hand to indicate the entirety of the outdoors.

"You know," said Pansy, "things will be very solemn after we get to town, what with the mourning of Sister Gravity."

Auguste ceased walking. "What we did was horrible."

Pansy inhaled as if to speak. But she could only offer a weak nod.

"Will they be angry at us, Pansy?"

"Oh, no. The people of Solemn are gentle folk. He who casts the first stone, and so forth."

"Sister Gravity was the nicest person I ever met."

"Obviously. She saved your life."

"And yours. Don't you feel guilty?"

"I feel sad," said Pansy. "But Solemnites are taught not to punish ourselves for our sins. Like Captain De Saune said, guilt will eat you up."

"I'm still awfully sad." The boy raised a finger, as if he'd had a thought. "Do you mind, Pansy, if we cry for a bit?"

"Yes, but only a little."

After they'd cried for a bit, Pansy said, "I have to pee."

"So do I," said Auguste.

"You go that way and I'll go this way and we'll meet back here."

Auguste made note of their spot and he walked until he could no longer see Pansy's retreating form. He untied his rope belt and emptied his bladder on the soft soil. As he was re-tying his britches, a footstep snapped a branch behind him.

He turned to discover a lad, roughly his age, dressed in clothes more ragged than his own, bare feet, leaves in his hair. A long-barreled musket leaned upon his shoulder, a string of dead squirrels hung from a rope strung around his waist.

Moments ago, these woods had seemed empty, as if they'd existed solely to welcome Auguste into this new world. And now there was a lad with a musket, and Auguste understood that it was himself who had no business here.

The lad remained still. His eyes and freckled face and shirtless overalls and the dead squirrels and the gun were uniformly uninviting.

A stomping, a flash of yellow fabric, and then Pansy's voice, "Hello, Delmar." She stepped behind the lad and flicked the barrel of his gun.

The lad spun around.

"I'm Pansy. You're a Methodist, you probably don't know me. But I know you. Your grandma and my mamma used to snap beans together."

The lad eased up a little.

"You got yourself some squirrels."

Delmar ran a finger along the heads of the five corpses hanging from his waist. "I set out for the bair, but all's I've shot is these'uns."

"You say 'the bair', as if it is a well-known creature."

"It's a downright notorious oppugner of man and beast. Where you been?"

"I've been missioning on a whole 'nother continent. It's where I found him."

Auguste felt the conversation turn his direction. As spoken by Delmar, English words had grown new syllables and attained vowels that his mouth had never formed and his ears had never heard. And Pansy was mimicking him.

"This here's Auguste. He's French. Maybe you don't know where France is. That's a country all the way on the other side of the world. That's where I've been for the last year. Auguste is dressed like French person. Those little britches of his are called a *pantalon*—singular, not plural—in his country. He spoke a whole different language of what we do. Say hello, Auguste."

Out of the corner of his mouth, Auguste murmured to Pansy, "*Je ne comprends rien.*"

"*Dis-lui* hello. *N'aies pas peur.*"

Auguste said to Delmar, "I em Auguste Lestables. I em much pleased to meet you."

Delmar said to Pansy, "You was amongst those who waint on that train last year."

"Indeed, I was."

"That boy thar talks lack a sissy."

Pansy said, "You said you were hunting a bear. What sort of a bear?"

"They say she's a female. No one knows for shore. She sorta lurks around. Only a few's seen her. You'uns never haired about her? This bair, she's got hersuf three airs and she can hair you coming from a long ways. And when she hairs you, she don't flee off; she comes to. So they say. Goodbye now."

Delmar walked away into the trees. The squirrels had oozed some droplets of blood on the ground.

Pansy said, "Don't pay attention to Delmar."

Auguste said, "I didn't understand very much of his words."

Pansy switched to French and explained that Delmar claimed

he'd been hunting a *three-eared* bear sow. Back to English, she said, "There is no three-eared bear. Delmar is an onerous rascal with a primitive accent."

She led on, naming wildflowers, pawpaws, raspberries, the clouds, and warning of the dangers of copperhead snakes. For a boy who had been learning English for less than four weeks, Auguste had achieved quite a lot. But Pansy's monologue far exceeded his comprehension, and he soon tuned her out. Instead, he imagined that he was stalking a three-eared bear.

As they crossed a low spot, Auguste, deep into his ursine fantasy, dropped his gaze to the muddy ground and saw two eyes open up, as if the mud itself were alive. He gave a start. Pansy plunged her hands into the mud and pulled forth the largest frog Auguste had ever seen. The thing was bigger than his porridge bowl.

Pansy said, "It's called a bullfrog. You'll see more of these than you will bears."

The frog spasmed its legs and sprung from Pansy's fingers. It landed with a *splat* at Auguste's feet.

"Come. We're almost there," said Pansy.

They walked a little farther, and, suddenly, there they were.

"As you can see," said Pansy, "Solemn was designed very deliberately."

"It's more round than I imagined," said Auguste.

The village was laid out in concentric circles; as if it had been designed so that, when viewed from the lofty heights of heaven, it would provide a conspicuous target upon which the Lord could fling his darts of righteous glory.

A ring of buildings—two dozen-odd houses, a cobblehouse, a smithy, a feed store, a pantry, and the chapel—faced inward to a large common space where chickens and geese roamed freely. In the center of the open space—the bullseye—was an expansive garden of pole beans, squash, potato, corn, rye, and so forth.

Virtually all of the buildings were unpainted clapboard, oozing sap from the dimples of square-headed nails. On the far side of town, set off by a hundred yards, was a great red barn. Next to it, a split-rail fence hemmed a pasture of braying donkeys.

Milling about the town were various Solemnites, men in wide hats, women in plain dresses, all of them whistling. They waved to Pansy as the children approached. No one smiled.

Auguste said to Pansy, "Where is our mothers?"

"Where *are*. I expect they're at Sister Gravity's house." She pointed to a tidy domicile in the outer ring. "Oh, it's wonderful to be home!" Pansy took a few jaunty steps and then froze, for the bells of the Chapel of Solemn had begun to ring.

Chapter Twenty-Two

WITH THE SOUNDING OF THE BELLS, THE VILLAGERS BEGAN STREAMING toward the chapel. It was the only painted building in Solemn, whitewashed, one storey tall, topped by a bell tower.

Pansy said, "The bells are only shaken under the most solemn of circumstances, or to share glad tidings."

"Which is it?"

"Both, I expect." She quickened her pace.

Pansy and Auguste were the last to arrive. Heads turned as they entered the chapel. Drip-glass windows, rows of pews, a basket of chip-board fans. A segment of a hickory trunk served as a pulpit. Behind the pulpit, a small man in an undersized grey sack suit was tugging a rope that dangled from a hole in the ceiling.

"That there," said Pansy, "is Reverend Celicius Steadfast. You'll get to know him pretty well. Oh! Our mothers!"

Honora, Temperance, and the widows were all seated in the pew directly in front of the pulpit. Pansy and Auguste rushed to join them. Reverend Celicius Steadfast released the rope and the bell rang itself out.

The Reverend raised his hands. The congregation quieted, and then puckered their lips and whistled. A drone rose and crab-walked itself from one throbbing harmonic intersection to another. The Reverend lowered his hands and the whistling stopped.

"I've summoned you today under circumstances of both tragedy and joy." Auguste elbowed Pansy to acknowledge her prescience. "A reminder that God's perfection is as mysterious as it is miraculous. We are but feathers floating—sometimes toward the sun, but always, eventually, we shall settle to the earth."

The congregants whistled in agreement.

Reverend Steadfast said, "Let us first acknowledge a moment of floatation. Sisters, would you stand?"

Sisters Honora, Temperance, and Pansy, complied.

The Reverend continued. "After nearly a year in France where they dutifully spread the good news of Solemnity, our courageous missionaries have returned with three very special guests. Friends, please welcome these new citizens of Solemn, refugees of poverty and intolerance; stalwart, strong, and decent. Stand, Euphémie Deplouc. She's tall, ain't she? Stand, Annie Lestables. Stand, young Auguste Lestables. You are amongst friends. Your travails are concluded. The journey of our missionaries, taken at great risk and expense has borne fruit. Let us praise the Lord's heavenly wisdom."

Auguste looked to his mother. He had understood only a few moments of the Reverend's speech. Amongst those had been the man's attempt to pronounce their names. *Annie* had more or less survived intact. *Auguste* had migrated into the back of the Reverend's throat, but nevertheless remained recognizable. *Lestables* had been twisted into *Luh-stay-blays*. As for *Euphémie Deplouc*, the indignities were too horrific to detail.

In the mouths of all but the women who'd smuggled them out of France, these were to be their new names for this *nouveau Monde*.

The Reverend said, "You may be seated." The congregants obliged. The sermon continued. "Our numbers have grown, the feather has flown. But, alas, numbers will wane as well. Disease—let us remember the sad demise of Brother Gravity—and injury and age devour us all. There is much in this world that would reduce us. And today our missionaries, who have brought the gospel of Solemnity to the Old World, and who have returned with three new friends, have informed us that our dear Sister Gravity has joined her husband in the afterlife."

Gasp.

"Remain solemn, friends," said the Reverend, "as I invite Sister Honora to address the passing of Sister Gravity." He retreated to a logstump chair directly below a pinewood cross, from whence hung a papier-mâché Christ with hand-painted eyes and straight, scrawny limbs.

Sister Honora approached the pulpit. "It is with profound grief that we learned some weeks ago via a letter that Brother Gravity had been consumed by sickness. I am further grieved to inform you that, only a few days ago, dear Sister Gravity was consumed by a monstrous large narwhal." Honora added, "A narwhal is a sort of porpoise, a sea-fish which breathes air and which has a horn growing out of its face. This particular narwhal was unnatural, the size of a whale, and, after a mighty storm which nearly destroyed our vessel, it swallowed our colleague whole."

This inspired several low whistles.

"Sister Gravity gave her life for the two children you see here. They had been caught topship during a maelstrom. It was Sister Gravity who ushered them to safety. Alas, once they were out of danger she was taken by the beast, a sacrifice as noble as it was tragic. As we mourn, let us also celebrate. For I assure you, these two children will prove worthy of her sacrifice."

The congregation craned their necks to view Pansy and Auguste. Pansy, who understood her mother's words, waved timidly. Auguste, who had not, imitated her. It was hard to guess the emotion behind the grim faces of the congregation. But one assumes that not all of the Solemnites agreed that two children were worth one Sister Gravity.

Sister Temperance was now invited to the pulpit, where her breezy cheer might elevate the mood.

"Let us thank the Lord that Sister and Brother Gravity were unable to produce children, for there is no greater loss than the loss of one's parents. God has shown his wisdom, as always. What was once considered a tragic barrenness can now be called a mercy."

Temperance now beckoned Annie to the pulpit, and, though she had not expected this, she complied. Speaking a close approximation of English, and shaking with nerves, Annie said, "I am thank you. My friend, Euphémie, is thank you. My baby is thank you. Solemn is good and safe."

She shuffled back to the pew.

Reverend Steadfast then led the church into an excruciatingly long silent prayer. Some unknowable time passed—during which Euphémie unsuccessfully prayed for a line of ants to walk across her foot—before Steadfast finally uttered, "Amen."

The entire congregation exhaled. Reverend Steadfast leaned against the pulpit. "Isaiah declared, 'One day the Lord will whistle for the fly that is at the end of the streams of Egypt, and for the bee that is in the land of Assyria.' Let us now whistle in honor of those we have lost and of those whom we have discovered."

The Reverend puckered his cheeks and a slow noise rose from his lips, less of a whistle, and more of a piccolo. The congregation joined him, eighty-odd sets of puckered lips in a harmony of mood moreso than of pitch.

The Reverend raised his hands and the chorus settled into a final, breathy wind. He declared, "Solemnity in all things."

In unison, the congregation answered, "And all things be solemn."

As the flock exited the chapel, Sister Temperance whispered to Annie and Euphémie, "Welcome home."

Chapter Twenty-Three

THERE WAS BUT ONE VACANT BUILDING IN ALL OF SOLEMN: THE clapboard house that had belonged to Sister Gravity and her husband, Brother Gravity. It was across the circle, directly opposite the chapel, whose bell tower was visible just above the village's inner garden.

Sister Honora led the Sanvisians to the Gravity house and pushed open the front door. As with all of the homes in Solemn, this one had two entrances. The front entrance opened to the village's inner circle, and was considered a public place. The rear entrance led to a private sitting area that faced the forest that encircled Solemn.

As with everyone else in Solemn, the Gravitys' aesthetic had been plain. Unfinished furniture, whitewashed walls. A cast iron pan, copper kettle, fireplace, washbasin.

"Two rooms!" cried Auguste, skipping about the orphaned home.

Annie said, "We do not deserve such luxury."

Sister Honora, serene in the doorway, said, "You may refuse, but I believe Sister Gravity would have wan—"

From the other room, Euphémie cried, "*Incroyable!*"

They found her reclined upon an enormous bed whose corner

posts were thick as pine logs. The bed was so tall it required a step stool to climb atop. And the mattress itself was vast and soft with down.

Euphémie said, "My feet don't overhang."

"Brother Gravity was a large man and an excellent carpenter," said Sister Honora.

Auguste belly-flopped onto the bed, rolled over, wiggled his dirty feet. "Mother, you must try it!"

Annie, being a good sport, climbed the stool and fell back upon the bed, her hair spreading upon the quilted bedcover.

Sister Honora, said, "There is room for all three of you."

"There is room for more than three!" said Annie. "Surely someone else needs this bed more than we."

Euphémie knelt before Annie and flattened her hands in prayer. "Heavenly Father, we thank you for inviting us into this home. We will honor the memory of Sister and Brother Gravity for as long as we stay. And we will sleep on your heavenly bed night and day."

Satisfied that the Gravity house had found its ideal tenants, Sister Honora said goodbye and good day and promised to visit them tomorrow.

Though it was only early evening, the stowaways remained in the bed, coaxed into sleep by unparalleled comfort. For fourteen uninterrupted hours, dreams weaved and mingled and merged in the minds of the widows. Auguste, snuggled in-between them, dreamt he was being chased by a three-eared bear thru a graveyard of wooden crosses and marble crypts.

They were awoken before dawn by rooster song, the sound of the sun, the clap of mothwings, by horses snorting and dogs barking. Midwest summer humid, morning glow peeking thru the shutters.

Annie stretched, yawned, itched. "Does anyone else feel like they've been dragged thru a field of nettles?"

Euphémie leaned over Auguste, who was still sleeping. Squinting, she plucked a small black spot from Annie's hairline, just above her ear. She squeezed the black spot until it made a faint pop and then she wiped the residue upon the quilted bedspread. "We must burn this mattress. It is infested."

Annie cried, "We will not do such a thing!" She reached under her armpit and began scratching.

Euphémie peered underneath the bed. In the sniffly voice of one whose head is dangling upside down, she said, "We may have to burn the whole house."

Auguste awoke and immediately began crying. His back was pocked with the swollen bites of bedbugs.

ᵐ   ᵐ   ᵐ   ᵐ

"It's not just you. The whole of Solemn is infested," said Sister Temperance, seated on a bench in front of the Gravity house. "It wasn't like this last year. Apparently, well, I don't know"—she broke off to scratch behind her ear. "Take heart, the Brothers and Sisters say our skin will toughen."

Euphémie and Annie were sitting upon an overturned log facing Sister Temperance. Euphémie said, "I like my skin as it is." She slapped at her knee.

The sun was well up. A breeze shifted the discarded shells of ground barley from one heap to another. The Solemnites had settled into their daily chores. Babies were napping. Dogs and cats slept soundly while free-range fowl trod amongst them.

Temperance said, "Where is Auguste?"

"Off with Pansy," said Annie. "Scratching each other's backs, I presume."

"I have been given permission to share this with him." Temperance presented to Annie a disintegrating, leather-bound book. "It is Sister Gravity's Bible. Goodbye now. I will check on you later today."

After Temperance had parted, Annie pressed the Bible against her forehead and sighed to Euphémie, "What am I to do about this?"

"You mean the fact that we've joined a clan of whistling dogmatists who want to turn your son into one of their own?"

"Precisely," said Annie.

Euphémie said, "Let him read it. Auguste is curious and kind and clever. Trust his heart."

Annie idly flipped the pages of the Bible. "I like it when you're wise."

"I like it when you take my advice."

Chapter Twenty-Four

AUGUSTE AND PANSY WERE NOT SCRATCHING EACH OTHER'S BACKS. Rather, they were in the loft of the village barn, trying to rescue a calico cat that they'd chased into the trusses. The cat had settled upon the toppermost of these trusses with its front paws under its chin, eyes half-closed.

Pansy found in the straw a hard clump of dirt that fit nicely in her hand. She winged it at the cat, missing spectacularly. The clod struck the ceiling and rained chunks of itself.

The air filled with *clickclickclicks*. A little brown bat slipped from between two ceiling planks and flew erratic, irritated circles below the peak of the roof. As its frantic flapping began to ease, Auguste felt in the hay for another clod of dirt and chucked it at the bat. The clod flew directly over the cat, startling it out of its meditation. The cat saw the flapping bat and sent forth a vicious left hook, which knocked the bat silly. It fell straight down. The cat closed its eyes and resumed its nap.

The children raced to the bat, which was flapping feebly in the hay before them.

Auguste said, "I want it."

Pansy said, "Do you know what it is?"

Auguste said, "It's a bald mouse."

"Pervert. It's a dead bat."

Auguste held it between two fingers. He felt the small chest expand. "It is alive. But sleeping."

The children played with the comatose animal, spreading the wings, examining the blood vessels in the translucent skin, poking a piece of straw at its bullish nose.

Before they descended the loft, Auguste slid the bat into his pocket.

That night, after some debate, the French newcomers opted once again to sleep in the supremely comfortable bed, bugs be damned. Before they climbed in, Annie presented Auguste with the Gravity Bible. Loose pages, bent corners, a perfume of Sister Gravity's sweat; Auguste's straight arms held the world-beaten book as if it were a bomb.

"I will read every word."

The next morning, no bites and no bedbugs. But an awful stink. Auguste watched innocently as Annie followed her nose underneath the bed. She reached an arm, waited for her eyes to adjust to the darkness, shrieked, and emerged holding a dead bat by its wing.

Euphémie stared at the bat.

Auguste stared at the bat.

Annie said to Auguste, "Yours, I presume."

Auguste, "Yes, mother."

Annie said, "You know better than to harbor dead mammals. Your father always said."

Auguste said, "The bat was not dead when I brought it home. It had been attacked by a cat, see, in the barn, and I wanted to revive it."

Euphémie said, "You frightened your mother."

Annie said, "Mildly surprised." She pinched a small insect off the fur of the bat.

Auguste said, "Father told me that evil draws evil and wisdom creates wisdom." The boy did not sputter, as most children would have in this situation. "So I put the bat under the bed."

Annie was dumbfounded by this foolishness. She dropped the bat to the floor and took Auguste by his arm and prepared to wallop him on the bottom.

Euphémie, staring at the corpse, said, "I think maybe you should not punish the boy."

Annie said, "I'll do as I please."

"Does it please you to know that your son has found a cure for bedbugs?"

And so the village captured bats and beat them senseless and put them under their beds. The dying animals proved to be deadly sirens. The bedbugs swarmed the bodies, drank the blood, and then died.

"We bore this plague for months," said Reverend Steadfast days later, during an evening church meeting, "and the Lord provided salvation in the figures of these three foreigners. Solemnity in all things."

The congregation replied, "And all things be solemn."

Euphémie whispered to Annie, "Lest those things be bats or bedbugs."

Later that evening, Euphémie and Annie lay in the pest-free bed with Auguste snoring between them. Here was the whispering time, when the widows uttered pet phrases in their native language.

"*Mon ange.*"

"*Mon trésor.*"

"We are in Eden."

"Auguste is certainly happy. And he adores Pansy."

"This bed is unbelievable."

"We do not deserve such good fortune."

"We can be as gods to these people."

"They would invite hornets to live in their mouths."

"We are not hornets."

"Yes. We are much worse."

"What price will we pay for our deliverance?"

Annie said, "I will not exchange Auguste's soul for our freedom."

"I have made a similar exchange with my own son, without regret."

"You are a formidable woman, Euphémie."

"Yes, I am. But in fairness, my son *had* no soul."

Annie said, "These people are good and kind and they have accepted us. We must accept their generosity."

"It's not their generosity that concerns me. It's their theology."

"A theology my son is embracing."

"The boy's skepticism will pull him thru this."

"We must keep an eye on him."

"They're harmless."

"The whistling annoys me."

Auguste, who was not asleep after all, shifted between the women. He said, "Father said that humanity is better served by honesty than by acquiescence."

Annie said, "You don't even know what that means."

Chapter Twenty-Five

PRIOR TO THE ARRIVAL OF THE FRENCH REFUGEES, THE PEOPLE OF Solemn had approached food as if it were punishment for living. But somehow, using the very same ingredients that the Solemnites typically dumped into a community cauldron, from whose perpetually bubbling depths one could ladle a gruel that frequently rewarded its consumers with the scours, our heroic widows generated actual food.

This was not *haute cuisine*; it was hearty, simple, and satisfying. In the hands of the widows, butter became creamier, meat more tender, and vegetables sharp and crisp. The widows were especially thankful to find in Solemn's garden a large plot of potatoes, the American versions being bigger and sweeter than the French. These they baked, boiled, sliced, buttered, mashed, and hashed into forms previously unimaginable to their ascetic hosts.

There was some question of the food being too delicious. Could culinary satisfaction safely co-exist with a colony of strict Solemnites? Reverend Steadfast was brought in to make judgment. At his request, the widows prepared a meal of their finest delights and, accompanied by Sister Honora, they laid it upon his table.

It was not long before every last crock, plate, and bowl of *repas de pommes de terre et autre choses diverses* had been licked clean.

Reverend Steadfast was raptly scraping mashed-potato droppings from the front of his sack shirt when Sister Honora discretely reminded him why they had gathered in the first place.

The Reverend looked about the room as a man caught *in flagrante delicto*, and solemnly declared, "Ecclesiastes, of the ancient Bible tells us , 'Go, chew your food with gladness, and swallow your wine without shame, for God approves, if you do it solemnly.'"

Thereby did the widows liberate the village from the great cauldron of gruel. In their gratitude, the Solemnites invited the widows wholly into the thousand tasks required of a self-sustaining community: gardening, animal husbandry, household repairs, and the rest.

᠁

The Doctrine of Solemn asserted that God favored the well-educated, and so, for four hours every Monday, Wednesday, and Friday, the Solemnitic Chapel became the Solemnitic School. Taught by a peg-legged septuagenarian called Sister Punctuality, the curriculum was a combination of practical education and religious indoctrination, emphasis on the latter.

As a schoolmarm, Sister Punctuality wasn't one of those knuckle-knocker types. Nor was she a kind-but-dim manipulable sap. Nor was she, strictly speaking, a teacher. This was her first season on the job—and her first employment since her leg had fallen off. It wasn't an overly demanding role; because of the Solemnites' aversion to pleasure, the village contained relatively few children, only thirteen, ranging in age from three to eleven, with Pansy and Auguste being the eldest of the lot.

The students sat in the first pew, in order of birthdate, with slates upon their knees, as Sister Punctuality stood at the hickory pulpit and improvised lessons. Pansy and Auguste were excellent students, well-liked by the other children, and so, one day Sister Punctuality invited them to teach simple arithmetic to a muddle-headed seven-year-old boy named Clemming.

Pansy: What's six minus nine?

Clemming (pondering): No such thing as a little number minusing a bigger number.

Pansy: Correct!

Auguste: In actuality, Pansy, there is no reason why you can't subtract nine from six. The answer is a negative number, also known as a debt.

Pansy: Don't let Auguste confuse you. A number less than nothing is not a number. It is a fantasy.

Auguste: I dispute this. For example, Hell is less than nothing, yes? It's on the other side of zero. Is hell a fantasy? Is evil at one end of a great ledger, and grace at the other end? If so, how does one determine the idea of neutrality? Or is evil on an entirely different spectrum, independent of grace? Is the nature of God to bring these two spectra together? Or is it the duty of man to keep them separate? Do bats and bedbugs have their own, respective, ideas of moral neutrality?

Pansy (to Clemming): Ignore him.

Sister Punctuality overheard just enough of this to convince her to never again ask Auguste to assist in her duties.

The boy was capable of upending any lesson at any moment. In the midst of a discussion about possessive plurals, Auguste stated, "I do not understand what is a Holy Spirit. It seems to be

an unnecessary concept. Isn't the god"—he referred to it as *the god*
—"capable of doing himself the work that is attributed to this
Spirit? How does the Spirit communicate with the god? If it's a
mental conversation, and if the Spirit is bodiless, then couldn't we
just as well describe the Spirit as an extension of the god's omni-
science? And prayer. How does the god choose which prayers to
answer? If I pray for rain and my neighbor prays for clear skies,
whom does he reward? Is it a democracy? Does the god count
prayers?" He paused for breath. "I find this all very concerning."

"In the Solemnitic church, we address our concerns thru
solemnity."

"But wh—"

"Nothing is frivolous, no creature is to be mocked, no creature
is to be harmed unless it's for the betterment of the world. Which
is why we allow for the bats."

"My concern remains unwaveringly intact."

"Your concern is perfectly natural; you are a young refugee in
a new world, learning a new language, discovering a relationship
with the god. God, I mean."

"My father would say that Monsieur Comte would say that
religion is a phase of human social development."

"I would agree."

"And when the time is right, we'll replace religion with supe-
rior behaviors based on the principles of mathematics and
gravity."

The other students were studiously pretending not to listen.

Sister Punctuality said, "You are perilously close to heresy."

Pansy sought to distract. "Sister Punctuality, how does one
spell *Emmanuel*? Does it commence with an *I* or an *E*?"

"*E.*"

"Thank you. One *m* or two?"

"Two. E-m-m-a-n-u-e-l."

"In actuality," said Auguste, "I've seen it written with vari—"

Sister Punctuality said, "Young man, the people of Solemn
have welcomed you and your mother and her friend into our

home because all are welcome here." Her soft voice had risen slightly, her ancient vocal cords wavering in the effort. "We act with charity and kindness. And we do so without cruelty, for we are righteous. And so, it is without cruelty, but rather with a desire to impart wisdom unto your heart, that I ask you what sort of student you wish to be. Would you debate every word from the mouth of your instructor, or would you remember the value of solemnity? Would you consider that, perhaps, your father's philosophies are imperfect?"

Auguste reddened. "You will not speak thusly of my father." He gathered his slate and his Bible, and tucked them under his arm and marched past his shocked classmates and out of the school.

Chapter Twenty-Six

EARLIER THAT SAME MORNING, AFTER AUGUSTE HAD HEADED OFF TO school, Annie had said to Euphémie, "Remember that loaf of bread in Le Havre?"

"The one Sister Temperance gave me when we were starving?"

"I don't think she baked that bread."

"Because it was delicious, you mean?"

"Every loaf she's baked in Solemn tastes like a brick."

"She claims it's the same recipe."

Annie's eyes alit. "It's because here they bake their bread in metal pots, Dutch style. That's like asking a chicken to pull a plow. She must have gotten access to a proper oven in France. Tell me, Euphémie, have you ever made a clay oven?"

"I've seen it done."

Annie said, "They say watching is nearly the same thing as learning."

"Then we need to find some clay."

After scouting various creeks and sludgepuddles, they settled on a clear pool in a basin of mud that slid easily between the fingers and dried under the sun into a white crust.

They hauled several barrowloads of the mud to their front yard and stomped it, along with handfuls of straw, into a cob mixture. Then they formed the mass into the shape of an igloo that would have served as a comfortable home for a cocker spaniel.

This completed, they reclined before their curing masterpiece and watched as wasps stole mouthfuls of the mixture for their larval nurseries.

This moment of hard-earned happiness was interrupted by the trudge of Auguste's feet, home three hours early.

He said, "Greetings, Mother, Euphémie. How goes your day?"

"We have fashioned an oven. Why aren't you in school?"

"Sister Punctuality is delusional."

Euphémie cast a glance at Annie, who said, "Delusion is relative. We live in the house of a woman who was swallowed by a horned whale. Are *we* delusional?"

Auguste persisted. "But we saw the whale swallow her. It happened, therefore, the horned whale is not a delusion. The things Sister Punctuality describes are literally unseeable. Today she claimed that we are guided by a ghost!" He flopped his boyish self to sit upon the ground. "I like Sister Punctuality. I like her stories, and I like being here in Solemn, in America. Sincerely. But their dogma lacks consistency. Father would not tolerate this arrangement."

Annie said, "Your father was intolerant."

Euphémie added, "And frequently intolerable."

"My father was a scribe to Comte."

Euphémie said, "According to himself and no other."

Auguste's voice grew sharp. "I beg your pardon, Euphémie, but my father died out of honor for you. I don't see you grieve him. All I see is you working and sleeping alongside my mother. You are not my mother."

From behind, a voice said, "Please."

Pansy stood there, hands crossed in front of her belly. "The entire village can hear you. Your agitation is making people nervous."

"It's a private discussion," said Euphémie.

"Raised voices enjoy no privacy," said Pansy. "Listen."

The air hummed with the type of whistling one normally reserved for a lonesome walk home on a windless night.

Pansy said, "You think we whistle simply for the pleasant noise? We whistle to gather ourselves into a cloud of strength. We have done this ever since our founders said it must be thus. Like you, we Solemnites have suffered a great deal in our journey to this place. And here we have found peace. Please don't disrupt our peace." Pansy covered her round face with her arm and made weeping noises. "Auguste, come back to school. Sister Punctuality is mortified. She promises never to speak of your father again."

Auguste said, "Why doesn't she tell me herself?"

Pansy said, "It's hard to chase little boys when you only have one leg."

Annie said, "Your teacher is a cripple? Good lord, boy." She swatted her son on the back of the head.

Pansy led Auguste away.

Euphémie looked to Annie. "This village is a collection of simmering kettles."

Chapter Twenty-Seven

SISTER PUNCTUALITY WELCOMED AUGUSTE BACK TO CLASS WARMLY, but not so warmly that the rest of the students might guess just how relieved she was that he had returned.

For his part, Auguste endured the remains of the lesson without subjecting his teacher to any further doubting-tomfoolery.

When the day was concluded, and after the students had quick-walked out of the chapel, and as Sister Punctuality was hobbling about and tiding up her papers, she was startled to find Auguste standing at the back of the chapel, arms at his sides.

In a small, polite voice, Auguste said, "I am sorry, Sister Punctuality, for disrupting class today. Your reaction to my unsolemn behavior was perfectly justified. Please forgive me."

In the face of Auguste's contrition, the schoolmarm melted. "I'm not without blame. It was unsolemn of me to mention your—"

"It's okay."

"—father."

"You're a fine teacher," said Auguste.

"And you're a good boy." Sister Punctuality hoisted her satchel over her neck.

Auguste said, "Can I help you carry anything?"

"No, dear. I'm fine."

"Well, I just wanted to tell you that."

Auguste exited the chapel and joined Pansy where she awaited him on the front step.

She said, "How did it go?"

"You were right," said Auguste, "As soon as I said I was sorry, she apologized back to me."

"Grown-ups don't hate us as much as we like to think."

"Let's walk around some," said Auguste.

Pansy took his arm and they did just that.

The children had seated themselves upon a patch of warm grass atop a rounded hill. Although they would not have described the scene as romantic, it surely was so, with their soft faces reflecting the salmon-glow of the sun as it began its approach toward the horizon.

Their conversation flowed independent of purpose, swiftly passing beyond the day's humiliations and into such subjects as the dietary benefits of squirrel meat, and the weight of clouds, and, eventually, into a vigorous debate about the definition of a sunset.

Pansy said, "A sunset begins the moment the bottom of the sun touches the horizon and it concludes the moment the top of the sun goes below the horizon."

"In France," argued Auguste, "a sunset begins once the sun is below the horizon and it only ends once the sky has gone dark."

"French definitions do not apply in America," said Pansy chirpily. She enjoyed this sort of back-and-forth.

Auguste usually enjoyed this sort of back-and-forth as well, but not today. "I am in America, and yet I am French. One of the things that defines me as French is my French definition of a sunset. It is a distinct part of my self."

"You are eleven years old. You barely even *have* a self."

"In France, eleven is an old man," said Auguste irkishly. "Did you learn nothing in my country?" He was clearly still feeling the sting of his confrontation with Sister Punctuality.

"*Moi, je pense que oui*. You've been in America for how long? Six weeks? What have *you* learned?" Pansy had not yet registered Auguste's lingering frustration.

"I have learned your language."

"How can you say that?" said Pansy. "You don't even know what a *sunset* is." She thought this hilarious.

Auguste said, "You are impertinent." He meant this sincerely.

Pansy said, "I am your only friend." She meant this ironically.

Auguste became cross. "I'll find others."

Finally understanding that Auguste was genuinely upset, Pansy said, "You are arguing with me about sunsets. This is irrational."

Auguste stood. "Very well. I have irrationally decided that I shall sit somewhere else."

He descended the hill without looking back.

Basking in his second dramatic exit of the day, and also confident that he and Pansy would patch up their relationship just as soon as the girl agreed that a sunset lasts from the time the bottom of the sun strikes the horizon thru the moment the top of the sun disappears—or, no, was it the other one? Anyway, Auguste was angry and so he committed himself to a life of solitude. He would wander these woods alone for the rest of his years.

Auguste Lestables, son of the scribe to Auguste Comte. Irrational? A preposterous notion, one which he could have easily rebutted if he'd still been in possession of his father's papers, if only his mother had allowed him to chase down the ruffian who'd stolen their trunk in Le Havre.

Because solitary wandering children require a purpose, and because there remained at least another hour before the sun would actually set, Auguste resolved to find and slay the elusive three-eared bear—the one Delmar the squirrel-hunting boy had described to Auguste and Pansy on the day they had arrived in Solemn.

Auguste was walking along a stream, searching for bear footprints when Pansy appeared from a clump of trees. The life of solitude had lasted less than half an hour.

Pansy said, "Are you feeling better?"

"I'm looking for the three-eared bear."

"Oh, Delmar's silly fantasy!"

Auguste smiled maliciously. "A three-eared bear is very frightening."

"Then I must accompany you, to keep you safe."

Auguste did not object when Pansy took his hand. Nor did he object when she said, "Your day has been difficult."

"It has been."

Pansy squeezed his hand, "The day will soon be over."

Pansy's affection washed over Auguste, dislodging fragments of the mournful grime that had been accumulating inside himself these past few months.

Pansy sensed the boy's gratitude, accepted Auguste's desire to let subtext remain subtext, and continued accordingly. "I'm quite certain we're not going to find any bears this evening, but there is something."

Auguste understood perfectly well that Pansy was trying to cheer him up, and he adored her for this unvoiced awareness. "Something what?"

Pansy gave Auguste's hand one more squeeze and then she released it. They were in concordance now. "My grandfather died in a coal mine just over that hill."

Pansy mistook Auguste's look of concern for confusion. "A

mine is a hole where people look for black rocks which can be burned."

"I know what a mine is."

"Except sometimes the blasting caps explode before the all-clear is given. My people used to work in the mines, before Solemn."

"This mine is nearby, yes?"

"Over that hill. But we're not allowed. After the explosion, the whole area was declared a Site of Maximum Taboo."

"Why, then, did you mention it?"

Pansy said, "My dear friend, do you know what 'Maximum Taboo' means?"

The sun had now begun to set, by any definition.

Chapter Twenty-Eight

AUGUSTE AND PANSY WERE CROUCHED BEHIND A MULBERRY BUSH, peering at a haphazard pile of violence: chunks of shale the size of a piano, crumbling sheets of limestone, and splintered roof timbers and warped and ripped and rusted remains of ore carts and shovels and other human inventions, including a pair of rail-tracks that had been twisted into awful scribbles.

All of this was overlain with ominous, late-day shadows.

The epicenter of the rubble was the caved-in entrance to the coal mine itself.

"As you can see," said Pansy, "the explosion was quite vigorous."

"How deep is a coal mine?"

"This one was so deep they had to pump in the oxygen so the workers could breathe."

Subtle, white exhalations were clouding out from the rubble pile.

Auguste said, "Is that steam?"

"It's smoke. The explosion started the coal to smoldering. It'll burn for another hundred years."

"It reminds one of—"

"Of hell?"

"I was thinking more of a kitchen of some sort. Or the bread oven my mother and Euphémie made today."

"Nobody wants to eat bread baked in a grave."

"Your grandpa's in there?"

"There were seventeen people in the mine when he dropped the blasting caps. Sixteen of them, including Grandpa, were never recovered. There was one fellow, though, at the front of the mine. The explosion sent him flying like a cannonball. He landed in a tree." She pointed. "That one. When the villagers came to see what the ruckus was about, they thought he was dead. But he opened his eyes, white under that soot, and started whimpering. Scared the dickens out of everyone. He died as they tried to take him out of the tree. He'd gotten a branch right up his tooter. That branch, right there." She pointed again. "I cannot overemphasize how awful this was, according to the people who claim to have witnessed it. His last words were, 'The juggling fool.'"

"Referring to your grandfather."

"Presumably. Grandpa was a circus-type. Always juggling. He could keep five items aloft at once. But juggling blasting caps? In a confined space? Right near crates of dynamite that should never have been stored down there anyhow? A complete lack of solemnity, that's what it was. And it's what undid this mine. Or that's the accepted theory."

Auguste said, "Why are we hiding behind a bush?"

Pansy said, "Out of respect."

"I want to climb on those rocks."

Stars were beginning to dot the eastern sky.

"It's warm," said Auguste. He was seated upon a teetering block of shale, sniffing a tendril of smoke, the scent of a dead star.

"Like I said," said Pansy, safely at the foot of the pile of destruction, "the coal's on fire. Come down now. We'd best get home."

Auguste said, "If I was a bear, I would spend the winter in a warm cave."

"Bears, bears. Listen, the three-eared bear is a silly kids' story. Nobody's seen footprint nor hair of it, ever. People make things up, you know. But if the thing *were* out there," she broke off, swallowed hard, "which it isn't, you'd be crazy, looking for it."

Auguste bounded down the pile, landing in front of Pansy. He crossed his arms, raised his chin. "I'm courageous."

"Solemnites aren't impressed by vengeful acts, especially those directed toward mythical animals."

"Maybe I just want to see a three-eared bear, is all."

"If you find it, you'll be seeing it from the inside."

"Just for imagination," said Auguste, "imagine you were a bear. Wouldn't you want to sleep someplace warm? And isn't this place warm? If I was a bear, I'd live right here. Especially since people don't come up this way."

"How's a bear supposed to get inside a collapsed mine?"

"Maybe it dug out a den somewhere else on this hill."

"Maybe so. But we're not going to find out. Let's go. This place is frightfully dreary, especially under this sky."

"Bleak," agreed Auguste.

"Good word," said Pansy. "You've been studying."

"Thank you."

"On the way home, I'll tell you how the explosion birthed the Church of Solemnity."

INTERLUDE

How the Baker Mine Explosion Birthed the Church of Solemnity
as Explained by Pansy to Auguste on the Way Home

PRIOR TO THE SLAVERY WAR, SOLEMN WAS KNOWN AS SECRETION. There was a rich man in Secretion and he owned the Baker Coal Mine. All the healthy menfolk worked in the mine.

But then the mine exploded and Secretion lost half its male population and all of its income. My grandma, being the widow of the man who started the explosion, was shunned by the rest of the Secretionites. It was very mean of them. Nobody would talk to her or her young daughter, who would eventually become my mother.

One day, Grandma had a vision in which the Lord told her to go to church more often. At the time, the church in Secretion was some sort of Pentecostal deal, with all the testifying and shouting and whatnot. Anyway, Grandma brought mamma to church. Together they begged God's forgiveness for Grandpa's foolish and frivolous attempt to juggle explosives. A young man named Celicius was in the congregation that day, and he overheard Grandma's pleas. Celicius had lost many friends in the explosion and he was greatly moved.

That very night he received a vision from the Lord; the Solemn Vision. We'll skip ahead here, because I'm not sure how Celicius talked the Pentecostal preacher into letting him take over, but the upshot is that Celicius remade the church and remade this town. He also remade himself...as Reverend Steadfast. They're the same person!

There's a lot else that happened, but the upshot is that Solemn was born. Now we live with the land rather than off it. You notice no one burns coal in Solemn—except the blacksmith, of course.

And *nobody* juggles.

Chapter Twenty-Nine

A WINDLESS EVENING SETTLED OVER THE VILLAGE. THE FIREFLIES HAD begun to ignite, oil lamps were hung in opened doors, shavings of green cherrywood smoldered within clay pots dispersing a sweet haze intended to frighten away mosquitoes. Prayers and ghostly whistles mingled with the buzz of lonesome frogs.

In the small courtyard behind the Gravity house, Annie and Euphémie sat upon their log bench, cheerful lovers watching fat drip from a skewered rabbit over an open fire. On the other side of the fire, opposite the widows, sat Sister Temperance. It was she who had snared and skinned the rabbit, and was she who was proudly roasting it for her friends.

All present were flapping kerchiefs around their ears to ward off the clouds of mosquitoes that had no aversion to cherry smoke.

Neighboring dogs began to bark half-heartedly at the arrival of two small figures who emerged from the dark, hand-in-hand.

"Here they are," said Sister Temperance. In spite of her Solemnitic principles, Temperance had been especially cheerful this night, and the appearance of Auguste and Pansy only made her more so. Temperance lifted Pansy to her lap. The growing girl was approaching the end of her days as a lap-sitter, and yet, almost-too-big as she was, she still rested lightly upon Temperance's thighs.

Auguste climbed onto the log, squeezing in-between Annie and Euphémie. After a ruffle of his hair, Annie handed him a knife and a serving dish. He leaned over the fire and carved chunks of rabbit flesh and placed them upon the dish, which he then presented to all. Also on the menu: strawberries, cider, and the very first loaf from Annie and Euphémie's brand-new bread oven.

Temperance devoured half of the loaf herself. "You've brought me back to France." She kissed her fingers. "*Magnifique.*"

Annie said, "I should have let the dough sit longer."

After the food had been devoured, and the cider sipped, then did Sister Temperance thank the Lord for that which they had received. Bellies were slapped, belches were released behind cupped hands. Beyond the edge of the village, two cats copulated loudly.

Recalling her son's difficult morning, Annie asked Auguste how his afternoon had fared.

The boy perked up. "Pansy I went back to school and I apologized to Sister Punctuality and now we're friends again."

This pleased Annie greatly.

Pansy, from her side of the fire, began desperately beaming telepathic messages instructing Auguste to keep his trap shut about the coal mine.

Auguste did not receive these messages.

"And then, after school, Pansy and I went to an old coal mine."

Sister Temperance said, "The Baker mine is forbidden!"

Auguste felt Annie stiffen beside him.

Euphémie, oblivious to any tension, licked rabbit grease from her fingers. "Delicious."

Sister Temperance acknowledged the compliment with a tip of

her head, and then spoke to the girl seated on her lap. "Pansy, you know the mine is a Site of Maximum Taboo. None shall enter that area, none shall look upon the area, and none shall frivolously discuss the tragedy that befell those who perished in that area."

Pansy sought an excuse. "But Auguste thought *taboo* meant *tattoo*. As his primary English teacher, it's my responsibility to provide the clearest possible definition for unfamiliar words. In this case, I showed him a physical example of a taboo. Have I done wrong?"

Sister Temperance said, "Do not be coy."

Pansy lowered her eyes.

Auguste said, "It's my fault. I wanted to see the three-eared bear."

Annie, decidedly unhappy, said, "So there's a bear, now?"

Euphémie said, "I'm still waiting for someone to explain the coal mine."

Annie said, "Furthermore, one does not look for three-eared bears unless one wishes to be eaten by three-eared bears."

Auguste took refuge in the sort of pragmatism favored by his late father. "If one wishes that the bear eats no other, then one must find the bear and slay it."

Euphémie, smiling because she wasn't one whit concerned, said, "If one is eleven years old, one does not slay bears, *especially* those with three ears."

Auguste, at the edge of a pout, "My father was a great hunter, like Nimrod."

Annie said, "Your father threw stones at ducks and struck only frogs."

"You say cruel things," said Auguste.

"I say true things, and I expect you to do the same. And why are we talking about bears? Is there a bear, Sister Temperance?"

"Not that I know of. Certainly not with three ears. But the mine is very real."

Euphèmie said, "Yes. The mysterious, dangerful mine."

Pansy hurried to speak. "It's not *dangerous*. You can't even get inside. As for the bear, it's just a story made up by silly boys."

Sister Temperance said, "The mine is a black memorial to dead men. We avoid it."

Annie said, "How great of a transgression are we talking about? Shall I punish the boy?"

Sister Temperance considered for a moment. "A violation of Maximum Taboo is serious business. If the town council learns of this—and I remind you, Pansy, that your mother is on the council —*when* the town council finds out, my guess is that you will be deemed insincere."

"What's that mean?" said Annie.

"No one knows. It's never happened."

Euphémie said, "I hate to be contrary, but—"

"You are only ever contrary," said Annie.

"—this mine you're speaking of, it's a place, not a behavior. To *be somewhere* is different from *doing something*. Perhaps it's time to release the mine from its burden—whatever that may be—and turn it into a place of reflection."

Auguste glanced at Euphémie to let her know that he appreciated this argument.

Sister Temperance was less appreciative. "There is little to be gained from reflecting upon a site of seventeen gruesome deaths."

For the benefit of the widows, Sister Temperance recounted the mine accident, including explanations of the ever-burning subterranean fire and the invention of Solemnity. Her version was far less succinct than that of Pansy.

Gruesome deaths or not, Euphémie continued to advocate for the accused. "Tragedy, intrigue, fire, ruins, religious epiphany; all reasons for a child to visit the mine. Temptation has led to far greater evils than this."

Annie kept her mouth shut and hoped that Euphémie could carry this one across the finish line.

Sister Temperance thinned her lips. "As Solemnites, it is not our place to judge things evil and wise. That burden lies within the—"

Auguste finished the sentence, "—purview of God alone." He sat upright.

Pansy, with a glint both mischievous and wise said, "These words are as true now as they were when the Reverend received them from God himself. And in the name of truth, I confess my sin to all present. I led this innocent child"—meaning Auguste —"to a site of Maximum Taboo. I beg the forgiveness of God. I shall submit to his judgment."

Seeing the favorable impression of Pansy's words, Auguste attempted some repentant rhetoric of his own. "It pains me, Sister Temperance, that we have burdened you with the knowledge of our violation of the taboo. I, too, beg the forgiveness of God and submit to his judgment. Though, given the breadth of my life's experiences, I would hardly consider myself a child, innocent or otherwise."

Pansy's turn. "As a young woman mature beyond her years, I trust that the Lord's justice shall be as swift and fair as any punishment that could be imposed by the council."

Euphémie said, "These young persons—be they children or innocent or something altogether different—make a persuasive argument. All of us here, on this lovely evening, we ought to accept the humility of Pansy and Auguste; we should applaud them for their candor—after all, they could have lied to us—and we can, all of us, submit to God's eternal wisdom."

It was as impressive a string of words as any she'd spoken since their arrival in Solemn. Annie nodded her approval.

Sister Temperance stared at the fire for a long moment. Various insects dove into the flames. "Pansy, I am moved by your solemnity, humility, and grace, if not also by my own adoration for you. If you and Auguste can promise never to return to that spot, if you promise to never again speak of your trespass, I promise I will not tell the council."

Pansy said, "You would do this?"

"If you were sincere in your intentions and if you are sincere in your promise, then I declare you free of guilt."

Pansy said, "Not only do I sincerely promise not to return to the Baker mine, but I sincerely apologize to Auguste for leading him there."

"I accept your apology, Pansy," said Auguste, "and am grateful to the mercy shown by Sister Temperance."

Annie said, "And by your mother as well." She offered Auguste a chummy elbow in the ribs.

"*Chère Maman, je vous remercie mille fois*," said Auguste, wincing fondly.

"A happy ending!" said Pansy. "And now I wish you good night. I promised Mother I'd be home for dinner."

She skipped into the dark.

Auguste grew tired; it had been an emotional day. "May I go to the bed?"

Annie shooed him away. "It's late."

As Auguste slumbered toward the house, Sister Temperance called to him, "Tell me, boy, is the mine still smoking?"

"Yes, Sister Temperance. As if it were hell's chimney."

Chapter Thirty

THE VILLAGE DIMMED ITS FLAMES, DOGS SNORED, CATS CREPT IN shadows. From the north hills, a barn owl howled amorously. Stars flickered and dropped out of the slow rolling sky.

After cups of tea, after giggling at the widows' attempts to pronounce *squirrels* and *sheets*, after the village's ambient noise—with the exception of Auguste's snoring—had turned down to zero, Sister Temperance said, "There is news."

Euphémie said, in her charmingly irreverent voice, "The messiah has returned?"

"You aren't far off." Sister Temperance bit her lower lip, and her freckled cheeks dimpled. "After chastising the children, I have no right."

Euphémie said, "If you're going to refuse to disclose, then don't disclose that you've something to disclose. Speak."

Sister Temperance looked all about, leaned in. The widows leaned in. Temperance whispered, "After much delay and drama, the committee to choose the site of this year's All-Tent Revival has made a decision!" She covered her mouth and whispered behind her hand, "Forgive me, Lord, for my zestful ejaculation."

The widows sat upon their log in uncomprehending bemusement. Euphémie spoke first. "You presume we have the faintest idea of what All-Tent Revival is."

"Oh!" said Sister Temperance, who was valiantly attempting not to giggle. "It's a great festival of religions; a gathering of ideas; a moment of brotherhood and sisterhood; a marketplace for an exchange of Biblical proportions." Here she became serious. "Or so they say. I've never been."

"You said the committee has chosen a site," said Euphémie.

"That's the exciting part. They've chosen Restive!"

"Which one's Restive, again?" said Euphémie.

"That's where we got off the train." said Annie.

Euphémie stared at her blankly.

Annie said, "Where we hitched a ride in that wagon full of wood."

"Of course!" recalled Euphémie. "The bachelor whose bride got lost in the mail."

Sister Temperance said, "One wonders what became of him."

Annie said, "One wonders what became of *her*!"

Tee hee hee.

Sister Temperance cocked her ear to the silence of the village. "I should bid goodnight"—flames twinkled in her eyes—"before anyone else divulges their secrets." She stood and bent low. "God-speed your oven."

Side by side upon their sideways log under this starcrackle sky on this blessedly cool evening, Annie and Euphémie watched as Sister Temperance's straight body in her straight dress disappeared into the night.

Annie took Euphémie's hand. "Let us wander the forest like fairies."

"The forest is dark."

"Eyes adjust."

They entered the woods via a well-trodden path. Their eyes adjusted to the blue-black of night, and their ears adjusted to the animal noises that occasionally burst from the trees. Their feet, shod in leather shoes made by the village shoemaker Brother Discretion, probed the path, avoiding the dead branches that littered the way.

They followed a subaquatic clattering of rounded stones until they alighted upon the bank of the creek where, in the daytime, women washed clothes and children threw fits, but which was now just a place where the vegetation had been stomped flat.

The widows lay back, watching stars framed by treetop silhouettes.

"I like it here," said Annie, "in Solemn."

Euphémie did not reply, but raised up on one elbow and lowered her lips onto Annie's, which received them with familiar ease.

Chapter Thirty-One

THE NEXT DAY, AT CHURCH, AT THE COMMENCEMENT OF THE SHARING of joys and concerns, Reverend Celicius Steadfast invited his wife, Sister Rainbow Steadfast, to the pulpit.

"Darling, tell the folks the news."

Sister Steadfast ascended from the Steadfast family pew, handed her latest infant to her oldest child, and joined her husband at the pulpit. With an expression a few ticks short of paralysis, she summoned from her lungs a monotonic voice. "Restive will host the 1885 All-Tent Revival."

The entire congregation gasped. Realizing this indiscretion, they immediately whistled the Dirge of Emotional Overreach.

"Thank you, Sister Steadfast," said Reverend Steadfast as his wife small-stepped her way back to the pew where she retrieved the infant.

The Reverend leaned forward. "This is a big one, folks. Details are still being sorted out, but here's what I know so far. The All-Tent Revival is overseen by the All-Tent Revival Council. This council favors a host-site with a train depot, as they believe a train will allow more folks to attend. Restive has a depot, along with various shops and liveries and so forth, not to mention they're a Christian community. So, that's why the board chose it. Now—

and this is quite interesting so prepare yourselves—the *actual* festival grounds will be located a half-hour's walk south of Restive, which is a half-hour's walk north of Solemn. According to this postal letter"—he waved a sheet of paper—"there will be a planning meeting tomorrow, in Restive. Invited are representatives from any communities that may be affected by the Revival. This includes Solemn. Naturally, I will go. Sister Honora will accompany me. She has demonstrated excellent judgment both as a missionary for Solemnity and as a member of our town council. Any objections?"

Unmoving faces indicated their approval.

"There's one more thing, somewhat peculiar. The Revival will span the final four days of December. The timing seems odd, given our winters, but this is what the council wants. Anyway, now's a good time to start praying for a warm winter. With that in mind, let us bow our heads."

After a lengthy prayer, the Reverend bade his flock a blessed day and the chapel emptied.

Shortly before sunrise on September first, 1885, Sister Honora and the Reverend Celicius Steadfast trotted a pair of ponies two miles north into the town of Restive, Indiana for the *County-Wide Conference to Plan and Prepare for the 1885 All-Tent Revival Celebrating the Divers and Various Approaches to Holiness Within the Tri-State Region of Indiana, Ohio, Kentucky, and Elsewhere, as Hosted by the Town of Restive, County Seat of Gore County, Indiana.*

The meeting would take place within the County Courthouse, located in the dead center of Restive's town square. The courthouse was a two-story brick building accessorized by a handsome white bell-tower. On the front lawn, a pair of discarded Civil War cannon—one Union, one Confederate—had been arranged so they faced one another like two lovers puckering for a kiss; a makeshift memorial to those four awful years.

Inside the courthouse, limestone columns supported the ceilings, limestone stairways curved down to the limestone floor, and portraits of men on horses hung from the limestone walls. Every ounce of this limestone had been quarried in Indiana.

Across a carpet, up limestone stairs, thru a limestone doorway, and into the Great Hall there were gathered sixty-eight preachers, pastors, reverends, and laypersons representing thirty-four neighboring towns, hamlets, and villages.

Overseeing the event from a wide, shallow table, were the Gore County Commissioners as well as the three members of the All-Tent Revival Council who had ridden into town from Louisville the night before.

To plan an All-Tent Revival was no small thing. The areas around Restive would have to accommodate thousands of attendees representing a range of religious sects whose variety beggared the very idea of monotheism. The assembly of commissioners, councilmen, preachers, pastors, reverends, and laypersons had only this single day to arrange for infrastructure, volunteers, schedules, and so on.

The first two hours of the morning session were dedicated to opening prayers—every preacher in the room wanted his say. The next two hours consisted of the same disorganized banality that has plagued planning meetings from the dawn of time. Resolutions were proposed and then instantly forgotten as members of the congress spoke out of turn, worried over impossible dangers —tornados, mainly—and shared one meandering, irrelevant anecdote after another.

Reconvening after the lunch recess, the commissioners and councilmen sat at their wide, shallow table and watched helplessly as the representatives jawed about horse-feed, pitch-ins, and whether or not to hire the notorious (and entirely mythical) Blodgett Gang for security. Just when it seemed that the 1885 All-Tent Revival would collapse under a barrage of *non sequiturs,*

Sister Honora abruptly volunteered the services of the entire population of Solemn to thousands of hours of labor.

"We will arrange for sanitary middenfields. We will divert rivers for water and for sewage. We will design and create the main stage. And we will clear trees for campsites."

The other representative looked on in awe, and not a little relief. Those Solemnites sure were decent folks, taking on all that burden. Reverend Steadfast nodded along and prayed that it would be Honora—and not he—who would inform the folks back home that they had been conscripted to months of labor.

A motion to vote, seconded, the ayes have it, gavel struck, and Solemn was awarded the honor of providing virtually the entire infrastructure for the All-Tent Revival.

Motion to adjourn, seconded, the ayes have it, gavel struck.

And so it was that, on the evening of September first, 1885, Sister Honora and Reverend Celicius Steadfast returned to Solemn to share the triumphant news that, blessed be the Lord, all of you have been volunteered to work like mules for the next four months.

Reverend Steadfast's concerns had been unfounded; within moments, the air of Solemn was filled with industrious whistling. Within hours, blueprints were being scratched in moist dirt. Within days, Solemn had become a fully functional festival factory.

Chapter Thirty-Two

ALL TWENTY OF THE VILLAGE'S HEALTHY ADULT MALES WERE
immediately assigned to the design and construction of the
festival site. With the menfolk thus employed, everybody else—
old-timers, women, and kids—had to re-jigger their routines to
compensate. It meant a greater workload, but the people of
Solemn were capable of great works.

The livestock were seen-to, the garden was tended, and, in the
pursuit of efficiency, food management turned to mass-
production.

Naturally, Annie and Euphémie became the village breadmak-
ers. Every day, from dawn until late afternoon, they mixed and
kneaded and baked loaf after loaf of golden bread, enough to
meet the needs of all eighty-odd Solemnites. They built two more
ovens, churning out as many as forty-eight loaves per day. They
enjoyed working with flour and fire, and they were perfectly
happy to play their roles in this odd pageant.

Auguste and Pansy were tasked with the production of yarn. It
was an indirect service to the cause. Years ago, Reverend Steadfast
had established an arrangement with the mercantile shop in
Restive; every week he would bring a wagon to town and
exchange fine Solemn yarn—and eggs and anything else that they

had in abundance—for flour and nails and anything else that they lacked.

Assigned a pair of foot-powered spinning wheels, Auguste and Pansy had permission to work anywhere they pleased as long as they finished one basket of wool per day. Warm weather would find them outside, at any level place where they could feed the wool, work the treadles, and converse.

Weeks went by, rains came and went, days grew shorter, September slipped into October.

On a particularly pleasant morning, Auguste and Pansy set themselves up at the edge of the village's great garden where they could listen to the bees and bask in the sunlight.

"Look, Pansy," said Auguste, "my blister is healed." He was referring to a finger wound that had been a subject of fascination for the past two days.

"You are welcome," said Pansy.

"I do not understand."

"I prayed for your finger to heal."

"It was a blister," said Auguste. "It did not require prayer."

"Obviously, but it healed *faster* because of my intervention. You are therefore welcome."

"I find the theories of prayer to be perplexing."

"Here we go," said Pansy.

"A prayer is a request for the god to direct its infinite powers in a specific direction. In this case, you prayed that my blister would heal."

"That it would heal *more quickly*. Also, God is a *he*, not an *it*."

"And then, at your request, the god used his infinite powers to mend my wound, yes?"

"More quickly, yes."

"And you are taking credit for this miracle because it was you who requested it."

"I'm not vain, but, yes, I always appreciate gratitude."

"My question is this. Who is responsible for the miracle? You, for requesting it? Or is it the god, for granting that request? No, wait, let me finish. Assuming that prayers really do work—let me finish—assuming prayers can lead to miracles, then this implies that prayer grants a person the same powers as the god. Let me *finish*. And therefore, one who prays is the equivalent of a god."

Pansy fiddled with a knob on her wheel. "I'd accuse you of trying to be funny, except that wasn't funny."

Auguste thought it was, at minimum, food for thought. "Henceforth, Pansy, I request that you do not waste your prayers on blisters. Instead, please pray that I can learn to whistle."

"There's only so much the Lord can do." She dimpled her cheeks in her solemn/not-solemn smile. "Your English is getting much better, you know."

Smirking, Auguste said, *"Merci, professeur."*

Not-smirking, Pansy let her foot off the treadle. "You hear that?"

Eighteen black men emerged from the woods, walking two abreast, each with an axe or a saw or a pick leaning upon his shoulder. They were dressed much as the Solemnites: linen trousers, canvas shirts.

The column of workers marched straight thru Solemn's outer ring, thru the open space where the chickens were milling about, just past where Auguste and Pansy sat, and then into the garden at the center of the village. There, they broke ranks to pluck apples and tomatoes and beans and whatnot from those stems that had not yet succumbed to the cooling weather. They exited the garden on the opposite side and crossed north out of Solemn altogether.

⁙   ⁘   ⁙   ⁙

"I've never seen so many Negroes!" said Auguste. "Where did they come from?"

Pansy said, "You've been playing in these woods for the past three months and you've never been to Second Solemn?"

"I do not know what that means."

"Unbelievable."

Auguste shrugged.

"There's a whole 'nother Solemn over that hill." Pansy pointed west, from whence the eighteen black men had come. "It's not even a mile away. That's where the Negroes live. Those you just saw are headed toward the Revival grounds, to help with construction. My mother says the white Solemnites are behind schedule and so the Second Solemnites are pitching in."

"Are they slaves?" said Auguste.

"They've been free for almost twenty years. You learned that in school."

"Yes, but—" said Auguste.

"The Second Solemnites wouldn't work for free and we wouldn't ask them to. We let them pillage the garden coming and going. It's a pretty good deal; free food for digging a few trenches."

The next morning, Auguste and Pansy watched from their spinning wheels as the Second Solemnites again passed thru town.

"I still can't believe it," said Auguste.

"Which part?"

"That they live so close to us."

"They're not dangerous, if that's what you're worried about," said Pansy. She added, "Although they're eating all our apples."

"Why don't they come to church?"

"They have their own."

"We could at least partake in fellowship together. Whistling or sharing a meal, maybe."

"It's better this way. Everyone agrees."

"I want to talk with one of them."

"They speak English, same as you and me," said Pansy. She watched Auguste feed wool into his bobbin. "You're getting quite good at that."

Auguste said, "What are the Negroes doing, specifically?"

"You're obsessed."

"They're our neighbors. I want to know them."

"Mother says they're clearing trees for the Great Stage. The white Solemnites could do all that stuff, except they're so busy milling lumber and digging trenches and I don't know what-all."

Auguste couldn't believe it. A village of negroes, all this time, just over the hill.

Chapter Thirty-Three

AUTUMN WITHERED THE LEAVES AND GLAZED THEIR RUSTED SKINS with morning frost. By late October, the trees were creaky and bare. Birds had gone equatorial, the bedbugs remained vanquished, and Solemn's dwindling population of brown bats huddled together in the recesses of the village barn.

The All-Tent Revival was two months away. Construction was on schedule, thanks to the assistance from the Second Solemnites, who continued their morning-and-evening marches thru town even as the Solemn garden lay down its frost-softened stalks.

🐎　🐎　🐎　🐎

With the cooler weather, Auguste and Pansy installed their spinning wheels permanently in the Gravity house. Squeezed into a corner of the bedroom, they spun yarn while the widows baked bread in the other room.

"Auguste?" called Annie. "Can you and Pansy please keep an eye on the ovens? Euphémie and I are going out."

"Yes, Mother."

"We'll be back in an hour or two. With mushrooms."

"Yes, Mother."

. . .

"Pansy," said Auguste, "I've been thinking about religion."

"As you should."

"I accept the teachings of Solemnity—"

"As you should."

"—because, although they lack coherent explanations, they are a necessary path toward the great rectification."

"You made that up."

"My father—"

"Have you ever noticed that I don't speak of *my* father?"

"I had assumed this was because he was uninteresting."

"I wouldn't know. I never knew him, remember?"

"Oh."

"Auguste, your father was special, but you should think your *own* thoughts."

"But he—"

"—studied under the great philosopher Comte. I know."

"My father's teachings reconcile the vagaries of Solemnity with the infallibility of science."

"I sometimes wonder if you are a true Solemnite, or if you remain here just so you can someday bear witness to a non-existent three-eared bear."

"A person can want two things at once."

"You can't *believe* two things at once."

"I object. For instance, do you not simultaneously believe that your father is dead, and also alive in heaven?"

"Those are distinct states!"

This debate would have continued for the rest of their shift, but it was interrupted when two black children sprinted into town, clanging a pair of handbells.

"Grim tidings from Second Solemn!" *Clang-a-langa-ding-ding.* "A bear has taken a ewe!" *Clang-a-langa-ding-ding.* "Location of bear is unknown!" *Clang-a-langa-ding-ding.* "Grim tidings from Second Solemn!"

The children, a boy and a girl, raced around the inside of Solemn's outer ring, shouting into opened doors, waving their bells at industrious workers, and then they were gone into the woods, sprinting back toward Second Solemn.

Pansy and Auguste threw down their wool and rushed out of the house in pursuit. The rest of Solemn's population followed, somewhat less hastily. Cows were left dripping milk into unattended buckets, coal smoldered in the smithy, and nine loaves of bread began to blacken in three clay ovens.

Pansy and Auguste ran along an overgrown path, following glimpses of the black kids clanging their bells thru the trees.

"What is happening?" said Auguste, huffing and puffing.

"It is an Other-Solemn Alert," said Pansy. "By mutual agreement, the alert is triggered by any one of the following: wildfire, murder, plague, or a bear attack. If any of these tragedies occurs in either Solemn the other Solemn must be alerted."

"So we might see a bear?" said Auguste.

"Run harder. We can catch them."

Indeed, the black kids were rapidly losing steam. After all, they had just sprinted all the way from Second Solemn and were now sprinting back. Of the two, the boy, who was the younger of the pair, was losing steam the most quickly.

The rest of Solemn's citizens—those who were not occupied with revival construction up north—had by now begun to filter into the woods behind Pansy and Auguste.

Auguste said, "I'm surprised that all these people"—he glanced backward to indicate the quick-marching crowd behind them—"would abandon the village on the word of two Negro children."

They had nearly caught up to the boy, who now slowed down until he was abreast of Pansy and Auguste. He turned to Auguste, "I couldn't help overhearing. Are you implying that, because we are Negroes, my sister and I are untrustworthy?"

Clang-clang.

"To the contrary," said Pansy, "I think my friend was suggesting that, given the historically cruel and dismissive treatment of your people by my people—slavery being only the most obvious example—he is pleasantly surprised that so many of the adults behind us"—she inhaled—"would so quickly assemble as one to follow you to the site of an alleged bear attack. Hello, my name is Pansy."

The black boy ducked a low-hanging hickory branch and said, "Do you agree, Pansy, with your friend's cynical assessment? My name is Kermit. Up there, that's my sister."

Clang-clang.

"As you can tell from his accent," said Pansy, "my friend is a foreigner. He's not well-versed in the local social dynamics. But, given his limited experience, I think his cynicism is merited."

Auguste said, "I am Auguste Lestables. You are the first colored person I've ever spoken with."

"Kermit Stovepipe. You're the millionth white person to tell me that."

Clang-clang. Clang-clang.

The trio caught up with Kermit's sister, who was by now getting a case of jelly-legs. To Auguste and Pansy, she said, "Just to be clear. Y'all are chasing us because you want to see evidence of a bear mauling; not because you want to string me and my brother up for trespassing in your village? Not being paranoid or anything."

Pansy said, "We haven't formally met. I'm called Pansy."

Harriet said, "Harriet Stovepipe, twelve years old, older sister to Kermit. But my question."

Clang-clang.

Auguste said, "We are here for the bear."

Pansy said, "He's bear-crazy."

"I'll take that over the alternative," said Harriet.

Pansy said, "You have nothing to fear from the Solemnites. We are here out of Christian duty; you have issued an Other-Solemn Alert, we shall answer."

"I'm pleased that you took the time," said Auguste, "to alert us. This is the most exciting moment in my life."

Harriet said, "How'd you get this guy?"

Pansy said, "I found him in France."

Auguste said, "I want to see a bear so bad!"

Clang-clang.

They exited the woods and came to a split-rail fence, which they simultaneously hurdled. They landed in a sheep pasture on the eastern edge of Second Solemn. At the far end of the pasture was a barn identical to the one in Solemn. A number of Second Solemnites had gathered near it. A vortex of buzzards circled above. From the barn came the bleating of a flock of sheep that had been sequestered for their safety.

Clang-clang.

Clang-clang.

The crowd—old-timers, women, and children—their men, too, were up north working on revival projects—turned to watch the four children who were rapidly approaching from across the field. A woman, Henny Stovepipe, broke from the group and squatted to welcome Harriet and Kermit, who jumped into her arms.

Harriet said, "We sounded the alert, Mother."

Auguste and Pansy were standing nearby with hands on knees, lungs heaving.

Kermit said, "That's Auguste and Pansy. A whole bunch more of them are right behind."

"I am pleased to meet you, Ma'am," wheezed Auguste. "Is there really a bear?"

Harriet said, "Auguste is bear-crazy."

Henny chuckled. "I don't think you'll see it today. But you can witness its doings."

She led them toward the group of Second Solemnites.

Clang-clang.

"Y'all stop ringing the bells," said Henny.

The group of Second Solemnites spread to allow the kids inside, where they were rewarded with a fantastical sight.

Death and gore were nothing new to any of these children. They had all of them beheaded chickens, slaughtered rabbits, and watched adults reach shoulder-deep into cows' vaginas. They had mercy-slain gangrenous dogs, watched their parents weep over stillborn children, survived measles, mumps, scarlet fever, and they had seen humans in a wide and gruesome assortment of illness, dying, and death.

Tufts of bloody wool lay in a halo around a cadaver that looked as if it had been catapulted into their midst from some great height. The blood had not yet clotted.

The only remaining question, at least in Auguste's reckoning, was whether the murderous bear had two ears or three. Nothing at the scene offered any evidence one way or the other.

Snippets of conversation:

Bear, yes.

Helluva deal.

No one saw it.

I heard it. The sheep made an awful racket.

It sounded like bloody murder.

Who's tracking it?

No tracks to follow.

The white folk are gonna love this.

Here they come.

Led by Reverend Steadfast, the rest of the Solemnites arrived, pushing their way into the circle. The mood amongst the Second Solemnites switched from lively to subservient. Now that the white folk were here, they'd be stripped of their jurisdiction over the crime scene. It was how things worked. They knew better than to assume that the Solemnwhites had any interest in their cooperation, and so they courteously departed.

Harriet Stovepipe whispered to Pansy, "It was nice meeting you." Then she and Kermit went off with their fellow villagers.

The Solemnwhites circled the dead ewe and immediately attended to the idle speculation.

We need an Indian.

Didn't anyone see?

Broad daylight, after all.

There must be footprints.

I stand by my statement regarding the necessity of an Indian.

Thinking it unwise to expose children to such horrors, the adults of Solemn ushered Pansy and Auguste away from the sheep and deposited them outside the circle, where they obediently awaited further instructions.

"Pansy," said Auguste, "why did all the negroes go away?"

Pansy said, "They sent the alert, they did their duty, and we've arrived. Now they can get back to their work."

"It doesn't seem fair."

"It's how it's always been," said Pansy. Distracted, she said, "Say, what are *they* up to?"

Auguste followed her finger pointing to the figures of Harriet and Kermit disappearing into the woods at the edge of the meadow.

Auguste said, "I like those two. We should spend more time with them."

"Maybe," said Pansy. "Oh, rats. Here comes my mother."

Sister Honora had been doing paperwork in the chapel when Kermit and Harriet had raised their alert, and she hadn't acknowledged the commotion until the last of the Solemnites was leaving the village. But here she came now, her prairie dress dragging in the wet grass, grim jaw, imperturbable face.

The Solemnites parted to allow her access to the mutilated sheep. With barely a glance at the dead animal, she said, "Are there any witnesses?"

Pansy said, "Nobody saw it, but some people heard it, and nobody's found any footprints."

Auguste nodded in confirmation.

Sister Honora said, "We'll not find any footprints now that everyone's stomped all the grass." She looked around disapprovingly. "There's no point staring at a dead sheep all day. Everyone, let us return to the village and attend to our chores."

End of the party. The Solemnites dispersed.

Sister Honora took Pansy by the hand and led her homeward. Auguste remained behind for an uncertain moment.

"Oh, dear," he said, "the bread!"

Chapter Thirty-Four

AT THE EXACT MOMENT THAT AUGUSTE WAS REMEMBERING THE unattended ovens, Annie and Euphémie were returning to Solemn, having completed their mushroom hunt.

Mushrooming was a pleasant task, and historically important to the widows. A half dozen years prior, Annie had been walking the forests of Sanvisa, a basket hanging from the crook of her elbow, when she heard a scream from yonder up the hill. Annie raced over briars and brambles to discover an extremely tall woman, roughly her age—mid-twenties—giggling maniacally at the foot of a recently-toppled hazel tree. The tree itself was uncommonly large for a hazel, with a trunk thicker than an elephant's leg and a canopy that must have lofted out at forty or fifty feet. The cause of its demise could be deduced from the state of its roots, which had been rendered visible by the tree's supine state. An overlong life had led to sickness that had left the roots corkish and vulnerable to the miniature *mistral* that had blown over the hills just the night before.

The screaming giggler, whom Annie had previously known only as the tall woman who obediently followed her husband to and from church, was sitting splaylegged at the edge of the ragged hole from whence the tree had been torn. The reason for the giggling—as well as the scream—was poking out of her mouth: a ball the size and hue of a sheep dropping. It was a black truffle. The woman gobbled it with ferocious bites. She reached her hand wrist-deep into the earth, extracted another truffle and, without even wiping the dirt, stuffed it into her mouth.

Seeing this, Annie screamed.

Euphémie, for that was the tall woman's name, saw Annie and screamed, spraying a mud of half-masticated fungi and saliva. Annie took a step backward, afraid that she had startled the woman, but Euphémie beckoned her to partake of this extraordinary discovery.

Annie partook of the mushrooms, and plenty more as well.

This day, in Indiana, the widows had quickly filled their pails with yellow chanterelles, shaggy boletes, and pearl oysters—no truffles to be found, alas—and then Annie had led Euphémie up a hill, under nests, over streams to a clearing littered with rubble that was inexplicably leaking smoke into the autumn air.

Annie said, "The impenetrable entrance to the deadly Baker mine."

Euphémie said, "Deadly and sacramental. Forbidden to all. Are you frightened?"

Annie answered this by unfurling a quilt to alight upon the soft bed of the forest just behind a chunk of the mine's exploded boiler. They were hidden here, and the ground was warm.

Laying upon the quilt, they took turns listening to one another's heartbeats and otherwise behaving in a manner that would have been frowned upon by their whistling hosts.

Upon concluding this moment of intimacy, they dressed and then they shook the twigs and dirt off the quilt. As they folded it, Annie said, satisfactorily, "*Ma chère*, we're committing sacrilege at an alarming rate."

"Alarming? I find the rate barely adequate."

No reply from Annie.

Euphémie added, in English, "What they don't know, can't hurt us. Did I say that correctly?"

Annie's face went slack. Slowly, she raised her right hand, and pointed an unsteady finger toward a hairy mass just up the hill.

Euphèmie's breath grew shallow and quick.

Crunch of branch, mucus snorting. A disinterred huckleberry bush flew thru the air and landed in front of the widows, scattering its fruit like a tipped over gumball machine. It was followed in a playful bound by a black bear. The bear landed upon the bush, flattening it, then seated itself on its bottom, with its feet splayed like a toddler playing with a rag doll. It was near enough that the widows could hear it fart.

The bear was not especially large, no heavier than a portly human. This was of no comfort to the widows, who had no idea how large bears were supposed to be.

The animal raised its head, and then grew perfectly still, save for the flaring of nostrils. The bear's black eyes were set in a round head the size of soup kettle. The eyes, with their tan brows, were trained on the widows, confused or curious or simply pondering the edibility of human flesh. Poised roundly upon the sides of the bear's round head were the customary pair of ursine ears.

Also—and this took a moment to register because it was so odd—the bear had a *third* ear growing out of the crown of its head. It was a perfectly normal ear in every respect, except for its existence.

Any threat posed by the animal was severely diluted by that third ear, which, now that Euphémie thought about it, was one of the goofiest things she'd ever seen. She pressed a hand tightly to her mouth. Annie was still pointing at the bear, but the fear had left her eyes, replaced by wary curiosity. A giggle escaped from behind Euphémie's hand. All three of the bear's ears swiveled toward her.

Euphémie whispered, "It's cute, no?"

"More adorable than cute," said Annie.

Euphémie said, "You want to hug it."

"Auguste would be so happy."

The bear snorted once more and then, convinced that the humans had no interest in its meal, took the huckleberry bush into its paws, casually rolled onto its back, and began devouring it as if it were an ear of roasted sweet corn.

Annie whispered, "*On dois partir.*"

With a post-coital combination of joy and awe, the women retrieved their mushroom pails and backed away from the bear and into the forest.

Homeward, hand in hand.

"We mustn't tell of this."

"We must."

"We were at a site of taboo. We cannot."

"Yes, but."

"And what we were doing."

"We don't have to tell that part."

"The bear is not our enemy."

"We have no enemies."

"We will have, soon enough."

"The bear spoke to me."

"Literally, or otherwise?"

"With its eyes. It said, 'I've been miscast in this role.'"

"A perplexing thing for a bear to say."

"For an animal with such a vicious reputation, I found it to be charming."

"I wasn't just the ear. The bear would remain a sweetheart with any number of ears."

"The beast transcends the prejudices of appearance."

"Let's not speak of this to anyone."

"Not even Auguste?"

"I think not."

"Agreed."

The village was empty. Eddies of wind spun dead leaves in little vortexes. Coals smoked in the farrier's forge. Deadwood fires darkened the bottoms of cast-iron roasters, the liquid inside having been reduced into a bubbling tar. Doors swung on hinges. A cow lowed from the barn.

"Ominous."

"A harbinger."

"The bread!"

The ovens were pouring smoke. One by one, Annie slid the paddle into the ovens and removed nine charred husks. The widows entered the Gravity house. The spinning wheels were unattended. Annie rubbed her temples. Euphémie kept a respectful silence for as long as she could manage, and then said, "We should put out the cook fires."

Annie, "Yes. They'll be back. Everyone will be back soon."

They snuffed the fires, tended the unmilked cattle, called for Auguste and Pansy. Then they sat upon the log outside their home and waited.

"The whole town."

"Not even a note."

"Indians?"

"A pied piper."

"A who?"

"A German flautist who mesmerizes rats and children."

"Someone's coming."

Annie said, "They sound jocular."

"Eerily similar to the audience at your husband's hanging."

Annie said, "You don't think—?"

"Not a chance. A society has to work up to that sort of thing. But listen. Nobody is whistling."

Beneath their efforts of solemnity, it was clear that all sixty-odd of them were enjoying this holiday from quotidia. Steps were bouncy, eyes were bright.

As delighted as Auguste was to have met two pleasant Negro children and to have seen Second Solemn and the remains of a dead sheep, and to be merrily jabbering about the bear with Sister Temperance and Pansy, he was equally anxious to find his mother, whom he hadn't seen since earlier in the day when she and Euphèmie had left to hunt mushrooms.

As the crowd neared the village, Auguste hurried to the fore and, yes, there they were, Mother and Euphémie, seated upon their log at the back porch. He sprinted ahead for the next fifty yards and jumped upon Annie's lap.

"Mother! Did you find mushrooms?"

"Oh, lots! And when we returned, we found," she swept her hand to indicate the vacant town, "this."

"Yes, Mother. There was an Other-Solemn Alert. The first in ten years! A bear ate a sheep in Second Solemn."

Annie's jaw clenched.

Words rushed out of Auguste's mouth. "They want to exterminate it. I think that the bear is no threat to us. It has clearly discovered that which we all know: sheep are delicious, and are more easily killed than humans. I was just telling Pansy and Sister Temperance that we ought to offer to the bear a sheep every week. It makes sense to me now, the idea of sacrifice. People don't sacrifice animals to gods; people sacrifice animals to devils. A well-fed devil doesn't eat people. Also, we made friends with some Negro children."

Annie kissed him smartly on the top of his head.

Euphémie said, "When did the assault take place?"

Auguste calculated. "Before lunch, probably."

Euphémie said, "Did anyone see this bear?"

"Not as yet, but there's no doubt that it was a bear that done it." He added, "Probably the three-eared bear."

Annie said, "You never know."

Auguste's attention went to the mound of smoking bread husks that Annie had piled in front of the ovens. Before he could speak, Annie said, "We'll make more."

Sister Temperance emerged from the oncoming mass of villagers and, holding her skirt above the grass, hurried to Annie and Euphémie.

Swallowing hard to reclaim her solemnity, Temperance exclaimed, "What an adventure!"

Annie said, "I'm sorry to have missed it."

Euphémie said, "Our regret is tempered by a successful mushroom hunt."

Sister Temperance said, "Oh, but you must have been frightened when you returned. Had you any idea where we'd gone off to?"

Euphémie assured her that they hadn't been frightened in the least.

Sister Temperance noted the state of the village. "You tidied up after us." She tilted her head, "I'm so glad you're here."

A piercing whistle paused all conversation. Standing before the chapel, Reverend Steadfast bellowed, "Friends, I applaud your bravery. The people of Second Solemn are surely grateful for your quick attention. And I assure you that the bear will be dealt with before it can spill another drop of blood. We will address this as soon as the men return from the day's labor. For now, I ask that you please return to your day. We've much to accomplish yet. Solemnity in all things."

"And all things be solemn," replied the congregants, who began to disperse.

Euphémie asked Sister Temperance, "How does the town council normally deal with murderous animals?"

Sister Temperance said, "They kill them."

Annie said, tersely, "And good luck to them. Meanwhile, Auguste, there is wool to spin."

The widows allowed their hands to brush. The bear was real, it had three ears, and it was theirs.

Chapter Thirty-Five

THE NEXT DAY, REVEREND STEADFAST AND SISTER HONORA WERE summoned to Restive for an emergency meeting at the county courthouse. No great hall this time. Instead, they were led to a humble sideroom. Less limestone, more wainscoting.

Reverend Steadfast and Sister Honora sat upon creaky wooden chairs and faced the three county commissioners. Without the distraction of an auditorium filled with bumpkins, the men seemed not so elevated as the Solemnites had originally thought. Dandruff, coat seams splitting, various skin conditions.

One of the commissioners said, "People are saying about this bear."

Reverend Steadfast said, "It took a sheep, sir."

Commissioner number two said, "They're saying it also took a man."

"Pure gossip," said Reverend Steadfast. "No one has gone missing in ages."

Commissioner number three said, "Has anyone actually seen this bear?"

"I'd say maybe, but no one of great standing."

Commissioner number one said, "They're saying it has three ears."

"A fiction, I am told, invented by the children of Second Solemn."

Commissioner number two said, "So it could be we're talking about *two* bears?"

"I'm sorry?"

"One bear took a man. Another took the sheep. No one witnessed either of the actual attacks, and the only people who *maybe* saw either of the bears are some nigger kids?"

Reverend Steadfast said, "I assure you, sir. There's only the one bear. And zero dead men. In fact—"

Sister Honora spoke. "We are prepared to address the situation."

Commissioner number three said, "Dadgum right it's a situation. This here county is a full-bore rumor machine. Word gets out that the Restive All-Tent Revival is being stalked by a man-eating, three-eared bear, why, pretty soon, the critter's gonna have *six* ears, *three* heads, and proclivities for white women. You know who comes to an All-Tent Revival that's being stalked by such a beast?"

"Niggers?" said the Reverend, who did not entirely follow this line of thought, but who nonetheless preferred to give an answer that might find accord with the commissioners.

"What we're saying, Reverend," said commissioner number one, "is kill the damned bear or the Revival's high council is a'gonna move the whole thing across the river to Kentucky." He squeezed his face tight, as if he were working a complex turd out of his rectum. "*Kentucky!*"

As they exited the city hall and mounted their horses, Reverend Steadfast said to Honora, "Next time, you do the talking."

The next day, Sunday, during the sharing of joys and concerns, the Reverend invited Sister Honora to speak.

She stood and addressed the congregation. "We have been instructed to slay the bear. Otherwise, the Revival will be relocated…"

The congregation absorbed this solemnly.

"…to Kentucky."

This was altogether too much, and the congregation made their displeasure known. The Reverend had to raise his arms to remind folks to be solemn. After a short iteration of the Song of Emotional Overreach, Honora said, "With vigilant hearts and the grace of God, the bear will be brought to justice. We can do this, for we are solemn."

Solemn's finest gunsmen and trackers were immediately taken off construction duty and organized into pairs that set out on coordinated patrols. At any given moment, day or night, at least two trackers were stalking the woods, guns on shoulders, eyes to the ground, jaws set hard against their unseen foe.

They may have been the finest of the lot, but none were very good. Several times per day, the entire citizenry of Solemn was subjected to the thunderous shock of a panic-fired blunderbuss, coachgun, or musket, followed by the equally-panicked fluttering of a flock of innocent crows scared up by the racket.

One person was shot, to no great damage. Sister Punctuality had been collecting vine flowers when she waggled the wrong bush and a jumpy fifteen-year-old tracker squeezed the trigger on his father's musket. The ball shattered Sister Punctuality's wooden leg.

For her bravery, Brother Fondly built her a new and sensuous limb of laminated hickory and pine, complete with a life-like, articulated foot over which Sister Punctuality could pull a stocking and tie a shoe.

· · ·

Out of respect for the site's status of Maximum Taboo, none of the bear-trackers went anywhere near the Baker Mine. Annie and Euphémie profited greatly from this oversight, as it safely allowed them to continue visiting the place for their "mushroom hunting" expeditions.

The bear was often present for these visits. It grew accustomed to the widows, and the widows became accustomed to the bear. It would sit nearby, atop a large, sun-warmed plate of stone, paws crossed under its chin, eyes closed, and listen contentedly to their whispered conversations, and the moments of heavy breathing and grunting and giggles and moans.

Said Annie, after a vigorous half-hour of cuddling, "It's bizarre, isn't it?"

"That we're making love at the site of a tragedy?"

Annie said, "We make love here because it's *convenient. Bizarre is*"—she gestured toward the bear lounging on the rock. It opened its eyes, yawned hugely, and lowered its chin to its arms.

"Her? She's no more bizarre than the clouds, the trees, the bugs crawling in our hair. She's nature."

"*Her? She?*"

Euphémie said, "I've yet to see a single testicle."

"Look at the way she listens."

The bear's three ears swiveled independently, tracking the birds and insects and humans. The bear, perhaps bashful at the attention, opened her eyes, stood, and walked into the darkness of the woods.

"*Au revoir, ma vicieuse,*" said Annie.

They dressed, stowed their blankets under the upturned mine-cart, retrieved their mushroom buckets, and started back to Solemn.

Chapter Thirty-Six

AUGUSTE SAID, "ARE WE ALLOWED TO ENTER UNBIDDEN?"

"From a legal perspective," whispered Pansy, "we can do whatever we want."

The boy and girl had ventured to the edge of Solemn's sister village, and were squatted behind a wooden sign that read, *Welcome to Second Solemn.*

"Then let's enter," said Auguste, straightening out of his crouch.

Pansy pulled him down. "The law doesn't account for courtesy. This is their town."

"But we were welcomed here just a few days ago."

"Because we were summoned by the alert. And we didn't actually go into the town proper."

"You're being cautious," said Auguste, "which I understand. You must feel horrible guilt after the years of oppression your people imposed upon their people."

"Don't say 'your people.' Those were *not* my people. They were southerners. The south is a good ten-mile from here. If you're going to lump a well-meaning eleven-year-old girl from Indiana in with a group of southern traitors simply because I am white, then you, too, as a white person, are one of *those people* and therefore are entitled a share of the guilt."

Before Auguste could counter this, a new voice piped in from the other side of the sign. "It's not guilt that's holding you back. It's fear."

Kermit Stovepipe poked his head out from behind the sign. "Come with me."

With a lithe step, Kermit led Auguste (also stepping lithely) and Pansy (more of a morally-uncertain shuffle) into the black settlement.

Auguste said, "This is just like our Solemn."

"Except," said Kermit.

Auguste said, "Well, the village is laid-out similarly. And there's chickens and a blacksmith, and a garden, all the same as Solemn!"

"Except," said Kermit.

"Except?" said Auguste.

"Except," said Pansy, "There's no white people."

Auguste said, "Except *us*."

"Therefore," said Kermit.

"Therefore," said Auguste, "the people of Second Solemn are prejudiced?"

Pansy groaned.

Kermit said, "He's joking, right?" He led them past Second Solemn's replica of the Solemn chapel, past a group of women shuttling up an Indian-looking blanket at a loom. Some of the women nodded hello, most paid no attention whatsoever. Zero whistlers. Instead, and it was not obvious at first, there was a low, humming drone.

Seeing Pansy's reaction to the humming, Kermit said, "We don't whistle like you folks." He shivered up and down his spine. "It's so shrill. Instead, we hum. And if you stick around for a while, and if people trust you, you might even hear someone sing."

"Blasphemy!" said Pansy.

"Y'all better get used to it. That revival of yours is gonna be jam-packed with choirs, chorales, banjos, accordions. There might be dancing. Hell, there might be drums. You're about to host a mob of sin. You ever think about that?"

"No, because it isn't true," said Pansy, arms crossed.

"You'll see," said Kermit.

"Well, anyway," said Pansy, "we welcome all kinds in Solemn, even those who don't whistle."

Auguste said, "What she says is true. *I* can't whistle, and they've taken me as one of their own."

Kermit said, "Can't whistle? I can fix that."

He brought them just beyond the town proper, to a decrepit chicken house, spongy with rot. Inside, it stank of ammonia and eggshells. Tiny snails climbed on the mossy walls.

"A whole building all to yourselves," marveled Pansy.

"It's a little messy, yet," said Kermit. "Harriet and I only got permission to use it a few weeks ago, after Old Man Drodger passed on." He moved some broken chunks of wood, uncovering a rusted tin can. "Here it is." He shook the can until several large teeth fell into his upraised palm. He extended his hand to Auguste. "Take some."

Auguste said, "These are from a goat?"

"Too small," said Pansy. "A horse."

"Nope," said Kermit, "Cow teeth. The biters, not the chewers."

"Incisors, technically." said Pansy.

Kermit placed one of the teeth in his right cheek and formed an *O* with his lips. A fluttering birdsong escaped his mouth.

Auguste said, "Do it again!"

Playing cool to Auguste's enthusiasm, Kermit slid a second of these carved cow incisors into his other cheek. This time, he exhaled a pair of notes, soft, low, flutelike. As Kermit shifted air from one cheek to the other, the notes diverged, overtones pulsated against one another. Then he spat the teeth back into the rusted can.

"Now you," said Kermit, handing Auguste a fresh pair of teeth.

Auguste placed them in his cheeks.

Kermit said, "Get 'em tight against your gums. Then loosen your cheeks and—"

From Auguste's mouth came the music of two birds flirting on a dewy morning. His eyes went wide, the flirting birds flew away, and, with chipmunk cheeks, he cried, "I ca' wishel! I ca' wishel!" Smiling ridiculously he carefully expectorated the teeth into his palm.

"Say," said Kermit, "he's a natural. You wanna try, Pansy?"

Pansy, playing at her own version of cool, said, "I can whistle perfectly fine without contraptions."

Auguste said, "Will you show me how to make some, Kermit? Please?"

"How about you just keep those two?"

Auguste said, "But they must be very difficult to construct."

"Oh, hell, I bore 'em out with an old drill bit. Doesn't take but a couple of hours."

Pansy said, "It's a skill that's been passed down for many generations, all the way from Africa."

Kermit said, "Hardly. I made this up myself. Came to me in a dream. 'Thou shalt create cheekflutes out of the teeth of the slaughtered ox.' Something like that, anyway."

Auguste said, "It's a miracle." He re-inserted the teeth and blew another series of notes.

"The miracle," said Kermit, "if there is one, is how quick you've figured 'em out. It took me a couple of days just to get a sound."

Pansy, who was still smarting from her wrong guess about the origins of the whistles, said, "We didn't come here to talk about teeth, boys. There are other matters; bear-related matters. Starting with the other day, Kermit, when the bear ate the sheep. After everyone started clearing out, we saw you and Harriet sneak off into the woods. What were you up to?"

Kermit made a non-committal noise.

Pansy said, "You know something."

Kermit said, "Only thing I know is that y'all Solemn*whites* are never going find that bear by stomping in the woods like dummies. Guns going off all hours. We hear 'em on our side of the hill. The bear hears 'em."

"Aha!" exclaimed Auguste. "So it does have three ears."

Kermit said, "That's one theory."

"Quiet," said Pansy. "Someone's out there."

Harriet poked her head thru the doorway. She said to Kermit, "Where'd you get these two?"

"They're the ones from the sheep deal."

Harriet said, "Right. Pansy and August."

"Au*guste*," emphasized Auguste.

"I gave him some of my toothwhistles," said Kermit. "Kid's a natural."

Harriet said, "Mom's waiting on you. Get a move on."

Kermit got a move on.

To her guests, Harriet said, "Mother is teaching him how to milk the goats." To Auguste, she said, "You talk funny. Where do you come from, again? Louisville?"

"France," said Auguste, "It's very far."

"Why'd you come all the way to here?"

"My father killed a man and was hanged for it."

Harriet said, "Hm." To Pansy, "Weren't you there, too? In the France?"

"I brought him back with me."

"You know what'll happen if the white folk find out you've been visiting with us?"

Pansy said, "Nothing will happen. The people of Solemn don't truck in that Confederate small-mindedness."

Harriet shook her head. "They'll feed you to the bear is what they'll do."

Pansy said, "They don't even know where the bear is."

Harriet lowered her voice. "Can I tell you something without you blurting it all about?"

Auguste and Pansy nodded.

"After that sheep deal, me and my brother went looking."

"We know," said Pansy. "I was just telling Kermit how we saw you go into the woods."

"He tell you what we saw?" said Harriet.

"You got here before he had a chance," said Pansy.

Harriet began to sense that Pansy might be one of those *know-talls* who can't help but point out every doggone thing. She said, "Here's what we saw."

Auguste said, "A three-eared bear?"

"Ease up on the ears, already," said Harriet, who sensed that Auguste might be one of those people who, once infected with a silly notion, will never be persuaded to give it up. She continued. "While all the white folk were lollygagging at our dead sheep and talking big about hunting bear, we Stovepipes got right to work."

Pansy said, "I figured. Didn't I say so, Auguste?"

Harriet continued, "We'd only walked about ten feet before we saw a sign, a drop of blood, just as plain as the sun shines on a sleeping cat."

Pansy and Auguste were open-mouthed.

"So we looked some more. Kermit found some wool, and then"—dramatic pause—"I found a footprint!" At that final phrase, Harriet clapped her hands with a loud pop. Her guests jumped at the noise. Capitalizing on the drama, Harriet lowered her voice to a whisper. "But it wasn't a bear print. It wasn't a panther print or possum or any other animal. It was the footprint of a human person who didn't have any shoes."

Pansy furrowed her brow. "There's lots of barefoot people in the woods."

"That's just what Kermit said. Until he found another foot-print, and another. All made by the same set of feet, headed in the same direction, and all of them accompanied by some evidence of sheep murder. Blood, wool, even a kidney."

Pansy said, "Yes, but—"

"—it coulda been that someone set out for the bear just before we did? And his footprints were just following the bear's tracks?"

Pansy said, "Precisely."

Auguste appreciated the girls' mutual affection for problem-solving.

Harriet said, "There weren't any bear tracks. Nowhere. Just barefoot human tracks. They led like one of those scribbles that a termite chews thru wood."

"And then?" said Pansy.

"And then they stopped."

Pansy said, "How thorough did you check? Maybe he back-tracked or something."

Harriet said, "We crawled around like a couple of Indians."

Pansy said, "Did you look up? Maybe he climbed a tree. Or maybe there were rocks that he could have walked on without leaving prints."

"The tracks stopped. And something else. Kermit and I both felt—how to say it—we felt a *scare*."

Auguste said, "Naturally, after what happened to the sheep."

Pansy said, "This *scare*. Was it a real scare? Or was it a kid-scare? Like when you're afraid of the dark?"

Harriet pondered.

Auguste said, "I think Pansy means was it rational or irrational."

Harriet said, "It was supernatural. Devilish, even. Kermit would agree. It reminded us of how maggoty meat smells."

Pansy said, "How solemnly have you prayed about this?"

Harriet shook her head. "Our Solemn is different from your Solemn."

"But you pray."

Worried that the conversation was about to be derailed by a theological dispute, Auguste said, "Back to the bear."

Harriet didn't budge. "We're a little looser here than you folks. Some of us are dedicated to Solemnity, others don't even go to church. It's not considered a big deal either way." She sighed. "And prayer. Well, it might work for some folks. But it seems awfully passive, like begging. Maybe I'm cynical, you know, after all that's happened to us all."

Curtly, Pansy said, "So you don't pray."

"I do. But mostly to give thanks for food and good weather. Not for personal favors; I've never felt the need to pester God about my problems."

"That seems pretty solemn to me," said Auguste, who had his own divergent thoughts on prayer.

"I guess so," said Pansy. "But strange."

"Thanks for not judging me," said Harriet, semi-disingenuous, semi-grateful.

"We all know what they say about judging," said Pansy, semi-contemptuous, semi-flattered.

Auguste again attempted to steer them toward the original subject. "I'm unclear. Was the sheep killed by a bear or by the man with mysterious footprints?"

"I have a third option," said Harriet. *"What if the bear—"*

"Has three ears?" said Auguste.

"—can turn into a person?"

Pansy said, "You're talking about demons now."

"It's just a theory," said Harriet who had by now decided that Pansy was indeed a *knowtall*, albeit one who knew a few things.

"It's a silly theory," said Pansy, doing nothing to change Harriet's mind.

"Silly isn't always wrong," said Auguste. "I am thinking of a story Father used to tell me. Long ago, in a town called Gévaudan, there was a wolf that could change itself into a man. Or a man that could change himself into a wolf. In any case, it slayed a dozen men and women and children. Not all at once, but sporadically, over many months. Their throats were removed and the bodies drained of blood."

Pansy said, "You're talking about werewolves. That's fairy-tale talk."

Harriet said, "I've heard plenty of tales of werewolves. Ain't no fairies in those tales."

Pansy said, "You are suggesting that the sheep was mauled by a were*bear*?"

"It would explain quite a lot," said Auguste. "According to Father, the beast of Gévaudan, after it had fed, it would change back into a man and watch as the family wept over the corpse."

Harriet nodded knowingly.

"What finally happened to it?" said Pansy.

"The people of Gévaudan gathered all the reprobates they could find, twenty-three in all. Thieves, liars, adulterers, that sort of thing. They hanged them and burned their bodies. After that, the murders ended. My father was skeptical, though. He said it only proved that all men are monsters. He believed the beast still walked the woods and so I was to never leave the house on my own after dark. Not until I was ten years old."

Pansy said, "Adults do that all the time; making up stories to scare us into behaving."

Harriet said, "All the time."

Auguste flexed his eyebrows. "My father was no liar."

"I was just saying," said Pansy. As a concession to Auguste's father issues, she added, "Your theories do make a certain amount of sense, *vis-à-vis* footprints and so forth."

Auguste said, "A werebear is the most rational explanation."

"Rational or not," said Harriet, "who's gonna listen to us when we tell them we've got a werebear? It's bad enough that we're all kids—me and Kermit are *nigger kids*."

"What do we do?" said Pansy.

Harriet said, "It's not an emergency yet, not as long as the werebear sticks to sheep."

Auguste nodded enthusiastically. Harriet was awfully clever, and she hadn't even heard his theory about animal sacrifice.

"But if it doesn't?" said Pansy.

"We just have to stay smart," said Harriet. "Watch for signs, keep in touch."

"Vigilance," said Auguste.

Pansy said, "That's an awfully passive approach. Shouldn't we at least look for it?"

Auguste said, "And end up like the sheep?"

"A few minutes ago, you were ready to hunt the bear all by yourself," said Pansy.

"That was before we knew it was a werebear."

Pansy said, "So, if we tell the grown-ups they need to look for a werebear, we'll be laughed at. If we try to find the werebear, we're dead. So the wisest thing is to keep quiet and stay aware."

"And be smart," said Harriet. "Remember, this is a half-man, half-bear. It can hear your eyes blink from the other side of the county. It can smell your earwax even when it's sleeping in its denhole. And it can swallow a man's head in one gulp."

Pansy shrugged. This whole business was silly.

A voice called from outside.

Harriet said, "That's my mom. I gotta go. You know the way out."

Auguste blew his tooth whistles practically all the way home. He removed them from his cheeks only once, to say, "I don't suppose there's a *Third* Solemn? Just for Indians?"

"There ain't enough Indians left to fill a wagon, much less a whole town."

Auguste returned the whistles to his cheeks. Before they reached Solemn, he had managed a reasonable facsimile of the goldfinch that had followed them thru the forest.

Chapter Thirty-Seven

ANNIE AND EUPHÉMIE CONTINUED TO VISIT THE BAKER MINE EVEN AS the weather grew colder and as the mushrooms grew scarce. Toward the end of their most recent tryst, as dried leaves settled from branches and stuck on their sweating skin, the bear, who had been watching from her rock ledge with her paws crossed under her chin, gave a loud snort.

The volume of the bear's vocalizations tended to match the amplitude of the widows' sexual enthusiasm. On this particular day, the bear snorted especially loudly and then stared at them with her smoky eyes, and wiggled her goofy ears. She turned and walked away from the couple, then she paused and gestured with her head as if to say, "Follow me."

Annie raised her eyebrows at Euphémie.

Euphémie said, "You think?"

The widows pulled on their dresses. They followed as the bear padded between shrubs and young trees. She led them to a large stand of raspberries, woody canes bunched together, fruit devoured by bird and bug and bear and frost.

The bear plunged into the raspberries and disappeared. A moment later, she poked her head out, wiggled her ears, and beckoned again.

The widows entered the bush, which smelled faintly of coal smoke.

They emerged some time later, and walked home, holding hands and gaily swinging their empty mushroom pails.

Chapter Thirty-Eight

ONLY ONE DAY REMAINED BEFORE THE REVIVAL COUNCIL WOULD BE forced to relocate the entire kit-and-caboodle to Kentucky on account of the bloodthirsty bear, which had not been seen by *anyone*—other than the pair of French *immigrées* who so much enjoyed fondling each other in front of its adorable mug at a disaster site that they couldn't be bothered to disclose its presence to the very people who had brought them across an ocean and welcomed them to their sylvan sanctuary.

On the afternoon of this portentous day, the *immigrées* in question were happily kneading dough when a swell of whistles floated in thru the window.

"Which one is that?" asked Annie, "The incoming-storm-announcement or the please-gather-at-the-chapel call?"

Euphémie said, "I'm inclined toward another-of-our-mighty-hunters-has-accidentally-sent-a-ball-into-Sister-Puntuality's-new-wooden-leg."

The widows leaned out the window to see a soft-skinned,

angular young man enter the town, followed by an audience of whistlers.

This was Brother Courage, the nineteen-year-old husband to Sister Courage, with whom he'd created two daughters. He was an avid hunter of the bear, and he was walking proudly, with a patch of black fur flagging off the end of his shouldered musket.

"I got him! He's down in the yonder. Too big to carry."

The whistlers redoubled their song, adding to it the sonic equivalent of exclamation points.

Annie grew pale.

Euphémie said, "Don't worry. There's no way that runt killed our bear."

Reverend Steadfast heard the commotion from his desk in the chapel. He abandoned the sermon he was writing and hurried out to the growing crowd, which parted in order that he might assess the news up close.

"Brother Courage," he said, "what have you?"

Brother Courage said, "I have slain the beast. A great creature it was. But the Lord steadied my hand and I fired true. It yonder lays dead in its own red mud."

Reverend Steadfast gestured toward the patch of fur hanging from Courage's musket. It wasn't much larger than a handkerchief. "And this is its hide?"

Brother Courage's voice wavered. "There is much more to be had."

The Reverend snatched the fur from where it hung and he held it to his nose. "Brother Courage. This is no bear."

The Reverend passed the fur to Sister Courage, who, with her daughters, had appeared at the side of her husband. She sniffed once, and cast the fur to the ground. "Husband! A skunk?"

The gathered crowd released a deflating whistle.

"You are mistaken, Sister," said Brother Courage.

"Take me, then, to the red mud in which the rest of this creature resides."

Brother Courage opened his mouth, then closed it. Then he opened it again, and then he closed it again.

Sister Courage said, "Can you not smell?"

Brother Courage stammered, "I meant only to save the Revival."

Sister Courage said, "You have shamed your family."

Reverend Steadfast addressed the crowd. "A town meeting will commence in ten minutes."

To Brother Courage he said, "I am displeased."

Still leaning out their windowsill, Euphémie said to Annie, "At least he didn't shoot anyone."

Annie called into the bedroom where Auguste and Pansy were supposed to have been whirring their treadles, but from whence the sounds of industry had ceased several moments prior. "Children! Come, there's another meeting at the chapel."

𝕽   𝕷   𝕳   𝕸

After a half-hour of opening prayer and humble entreaties to the wisdom of the Lord, Reverend Steadfast laid his hands upon the pulpit. "Friends, there are impediments, and there are those of us who can overcome those impediments."

Sensing that he was about to embark upon a multi-hour theophilosophical journey, Sister Honora asked to be recognized. A close observer would have noticed a loosening of Reverend Steadfast's features as he nodded in acquiescence.

Sister Honora took to the pulpit. "Let us not cast blame upon Brother Courage. As we stand on the cusp of our reckoning with the bear, I ask you to consider that our brother's ambition was to help us. Even if his actions were regrettable." She cast her eyes upon Brother Courage, who was seated upright in a wooden chair immediately left of the pulpit. His face was a blank mask. Honora said, "Am I correct, Brother Courage? Do you feel regret?"

Courage's lips remained sealed even as he opened his jaw, stretching until they finally parted with a little *pop*. "I mistook the skunk for a bear and I shot it. In my excitement, I lost my sense of solemnity and I..." He slid his unfocused eyes over the assembled crowd. "In my desire to prevent the re-location of the Revival, I deceived myself." He swallowed noisily.

Honora said, "Brothers and Sisters, it is no small thing to welcome a thousand strangers into our small county. But we are up to this task. Witness the progress we've made in all manner of things. Hundreds of trees have been cleared; the campgrounds are finished; the Village of Godly Illumination is nearly finished. In the coming days, the Second Solemnites will begin work on the Great Stage. The revival is coming, and we will be ready. All we lack is a dead bear. A bear! A simple beast that lives in a cave and which leaves footprints and deposits scat. We're not talking about the giants of Gath, or Saph, or even of Ishbibenob. We can defeat this enemy, but only if we remain solemn."

A voice from the rear shouted, "We need an Indian!"

"We need a dead bear," said Sister Honora. "Today."

Sister Temperance's eyes widened and she barked a single, embarrassed laugh. Eighty-odd pairs of eyes swiveled to regard the source of this outburst.

Sister Temperance said, in her timid voice, "I would suggest that our troubles are over."

Excited murmuring.

Temperance continued, her voice a little stronger, "Does the Revival not commence on December twenty-eighth? Do bears not sleep during the winter? Would a bear not feed immediately before entering its hibernational state?" Temperance's timidity was eroding. "Would a sheep's flesh not sustain a bear until spring?" Giving way to full-throated declaration. "People of Solemn, the All-Tent Revival needn't worry about a bear. The bear will be snoring!"

In the silence that followed, Pansy flicked Auguste on the wrist. *Should we tell them about the werebear?*

Auguste shook his head.

Reverend Steadfast said, "Sister Honora, saddle a horse and bring this news to Restive. The All-Tent Revival will go on."

If this had been any place other than the Church of Solemnity, the room would have erupted in applause. It was not, and so it did not.

Pansy and Auguste held hands tightly. These people had no idea.

Or maybe they did. Because, as the churchgoers were raising themselves from their pews, an elderly man, Brother Cleanly, spoke in his jackdaw of a voice, "I been hearing of chickens."

The Reverend raised his arms for quiet. He was familiar with the vocalized spasms of Brother Cleanly, who was half-deaf and still insisted on sitting at the very back of the chapel, often interrupting sermons by shouting to his equally-deaf wife, "The man don't enunciate!" Occasionally, an incomplete sentence would spring from his lips as if it were a garbled transmission from the heavens above. *The wolf and the lame! Damascus wilts in sometimes!*

Typically, after Cleanly realized that one of these fragmented thoughts had escaped his mouth, he'd tilt his head toward his lap and docilely allow his wife to pat his hand. But this day, Cleanly persisted. "Some of the coloreds in Second Solemn been losing chickens. Someone been stealin' 'em, I hear, and it warn't no bear. They's been seen footprints of shoeless feet. Human feet. And clothes been stolen from drying lines. Lord knows what-all the manner!"

Reverend Steadfast was briefly taken off-guard at this unusually long stretch of coherence. "I've heard the rumors, Brother Cleanly." General agreement from the congregation, who were caught between standing up and sitting back down. The Reverend continued. "It's most likely some of their own doing it."

A voice called out, "Or a Indian!"

"In any case, we can let them handle their own troubles, and we can be thankful that our bear troubles are over."

Another voice called out, "At least until spring!"

. . .

Filing out of the chapel, Auguste and Pansy agreed that, yes, these people really had no idea; and that, no, he and Pansy had no idea how to convince them otherwise.

Auguste slid his cow teeth into his cheeks and tweeted a quail's inquisitive call.

Chiou...wheet?

Chapter Thirty-Nine

THE BEAR HUNT WAS IMMEDIATELY CALLED OFF. THE NEWLY unburdened bear hunters rejoined the labor force for the infrastructure project, which allowed for the rest of the Solemnites to end their work days earlier, a blessing in the crisp and cool days of November.

With the changing weather, Sister Temperance and the widows began to meet inside the Gravity house every evening for post-dinner tea and kibitzing. They'd gather around the cast-iron stove with knit blankets over their laps and converse in French.

The children tended not to join in these sessions; they had forged their own post-dinner routine of hiking to Second Solemn to visit their friends, Harriet and Kermit Stovepipe.

On this particular evening, after their shifts at the spinning wheels and a bite of bread, Auguste and Pansy walked to Second Solemn. They'd grown familiar with—and familiar to—the residents of Solemn's sister village. Their trepidation had by now been replaced by a routine of cheery *hellos* and easy waves.

The Stovepipe kids, with assistance from Pansy and Auguste, had made several improvements on the chicken house. These included four logs that served as stools, wall decorations made from fabric scraps, and a floppy tin door that swung on leather hinges.

When they pushed open the door this chilly evening, Pansy and Auguste were greeted by the crackling of burning wood.

"A stove!" said Pansy. She and Auguste hurried to warm their hands at the barrel stove that now stood in the corner.

Kermit grinned proudly from his log-chair. "I found it under that old fell-down shack down by the river."

Auguste, attempting an English pun for the first time in his life, said, "Every Stovepipe requires a stove."

Pansy recognized this great milestone, and then stomped all over it. "Oh, but Auguste, that would mean Harriet and Kermit are still one stove short. Because there are *two* Stovepipes, see, and only *one* stove; and you've just said that *every* Stovepipe requires a stove."

Harriet, seeking to profit from Pansy's misfire, said, "You've made a good joke, Auggie. Now let us settle in for an evening of fellowship."

Simultaneous to this, Sister Temperance was being welcomed by the widows into the Gravity house, which had a crackling fire of its own.

"Friends," said Temperance taking her seat at the table, "may I present the season's first batch of Brother Providence's celebrated venison jerky."

After Annie and Euphémie had formally agreed that Brother Providence's jerky was worthy of celebration, Temperance crossed her hands on her lap and hazarded a question that had been on her mind for some time. "What is it like to create a baby?"

Euphémie quickly turned to Annie, whose eyes were wide in surprise.

Blushing, Sister Temperance said, "I should not ask such things."

Annie's eyes softened. She had never thought of Temperance as a woman—moreso as an adorable pet—and here she was asking about human sexuality. Simultaneously, Euphémie and Annie leaned forward and patted her upon the knee. Annie said, "Sister, you may ask us anything."

"I don't know what to ask."

"Are you pregnant?" said Euphémie.

"Goodness no!" cried Temperance. Meekly, she added, "But one day I may wish to be, if it's not too much of a chore."

Euphémie said, "There's a whole lot involved in creating a child. Of which parts do you lack in knowledge?"

Sister Temperance said, "I'm not entirely ignorant. I've seen the process in animals; from the coupling between the male and female all the way to the birth and then the mother eats the after-birth and then she allows the child to drink from her teat. But I want to know what it's *like*, all of it. From a human perspective."

Annie said, "Starting with...?"

Sister Temperance said, "From the coupling."

Annie said, "In fact, it starts prior to the...coupling."

"Of course," said Temperance. "A man and woman must first marry and build a house. This is all known to me." She cast an eye toward the great Gravity bed. "What I don't understand is what happens to a woman during—"

Euphémie spoke, serious and kind, "I never much cared for it —I had a son, you know. My husband was not my friend. He was my master. And I was never attracted to him, not in a coupling-way."

"But you did it?"

"It was not optional."

"Did it give you no pleasure?"

"The same pleasure one derives from sticking oneself with a needle."

Sister Temperance nodded wisely. "This is the sort of man I wish to couple with. A man without pleasure."

Euphémie and Annie were accustomed to Sister Temperance's

counterintuitive proclamations, and so they kept their mouths shut and waited for clarification, which she offered immediately. "A child's life should not begin with a bestial outburst of lust. Forged in heat, iron becomes soft. Soft iron is easily shaped into a sword. I do not wish to be a mother to a sword. This is a lesson of solemnity."

Euphémie swallowed hard. "When my son was forged, there was no heat, there was no softness. At least not for me; I was weeping, as solemn as you could imagine. And the boy, yes, grew up hard. But he was never a sword, only a lump of metal, something to trip over."

Sister Temperance said, "This is why you abandoned him?"

"I did not abandon him. I fled him. He had turned into his father." Her voice began to quaver. "If you wonder, do I feel remorse, I do not. It pleasures me to imagine him miserable and alone."

Sister Temperance absorbed all of this, then turned to Annie, "And your son. Was Auguste forged with heat or was he forged with solemnity?"

Annie thought for a moment. "I suspect, Sister Temperance, that it's not a question of solemnity. It's a question of whether both parties are of the same mind at the time of the forging. Euphémie's child was an unfortunate product of a man's desire colliding with a woman's despair. And, while I cannot recall the exact moment of his conception, my child, whom we can agree is a sympathetic creature, was the product of like-minded parents."

"And what were your minds like?"

"At that precise moment, our minds were a rollicking, bestial outburst of lust."

Annie winked at Euphémie, whose head twitched slightly, as if to say *I appreciate the manner in which you've just altered the tone of this conversation, but I'd rather not hear another word about the sexual relationship between you and the late Mr. Lestables.*

In the ponderous silence that followed, Annie extended an

index finger and gently stroked the outside of Euphémie's thigh, an act of fondness beyond the view of their curious guest.

"I suppose none of this matters if I cannot find someone to couple with," said Temperance. "Perhaps you could give me some council on the subject?"

To the widows' relief, there came a knock upon the door before they could reply.

Chapter Forty

MEANWHILE, IN THE CHICKEN SHACK, THE CHILDREN HAD DIRECTED their conversation to the recent string of misdemeanor larcenies that had been plaguing Second Solemn; these being the crimes that Brother Cleanly had recently described after Brother Courage had unsuccessfully transubstantiated a dead skunk into a bear.

Chickens were disappearing, about one per week. Other things as well, less-significant items like matches and knives and pillows. According to Harriet, one morning, after a hoary frost, one of her neighbors had seen footprints in the grass, leading away from a chicken roost, from which a chicken had been stolen. The prints had been laid by unshod human feet.

As the nights had grown colder, a pair of boots disappeared off a back porch. The next time footprints showed up in the hoar frost, they were of boot soles. These led into the forest, wound about, and melted as the sun rose.

After Harriet had finished, Auguste said, "Would the werebear wear the boots on its front feet or its rear feet?"

"Don't be silly." said Harriet, "It only wears shoes when it's in the shape of a human."

"Which it wears on its feet, not its hands," added Kermit helpfully.

Pansy said, "According to the grownups in our Solemn, the thief's a Negro. As long as he sticks to stealing from other Negroes, the problem is Second Solemn's to worry about." She added, "I do not share their opinion."

"But the thief is not just a thief," said Kermit. "He's a werebear."

Pansy said, "Yes, and we agreed to keep our mouths shut about it unless it did something worse than kill a sheep. I don't think a stolen pair of boots meets that criterion."

"Personally, I don't care about the werebear," said Harriet. "I care about the fact that the grown-ups of White Solemn blame the Negroes any time something goes sideways."

Pansy harrumphed. "It was those same white folk who gave you this town. It was those white folk who freed you from the bonds of slavery."

Harriet lowered her voice to a rumble, "You all haven't saved anybody."

This was news to Pansy. "We saved you from the 'federates. Sister Punctuality said so."

"What's a 'federate?" said Kermit.

"The ones from Kentucky," said Harriet. "The ones who thought our people were cattle. The war proved them wrong, but being *proved* wrong never stopped a white man from *doing* wrong." She looked to Pansy. "There's some things about our Solemns that you maybe never heard."

Pansy crossed her arms. "I'm listening."

Chapter Forty-One

THE HINGE SQUEAKED, CANDLE FLAMES LEANED TOWARD THE BRISK pull of the door, and Sister Honora entered the Gravity house. She stripped off her wool cape, flipped her hair behind her ears, fluffed her skirt, and seated herself at the table. Then she blinked as if she were just now realizing where she was. Thru thin lips, she said, "I apologize for my outburst."

Annie had by now learned that, in Solemn, not-saying-hello could count as an outburst. She reached across the table, offering the harried woman a stick of deer jerky. "Speak, Sister."

Honora bit off a nub of the jerky. "A man has come to Restive who would build a *Pleasure Wheel*."

Considering the nature of the earlier conversation, this was cutting a bit close to the cloth. After a quick gasp, Sister Temperance said, "To what end?"

"Obviously, something decidedly lacking in solemnity," said Honora.

Over these past months, Euphémie had learned how to maintain a straight face even in the most ludic of situations. The phrase *Pleasure Wheel* was pushing the limits of that control. With lips that oscillated between the opposing forces of gravity and depravity she managed to say, "More information, please."

Sister Honora gnawed off another inch of the jerky and swallowed it without chewing. Euphémie, Annie, and Temperance all gaped as the lump slid down her throat.

"I have just returned from a council meeting in Restive. They have granted permission for a Californian to construct a mechanical device called a Pleasure Wheel." Honora raised a palm to forestall the inevitable query from Sister Temperance. "Its purpose is to convey festival-goers in a vertical fashion to great heights and then to return them unharmed to the pediment. I cannot believe this will be allowed."

Annie said, "As long as the device does no harm then it would seem to be harmless."

Sister Honora said, "I've seen drawings of this...contrivance. It resembles a great water wheel, except, rather than paddles, it will have carriages upon which people can recline themselves."

"A person-wheel?" said Temperance. "There must be better ways to operate a mill."

Sister Honora ignored this comment. "The Californian claims that he will bring the masses closer to God. Apparently, the wheel is exceedingly tall, over thirty feet." This impressed the widows. "But I know his true motivation. The council has granted him permission to charge one ha'penny per rider of the wheel. Half of this profit will go to the Revival's general operating fund. Fie! After all our industrious contributions to this great gathering, we have become blinded to the obvious truth. We would exchange integrity for notoriety, and solemnity for Sodom."

Temperance said, "You raised these concerns with the council, yes?"

"I raised my concerns. They explained to me the following. An All-Tent Revival welcomes all sorts of beliefs. It is a *détente*, it is a summit, it is—and here they were especially blunt—not a referendum on the perfection of Solemnity."

"But," said Temperance.

"Exactly," said Sister Honora. "Those condescending—Lord forgive my tongue—those men of the council explained that the

Revival shall be a marketplace for God. And all parties attending are asked to willfully suspend their exclusive belief in the one true way. It is, they claim, a test of a greater form of righteousness."

Temperance may or may not have been getting the details, but she was catching her colleague's vibe. "Gracious," she said. "This is entirely unreasonable."

Annie handed Honora another strip of jerky, then said, "I think this is not so awful as it seems. Permit me to explain. The Lord is known to test his subjects, no?"

Honora's chewing slowed.

"And yet the Lord stayed Abraham's hand, and the fish spat Jonah upon the shore, and the Israelites were freed, and Job was rewarded with a thousand asses."

Euphémie was amazed, and slightly disturbed, that Annie had retained so much from Reverend Steadfast's sermons.

Honora rebutted, "And when Satan told the Messiah to leap from the temple so that angels might catch him, what did Jesus say in reply?"

"Um..."

Temperance raised her hand. "I know! He said, 'Do not put the Lord to your test.'"

Euphémie, who cared not a whit about any of this, said, "But this *isn't* us putting the Lord to a test. The Pleasure Wheel is the Lord's way of testing *us*. It's consistent with his methods. He tests us thru death and anger and poverty—"

"—and unquenchable desires for flesh!" said Temperance, knocking her freckled knuckles against the tabletop.

Sister Honora, who had never known Sister Temperance to speak of desires, quenchable or otherwise, gasped so violently that she inhaled the morsel of venison she'd been gnawing, and then immediately projectile-coughed it across the table, just missing Annie's right ear, to splat against the far wall, where it clung for a moment and then slid to the floor like a weary slug.

This was all too much for Euphémie. Biting sharply upon her

left thumb, she sprinted into the cool night and plunged her head into a frigid washbasin and screamed her laughter into bubbles.

Temperance shrunk into herself. "I apologize for my outburst."

Annie assured her she had nothing to worry about. At least this outburst, unlike Honora's, had included actual sounds.

Honora inhaled as if to swallow all the tension in the room. Her face relaxed into a state so solemn that it approached beatitude. "I'm a fool. I've come here unbidden and I've infected you with my passion. In spite of all things, Solemnitic Christianity is the true path to God. A perverted wheel to the heavens will not alter that."

"A wheel travels in circles," said Annie. She had meant nothing by it, but the statement provided an opportunity for all present to nod wisely, as if the roundness of a circle was a metaphysical revelation. The mutual agreement on this principle of geometry presented an adequate coda to the conversation. Honora led Temperance out the door and past the wet-haired Euphémie, who could only offer a half-hearted wave to her friends as they marched to their respective places of slumber.

The night remained young, but their day had been long and so Annie and Euphémie went straight to bed.

Chapter Forty-Two

MEANWHILE, IN THE CHICKEN SHACK, HARRIET SAID, "HERE'S THE Solemn-story that Sister Punctuality didn't tell you. Prepare yourselves; it's a major deviation from the fib your white folk been propagating.

"In 1862, there was a man named Clawdy Baker, lived just across the state line, in Sidehaul, Kentucky. This was during the war. Baker owned what they call a deep-shaft plantation. Deep, deep coalmines operated by work-slaves. One night, one of his mines got captured by abolitionists. They set it afire. Nobody inside, but the operation was destroyed.

"So Baker moved north. He found himself a place to dig and relocated the whole plantation—slaves and all—right here in this so-called free state of Indiana.

"He called this new plantation Secretion, because it was a secret; so well-hid that nobody in Indiana even knew he was there."

Auguste said, "Excuse me. Does *secretion* mean the same in English as it does in French?"

"Yes, liquid ooze," said Pansy, who was not hating this story as much as she'd anticipated.

Kermit said, "Mr. Baker was not a vocabularious man."

Harriet recommenced, "For a year or so, nobody had a clue what he was up to. Not until that dumbass blew the mine to smithereens."

Pansy said, "Please don't call people names. The dumb...bottom was my grandfather, and, as tragic as it was, his frivolous behavior did lead directly the founding of the church of Solemn."

Harriet said, "Did you know that, in addition to the seventeen white folk who died, twenty-six Negroes got blown up? Sister Punctuality didn't teach you that, I bet."

Pansy's face teetered at the edge of the cliff of indignance.

"A few days after the explosion," said Harriet, "word got out that Lincoln had already freed the slaves several months prior. Baker had known about the emancipation from the beginning, but he'd kept it to himself. So those twenty-six dead Negroes had been free men in a free country, slaving for a rotten liar." To Pansy, she said, "You don't object if I call Baker a liar?"

Pansy said, "If what you're saying is true, call him as you please."

"The remaining population of black folk—the ones who didn't get blown up—told Baker to go to hell and they all moved out of Solemn and started their own town. And that's how Second Solemn came to be."

Kermit said, "I bet you never knew all that."

Auguste said, "I am reminded of my father's words, 'The fictions of religion will unite society only so long as society agrees to ignore facts.'"

"Facts is right," said Harriet.

Pansy said, "Have you any proof of this allegation?"

Harriet said to Kermit, "Show them the paper."

Kermit reached his hand thru a crack in the wall, from which he extracted a crinkled sale bill.

He handed it to Auguste, who lingered over the bill's crude woodcut of a black man.

Pansy said, "It's a sale-bill. What's your point?"

"The point is," said Harriet, "that the buck and the wench on that poster were our grandparents. They were bought in 1847 by the Baker family. In 1865, after the mine accident—and after the surviving black folk founded Second Solemn—the Baker family changed their name to Steadfast, which happens to be the name of your preacher. It was his kin who enslaved my kin. It was his kin who stole us into Indiana. It was his kin who worked us to death."

"False," said Pansy, arms crossed. "Indiana is a free state, and Solemn is a free town. Always has been."

Auguste said, "Yes, Pansy, but Solemn *used* to be Secretion."

Pansy said, "It has been Solemn ever since the Epiphany of the Explosion. That paper doesn't prove anything."

Harriet said, "You go home, look at your church ledgers. Look it up. I promise you, around 1866, you'll see that all the Bakers disappear, replaced by a family called Steadfast, all of which have the same first names as the used-to-be Bakers."

"Even so," said Pansy, "That don't mean Reverend Steadfast has the same evil as his prior kin."

"Sure," said Harriet, "except, did you ever wonder why all our menfolk are busting their backs for a revival *they won't even be allowed to attend*?"

Pansy considered many responses, and none of them gave her satisfaction. She opted for, "No."

Harriet said, "You didn't know we weren't invited."

"Of course you're invited!" said Pansy. "*All are welcome.*"

Harriet shook her head. "Nobody's gonna declare this out loud, but, trust me, you're not gonna see a single dark face at your friendly little festival."

"Sounds like sour grapes to me," said Pansy.

Auguste said, "What are sour grapes?"

Harriet said, "Pansy thinks we don't wanna go on account of we're spiteful and ungrateful."

"If that's not it, then why?" said Pansy.

"Because," said Harriet, "colored folks have their place. Nobody has to tell us; we understand what's expected. And none of your kind expects us, or any other darkies, to stick our big ol' noses into your handkerchief of Christian brotherhood."

Auguste said, "What is a handkerchief of Christian—"

"She's saying," said Kermit, "that there's an unwritten rule."

Pansy rubbed her temples. "This is, maybe. It could be true. It's hard to think. No, I've got it. Auguste, you know how dogs aren't allowed inside houses?"

"I like dogs."

"Everybody likes dogs," said Pansy. "But—"

"But," said Harriet, "dogs have their place. And it don't take long for a dog to figure out that it's gonna get its ass beat if it tries to cross the threshold into your kitchen."

"It's like when we hid in that box in the ship," said Auguste.

To Harriet, Pansy said, "But can't you just go to the festival anyway?"

"Sometimes you have to be smart," said Harriet.

Kermit said, "Being smart means you don't go where you aren't welcome."

"So, why are your men helping us?" said Pansy.

"It's not for the vegetables, I can tell you that," said Kermit.

"It's because of wool," said Harriet. "We grow sheep, we shear the sheep, and then you all turn the wool into yarn."

"I'm a very good spinner," said Auguste, proudly.

Harriet continued, "And then Reverend Baker—I mean Steadfast—hauls that wool to town and trades it for lamp oil and fabric and windows and all that other stuff none of us can make. The old bastard at the Restive Mercantile doesn't trade with coloreds; without your kindly white reverend as our deal-man, we'd be up a crick. And he doesn't give us a proper share as it is. And so, when he comes to us and says, 'Boys, I need your help or we won't be able to pull off this revival,' we know, even without him saying it, that our men had better get to chopping trees or pretty soon we'll be stuck with a whole lot of wool that we can't trade."

Pansy ruminated on this. "It's not right."

"But it's real," said Harriet.

"What do we do about it?" said Pansy.

"I don't yet know," said Harriet. "Don't you worry on our account. We're tough. Spin your yarn, go to your revival. We'll survive."

Auguste said, "My father used to say that the best thing about history is that it's over with. But I wonder, how do you know when it's over with?"

"Believe me," said Harriet, "We'll know." She exhaled loudly. "You mind if we stop for tonight? If we keep on about this, I'm going to have nightmares."

Kermit said, "My sister gets bad dreams when she thinks too much."

Pansy said, "I shall have to think on all this."

. . .

Normally, on the walk home from Second Solemn, Auguste and Pansy's conversation would have been dominated by werebear talk. After Harriet's story, Pansy was not in any kind of mood for fanciful monsters. At the base of it all, she understood that Harriet had spoken the truth, and this bothered her. So she walked silently and hugged herself against the chill air.

Auguste kept a few steps behind and blew his cheek whistles softly.

Upon reaching Solemn, Auguste left Pansy at her house, which was dark. Gently sounding his whistles, he continued toward the Gravity house. Midway, he nearly crossed paths with Sister Honora as she was returning home from the Gravity house. At the sight of her, marching thin-lipped and deep in thought, he ceased his song and froze in place. Honora strode past close enough to touch, and took no notice.

Auguste entered the darkened house. Annie and Euphémie were snoring in bed. Walking carefully, he climbed atop the bed and attempted to work his way in-between the slumbering widows whose arms and legs clung tightly to one another. His attempts to peel them apart were met with irritated groans and dismissive elbows.

Ever thoughtful, Auguste carefully removed one of the two patchwork quilts and dragged it underneath the bed, where there was just enough room for him to lay on his back with his nose nearly brushing against the wooden bedframe. Other than the hovering flecks of straw and feather—and a faint odor of dead bat —it wasn't so bad. In fact, it was downright cozy. Nothing could get at him here, at least nothing more than ten inches tall.

Listening to his breaths bounce off the bottom of the bed, Auguste relived his day with as much detail as he could muster. It was a habit he'd picked up since moving to America, an opportunity to analyze conversations for English nuances he'd overlooked, to relish moments of joy, to decipher the world.

He had always half-assumed the werebear was a fantasy, just as he'd half-assumed the Jesus stuff was a mass delusion. In both cases, he had assumed that everybody involved was okay with these mutual fictions. But the fictions were no longer mutual. And with Harriet's revelations about the Baker mine, the history of Solemn itself was now in dispute.

Back to the words of his father. *When the fiction breaks down, so does the society.*

America sure was complicated.

Chapter Forty-Three

EVERY MORNING, THE COCKS OF SOLEMN BEGAN THEIR *COCORICOS* well before dawn, and they continued with the racket until sunrise. Euphémie and Auguste had learned to sleep straight thru this. Annie had not, and so she spent her early-morning hours in bed, staring at the whitewashed ceiling, wishing death upon the obnoxious American fowl. When the sun eventually did come up, she'd roll over and stare at Auguste's face, inches from her own, his breath a bacterial fire, remarkable for its potency even in that era of hygiene.

Auguste slept with his eyes open, and, every few minutes, his eyelids would lower like those of a basking lizard and pause at their close-point, just long enough for Annie to imagine that this time they'd stay shut. And then they'd snap open, wide, white around the irises, and, as Annie regained her sense—for this shocked her every time—the eyes would settle into a contemplative gaze, which, as the years thinned his fat, more and more resembled that of his father.

The eyes, the boy's metamorphism into the man whose sperm had survived the rigors of her cervix, and the cynical sensual sweetheart snoring on the opposite end of the bed—all of this had been on Annie's mind for several weeks. Their sleeping arrangements needed to change.

But when she rolled over this morning, no Auguste.

He'd probably gone out to pee. He'd be back soon.

Later, long enough to not be soon anymore, he still hadn't returned. Had he even come home last night? Of course he had. He'd climbed on the bed. And then she'd elbowed him.

Should she wake Euphémie? The woman could sleep all day. Annie sometimes allowed herself to imagine that sleeping Euphémie was dead Euphémie. Rehearse your grief and it becomes tolerable. Annie had imagined her husband's death every night since they'd married, even on the good nights.

Arthur's actual death had been far more tragic than any of her fantasies. But the events that led to it—primarily the drowning of the man who'd broken Euphémie's fingers, and Arthur's casual courage during their shared week in that awful jail—well, Annie'd had no idea that her husband was capable of such—she had no other word for it—goodness.

She truly regretted that she hadn't been able to witness his death. Assuming Euphémie's telling of the events had been accurate, it must have been glorious: Arthur's ascension of the hanging-rope; his bile toward the idiot vicar, the judge, and the ghastly audience; the quip about Henri Deplouc's inability to swim. Arthur's redemptive coda had re-cast his forgettable life into something verging on the noble. And she did miss him on occasion.

The boy, too, had witnessed Arthur's death. Annie reminded herself to someday ask him what he'd thought of the whole ordeal.

Where was Auguste?

Snoooorrrrrrrrrrrrrrrrk.

A minor earthquake, a deviated septum, a soft palate—an eleven-year-old in the midst of a dream.

Annie leaned over the edge of the bed, peered underneath. So that's where the quilt had got off to.

Relieved, and now playful, Annie began gently bouncing upon the mattress. The agitation was a game; whom could she awake first?

Euphémie sat up, hair hanging into her eyes.

Annie giggled.

Euphémie looked around. "Where's the kid?"

Annie pointed downward, toward the mattress. Euphémie was confused. When she opened her mouth to express this confusion, she was interrupted by a *snooorrrrraaaakkkkggggghhhhhh*.

"Oh," she said, "I've been telling you, the boy needs more privacy." She kissed Annie on the cheek. "Us, too." Sliding closer, she said, "Surely we can get him a room of his own, somehow."

Annie said, "Peasants do not enjoy such luxuries."

"Be if we *could*, we could make love right here, without having to hike up a hill and entertain a bear, whom I believe is a pervert."

Annie touched Euphémie's nose. "You adore the bear."

"You are correct."

"And I agree; it would be nice to explore the full potential of this mattress."

"Even though the Site of Maximum Taboo does have its charms."

"It's not so bad."

"Once you get past the raspberries."

"And the darkness."

"Kind of tight in there."

"Perfect for a three-eared bear."

"A rotten place to die."

"A rotten way to die."

"You mean the *plouc* who blew the place up by juggling explosives?"

"I mean getting eaten by a bear."

"We don't have to worry about the bear."

"That was something, yesterday, how she just laid down and started snoring."

"Fat little cow. She's out for the winter."

"After Auguste gets his own room—maybe this spring—we'll still go up there, right?"

Euphémie tilted her head. "Quiet."

"Quiet, why?"

"Your son has stopped snoring."

A muffled voice. "Mother, I would like some porridge, please."

Chapter Forty-Four

A CRISP, MID-DECEMBER AFTERNOON. THE WIDOWS WERE CLEANING out the earthen ovens when a massive wagon, drawn by a quartet of draft horses, rolled into Solemn. It was piloted by a man in a top hat, black vest, watch chain dangling from his vest pocket, a pince-nez crooked on his nose; the official uniform of an entrepreneurial Yankee fop. And yet, he handled the reins with the casual competence of a westerner, possibly even a Californian.

Sitting next to him was a teenaged boy, bouncing lightly upon the springed seat. He was dressed in too-short trousers, a too-small suit jacket, and a floppy, drooping, fifth-hand prospector's hat.

The kid's limbs appeared to be growing longer. Take an eye off an arm or a leg, look again, and it would be poking even more awkwardly out of its sleeve or pantleg. He seemed to have between three and six elbows. And his poor face was a landscape of volcanic acne emerging from the pits of smallpox scars.

The wagon creaked under its burden; timbers, roughcut and large enough to support a cathedral.

"It hardly resembles a Pleasure Wheel," said Euphémie, slapping flour off her apron.

"Oh, so you've seen one?"

"I have a vivid imagination."

Also aware of the wagon's arrival: everybody else in Solemn. Work ceased as folks stood and watched. The waggoneers had not been warned of the stone faces and soft-whistling that greeted them, but the Yankee-fop-by-way-of-California did not seem flapped.

Reverend Steadfast exited the chapel and marched to the driver of the wagon, shook his hand. From where they stood, the widows could not hear the conversation, but the body language was genial. Steadfast pointed north, toward a clearing that had been designated for the wheel. See, there's water for the horses, hay, firewood.

The driver tipped his hat, muchly obliged, snapped the reins, and the horses drew the wagon away into the clearing.

"Lookee," said Euphémie, nodding toward the chapel.

Sister Honora's face was framed in one of the windows, her lips pursed like a cat's ass of silent foreboding.

The next day was Sunday. After church, the adults gathered at the south edge of the clearing, smoking pipes, watching as the man and the boy unloaded the wagon.

Folks offered to help, but the Wheelers, as they were soon known, declined, much to the relief of the Solemnites, who generally avoided work on Sundays. The Wheelers did accept gifts of bread and cider, consuming them while wiping sweat from their foreheads.

With calm efficiency, the man and the boy laid out the timbers, roping and pegging them together into a pair of enormous eight-sided stars. Heavy lifting was accomplished via a block-and-tackle and a gin pole and the assistance of the draft horses. It was a two-man, four-horse barn raising, and a lesson in Archimedean engineering.

*   *   *   *

"Auguste. Auguste?"

"Whu?"

"Come back to us."

"Sorry. It's so fascinating."

Auguste and Pansy, along with the Stovepipe siblings, were seated on the grass at the far edge of the clearing, out of sight of the Solemnites. This was the first time the children had met up since Harriet had shared her history of Second Solemn and the invisible shroud that separated their two villages. Since then, something had changed, especially between Pansy and Harriet. The not-quite respect that had underlain much of their previous discourse had been replaced with something more cooperative.

Harriet said to Auguste, "You were talking about your mother and the bear."

"Right. I was under the bed yesterday morning and I woke up and I heard Mother and Euphémie talking about the Baker Mine and—"

"What were you doing under the bed?"

"I slept there."

"Is this common?"

"That was the first time. I heard them talking about the bear. It's in the Baker Mine!"

"The Baker's off-limits," said Kermit.

Auguste shrugged. The Wheelers were now assembling a pair of enormous wooden gears into a right-angle power transfer mechanism. It was beginning to resemble the horse-powered flourmill back home in France. Auguste lightly blew one of the tooth whistles that bulged in his cheek.

"Auguste, focus!" said Pansy.

He spat the whistles into his palm, then wiped them on his

britches before stuffing them into his pocket. "Right. They know it's a site of taboo. Probably, they were looking for mushrooms, got there on accident."

"Ain't no mushrooms this time of year," said Harriet.

"The mushrooms are irrelevant!" said Auguste. "Listen to me. My mother and Euphémie saw the bear! They found a way into the mine, and, inside the mine the bear lay down and fell asleep. They said the bear was nice. And that it had *three ears!*"

This did not provoke the reaction Auguste had expected.

He added, "Also there was something about a raspberry patch."

Harriet rolled her eyes. Pansy sighed. Kermit managed a mild, "Is that so?"

Auguste was uncertain whether his friends had understood him. He clarified, "The three-eared bear is real. My mother saw it."

"We heard you," said Harriet.

"Does this not fill you with zeal?" said Auguste.

Pansy said, "There's just so many other things happening."

"Things that are *real*," said Harriet.

"But my mother—"

"Do you know what you sound like?" said Pansy.

"I'm not a liar," said Auguste, growing cross.

"Of course not," said Harriet. "But, seriously? You were sleeping under a bed? And you overheard your mom and Euphémie confess to visiting the Baker mine? And they went inside? And saw a three-eared bear?"

Pansy said, "What did your mother say when you asked her about it?"

"I didn't ask her about it. I crawled out from under the bed and ate my porridge."

"Seems you could have said something," said Pansy.

Kermit said, "Dreams always seem the most real in the morning."

Auguste pleaded, "But it could be the werebear."

"Listen," said Harriet, "the bear stuff was fun. But it's kid stuff. As of two days ago, I'm a full-grown woman. I got no time for silliness anymore."

Kermit clarified, "She just turned thirteen."

Pansy said, "I'll be twelve in just a few weeks."

Auguste frowned. Pansy took his hand and spoke with the genuine affection of a mature girl, "Please, please promise me you won't go near that mine. Not on your own."

Auguste was silent.

Harriet said, "Who knows, maybe the bear *is* up there. Best to do it together, later."

Pansy said, "After the Revival."

Kermit said, "You'd think it'd be safe to sneak in on a bear when it's winter-sleepin', but," he shook his head, "nope."

Auguste huffed. If Harriet and Pansy said it must be so, then it must be so. "I agree to this, but without enthusiasm."

"That's more like it," said Harriet. She patted him on the head.

Auguste knew he hadn't been dreaming. He knew his mother and Euphémie had seen the bear. He also knew his friends were correct; the three-ear werebear was almost certainly fantastical. Until one scenario or the other was proven to be true, he would simply have to believe in two things at the same time.

Chapter Forty-Five

IN THE EARLY MORNING OF THURSDAY, DECEMBER TWENTY-FIFTH, Pansy awoke to the crackle and scent of oakwood burning in the fireplace. Her mother had lit the fire some time earlier and the chilly house was slowly warming.

"Mother," said Pansy, still under the covers, "may I stay in bed all day long?"

"You say this every morning," said Honora, who was at the table drinking tea.

"And you say *that* every morning."

"And what do I say every morning after you say *that*?"

"You normally just walk outside. And then I get up."

Honora sat on the bed next to her daughter. "What if today was different? What if today I said yes, stay in bed?"

"I would enthusiastically obey."

"Of all the sins, sloth seems to come most naturally to you," said Honora, giving Pansy's hair a tussle. She sighed. "I miss you, darling. These past months have been so busy: the trips to Restive, the planning committee, the nonsense with the bear. I'm eager to be done with it."

Pansy said, "Don't worry, mamma, it'll all be over in a few days." She looked out the window. "Is it ever going to snow?"

"Hopefully not until the end of the Revival."

"Why aren't they doing it in the summer?"

Honora said, "It seems odd to us, sweetheart, but some religions believe they know what day Jesus was born. And they treat his birthday with great reverence."

Pansy said, "Like one of those celebration days that Sister Punctuality talks about?"

"They call it Christmas, which happens to be today. They make a great pageant out of it. Pagan rituals, hymns, re-enactments of Christ's birth."

"That sounds peculiar, mamma."

"We used to celebrate it when I was a little girl, before we became solemn."

"Do you remember those days?"

"They were full of indulgences, best forgotten."

"Do you remember Grandfather?"

"No."

Pansy said, "Was he a bad man?"

"He never meant to hurt anyone, if that's what you mean. The explosion was tragic and nothing more."

"Except it inspired Reverend Steadfast's divine vision of Solemn."

"Except that."

Pansy had nudged the conversation ever-so-close to Harriet's worrisome revelations. And yet she couldn't bring herself to ask about the twenty-six dead black men and the ignoble origins of Second Solemn. Not when her mother was being so gentle. So Pansy tacked back to the original subject. "And we don't celebrate Christmas because every day is equally worthy of praise."

Honora welcomed this return to the unimpeachable truth of Solemnity. "Correct."

Pansy sat up. "And that's why the Revival will take place in December. To celebrate the alleged birthday of Jesus."

"Clever girl."

"I suppose it makes sense," said Pansy, "but I still think revivals are more suited for summer."

"I agree. But we're in the minority, and so we solemnly go along." Honora crossed the room to the pantry. She returned with a small crock and a spoon. "Would you like some applesauce?"

"In bed?"

"Today only."

"Because it's Christmas?"

"Because I'm fond of you."

Pansy spoke between bites. "We used to eat applesauce all the time in France, remember? I loved it there. We had adventures! I miss being with you like that."

"Things will be normal again after the Revival."

Pansy said, "May I tell you that I love you?"

Honora's eyes wetted. "Yes."

"I love you, momma."

Honora said, "I love you, Pansy." She hugged her daughter and then said, "I've got to go recruit some volunteers. Because you are such a wonderful girl, I give you permission to stay in bed until I return."

Pansy slid under the covers and made purring noises. As Honora exited, she said, "Solemnity in all things."

Pansy's muffled voice, *"Et que tout soit solennel."*

Sister Honora hurried thru the waking village. She strode past the wintery remains of the garden and intercepted Sister Temperance who was heading to the creek with an empty bucket.

"Good morning, dear," said Honora.

Temperance said, "Once again, the Lord has outdone himself."

"I wonder if you might accompany me on some business."

"Of course, Sister. Where to?"

"The chapel, and then to the Gravity house." Noting the empty bucket in Temperance's hand, she added, "I'll see that you get some water."

Annie, Euphémie, and Auguste were inside the Gravity house, breakfasting on garlic soup and yesterday's stale bread.

"Do you think it will snow today?" said Auguste.

Euphémie said, "Doubtful."

"How would you know?"

"Because I've seen snow," said Euphémie, "and so has your mother." She broke off a piece of bread and dipped it into her soup.

Auguste said, "In Sanvisa?"

Annie said, "It was 'seventy-two, I believe. Huge storm. It lasted all morning, and the snow didn't melt until the next day."

"It was up to our ankles," said Euphémie. "Everyone played all day long, even the grown-ups. We made a snowman, taller than me."

"She was tall even then," said Annie.

Without knocking, Sister Honora entered the house, followed by Reverend Steadfast and Sister Temperance.

"Good morning."

"Lovely home."

"What a pleasant surprise."

"Sorry we haven't any more soup."

"Would you like some stale bread?"

"Very kind. No."

"Please sit."

"Thank you."

Sister Honora crossed her hands on her knees. "We've a serious matter to discuss." She glanced at Auguste, who was standing in the corner awkwardly. "Auguste, there's a pail just outside the door. Would you be a dear and bring it to the creek and fill it for Sister Temperance?"

Auguste loved any excuse to go to the creek, and so he was immediately out the door.

Annie called after him, "Mind you don't spill!"

Reverend Steadfast led them in a refreshingly brief silent prayer. After the *amen* and the *and all things be solemn*, he cleared his throat and said, "Annie, Euphémie, Temperance, we'd like the three of you to serve as Solemn's emissaries to the Revival."

Honora said, "It's a straightforward job. You would remain on the Revival grounds for all three days, and you would be asked to share the virtues of Solemnity with as many persons as possible."

Annie and Euphémie shared a look. *These people are nuts.*

Sister Temperance said, "Are you certain we are suited to this task, Reverend?"

Reverend Steadfast said, "Who amongst us is better suited?"

Sister Honora said, "Certain of the Revival's attendees will represent churches that endorse levity, boisterousness, even ecstasy. Furthermore, with the arrival of the Pleasure Wheel, I'm concerned that the event will devolve into a vulgar faith-market. We need emissaries who can endure challenging circumstances while simultaneously offering deliverance to those sheep who've never tasted the grassy pastures of Solemn."

The Reverend said, "The three of you have spent considerable time in the vulgar world. You know how to negotiate the temptation of sin. And," he added, "you make excellent bread."

Sister Honora said, "You grasp our doctrine, and your mellifluous voices can explain it with an elegance that we cannot match."

Euphémie understood that they could not possibly decline this post. Anyway, it sounded like a hoot. She placed her hands upon her sternum and said, "I would be honored to testify to the Lord's solemn grace on behalf of Solemn."

Reverend Steadfast said, "You will face temptation. There are those who would dance and sing and commit other acts of treachery."

Taking her cue from Euphémie, Annie said, "We have lived in the world of treachery, we have survived an oceanic journey within the copper skull of a colossus, and we have emerged with our faith intact. We will do as you please."

Sister Temperance, suppressing her uncertain instincts, said, "I, too, will do your bidding."

Reverend Steadfast said, "We ask as well that you include the boy. His curiosity and uncanny intelligence will be appealing, we think."

Sister Honora said, "But a child should not be alone. I ask that Pansy accompany you as well. You've been her surrogate family these past months while I've been preoccupied with the Revival. She adores you, all of you. And, as a Coordinator of Revival Activities, I'll be too busy to keep an eye on her. It would comfort me to know that she is nearby and that she's under your care."

Temperance said, "We would do so gladly."

Honora said, "I honestly don't know how much *practical* help the children will bring to your mission, but I do know that Pansy's sunny demeanor was a formidable asset in our year in France."

Temperance nodded. "Her good cheer carried us thru many a dreary time."

Honora said, "There is much she can offer, especially when paired with Auguste."

Reverend Steadfast, "We might as well add that we hope they will marry. Let us start them on that path."

Annie said nothing to this, but she noted that she was not entirely opposed to the proposition.

Euphémie said, "This is off-subject, but has there been any word on the thievery that's been plaguing Second Solemn?"

Reverend Steadfast said, "We are choosing to ignore it until after the conclusion of the Revival. The crimes are minor, and confined to the Negro town. We cannot risk another inducement of panic, such as the bear did earlier impose."

Sister Temperance said, "Let us thank the Lord that the bear is asleep."

Sister Honora stood. "Reverend Steadfast and I are quite pleased. We will leave you now."

As Honora and the Reverend and Temperance were exiting the house, Auguste arrived, out of breath.

Proudly, he handed the water pail to Sister Temperance. "I spilled only a little."

Chapter Forty-Six

TWO DAYS LATER, AT THE CONCLUSION OF THE SUNDAY SERMON, Reverend Steadfast asked the congregation to stick around for a minute.

"Friends, these past months we have planned, we have built, we have overcome the bear crisis, and we have cooperated with the Negroes." He raised his voice a notch. "As of this morning, Sister Honora informs me that the preparations for the All-Tent Revival are complete. Every last tree has been cleared, every trench has been dug, and every board has been measured, sawn, and hammered. The Great Stage, the East Campground, the South Campground, and the Village of Godly Illumination are all finished. Thanks to your unflagging efforts, the All-Tent Revival of 1885 shall be a success. God has smiled on us. For this, I hereby declare a one-minute reprieve from solemnity. I invite you to congratulate yourselves, to feel pride, to express yourselves with your voices and your faces. You may begin…now."

The reprieve from solemnity commenced with timid murmurs of happiness, and it continued in that manner until, at precisely sixty seconds, and without a sign from the Reverend, the celebration ceased.

"God is good," said Steadfast. "A few more items. There will many temptations at this event. Not all religions are solemn. Some are downright jubilant. Because of this, I encourage you all to limit your exposure to the Revival. In fact, I would ask that you avoid it altogether."

There was the barest hint of a collective groan.

"I know. I know. After all your hard work. But there are lines we must not cross, temptations we cannot risk. For that reason, I am declaring the Revival to be a Site of Maximum Taboo."

The congregation sat, unmoved. The Reverend paused. There was a line that he mustn't cross either—a different line, but one no less treacherous. "You may ask, 'If this All-Tent Revival is to be so dangerous, then why have we contributed to it so much of our own energy?'

"Prior to this morning, I would have shared this sentiment. But God spoke to me last night, in a dream. I make no claim to prophecy, but I do heed the word of our Lord. And to me he spoke clearly. *Protect your flock, Reverend Steadfast, for they are Solemn. What they have built, they have made strong. They will be present in their works. I will be present in my holy spirit. Together, we shall shine a light.*"

In a soft voice, Steadfast said, "Because we are Solemn, we fell the tree and we wield the hammer. The rendering of wood into human geometry is our voice. Our voice is low, but it rings as brightly as the rainbow glows." Softer still, he said, "As the angel Girondel declared, 'The sparrow need not know the nut that birthed the tree, only that the tree welcomes her nest.'"

The Reverend braced himself, but none objected. They trusted him. His love for his flock had never been so great as it was in that moment.

From the rear of the chapel, half-deaf Brother Cleanly suggested to his wife that the Reverend ought to stop the confounded whispering. The doddering from this beloved old man seemed to leaven the air itself, and it was with that same air that the Reverend filled his lungs and declaimed, "Having said this, the Church of Solemn *will be present*. Sister Honora will be at the Revival for the duration, serving on the administrative committee. Also, we will be sending some folks to represent us in the Village of Godly Illumination."

He gestured for the emissaries to stand.

"Our friends from France, along with Sister Temperance and the children Auguste and Pansy will share Solemnity throughout the Revival. Having traveled the world and having passed thru the fires of sin, they are hardened like iron. I think they'll do wonderfully."

The congregation agreed.

"As for me, I will remain here in Solemn for the balance of the four days. My duty is with my flock."

The Reverend bowed his head. "Thank you, friends for your attention. I now bid you to go with grace toward this beautiful day. How fortunate we are that the Lord's mild autumn has led to a mild winter. Solemnity in all things."

"And all things be Solemn."

Part Three

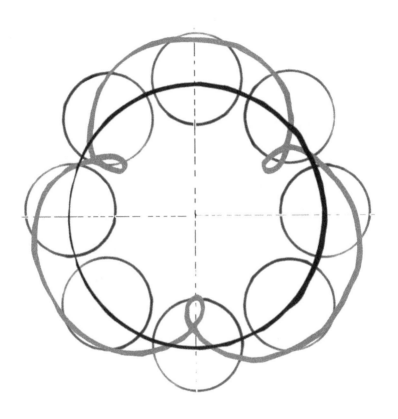

Okay, Tito, you got it.

— THE JACKSON FIVE, *GOING BACK TO INDIANA*

Chapter Forty-Seven

ON DECEMBER TWENTY-EIGHTH, 1885, SISTER TEMPERANCE AWOKE before dawn. She stretched, exhaled coldsteam breaths, rubbed her hands, warmed water, drank tea, pulled on her mittens, and then exited her one-room home with her travel bag in hand. She carried it thru the sleeping village to the Gravity house where the windows flickered with busy silhouettes. Pansy greeted her at the door. "They're almost ready! Come inside."

While Annie and Auguste encouraged grumpy, yawning Euphémie to pull on her shoes and get a move-on, Temperance chatted with Pansy. "Is your mother here?"

"The Reverend brought her up yesterday. Coordinating a revival is very busy business."

"With all this back and forth, the Reverend shall have to add *chauffeur* to his title."

After Euphémie's feet were finally shod, the emissaries gathered in front of the Gravity house to await their wagon. Auguste inserted his toothwhistles and began a light tune whose notes expanded like ice crystals into the morning dark. Pansy marched in place to warm her feet.

Auguste quieted his song. Horses snorted, hooves clopped,

and iron-rimmed wheels crunched on the cold ground. Reverend Steadfast rolled up in a buckboard wagon.

The emissaries loaded their luggage and climbed aboard. Temperance sat up front, next to the Reverend. The others squeezed together in the rear.

As the pair of horses pulled them thru the village, window shutters began to open. Faces appeared, hands waved, and the entire population of Solemn whistled to them a tune of good fortune.

Chapter Forty-Eight

THE WAGON ROLLED NORTHWARD. THE AIR WAS BRISK, THE CLOUDS low and dark. Auguste regarded the sky longingly. He was the only person within one hundred miles who had never seen snow. Seated next to him, Pansy said, "It's going to happen today."

The dawn progressed, the clouded sky began to glow, winterbirds chirped, and the horses' hooves plodded in the verdigris cool.

A half-mile outside of Solemn, they passed the field of mown grass in which the Pleasure Wheel stood fully assembled, a thirty-three-foot tribute to pinewood, improvised architecturalism, and the promise of paying customers. In front of the contraption, Mr. Wheeler and the boy were smoking pipes, sipping coffee from steaming cups. A campfire flickered between them. Their draft horses chewed grass. By the afternoon, if all went well, those horses would be hitched to the wheel engine. They would march in circles, spinning a shaft that ended in a beveled gear whose teeth interlaced with another beveled gear, which turned a horizontal shaft, which ended at a small wooden gear, whose teeth interlaced with a larger wooden gear fastened directly to the axel of the great wheel.

The Wheelers raised their cups to our waggoneers. The Reverend acknowledged this with a polite shake of his whip.

The Solemnites rolled forth. To the disappointment of no one but Auguste, the clouds soon gave way to blue sky and cotton nimbus.

The road began to fill with revival pilgrims. They came from every path, some on horses, mules, others on foot. It was early yet, and many of these people had been traveling for days; they had the look of marathoners at the final mile.

Stray dogs followed, as if they knew something.

Reverend Steadfast guided the wagon past the entry gate, waved along by several men and women dressed all in white. These were the Friends of the Revival. They shouted cheery greetings in the direction of every soul who entered the grounds.

"Hope you had a wonderful Christmas!"

"God bless this weather!"

"You folks need a hand with anything?"

Parents squinted at typeset schedules-of-events as herds of children tugged their skirts and trouser legs. A crowd had gathered to watch a crew of bearded Mennonites raise a twenty-foot wooden cross just outside the entrance to a circus-like tent from whose canvas hung a banner: *Welcome Revivalists - Information and Registration.*

The Reverend reined the horses to a stop near a water-trough. "You all get signed-in. I'll await you here."

The Solemnitic emissaries entered the information-and-registration tent. There, amidst an atmosphere of eager anxiety, they found a queue that led to a table under a sign that read *Those Who Would Represent Their Church at the All-Tent Revival's Village of Godly Illumination.* The queue eventually led them to a red-cheeked Friend of the Revival who took their information, assigned them a lot-number ("your address" she called it), and then asked them to please raise their right hands and recite the Pledge of Cooperation.

I shall not speak ill of any other faith. I welcome all. I respect all. So swear I before the gaze of our Lord.

Papers in hand, they exited and climbed back aboard the wagon. The Reverend guided them to the Village of Godly Illumination, two acres of clearing laid out in a grid. Handpainted signs denoted neighborhoods (named for books of the Bible) and addresses (chapter and verse). Tents were being staked, neighbors acquainting themselves.

The Solemnitic Church had been assigned Psalms, Chapter Forty, Verse Three at the end of Old Testament Lane. Their lot butted up nearly to the woods that bordered the west end of the village.

"Home," said Sister Temperance.

The Reverend helped unload their supplies and then he bade the emissaries goodbye and God bless, and then he snapped the horses southward to his flock.

The Solemnites raised their tent, arranged cots and cookware, and staked a handpainted sign reading *Solemnity: What is it?* The widows then set to work behind the tent, building a brand-new oven. By now they were experienced oven-makers, and so it went quickly. They'd brought with them clay and straw, and Auguste and Pansy and Temperance happily joined them to fetch water and stomp the cob. Once they'd formed the oven into shape, they lit a fire and set it to curing.

It was night, now, so the emissaries climbed into the tent and under their blankets and silently wondered what they'd gotten themselves into.

Chapter Forty-Nine

NEXT MORNING. HELD ALOFT BY SOFT FEATHERS AND WARMING AIR, A candy-apple cardinal circles above the brand-new village, uncertain of this transformation of the woods where she had hatched her first clutch of chicks only a few months prior.

Clumps of women, clumps of men, horses and dogs, mallets striking tent stakes, sound arriving after sight. Lard and horseshit and honey, and smoke spilling from bronze censers.

The cardinal spies a group of crows leapfrogging its way thru the collection of tents, grabbing what crumbs they can and then fleeing before the threat of broom-wielding maidens.

Inspired by her corvidian cousins the cardinal reduces her altitude. With spare movements of her wingtips, she glides over tents, veers toward a little girl carrying a large slice of poundcake. The girl's hand squeezes too tightly and a crumb is liberated.

Swoop. Before the crows can notice the morsel, the cardinal has snatched it mid-air. She wings upward, gulleting the crumb, and zeroes on a linked rope of sausages dangling from the hand of a hatless, white-haired zealot, poised just outside his tent.

Now a half-starved hound springs forth. The zealot, whose disordered hair would have made a handsome nest, yanks the sausage rope upward and beyond the reach of the dog. The whipping motion snaps a link of sausage from the rope, flinging it directly toward the cardinal's conical beak.

The bird snags the sausage by the tiny umbilical of intestine that dangles from one end, and hastily spirits the aerodynamically inconvenient treasure to alight safely upon the peak of a tent in front of which five humans are sharing a loaf of day-old bread.

"You see that?!?" This, bursting from Euphémie's mouth in a spray of crumbs and unrestrained mirth. "That crazy bird just caught a flying sausage."

Sister Temperance, though she, too, was amused by the acrobatics of dog, man, sausage, and bird, offered her friend a familiar glance. *Cool it, sister; we're trying to sell* solemnity *here.*

The bird attempted to flip the sausage into its mouth, but the meat was altogether too girthy for her beak, and she watched ruefully as it slipped from her mouth to tumble down the canvas of the tent and into the lap of Pansy.

The cardinal flapped away.

Pansy held the sausage to her nose. "We shall boil it for breakfast."

Sister Temperance shook her head. "It is not ours to boil. Be nice and return it to the man."

Pansy looked to Annie and Euphémie for support, received none, and walked Old Testament Lane to the flustered nest-haired preacher, who accepted the link without a word.

The evangelizers multiplied. Outside of each tent, men and women clutched Bibles, imploring passersby to enter their cloth chapels, to repent, confess, learn the true word of God, accept the gift of everlasting life.

"Bathe in the kindness of the Lord."

"All are welcome!"

"Army of God!"

"Remember the Magdellites!"

"Complimentary biscuits to all who would join us!"

The cries were soon ringing from all directions. Pilgrims were now wandering the lanes and avenues and boulevards of the village, lookeelooing, calling for wayward toddlers.

Behind the Solemnitic tent, the widows mixed starter, buckwheat flour, eggs, and salt for their first batch of bread in the new oven. Soon, this bread would be shared with new converts to Solemnity.

Meanwhile, streetside of the tent, Sister Temperance was floundering. Here she was, in her wool dress, solemnly trying to compete with the nearby loudmouths bleating solicitations at the pilgrims who poured down the avenue.

If a passing pilgrim engaged with one of these barkers, or made eye-contact with him (they were mostly men), or so much as slackened their pace, a woman (usually the barker's wife) would take the pilgrim by the elbow and usher him or her into a canvas chapel. "Welcome to our sanctified tent." The greeter-woman would press a pamphlet into the guest's hand. "You'll find this enlightening. Can I interest you in a morsel of food? It's made with the whitest of flour. Have a seat. I'll be right back."

This greeter-woman would then hurry outside to usher in another potential convert. Once the tent was sufficiently peopled —no less than half of the available seating area—the husband and wife would switch places. She, outside, cajoling; he, inside to extol their particular subsect of monotheism.

But for Sister Temperance, no pilgrims stopped, looked, or listened, even as she diligently read from her script as prepared by Sister Honora.

*What is Solemnity? Solemnity is liberation. Liberate yourself
from frivolity and foolishness. Embrace the soul unadorned.
Embrace the divinity of Solemnity...*

Her small voice was barely heard over the din of dogs and donkeys.

Things changed once the widows joined her to lure pilgrims with fresh-baked bread. Whether it was the scent of the bread, or the French accents, or Euphémie's impressive stature, passersby started approaching the tent. Alas, after accepting the bread, they universally continued on their way.

At the noon break, safely inside their tent, Sister Temperance said to the widows. "I'm not suited to this. How can Solemnity compete with all these screaming prophets?"

Euphémie said, "The bread is popular."

Annie said, "We'll get them tomorrow when they come back for more."

"It's altogether discouraging," said Sister Temperance, then, looking about, "Where have the children gone off to?"

Annie said, "They fled after breakfast, I think. I assume they're spreading the word amongst the diminutive crowd."

Chapter Fifty

Pansy and Auguste had spent the morning walking the village, eavesdropping on those who would hawk inferior versions of Christianity.

Overheard from a pair of straightbacked Anabaptistas:

"Why must we do this in the winter?"

"If Mary can birth a child in the winter, we can celebrate our Lord in the winter."

"I don't think it snows in Nazareth."

"Bethlehem, you mean."

"He was born in Nazareth."

A passing stranger, "You might be happy to learn that the Bible cites *both* Nazareth and Bethlehem as the birthplace of the Heavenly Son."

"So we're both right."

"We've a saying in the Church of Intratextual Consistency, *Trust Matthew, but trust Mark, Luke, and John moreso.* Have a blessed day...and evening."

Pansy and Auguste ventured as far as Revelation Street, where the Revival's organizers had elected to stow the most rapturous, apoplectic, fire, brimstone, sulfur, tooth gnashing, and trichotillo-maniacal of the froth-spitters.

"Are you amongst the one hundred and forty-four thousand?"

"Will you concede to be Christ's loyal slave?"

"Join the Church of Many Baptisms. Be born again, again!"

"Circumcision is only the beginning! We offer cuttings, complete, for those who would remove from themselves the source of sin."

"We have discovered a formula which will lay bare the evils of those whom you trust."

"*Herpoculous devinium ceranium violatendant mater inifintorae sploink paxexidum bibendum!*"

The children soon received their fill of apocalyptica, and so they exited the Village of Godly Illumination and ventured to the East Campgrounds where hundreds of pilgrims had set up tents. A steady stream of women with buckets walked back and forth, sloshing water and dumping it in basins. Babies cried and crawled. Cats and pregnant dogs argued over scraps of biscuits.

Independent of familial affiliation or theological preference, groups of children had clumped together. The clumps accorded to the hierarchies of youth; age, footspeed, ability to throw stones over tall trees. Pansy and Auguste observed all this from a distance, not yet willing to immerse themselves in this unsolemn chaos.

"Pansy?"

"Yes, Auguste?"

"After much consideration, I think I understand why the Negroes aren't here."

"Yes?"

"It's because they wouldn't be having any fun."

Pansy said, "True enough."

It was late afternoon when they returned to the Solemnitic site. Their arrival provided an excuse for Sister Temperance and the widows to abandon their futile attempts at wooing pilgrims, and to instead relax inside the tent while Pansy and Auguste recounted their day's adventures. Marveling at the descriptions of Revelation Street, the Solemnites conceded that they were in the midst of a great gathering of oddballs.

"I suppose," said Euphémie, "that our presence here means that we, too, are oddballs."

With the arrival of night, and its attendant drop in temperature, the Village of Godly Illumination gradually grew quiet. One by one, the carny barkers retreated into their tents, until all that remained were a pair of unquenchably frantic screamers whose voices echoed from Revelation Street.

Annie tasked Auguste to start the evening's fire. Since matches were valuable, and since their neighbors' fire was already crackling, Auguste asked them if he might borrow a flame. He returned with a burning stick with which he alit the ball of wood-shavings Pansy had placed under a pyramid of knee-broken branches.

As the flames crept upward, Auguste explained, "Our neighbors are Nimrodian Protectorites. Very nice people. They seek to bless cotton with the power of Adam and Eve. They sew their cotton into garments that are as impervious as Nimrod's armor. I am unclear on much of this."

The Solmenites dined, enjoyed the warmth of the campfire, settled into their own thoughts. These thoughts were interrupted when a friendly voice cried out from the dark, "What ho, Solemnites."

Sister Honora stepped into their circle.

Temperance said, "Welcome, Sister. Come, sit with us. I'll fetch you a blanket." She ventured toward the tent.

Pansy hugged her mother. "You wouldn't believe half the things we saw today."

Honora petted Pansy's head. "I believe you, darling, and I'm glad you're getting along okay." In a weary voice, she added, "And now, it's bedtime."

Unusually for her, Pansy agreed to this without complaint; the day had been exhausting.

Auguste, also exhausted, volunteered for bed. He and Pansy arrived at the tent as Temperance was exiting, blanket in hand. Passing them, she whispered, "Sleep well, dearies; we'll expect some proper work from you tomorrow."

The women placed themselves around the fire, blankets over their shoulders. Sister Temperance said, "How goes the Blessed Station of Administration?"

Honora said, "I was witness to squabbles, emotional outbursts, unneighborly neighbors, and complaints about the weather."

Temperance said, "The weather? But it's been so pleasant, especially for December."

"Apparently, that's the problem. A young man from the Church of Jobian Agony approached me this afternoon and declared that the day had been too warm. He demanded that I organize a camp-wide pray-in."

"To change the *weather*?" said Euphémie.

"I told him it was a reasonable suggestion and that I would be delighted to assist him"—almost imperceptibly, one of Honora's eyebrows raised—"just as soon as he convenes a tribunal of all the pastors present at the Revival, shares with them his proposal, and then gets them to elect one of their number to lead this prayer. He has not since re-appeared."

"You've the wisdom of Abigail," exclaimed Sister Temperance. The others looked at her, confused.

"Abigail," said Temperance. "Wife of David."

Stares.

"She's my favorite," said Temperance, defensively.

Honora said, "Well, after today, *I* felt like the wife of *Job*." She sighed. "Solemnity in all things." She addressed the emissaries. "I pray you've fared better than I."

Temperance dipped her eyes. "It was slow."

Euphémie said, "They liked the bread."

Honora said, "Ours is a subtle theology. Give yourselves time. We're all new to this." She stood up. "Goodnight friends. Tomorrow will be better." She took a few steps, turned back. "Not a single new member?"

"Not as yet," said Annie.

Honora parted. Save for the rapturous revelators, the village was silent.

Chapter Fifty-One

UNDER THE QUILT, AUGUSTE AWOKE, HIS HAIR HEAVY WITH SWEAT. Next to him, Pansy breathed shallowly. The widows and Sister Temperance creaked occasionally on their cots.

The last of the revelators had finally ceased their racket. Other than the ambience of his sleeping tentmates, the only sounds were the tent-walls' breeze blown convexions and concavations, and the frog-like snoring of the multitudes in their respective abodes.

Lord almighty, he needed to piss.

Clad in his nightgown, Auguste salamandered out from under the tent-flap. His breath clouded before his eyes. His sweated hair channeled the night chill directly into his scalp.

Rather than venture all the way to the middenfields, he whizzed in the middle of Old Testament Lane. After the final drops emerged from his boytube, Auguste closed his nightgown and began walking carefully toward the tent.

A crunch of shoesole on cold grass, Auguste turned toward the sound. There, not ten feet away, stood a hominoidal creature, its head a confusion of unshorn, unkempt hair that blended into an unshorn and unkempt moustache-and-beard. From within this mess, a pair of wicked eyes and a beak of a nose strongly implied —although by no means confirmed—that the creature was of human origin.

The creature breathed wetly thru its nose. Auguste noted the shine of mucus on its moustache.

"*Bof,*" said the creature. Then it jogged away, dodging between tents, until Auguste could neither see nor hear it.

Auguste crawled sleepily back into the tent and slid under the quilt and returned to his slumber.

By the time he awoke the next morning, the incident had faded into the merest hint of a dream.

Chapter Fifty-Two

THE WIDOWS AND SISTER TEMPERANCE AND PANSY WERE PLEASED, upon exiting the tent that morning, to see that Auguste had awoken early and started a fire and was warming a pot of porridge sprinkled with dried blackberries.

The boy greeted them by asking if anyone had seen one of his toothwhistles.

"Nope," said Pansy, "did you check your pockets?"

"I looked everywhere. One of them has disappeared."

Annie said, "I heard you go out last night."

"I had to pee."

"Maybe you dropped it."

"Maybe."

"We'll be vigilant," said Sister Temperance.

Auguste blew a lonesome note on his remaining whistle.

As the Solemnities breakfasted, the sun crept over the trees, burned away the frost, warmed toes, revived stiff muscles. Throughout the camp, morning hymns clamored around searing pig meat.

Before long, tortured cries of vigor and sin began to float from the direction of Revelation Street. First one, and then all the rest, as if they were cicadas aroused by a summer afternoon. This was greeted with an involuntary groan from the rest of the village.

By mid-morning, groups of children, having gained permission from their parents to explore the festival grounds, had begun to form into diminutive mobs that raced thru the village's streets.

Pansy, hoping to distract her friend from his missing whistle, volunteered herself and Auguste to fetch a pail of water from the creek.

"Don't linger," said Annie.

As soon as the kids had trotted away, Euphémie said, "They'll linger." She caught a whiff of coffee from their neighbors. "I shall introduce myself to the Nimrodians." She marched away, swinging an empty copper cup from her index finger.

Meantime, Annie watched patiently as Sister Temperance practiced her pitch-script. "'The Lord hath made a solemn promise. He sent his only begotten son to die. We live in solemn observation of his words. All are welcome.'" She sighed. "It's no good. This feels like France all over again."

"Except it's not."

"Sister Gravity, *she* had the knack."

"She's inside a great fish now."

A moment of Solemn silence.

Annie said, "It's possible that we're being a touch *too* solemn. Perhaps if you did some shouting?"

Sister Temperance's eyes jittered. She said, "Solemnites do not shout."

Euphémie returned, her cup now overfilled with steaming coffee. "Based on those jokers over there, and there, and there"— she pointed at the nearest and loudest of their competition —"screaming at the top of your lungs might be in order." She gestured in the direction of a particularly apoplectic one-legged man who was not only balanced upon a cream can, but hopping upon it, all while howling, "Sinners, beware!!! Devotees, beware!!!! Not even Job was exempt from the taunting power of the devil. *Blarghity doop flannious skunkaboo.*" A reasonable-sized crowd had gathered. They gave him an *amen.*

Sister Temperance said, "Reverend Basil Thierry, founder of the Church of Futile Hope. His sermons are consistent with his cynical outlook. We are not cynics; we are Solemnites."

A pair of giggling teenaged girls approached Reverend Thierry. He exhorted, "My tent is open to all comers! Anybody want a crumpet?" The girls slipped inside, followed by several broad shouldered, smiling men, followed by their narrow-shouldered unsmiling wives.

Reverend Thierry screamed, *"Thangolly weegland fantafeel glossib sproill serum!!!!"* Then he hopped off his cream container and followed his latest audience into his tent.

Euphémie said, "What's with the gibberish?"

Sister Temperance said, "It's...I don't know." She put her hands together. "Sisters, I am not suited to this task."

Euphémie drank from her cup, wiggled her face left and right so her mouth flapped loosely back and forth. One half-expected her to shout "YOWZA!" She did not. Instead, she pressed a large hand on Temperance's shoulder, which was sagging under the weight of her responsibilities, and said, "We're competing against screamers and shouters and death rattlers with crumpets. Crumpets! The Church of Solemn is serenity and free bread. No matter how warm the smile, no matter how delicious the bread, it's ordinary. Nobody wants ordinary. They want danger, devils, a sword both gleaming and righteous."

Temperance said, "People want peace."

"Peace is achieved by shouting louder than everybody else."

"That won't do," said Sister Temperance. Her eyes brightened. "Perhaps I could whistle."

Annie and Euphémie endorsed this tack. Temperance, now emboldened, stood before the tent, pursed her lips, and loosed a series of long dorian tones that soared and slithered above and within the threatening cries of the other three hundred would-be convertors in the Village of Godly Illumination.

Seeing that Temperance's mood had lifted, and hoping to postpone their inevitable turn at ballyhooing, Euphémie said, "You're onto something, Temperance. Say, Annie and I are gonna roam a little. Keep it up. We'll be back before lunch. There's bread in the oven."

Sister Temperance, still whistling, nodded and accepted Euphémie's outstretched hand.

Euphémie said, "Need anything while we're out?"

Temperance shook her head.

Annie said, "The children will be back soon. You can put them to work."

After the widows disappeared into the crowd of bonnets and hats and horses, folks continued to rush past Temperance, but now they rushed a little less quickly, as if Temperance's whistlesongs were a sonic mud they had to trod thru.

Glory of glories, an elderly man wearing a bolo tie placed his knobby hand on Temperance's shoulder and said, "I'll go in your tent."

Still whistling, she beckoned him to enter. The man leaned forward and pushed his lips toward her face. Sister Temperance turned away, but he had her by the arms. The lecher stuck his tongue out and licked her forehead.

Sister Temperance flexed her biceps. "Disengage me, sir. I've no wish to harm you."

He did not disengage.

Sister Temperance said, "I have been across the ocean, I have seen things you never imagined. And if you persis—"

"Give me a kiss."

"Unhand me, devil, or I will make a great noise."

The lecher released her, blended into the mob.

Beaten, Temperance limped into the tent and lay upon her cot.

Walking hand in hand amongst the food vendors—*Cabbage! Potatoes! Hot cross buns!*—Euphémie said to Annie, "Where's the wine? Shouldn't there be wine?"

Annie said, "You're being moody."

Before Euphémie could offer further complaint, a joyous cry burst from the south, beyond a wall of forest. Following the noise, Euphémie saw the upper arc of a miraculous wooden contraption.

"Say, darling," she said, "How about we take a spin on Mr. Wheeler's Pleasure Wheel?"

Chapter Fifty-Three

AUGUSTE AND PANSY HAD INSTANTLY FORGOTTEN THEIR PROMISE TO fetch a pail of water. Instead, they had joined a parallel, younger, shorter version of the All-Tent Revival. This subculture of children had formed into a fluid-like substance that raced unnoticed around the legs of adults, playing tag, laughing, oblivious to everything save for amusement.

The field of play was limited to the Village of Godly Illumination. The grid-like layout of tents and streets provided an underlying order to the kids' chaoticism. Auguste and Pansy quickly sussed the rules. If someone gives chase, run. If a chaser successfully touches a chasee, the chasee is obligated to retire to a clearing at the edge of the woods dubbed Purgatory.

Auguste and Pansy established a cycle. Race about, split up, flee, get tagged, meet up in Purgatory, share breathless tales of danger, re-enter the scrum.

At one Purgatorial reunion, Auguste said, "This is very good fun!" Pansy noted that his accent was beginning to melt away. She regretted this; she'd always been fond of the boy's silly pronunciations.

Purgatory was getting crowded.

A cry went up. The last of the taggers had tagged the last of the taggees. The winner of this round, Auguste and Pansy were mildly surprised to see, was none other than the Wheeler boy, apparently enjoying some time away from his work at the pleasure wheel.

Dressed in his black suit and prospector's hat and sporting his not-ready-for-adulthood beard, the Wheeler boy cupped his hands around his pimpled mouth and shouted, "I win! Gather for the next round!"

The children of Purgatory cheered, crouched, ready for chaos.

Pansy said to Auguste, "Not fair. He's too old. His arms are too long."

The mass of children began a group countdown. *Ten* accelerated into *one*, and then they bolted every which way in a delightful panic that otherwise resembled a herd of antelope being attacked by a lion.

The Wheeler boy remained still until Purgatory had been completely purged, then he, with a blur of his numerous, flamingo-leg limbs, flew after a slow-moving herd of four-year-olds. Hunter and prey were soon absorbed by the adult portion of Revivalers.

Pansy and Auguste charged into the labyrinth of tents. They dodged church barkers, women carrying water buckets, and fellow youngfolk who were pinwheeling their arms and periodically looking over their shoulders. The excitement aroused the various feral dogs and cats who had gathered, contributing to the pandemonium that governed life under five feet. At higher elevations, the adults' bemusement mingled with irritation.

"Mind your step!"

"You're a mad lot!"

"Lord have mercy on their parents!"

"Return that apple, young man!"

Pansy and Auguste separated, reunited, paused behind a wagon. Auguste bent with his hands upon his knees. He was breathing heavily. Pansy raised him to stand upright. "Are you going to die?"

"Only," he coughed, "for a moment."

Pansy gripped his red face in her hands and pressed her wet lips against his forehead. A first kiss. Tilting Auguste's face upward, she planted a second kiss—a peck, really—on his little lips.

She said, "You ought to breathe more."

The Wheeler boy galloped past their wagon and cried, "I will eat both of you!" He tacked toward them, flailing his long arms. Pansy and Auguste unheld their hands, and rushed away, woodsward.

It had been inevitable that the game would expand into this new arboreality, and there they were, Pansy and Auguste, full sprint, surrounded by the savage flora and fauna of southern Indiana.

The clamor of the festival dimmed. It was just the two of them charging side-by-side thru barebranched trees, sycamore and beech and birch and oak and maple and cypress and dogwood and paw-paw and hackberry and magnolia. Red cardinals and blue bluebirds fled before them, squirrels dived, banana slugs observed from slimy perches. Moist loam softened their footsteps.

Auguste thought, I have been kissed. Did I do well? Yes, I am now a man. Pansy has very handsome ears.

Pansy said, "I'll go this way, you go that way." She veered.

Alone, Auguste continued running, savoring the delicious privacy of the forest and the imaginary threat of his pockmarked pursuer. He leapt logs, ducked branches, slipped between leafless shrubs.

He coasted to a stop.

Softly, he said, "Pansy?"

She was out of sight. Woodpeckers tapped the trees above him. "Pansy?"

In the distance, "Fee fi fo fum. I can smell you, little ones!" The Wheeler kid was persistent.

A gleeful Pansy-scream was followed by a triumphant "Gotcha" that contained within itself all the octave-leaping mystery and confusion of adolescence. Pansy had been tagged.

The Wheeler kid's voice said, "Where is your boyfriend?"

"He is not my boyfriend. He is my husband." This being the voice of Pansy.

"You do not know where your *husband* is?"

Pansy was really rushing things, relationship-wise.

"Help! Auguste!" Pansy was not in danger, this was clear. But this was a game, and so Auguste must rescue her.

He barreled forth. Spying an opportunity for a grand entrance, he grabbed hold of one of the woody vines that hung throughout the forest, and, with a bellow preminiscent of Tarzan, he leapt.

The vine in question was attached to the upper branches of an aging poplar tree. Decades ago, the tree had been struck by lightning, and this had compromised the root system, which had been attacked by fungi, which had been devoured by various bacterium, leaving the forty-foot tree mostly dead and extremely precarious.

And so it was that Pansy and the Wheeler kid watched as Auguste burst thru the foliage like a triumphant howler monkey, followed immediately by the great, groaning tree that his slight frame had unrooted.

The vine slackened, Auguste landed on his rump, and Pansy and the Wheeler boy gaped as the poplar fell thru the canopy, breaking neighboring branches, scattering squirrels and birds, and eventually laying itself down inches from where they were standing.

Auguste, still on his rump, gazed at the vine, which he still gripped, then turned to admire this giant he had felled.

"Impressive," said Pansy.

Chapter Fifty-Four

"SO WE ARE FORBIDDEN," SAID EUPHÉMIE. SHE WAS USING HER displeasured voice.

"Read the sign ma'am."

CHARIOT OF FIRE
WITNESS GOD'S CREATION FROM HEAVENLY HEIGHTS
SIX THRILLING REVOLUTIONS
ONE HA'PENNY - GENTS ONLY

Euphémie said, "The sign is lovely. Except, I thought your machine was called a *Pleasure Wheel*."

Mr. Wheeler said, "'Chariot of Fire' better describes the epiphanic nature of the device. Now, if you could step away."

Euphémie and Annie were at the head of a line of boys and men that stretched out some great distance behind them. They'd been waiting in this line for over an hour, inching forward as pairs of riders dropped their coins into Wheeler's white-gloved hand, climbed into one of eight gondola benches, rode their six revolutions, and then staggered away having witnessed God's creation from the dizzying height of thirty-three feet.

In the absence of his young assistant, Mr. Wheeler was tending to every aspect of this process. He was taking money; instructing his customers how not to plummet to their deaths; motivating the four horses to march in their clockwise circle; smearing hog fat on the contraption's wooden gears; sorting riders by weight so the wheel remained reasonably balanced; and all while maintaining an endless monologue about the origins of his invention and the glories it promised to all who would submit themselves to its creaking majesty.

Mr. Wheeler beckoned to the pair of men standing directly behind the widows. "Step in, good sirs."

The men climbed into the gondola, swinging gently. Wheeler clicked the horses, who began to plod. The wheel turned. Sixteen happy riders alternately ascended toward their god and eased to the firmament.

Seeing that the widows had not stepped away, Wheeler said to them, "Your accent—German?—suggests that you are new to our language, and so perhaps the meaning of 'Gents only' is beyond your learning. It means only men are allowed."

The widows *had* misunderstood. They'd thought *gents* was the English equivalent of their *gens*, or people. In retrospect, it did seem odd that any non-people would have endured the wait to board this contrivance.

Their solemn faces betrayed no hint of this realization.

"Where is Young Mr. Wheeler?" said Annie.

"Who?"

"Your son. I expect he's more acquainted with the state of American equality."

"I gave him a break. He deserved it. Also, he is not my son. Also, why do you call him 'Wheeler'?"

Another misunderstanding. Wheeler was not the man's name, it was his title, as bestowed by the Solemnites.

Annie, unflapped, said, "The sign says, 'Gents only,' but it doesn't state why our race is forbidden."

Euphémie added, "Also, we are not German."

The wheelman, now nameless, urged his horses to walk faster, then returned his attention to the widows. He pointed to their skirts. He pointed toward the top of the Wheel. Then he pointed downward to the mob of children who were racing and chasing hither and yon.

Euphémie said to Annie, in French, "What's this deaf-mute trying to say?"

Annie replied in English, loud enough for the man to hear, "I believe, Sister, that womenfolk are forbidden to ride the wheel due to the fact that the machine lifts its riders into the sky, where it would be possible for youngsters to peer up our skirts."

"*Françaises*, eh?" said the wheelman. "*Fichez le camp, s'il vous plaît.*"

A *mistral* of French burst from Euphémie. The gist was, "You know, we used to live in a place filled with corrupt and pious judgmentalism. Apparently, we have left that place for an equally pious place that also happens to treat the human body as if it were some defilement of nature. For fuck's sakes, grow up."

Annie, also in French, pleaded with her friend, "Euphémie, people are staring."

An audience had gathered to witness these women—one extraordinarily tall—arguing in a foreign accent with a known mechanical genius.

The wheelman had exhausted his French vocabulary with "*s'il vous plaît.*" While he hadn't precisely understood the widows, their tone had left little mystery as to their feelings. A pleasant smile undulated beneath his moustache.

Euphémie said to Annie, still in French, "His uncomprehending face betrays his simplicity." Then, in English, "What if I were to don a pair of breeches, sir?"

The wheelman rubbed his chin. "*Have* you a pair of breeches?"

"I do not," said Euphémie.

"Then your question is irrelevant." He raised his chin as if he'd landed a blow for Reason.

Annie was familiar with this look; she'd spent half her life married to a man who couldn't shut up about the Virtues of Reason. She said, "By banning womenfolk, you've deliberately reduced your ridership by half."

Euphémie loved it when Annie became indignant on her behalf.

The man nodded patronizingly. "In addition to being a man of science and the arts and sundry other disciplines, I am also morally sound. A woman belongs on a pedestal, yes, but not one so tall that children can look up her dress. And so, my dear lady, yes, you have rightly observed that by refusing to expose children to female undergarments—or worse, their pudenda—I've reduced my ridership by half." He haughtily adjusted his hat. "In so doing, I deprive Lucifer of souls to feed upon. Anyway, look at that line. I've no shortage of customers."

Euphémie said, "Your logic is impeccable, sir."

He replied, "Due to the manner in which your accent places stress on, shall we say, random syllables, I cannot tell if you are being sincere or otherwise. Luckily, I observe the Church of Integrated Newtonian Morality's *Doctrine of Self-Actualization Via the Most Desirable Interpretation of Ambiguous Statements*. Which is to say, I take your words as a compliment. Thank you, *mesdames*. Now scram."

Annie, having learnt English alongside Euphémie and having spoken French with her for years, correctly deduced that the man had utterly misinterpreted Euphémie's non-complimentary words. And now Annie correctly deduced that Euphémie was about to cause a scene.

And that is why Annie pre-emptively started a scene of her own. Surrounded by a gathering crowd of sundry evangelicals in the shadow of America's second-ever example of what would one day be known as a Ferris wheel, Annie removed her skirt.

Annie had never heard of bloomers. The fashion, which had already overtaken most of America, had never reached the village of Sanvisa, nor had it penetrated the righteous walls of this little part of Indiana. If she'd know about bloomers—the trouser-like undergarment that had nudged women's rights into a direction that would reach its destination six score later in the shape of skinny jeans—she'd have been wearing some at that very moment. Instead, as was her habit on chilly days, she was wearing beneath her skirt a pair of light linen trousers.

The removal of her skirt was met with twin cries of shock from the assembled masses. First, that a woman would disrobe in public. Second, and far louder, that she would have been secretly clad in a male garment all this time.

Annie folded the skirt and draped it over her arm. She strode past the wheelman saying, "As you can see, I am now clad like a man. There is no danger of my pudenda being exposed." She stepped forth, ready to board the next available gondola.

Euphémie, who was nearly as astonished as the rest of the crowd, joined Annie. "I'll ride with her, if you don't object."

A smartass in the rear shouted, "Will the tall one remove her skirt as well?"

Euphémie chuckled. "You do not wish to see my under-garments."

The crowd, righteous or not, was being entertained and so their sympathies swung now in the direction of the foreigners. The smartass in the rear shouted, "Come on, pal. Let the women ride."

General agreement from the peanut gallery.

Realizing he'd lost the battle, and unwilling to risk a scene, the wheelman halted his horses and directed a bemused father and son out of their gondola.

To the widows, he said, "In with you."

Annie led Euphémie into the repurposed porch swing. The wheelman, sensing an opportunity to turn failure into profit, said unto the masses, "Members of the female species are hereby invited to ride the Chariot of Fire. But there will be no mixing of the sexes upon individual benches. And no children younger than ten-years of age, regardless of sex."

The horses plodded around their drive shaft and the gears turned and the great Chariot spun its first female passengers.

Within moments, dozens of women had joined the line, doubling its length. An inbred compulsion for chivalry compelled the men in the front half of the line to cede to the women of the rear half. The wheelman was looking at a gender revolution. He collected his pennies, drove the horses, larded the gears. And he added a new cry to his pitch, "Knees together! Don't feed the cretins."

Indeed, a number of youngsters had diverged from the endless game of tagmob to crane their necks in hopes of witnessing whatever it was that womenfolk carried between their legs.

"Do you feel closer to paradise?" said Euphémie.

The widows were at the apex of the ride, this being their third loop around. The thirty-three-foot perspective was no small achievement in the age of horse-powered amusement park rides. The view extended beyond the leafless forest; they could see even Solemn from here, smoke rising from cookfires, small figures behaving solemnly.

"I feel like singing," said Annie.

"Then let us sing."

Together, they vocalized a wordless tune in the manner of a Solemnitic whistlesong.

At the completion of their six revolutions, Annie and Euphémie alighted from the gondola and made way for a pair of Neo-Pharoahnic Revisionist Nuns to take their places. The nuns, dressed as was their habit, in wool cloaks embroidered with cicadas and toads, whispered in the eerie unison that was also their habit, "Bless you, Sisters."

The wheelman extended his hand to the widows. "Dennis Dennison."

Annie accepted the handshake. "Annie Lestables." She nodded to her companion. "And Euphémie Deplouc."

Dennison said, "France breeds formidable women."

Annie said, "And California makes a fine engineer."

"No hard feelings?" said Dennison.

Euphémie said, "I'll reserve judgment."

"I'm not sure if you're being facetious," said Dennison.

Annie said, "She's always a little facetious. But I assure you, she and I both applaud the wisdom of your decision."

Euphémie added, "Even if it was motivated by greed."

Still holding Annie's hand, Dennis Dennison leaned close and whispered, "I like your spunk."

The widows marched away, grinning broadly, but not too broadly.

It was not until they were out of sight that the main axel for the drive wheel snapped. The Chariot of Fire came to a stop, tilted awkwardly. No injuries. The riders were led to the earth by a team of cooperative Samaritanians poised upon each other's shoulders. Dennis Dennison apologized to the riders, and to those in line who hadn't gotten a turn. Then he hung up his well-used "Out of Order" sign and fed the horses some straw. "Thank you, gentlemen and ladies. The ride is down until further notice."

Chapter Fifty-Five

STILL MARVELING AT THE TOPPLED TREE, PANSY AND THE NOT-Wheeler boy helped Auguste upright. He was covered with bits of branch.

"You okay?" asked the not-Wheeler boy.

Auguste nodded. "I am."

Pansy said, "In light of my companion's recent superhuman achievement, I call for a temporary suspension of hostilities."

The not-Wheeler boy bowed slightly. "Request granted."

After satisfying themselves that the poplar had been felled not by herculean strength, but by a rotted root system, the trio sat down, rested their backs against the lateralized tree-trunk, and had themselves a friendly chat.

The not-Wheeler boy's name was Gomar Himmelbaum. Mr. Wheeler's name was Dennis Dennison, and he was not Gomar's father.

Gomar's actual father was a deacon for the Church of Hemveria, a sect that had proven, via a new translation of the Protoevangelium of James, that Christ had not been a man at all, rather, he was a donkey.

"Is your father working a tent?" said Pansy.

"Naw. He's laid up back home with a broke knee."

"Where's home?"

"Athens. Athens, Alabama, that is." Haw haw. "I caught on with Mr. Dennison some time back. He was passing thru town with his Pleasure—excuse me, Chariot of Fire, and, well, I ended up riding with him. I'm his *protégé*."

Pansy said, "You run good for a smallpoxer."

Gomar put a hand to his cheek. "I was just a baby. Don't even remember it. Where're y'alls from?"

Pansy said, "I'm from Solemn, just to the south. Grew up there. I missionaried in France last year, though. Why France? Because everyone agreed that France could use some Solemning-up. And my mom, Sister Honora, studied French in grammar school. So we spent a year traveling the country, sharing the good news. *C'était génial!* And that's where I found Mr. Tree Toppler over there."

Mr. Tree Toppler waved.

"What's his name?" said Gomar.

"Auguste Lestables," said Auguste. "I am eleven years old."

Pansy said, "His last name means *the tables*. My name's Pansy. I am nearly twelve years old."

"*The tables*?" said Gomar. "That's a queer name."

Pansy said, "Not as queer as worshipping a donkey."

"That is strictly my father's thing," said Gomar.

The trio continued into the woods, no destination but conversation.

"What's your sect, again?" said Gomar. "Serenity-something?"

Pansy said, proudly, "We are Solemnites from the Church of Solemn. We embrace solemnity. And we helped put all this together."

Pansy gave Gomar a quick run-down on Solemnity, the ins-and-outs, the this-and-that, and the other. She concluded with, "It's a very good religion. Straightforward, sensible."

Gomar demurred, "I hold all religions to be equally impen-etrable."

"How do you mean?" said Auguste.

"Impenetrable," said Gomar. "Adjective.'Can't be pierced.' Me and Mr. Dennison often discuss the vagaries of religion. And I *think* about it all the time." His eyes brightened. "I've been putting together an allegorical model."

Auguste said, "Oh, please do share with us your allegorical model!"

INTERLUDE

An Orbitary View of God and Religion
as Professed by Gomar Himmelbaum
While Accompanying Pansy and Auguste on a Walk Thru the Woods

WE ALL KNOW WHAT THE SOLAR SYSTEM IS, RIGHT? SIX PLANETS circling the sun. Good. This is the basis for my allegorical model. First, we must replace the sun with God. We'll call this the Godsun. This Godsun is a great orb, similar in size to our sun, except it's made out of fantastically hot lard.

There are two components to the lard.

First, there's a thin outside layer, like the skin of fat that forms atop a broth when it's exposed to cool air. The "air" in this case is the *frigid ether of space*.

Underneath, protected by the skin, lies the second component of the Godsun: a globe of violent, searing, liquid lard, constantly churning and bubbling and rising. If it weren't restrained by the skin of cooled fat, this globe of lard would explode and splatter hot grease throughout the universe.

Imagine the liquid, bubbling, inner lard as the awesome *power of God*, capable of destroying anything it touches.

Now, imagine the Godsun's cooled skin as the *wisdom of God*. Without it, the boiling sphere of fat would explode and incinerate all of the solar system's planets.

The Godsun is a perfect balance between wisdom and power.

The Godsun is magnificent to the eye. The skin is translucent, and thru it you can see the cloudy, opalescent, swirling mass of hot, liquid fat. Let's add in some internal lightning sparks to make it even more visually stimulating.

Orbiting the Godsun are planets, but not just the six we're used to. There are *thousands* of planets, each representing one of the thousands of different religions here on our non-imaginary

Earth. Each religion-planet has a unique, incomplete view of the glorious, perfect Godsun, just as a thousand people standing on Earth would have a thousand different and incomplete perspectives of a single cloud in the sky. For instance, a humongous lightning flash in one hemisphere of the Godsun would go unseen by any religion-planet orbiting on the opposite side. A tiny reflection of a green swirl visible to one religion-planet may go completely unseen by a religion-planet only a few degrees away. Though the Godsun is perfectly beautiful from any perspective, it cannot be wholly seen. Which is to say, each planet can only see a portion of this perfection at any given moment.

Furthermore, the residents of each religion-planet universally assume that their perspective of the perfect Godsun is the *one true perspective*. But the Godsun is perfect from any perspective. And, anyway, no one person or religion could even *conceive* of the whole of the Godsun.

Meanwhile, we misinterpret the portions of the Godsun that we do see. We think that the *God* part of the Godsun is its interior —the rainbow inferno of lard churning beneath the cool surface skin. But, as I said earlier, the God part is the skin *and* the inferno. The inferno being a barely containable, infinite explosion. The crust of skin being all that prevents the inferno from snuffing out the planets as if it were smoke swallowing a swarm of bees.

Again, the inferno is *power* and the skin is the *wisdom*.

The planets, meanwhile, are always in danger of colliding with one another, and sometimes they do. When that happens, it's cataclysmic. Remember, each planet has its own infallible perspective of the Godsun, and each perspective contradicts that of every other, in small ways or big ways. And, within religions, even small contradictions can quickly grow overwhelming.

So, when planets collide, they destroy each other.

Think about the Crusades, or the history of the Jews, or the countless religions that once were, but are no longer. Religion-planets can co-exist, but they cannot integrate with one another.

They can't merge like balls of clay; they can't mingle like steam and coal-smoke.

In conclusion, all religion-planets orbit the same self-regulating Godsun—but their limited perspectives of the Godsun's opalescent masses of hot fat disallow them from any agreement upon what it is they're worshipping.

Chapter Fifty-Six

P ANSY WAS NOT IMPRESSED. "G OD IS NOT A BALL OF LARD."

Auguste said, "Gomar made it perfectly clear that the Godsun was merely an anal—"

"*Opalescent masses of hot fat*? Please shut up about this filthy nonsense, both of you."

Twenty paces later, Auguste said, "Excuse me, what is this thing I am seeing?"

They had reached a path lined with white pebbles recently laid. Gomar crouched, looking first one direction and then the other. "It's a fairy trail."

"Fairies don't need trails," said Pansy. "They have wings."

"*Fairies* don't need trails," said Gomar, "but their food does." He lifted one of the white stones, examined it, and then carefully returned it to its indentation. "One direction of a fairy trail always leads out of the forest. The other direction leads to a toadstool village."

"Neglecting the fact that you're making this up," said Pansy, "either direction sounds perfectly desirable."

Gomar shivered at the girl's ignorance. "A toadstool village is a vile place where fairies feed upon the rotting corpses of all who dare enter. Oh, from the outside, these villages appear as a fantastical joy; brightly-colored sprites dining on fresh melons, fairy voices reciting alliterative poems. But that's an illusion. Once inside the toadstool village, the spell disappears. The fairies swarm and bind you with fairy silk and suspend you by your toes. They plunge reeds into your eyes and drink the white fluid within. They deposit their eggs in your sphincter."

This kid is a strange bird prone to gibberish, thought Pansy. She said, "Gosh, if only we had a magic donkey to help us decide which way to go." She looked for Gomar's reaction.

He shrugged. "Again, donkeys are my father's domain."

At least he was a playful strange bird. Picking a direction at random, Pansy started the trio down the path.

The trail followed a bend, climbed a hill, and then quickly sloped until the kids were looking down upon a small, open glade. Within the glade, there stood a grey tent. It was similar to the ones in the Village of Godly Illumination, except it had six, rather than four, sides, like a miniature circus tent.

Arranged outside the entrance was a wooden stool, a fire pit, a kettle. Upon one of the tent's grey walls was a painting, slopped by a large paintbrush: a black outline of an opened hand. In the palm of the hand was an ichthys, the secret fish symbol early Christians would draw in the sand with their toes. In the center of the ichthys was an eyeball.

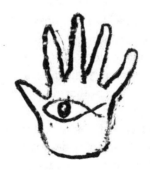

Gomar whispered, "I've seen enough. Let us depart."

"It's just another revival tent," said Pansy. "They probably worship solitude. Or are you truly afraid of fairies?"

Gomar said, "There are no fairies in that tent."

"Come," said Pansy, "We will say hello." It pleased her to wrest control from the fascinating pock-faced lard-worshipper.

"We oughtn't just barge in," said Gomar.

Pansy said, "I wonder if they have cake."

Auguste said, "Maybe they can point us back toward the festival grounds."

Gomar said, "Or they could drink the milk out of our eyes."

Pansy started down the hill. After only a few steps, she stopped abruptly, her breath caught in her throat.

The tent had begun to glow.

Chapter Fifty-Seven

WHERE IN THE DICKENS HAD THOSE WIDOWS GOTTEN OFF TO?

Sister Temperance had spent her morning growing more and more despondent. Whatever glories the Church of Solemnity had to offer, she had no idea how to advertise them without betraying her vows of solemnity.

This being the second day of the festival, the foot traffic in the Village of Godly Illumination was being diverted by a series of presentations at the Great Stage. An exploration of the overlapping exoticisms of Jews and Mosselmans; a theo-scientific explanation of the physics of Noah's ark; and something called *How the Faithful Might Draw Profit Thru the Eye of the Needle*.

Virtually all who did pass the tent accepted Temperance's bread-offerings and promptly marched away, oftentimes directly into one of the tents immediately adjacent to hers.

Annie and Euphémie had promised to return in time for lunch. They hadn't. By noon, Temperance's spirit had been effectively drained. "Solemn," she muttered, "solemn, solemn."

She was rescued by her neighbor, Resina Cotton, wife of Jimrod Cotton, First Minister of the Church of Nimrodian Protectors of the Impermeable Cotton. Mrs. Cotton took Temperance by the hand. "Sweetheart, bring me into that tent of yours and tell me all about your church."

Temperance wiped her nose on her sleeve and said, "I would be honored." Then she led her first-ever pilgrim into the Solemnitic tent.

"I swear. I says. I says, 'Honey, we can build a house from magic cotton, but ain't nobody going to live there. Look at all them other churches. The one with the one-legged preacher, they have crumpets. That's how you draw 'em in. You ladies are pretty, at least you have that. Look at me. I'm an old tater-sack. You'll not see me in public unless absolutely necessary. What I lack in wifely subservience, I make up with honesty. I tell him every day, who cares about magic cotton? But he loves ol' Nimrod. He claims he —meaning himself, Jimrod—can bless a blanket just like Nimrod, make it a shield against weapons and curses and all sort of things. But he—meaning Jimrod—can barely shake an egg out of a chicken. Did you hear? There was some sort of commotion at the Chariot of Fire. It were taken over by women! One of them even took off her skirt, I hear. But God's justice is as swift as his mercy, for, right after the commotion, he struck the wheel with a bolt of lightning and rendered it asunder. At least that's what..."

Sister Temperance had stopped trying to hide her yawns over an hour ago.

Euphémie and Annie, conquerors of the Chariot of Fire, liberators for the fairer sex, giddy with their own greatness, strode hand-in-hand into the Village of Godly Illumination. Annie had draped her skirt over her shoulders like a cape, and she wore her linen trousers so confidently that it almost seemed inoffensive.

Never mind that they'd been goofing off all morning and were late for lunch; these two were, in the words of the departed Arthur Lestables, squeezing the udder with four hands.

As they neared their tent, Annie said, "I don't see Sister Temperance."

"Perhaps she's finally given up," said Euphémie.

They pushed aside the flap went inside.

Sister Temperance greeted her truant friends with a cry of joy. Resina Cotton took one look at Annie's disgracefully exposed trousers, deduced her role in the incident at the wheel, and took this as a signal to skedaddle.

"Hate to tear out. You'uns have a day. Cotton beckons."

Exit Resina.

"Making converts of the Nimrodians?" said Euphémie.

Temperance said, "Her? She just came by to see if she could bore me to death." She placed a hand over her mouth. Speaking between her fingers, "Lord forgive me my ill-directed words."

Annie said, "The truth is ill only to those whom it sickens."

Sister Temperance said, "She was going on about a pair of loose women who forced the Lord to knock over Mr. Wheeler's wheel." Temperance tilted her head in the direction of the widow who was wearing her skirt over her shoulders.

Euphémie said, "Your guest spoke truthfully, mostly. It was indeed our dear Annie who liberated the great wooden wheel from the tyranny of men. As for the broken axel, I credit that to insufficiently solid lumber rather than a vengeful god."

Late or not, scandalous or not, Solemn or not, Sister Temperance couldn't help but adore these women. After all they'd been thru, and in spite of the fact that they'd thus far been useless as ambassadors for Solemnity—she could think of no others with whom she'd rather spend these days. Sister Gravity, maybe.

Annie said, "How goes it for you? Aside from the Nimrodian?"

Temperance said, "Let's see. I've received a proposal of

marriage from a palsied codger so advanced in his senility that, immediately after I declined, he asked me again as if for the first time."

Euphémie said to Annie, "Probably from that Methuselahian sect we saw earlier."

Sister Temperance did not digest this statement. "Then, as I was whistling my solemn best to share the word, a small dog approached. As you know, there are many stray dogs here. This one seemed more pleasant than most. And so I did not immediately kick it. Foolish me, the creature took my passivity as an invitation to. I'd rather not describe the act. After that, I pleaded with the Lord to guide his flock into this tent, as it's clear that my voice and my face will never bring them in. My prayers were answered in the shape of the gossip from next door."

Euphémie said, "It's okay, Sister. She's gone now."

Temperance practically wailed, "Why must proselytizing so resemble the mating call of flim flam?"

Euphémie said, "Annie, dear, let us be useful for once. Sister Temperance, you are excused for the rest of the day. We widows will take our long-overdue turn at the oars."

"Bless you," said Sister Temperance. She added, "But first, might I suggest, Annie, that you climb back into your skirt."

Chapter Fifty-Eight

"WE ALL PRAY TO THE SAME GOD."

The first time Sister Temperance overheard this phrase, she was passing a pair of pastors shaking hands, holding elbows. The men were clearly from different sects. One was bald, the other had hair down to his britches and a beard full of dead butterflies.

Chuckling, the bald man said, "I hear you, brother. You have one wife, I have five. What's it matter? We all pray to the same god."

"Amen, brother!" said the hairy one.

Temperance thought, I must remember that one; perhaps today I shall meet someone to whom I can say it.

As she continued along the flow of humanity, Temperance heard the phrase often enough that she wondered if *We all pray to the same god* was the official motto of the 1885 All-Tent Revival.

Brothers and sisters are we. The details don't matter, just so long as we pray to the same god. So sayeth the very people who had come here to establish that theirs was the one true path to glory.

Those sects that danced themselves into frenzies; or screamed gibberish; or that ate only insects; or that ate only on Sundays; or that celebrated a peaceful messiah; or marched in the vengeful army of Christ; or *whistled*—all of this from one god?

Fearing divine reprisal, Temperance's brain circled its wagons against this unwanted assault of skepti—

She couldn't even *think* the word.

A four-year-old girl proselytizing from a soapbox.

A Siamese cat that could—its owner claimed—sense the fear of God.

A legless girl, offering to wash the feet of strangers.

Endless iterations.

Toward dusk, Temperance risked a visit to the Chariot of Fire. Mr. Dennison had by then repaired the axel, this in spite of the continued, and now unexcused, absence of his young apprentice.

Dennison had hung sixteen lanterns to dangle from the wheel, one lantern on each side of each gondola. The effect, in the misty sunset air, was romantic.

A ring of lookeeloos had encircled the contraption, exhaling steam in the chill air, hands in mufflers or pockets or gunnysacks. Sister Temperance stood in the midst of this crowd, accepted a slice of fruitcake from a random hand, nibbled, and watched the start and stop of the wheel.

If only she'd had a ha'penny. Ha! None of that.

Look, listen, a man has climbed atop one of the draft horses, and now he's plucking a banjo as the horses trod their circle. The man is a Negro! So *they've* decided to show up. Clapping, clogging. Oh, mercy, who's this? It's Sister Honora, marching thru the crowd, straight to Mr. Dennison.

Temperance could not hear the conversation, but it was clear that Sister Honora was using her sternest voice. Calm, of course, but commanding. Honora pointed at the wheel, at the Negro on the horse, and the ring of soft-shoeing Revivalists who would have been better served by paying a visit to the Solemnites' tent.

Temperance worked herself close enough to hear.

"—no place for such revelry. This is an exchange of religion, not recreation."

"Ma'am, my exhibit was approved by the committee. Do you speak for the Restive Council?"

"I am *on* the Restive Council. Your application said nothing about banjos or females."

Now that Honora had mentioned it, yes, Temperance saw a number of skirts fluttering in Mr. Dennison's dangling chairs. Oh, those widows!

Dennison said, "As a member of the Church of Integrated Newtonian Morality, it is within my religious purview to offer the ecstasy of upliftment-by-mechanical-means. I took the Pledge of Cooperation, as I assume you did. Remember it? 'I shall not speak ill of any other faith.'"

"There have been complaints."

"From other decent folks who took the pledge, I suppose. Listen, every person on that wheel represents a quarter of a penny for your festival fund. If the council doesn't like it, they can take their profit and start their own, All-Tents-Except-Those-of-Which-We-Disapprove Revival."

Temperance could not believe that anyone, much less a wheel-man, would speak thusly to Sister Honora. She leaned closer, cupped one hand behind an ear.

Dennison continued. "Tell you what. I'm a man of experience. Been all around this country. Managed an opera house; owned a baseball park; sold horseless carriages. I managed Mark Twain for a couple of weeks. If I could handle that old cuss, surely you and I can work something out. I'll bump your take up to *seventy-five percent* of my profits. How's that? My soul profiteth not so much."

Honora, still angry, but no fool, said, "I'll speak to the council."

Honora turned and parted, to a smattering of applause.

Temperance could not tell which they were cheering, Honora's solemnity or Dennis Dennison's courage in testing that solemnity.

Temperance retreated from the crowd and stood alone in the darkness at the edge of the woods where she watched the hypnotic rotations of the lantern-lit wheel until the night's chill drove her back to the Solemnitic tent.

Chapter Fifty-Nine

WHEN TEMPERANCE RETURNED, THE WIDOWS WERE SIPPING SOUP AT the cookfire.

"How fares our fair Sister?" said Annie.

"It was a good walk. Many things to look at. Just what I needed," said Temperance, settling onto an empty stool next to Euphémie, who ladled her a bowl.

"You've just missed Sister Honora," said Euphémie.

"A shame," said Temperance.

Euphémie shrugged. "She did not stay long. She was in a mood." She placed the bowl of soup in Temperance's hand.

Annie said, "Agitated."

"Did she say why?" said Temperance.

"Who knows? Maybe she got another complaint about the weather," said Euphémie. "She asked where Pansy was, we told her she was out with Auguste, and then she stomped away."

Having witnessed Honora's confrontation with the wheelman, Temperance knew precisely why she had been agitated. Rather than mention this, she said, "Honora's duties are great and her rewards are few. But she wouldn't have it otherwise." She tipped the bowl into her mouth. "And you, Sisters? What have you learned today?"

"That we are no better at this than you," said Annie.

Euphémie said, "We even whistled."

"You make such beautiful melodies."

"My son," said Annie. "I believe he could bring a crowd with those cow-teeth of his."

"If we knew where he was," said Euphémie.

"Probably looking for his missing tooth," said Annie.

In fact, it had been several hours since Auguste had spared a thought for his missing toothwhistle, so occupied had he been by the day's excitement, and so occupied would he remain.

Chapter Sixty

STILL OVERLOOKING THE GLADE, PANSY AND AUGUSTE AND GOMAR had hidden behind a slab of jet-black slate that poked out of the ground like a leaned-over tombstone. They were maybe ten yards from the six-sided tent. Night had begun to fall.

At first, the tent had glowed with a yellow light, as if someone inside had lit a lantern. Then the glow faded, as if the lantern's wick had been rolled back, and then indistinct shadows began to shift around the walls of the glowing tent, an out-of-focus puppet play.

"What's that?"

"It's just shadows."

"Then go knock on the door."

"It's a flap, not a door."

"Shhh."

The shadows chased around the walls of the tent. The light flickered wildly and then the tent went dark, and with it the clearing and the sky and the whole world seemed gone into shadow.

"Welp," said Gomar, raising himself up, "Mr. D will be shutting down the wheel soon. I'd best get back. See you in the village!"

With no further comment, he sprinted away.

Pansy was disgusted. "Coward." She continued to stare at the darkened tent.

Auguste shifted around. "I'm hungry."

Pansy ignored him.

Auguste's stomach growled.

Pansy turned said, "Are you a coward, too?"

"I'm hungry. And it's cold."

"So go home."

"No, not alone."

"Are you afraid of the werebear?"

Auguste's eyes grew wide, his mouth dropped open. "Holy smoke! I think I *saw* it last night!"

"Saw what? And it's holy *smokes*, plural."

"What you just said, it reminded me, when I went out to—"

A voice behind them said, "I shoulda known it was you two."

It was Harriet Stovepipe, and her brother Kermit as well. Behind them was the fattest woman Auguste and Pansy had ever seen.

"Come on," said Harriet. "It's warm inside."

Chapter Sixty-One

"THEY SAID THEY'D BE BACK BY NOON," SAID ANNIE.

"They're fine, I'm sure," said Euphémie.

Temperance said, "Concerning, though. With the weather."

It was almost dark. The evening was cooling rapidly. Word on Old Testament Lane was that snow could alight at any minute. Knit hats, mufflers, sheepskin vests, and wool coats had suddenly become *à la mode* in the village.

Annie said, "Sister Temperance, do you mind watching the tent? Euphémie and I are going to walk around some. Maybe we'll find the kids."

Temperance said, "I would not mind at all."

"If they get back before we do, send them directly to bed."

* * *

The Revival had reached its groove. Preachers staged demonstrations of apoplecticism, testification, spontaneous synchronized prayer, and healing-by-the-laying-upon-of-hands. From a distance came the murmur of a hymn (*for there's no other way*), the voices ebbing and flowing (*to be happy in Jesus*), spreading thru the masses like a sweet aroma (*than to trust and obey*). Bonfires, flakes of ash, the undertow of screaming tagging children.

As Annie and Euphémie pushed thru the crowds, they were engulfed by a hand-linked line of dancing, shirtless monks from the Greco-Roman Catholic Church. Skipping and twisting, the men circled them once, twice, and then, with a cry of *Opa!* they moved on to harass some other innocent passersby, leaving Annie and Euphémie now to fend off a cluster of children-at-play.

Annie snagged a racing child and crouched before it. "Have you seen two kids?" Realizing the absurdity of the question, Annie added, "One's a girl, wearing a yellow dress. The other is a boy. He's wearing pantaloons and a blouse and he has an accent."

The child said, "Like yours?"

"Yes, like mine."

"Gomar chased them into the trees." The child pointed to the edge of the clearing.

"Who's Gomar?"

"The big kid from the big wheel. He's quick. I ain't seen him in a while."

Chapter Sixty-Two

THE SIX-SIDED TENT WAS LIT WITH KEROSENE LAMPS THAT HUNG FROM the pole-bracing. Much of the available space was taken up by a hexagonal table. In the center of the table was a clay platter upon which was poised a life-sized whitish waxen sculpture of a head. The head was leaned back, mouth agape. Within that mouth was a candlewick harboring a small blue flame. The head was crudely rendered but it was clearly intended to represent the Christian messiah. A ring of bent sawbrier sticks lay upon the waxen hair like a thorned crown.

The fat woman seated herself at the far end of the table. A pinkish robe was draped over her sloping shoulders. Her eyes bulged out of her head, and were pointed in different directions. This was not a simple case of lazy-eye; rather, the woman's ocular orbs seemed to move independently of one another, like a chameleon's.

Harriet and Kermit Stovepipe sat on either side of the woman, beaming pleasant smiles across the table at Pansy and Auguste, who, in the name of symmetry, had squeezed their chairs together at the edge of the table directly opposite the fat woman.

The Jesus-head candle sputtered. The first flakes of snow played a faint drumbeat on the canvas.

In search of the "big kid from the big wheel", Annie and Euphémie hurried south to the Chariot of Fire, which was positively charming, decorated as it was with sixteen lovely lanterns.

Snow had begun to fall. The low-clouded night sky glowed with the diffused reflections of campfires. Snowflakes melted in the teeth of beatific smiles.

The line for the ride extended in a chaotic squiggle of hundreds of eager customers, and just as many other pilgrims had gathered to watch the turnings of the great machine, as well as to listen to the Negro banjoist—the same one Temperance had seen earlier—who had dismounted from the draft horse and was now picking his frantic music in the midst of a crowd on the north side of the wheel.

Euphémie gestured toward to the banjoist. "That is precisely the sort of spectacle that would appeal to Auguste."

"Agreed," said Annie. "Perhaps we'll find him there."

As they headed toward the spectacle, the banjo stopped mid-song and the crowd uttered a collective cry of surprise.

"*Sacrebleu!*" cried Euphémie. "Is that Sister Honora?"

It certainly was, and she was far from solemn.

"Honey-water, anyone?"

The fat lady twisted her torso and lifted a serving dish from behind her. Upon it sat a ceramic pitcher and four copper cups. She placed it on the table. "Kermit, would you be so kind?"

Kermit filled all four cups, then slid two of them to Auguste and Pansy, who brought them to their mouths and sipped.

It was delicious, this honey water.

"So," said the fat lady, "you know my friends Harriet and Kermit."

Auguste and Pansy nodded.

Harriet cleared her throat. "If I may, ma'am, I shall familiarize you all with one another." Nodding toward the white children, she said, "These here are Auggie—"

"Auguste," said Auguste.

"—and Pansy. Pansy comes from White Solemn. Auguste is a refugee she picked up while she was in the France. They've been proselytizing with the Solemnite outfit at the Village of Godly Illumination. They found your tent on accident and were about to sneak away until we caught up to them."

Harriet spoke now to Pansy and Auguste. "This here lady is called Finoula. She's real pleasant, as you can see. She's here with the Revival, just like you folk. Different, though. You're wondering why she's set up all the way out in the woods instead of at the village. It's because they won't have her."

"But she's not a Negro," said Pansy.

Finoula said, in a honey-sweet voice, "Oh, but I'm much more frightening than a Negro!"

She and Harriet and Kermit shared a hearty laugh. Harriet said, "Really, truthfully, Finoula's just about the smartest, nicest person we ever met, right Kerm?"

Kermit nodded vigorously.

Finoula raised a shoulder in a half-modest shrug.

Harriet turned eagerly to Finoula. "How did I do?"

Finoula's eyes warmed the little girl. "Keep on."

Harriet addressed Pansy and Auguste. "Remember how we talked the other day about why us black folk don't exactly feel motivated to show our faces at your all-are-welcome party? Turns out, we coloreds are surprisingly curious creatures. For instance, Kermit and I have been watching from afar—"

"Hanging out in the woods, mostly," said Kermit.

"—and we're awfully proud to see so many people enjoying Second Solemn's many contributions to the fairgrounds. Right, Kerm?"

Kermit was proud.

Harriet continued. "Especially since, you know, we can't

comfortably enjoy our contributions in person. Returning to my point. Yesterday, in our lurkings about the woods, we found a trail lined with white stones—I presume you found it as well—and we followed it here. Same as you all, we hid behind that chunk of rock and spied. People came and went for most the day. Not a lot of people, but some. All of them were white womenfolk. They'd come to the tent acting embarrassed and scared. They'd go in and then they'd come out all aglow like they'd been washed in the blood of the lamb. Ain't that right Kerm?"

"Positively," said Kermit. "Scrubbed clean."

Harriet said, "Being courageous as well as curious, me and Kerm elected to see for ourselves what was the cause of this scrubbing. So, after this one lady came out, singing to glory louder than a skunk stinks, we climbed out from behind the rock and rattled the flap." She sipped from her honey water. "Now the good part. Have you ever been into a telegraph office? No? Me neither. But you know what a telegraph is, right?"

Finoula patted Harriet's shoulder. "I'll take it from here."

Harriet leaned back, pleased.

Finoula, scrunched her eyebrows. Her honey voice spilled from her lips, "Friends, this here is a telegraph office for the dead! You could call it a *mortigraph* office. *I* call it a Church of Spiritual and Material Integrative Communication. COSMIC, for short."

Pansy parenthetically explained to Auguste the concept of acronyms.

Finoula resumed, "As Christians, we recognize that the flesh is merely a vessel for the soul. Flesh filled with a soul is called life. Flesh without a soul is maggot food. On the other hand, a soul without flesh is something entirely different..."

She continued for several more paragraphs, weaving tenuous threads between the human hierarchy of needs, the resurrection of Christ, talking shrubs, ectoplasmic transubstantiation, heavenly ascension, and how all of this could be explained and manipulated if one applied Boyle's Law of Gaseous Interaction to the comings and goings of disembodied wraiths.

Upon concluding, she folded her hands upon the table. "Questions?"

Pansy had several, and she would have asked them had she not been distracted by Kermit, who was squirming with excitement. Finoula turned her eyes—both of them—to the boy.

Kermit burst forth, "She ain't kidding. She let us talk to our dead brother! He said he—"

"We used to have a big brother," said Harriet, "named Erasmus. He ate ants. He died from bad milk."

"I was real young," said Kermit. "I remember him being alive and then I remember him taking a long time to die and it was sad. Right, Harriet?"

"Very sad."

"And then Daddy tried to suicide himself over the ordeal."

Harriet said, "Don't tell that stuff, Kermit."

Pansy and Auguste, each, independently appreciated being told about that stuff.

"Anyway," said Harriet, "this lady here, she let us talk to Erasmus's non-corporeal essence. Did I say that right?"

"Spot-on," said Finoula.

"And he said he was proud of us," said Kermit.

Harriet said, "He said some other stuff, too, but you wouldn't understand it and it's none of your business anyhow. Not to be rude."

"It was private," said Kermit.

Harriet said, "That was yesterday. We came by again today. Miss Finoula just now let us talk to the woman I was named after, Harriet Tubman. Well, not her, actually, because she's not dead yet. But we did talk to her mother. She was also named Harriet. We never met her. She was a Methodist, and you can tell—boy does she cuss a lot. She told us—or, rather, her non-corporeal essence told us—that Harriet—her daughter—was only her second-favorite child, on account of she—the daughter—didn't ever give her—the mother—any proper grandchildren. Funny lady."

Questions jostled within the heads of Pansy and Auguste, with one being foremost. With the anticipation one would expect from a medium of any competence, Finoula put voice to that question. "With whom do you wish to have a COSMIC conversation?"

"You're speaking to Auguste and me?" said Pansy.

"Yes. Would you like a moment to talk about it?"

"No thanks," said Pansy.

Finoula raised an eyebrow.

"We want the same person," said Pansy.

"Who?" said Finoula.

"Yes," said Auguste, "who?"

"Obviously, we wish to summon Sister Gravity, who died sa—"

Finoula raised her hand. "Tell me nothing more."

"Buh, buh," said Pansy.

Auguste said, "Bif, bif."

"Silence," said Finoula.

Commence the séance.

Chapter Sixty-Three

THE WIDOWS STAYED BACK IN THE CROWD—JUST AS TEMPERANCE HAD done earlier under similar circumstances—and watched as Dennis Dennison wedged himself between Honora and the banjoist. Dennison pleaded for calm. Honora solemnly threatened to rip his eyes out of his skull if he didn't immediately shut down his sin-machine. The banjoist eyed a means of escape.

The Chariot of Fire loomed over them. Decorated with its sixteen lovely lanterns, it continued to rotate in fits and starts.

A peacemaker with an Amish beard attempted to calm Honora with some variant on "It's all good, sister." The man offered her a sip from a clay jug. Honora accepted the jug, brought it tantalizingly close to her lips, and then smashed it to the ground. Shards of jug, splash of moonshine. Confusion rippled the crowd. They were uncertain which party—Dennison or Honora—deserved the harshest judgment. Definitely not the banjoist. That colored boy was a damned good picker.

"What's she doing?" said Euphémie.

"She thinks," said Annie, "that she's spreading the word of Solemn. But she isn't."

"We must help her. Or stop her. Or something."

Annie had other concerns. "Our intervention would but

diminish the power of her message. No, we shall leave her be and look for the children."

Caught by a fit of compassion, Euphémie cried, "Sister Honora! The Lord begs of you a solemn heart!"

Honora started at this, and saw Euphémie's face above the mass of humans. Their eyes met for a moment—Euphémie's puzzled, Honora's stained red with divinity—before Annie dragged Euphémie away to the Chariot's horse-powered wheel engine where they finally found the kid, Gomar, who had recently, and tardily, returned to his post.

With his master engaged with Honora, Gomar was guiding the horses, taking the money, helping couples in and out of their gondolas. Also, he was on the verge of hyperventilation.

Annie walked straight to the panicking adolescent, took him by the ear and dragged him—and Euphémie, whose hand she still gripped—thru the parting crowd directly into the trees that marked the edge of the woods.

Satisfied with the privacy, and with dainty snowflakes alighting from the salmon-colored sky, Annie released both Gomar and Euphémie.

She put her hands on the boy's cheeks and, in a voice that Euphémie found admirably solemn, said, "Where is my son?"

Gomar didn't know who these women were, but he noted the similarity of Annie's accent to that of the kid who had toppled the tree. "Ma'am," he stammered, "are you the mother of a boy named Auguste Lestables?"

"Where is he?"

"I figured he'd be back by now."

"He isn't."

"I suppose I could lead you to him, assuming he hasn't gone anywhere."

"Yes, do this," said Annie.

Gomar said, "I will, ma'am, but first—"

"First, nothing! Move."

"—first, I must thank you—"

Unexpected.

"—for extracting me from that madness." He gestured toward Honora, who was now emphasizing her every word to Dennis Dennison with a stomp of her right foot. "That woman has lost her wits."

Gomar led them into the woods.

Chapter Sixty-Four

RIPPLES OF SNOW ACCUMULATED ON THE ROOF OF THE TENT AND SLID deliciously down the eaves as woodsy gusts florped the canvas. In two of the tent's six corners, coals glowed from within cast-iron pans. Exhalations were only faintly fogged. Noses only slightly red.

Finoula dimmed the lamps, poked her head outside to confirm that no one was lingering nearby, and returned to the table where the waxen mouth of Jesus flickered candleflame. She produced six stumpy candles and lit them from the Jesus fire and then she placed them in the table's six corners.

Finoula leaned back in her chair. "Let us form a circle of hands."

They did so.

"Let us pray. This is a long one, so if anyone needs to use the toilet, speak now. No? Good. Heavenly Father, hear these words uttered in humility." A hissing inhalation. "Lord, we beg of thee a few precious moments for a COSMIC conversation with"—speaking to Pansy—"name again?"

"Sister Gravity," said Pansy gravely.

"Sister Gravity, who escaped her fleshy prison at some untold year of her adulthood. Herewith do I beseech you, Lord. Summon the spirit."

To her guests, Finoula said, "Palms on the table. Stay calm." She gave a bark like a startled mutt, and then her chameleon eyes diverged and the six candles extinguished themselves, leaving the tent illuminated solely by the sputtering head of Jesus, whose smell reminded Auguste of bacon.

Finoula's honey voice became ancient. "I saw a great white throne and him who was seated on it. And I saw the dead standing before the throne. The king said unto them, 'Neither death nor life, nor angels nor rulers, nor anything else in all creation, shall separate us from the love of God.'

"Then the king summoned all the magicians, the enchanters, the sorcerers. 'Would any of you inquire of the dead on behalf of the living?' None stepped forth, so the king sent them away and demanded of his summoners, 'Seek for me a *woman* who is a medium, that I may inquire of her to divine for me a spirit and bring up for me whomever I shall name. As the Lord lives, no punishment shall come upon you for this thing.'

"And so a woman came and they were all filled with the Holy Spirit, for God grants a spirit not of fear but of love. Whoever has been perfected in love will not be visited by harm.

"And now, Lord, Jesus, effervescent Holy Spirit, I beseech you, in the name of love, please do me a kindness and guide to this sanctuary the voice of Sister Gravity."

Outside, the snow had settled upon branches and the birds that nested in them.

Chapter Sixty-Five

THE TABLE SHIFTED BENEATH THEIR HANDS.

"Oh!" cried Pansy.

Finoula said, "Palms down. Stay calm." A moment to settle, then Finoula filled her lungs and bellowed, "SISTER GRAVITY, WE WELCOME THEE TO THE COSMIC SANCTUARY."

The table shifted again. Calmness was maintained.

"Your friend is like a fish," whispered Finoula. "Her spirit bubbles up from great depths."

All followed Finoula's upward gaze. Appearing from nowhere, and supported by no hand, a gauzy mesh descended from the peak of the tent. The gauze jerked here and there, then floated toward Pansy. Unable to stop herself, the girl lifted her hand and reached toward it. The gauze jerked away to hover directly over the Jesus candle.

The tent was filled with the stench of dead fish. Noses scrunched. Auguste gulped.

And then, astonishingly, a disembodied, weary tenor exclaimed, "*I live. I see all. I venture within the sea, within the whale. I —wait a minute. Pansy? Auguste? So the ship survived! You're in America! How are the others?*"

"Go on," encouraged Finoula, "Talk to her."

Pansy swallowed and said, "Welcome, Sister Gravity. It is I, Pansy. Yes, we all made it. Save for you."

"*This pleases me greatly,*" said the ghost of Sister Gravity.

"You sound well." said Pansy.

"*It's not so bad here. It's like a womb. Warm and squishy. I've got all the cod I can eat, though I'm afraid I'll never get used to the smell. What's new in Solemn?*"

Auguste was growing restless. They were wasting time with small talk.

"You wouldn't believe it," said Pansy, "Restive is hosting this year's All-Tent Revival! Right now, we're in a tent with a woman named Finoula. She's real nice."

"*Finoula. Is it she who summoned me? A pleasant voice she has.*"

"An incredible voice," said Pansy.

Gravity said, "*So. What can I do for you, darling?*"

"Gosh," said Pansy, "I guess it's more of a what-can-we-do-for-you. I would start by saying Auguste and I are terribly sorry about putting your life in danger during that storm—say, *are you alive?*"

The gauze jerked up and down with ironic indignation. "*I'm talking to you, aren't I?*"

"I suppose so," said Pansy. "But really, since I've got you here, I just wanted to let you know that I regret my behavior and that I'd do anything to have you back."

"*Naturally. And if you and Auguste had died in that storm, I would have done anything to get you back. Of course, you didn't die, because I did everything I could to keep you from dying. Pansy, if you only take one thing from this conversation, I hope it's this: selfless sacrifices only count if you make them prior to the tragedy in question.*"

Pansy scrunched her eyebrows.

"*What I mean is, I wouldn't have had to make my ultimate sacrifice if you and Auguste had been able to make a minor sacrifice of your silly desire to go above decks in a tempest.*"

Pansy's chin trembled.

"*To be clear, I do not regret saving you. I am not upset at you or*"

Auguste for your frivolity. You are children, after all. Just promise me you'll steer clear of similar situations in the future."

Pansy, humbled, said, "I promise, solemnly."

At the mention of solemnity, Sister Gravity's gauzy manifestation jiggled wildly for a moment. Once it stilled, Gravity said, *"Sorry. I've developed a whole new relationship with*—chortle—*solemnity these past few months."*

Pansy said, "Have you seen the angels?"

"Not yet, I'm afraid. And before you ask, I haven't seen the Lord or Jesus or any holy spirits."

"But they're out there, right?"

"How's your mother? She still trying to carry the world on her shoulders?"

This was all silly chatter as far Auguste was concerned, and he could wait no longer. "May I have a word?"

Pansy glared at him, but the ghostly gauze jerked up and down in a permissive fashion.

"Sister Gravity, this is Auguste Lestables."

"I know."

"I am sorry you were eaten by the horned whale."

"I am aware of this."

"I really appreciate you saving us, same as Pansy."

"And of this as well."

"And I promise I will steer clear of similar situations in the future."

"This pleases me."

"And your house is really nice."

"I do miss that bed."

"It had bedbugs, but I figured out how to get rid of them. All you need is a dead bat."

"I knew you were special from the moment we met."

"I'm curious, though," said Auguste. "Can you talk to *other* dead people?"

"I presume that you're looking for the man who drowned Henri Deplouc."

"My father! How could you possibly know that?" demanded Auguste.

"Lucky guess. Also, he's standing next to me."

Pansy butted in, "What's *he* doing inside *your* whale?"

"Don't trifle with me, young lady."

In French, Auguste said, "Father? Can you hear me?"

"He can't speak," said Gravity. *"The noose left his throat in pretty rough shape. And he's missing a portion of his tongue. But, yes, he's nodding."*

"Papa," said Auguste, "even though you can't talk, can you maybe whistle?"

A smoky, flutish sonority filled the tent. It grew in volume, it split into two tones, and then those tones began a spiraling ascension, like starlings flirting into the clouds above. As the tones climbed, the sound faded until it finally merged with the sputter of the Jesus candle.

"It would seem," said the voice of Gravity's ghost, *"that he can whistle rather well."*

Auguste said, "Papa, do you know where my toothwhistle is?"

No reply.

"I love you, Papa."

The ghost of Sister Gravity said, *"He nodded."*

"He nodded?" said Auguste.

"To your question. The answer is yes."

"Thank you, Papa," said Auguste. "Where is the whistle?"

"He's shaking his head."

"As in, 'no'?"

"More like, 'It is up to you, son, to find your lost whistle.'"

"But, Papa!"

"Don't overthink it, Auguste. Ghosts are known for enigmatic behavior. Any other questions?"

Pansy said, "May I?"

With a permissive nod, Auguste ceded the floor.

"Mr. Lestables, my name is Pansy. I am your son's fondest companion. Except for one thing. We have a longstanding conflict that I hope you can resolve. Could you kindly tell us the true definition of a sunset?"

No response.

"I'm sorry," said Sister Gravity. *"It seems he's fallen asleep."*

"Wake him!" said Auguste.

"Not a chance. If he doesn't get his rest, he gets awfully moody."

"He always enjoyed his naps," said Auguste, wistfully. To Pansy he said, "Why would you ask such a silly question?"

In her honey voice, Finoula said, "Calm, please."

Auguste folded his arms in front of his chest.

The gauze floated toward Pansy. *"Sweetheart, I've a favor. Something I'd like you to write down."*

A whispering lilt entered Pansy's mind.

Finoula, who was familiar with this type of ghostly behavior, slid a pencil into Pansy's right hand and placed a sheet of paper under the pencil. Pansy's hand began to scribe small, neat letters on the paper. After a few moments, the pencil snapped and the room shivered into stillness.

Gravity's ghost said, *"That'll do. Thanks for the visit. Goodbye."*

The ectoplasmic gauze circled over their heads, then disappeared into the peak of the tent. The six candles re-ignited.

Finoula's chameleon eyes wandered madly and then aligned toward the Jesus candle. "So sayeth the dead."

Our principals blinked at one another.

Finoula said, "This concludes our session. You may exit via the rear entrance. If you enjoyed your visit, please tell your friends about Finoula and her Tent of COSMIC Wonders." She leaned forward and, with her delicate fingers, began reforming the soft features of Jesus.

At that moment, Annie Lestables crashed thru the front flap of the tent, half-crazed and covered in snow.

Chapter Sixty-Six

Finoula was not in the least perturbed, put-off, or intimidated by Annie's breathless arrival. She had long ago mastered the art of comforting desperate mothers in search of their *dead* children; winning over a woman who had entered the tent and immediately discovered her son alive and intact, that was duck soup.

All it took was, "Welcome to the Church of Spiritual and Material Integrative Communication. Have a seat. Enjoy some honey water."

Annie was immediately disarmed by the chameleon-eyed woman's mellifluidity. She settled upon the chair that Harriet offered her, and then she accepted a copper cup from Kermit. As Annie was sipping her honey water, Finoula said, "Please call your two friends in as well. It's cold out there."

Annie did so.

Euphémie and Gomar entered, shook snow off their shoulders, sat at the hexagonal table, sipped from copper cups, and warmed their hands over a skillet of glowing coals.

Within moments, everyone had slipped into a familial chat. The widows charmed Harriet and Kermit. Harriet and Kermit charmed the widows. Finoula charmed everyone with tales of famous ghosts. Of Napoleon, she said, "Terrible listener." Of Frederick Douglass, "Not as funny as I expected."

After the cups had been twice filled and twice emptied, Annie yawned. "We must go."

"Are you sure?" said Finoula. "I could summon Louis XIV for you."

"Not with this weather," said Annie.

Outside, bidding goodbyes.

Finoula placed a hand on Harriet's shoulder, master to apprentice. "I could show you how I do it."

"I'd like that."

Auguste approached Kermit. "I lost one of my toothwhistles."

"Happens. I'll get you another next time we're at the chicken house."

Finoula beckoned Pansy. She slid a folded piece of paper into the girl's coat pocket, whispering into her ear, "Don't forget."

The summoner-of-spirits gave a little salute and ducked the flap back into her COSMIC tent.

Harriet and Kermit bade goodbye to the white folk and started toward Second Solemn.

Auguste led the Solemnites and Gomar back to the revival, tooting his remaining whistle and skipping gaily in this, his very first snowstorm.

The snow was lovely, and only ankle deep.

Chapter Sixty-Seven

BY THE TIME THEY REACHED THE VILLAGE OF GODLY ILLUMINATION, the festival had gone quiet under the snow. Even the holy rollers had retreated beneath their sheepskin blankets, where they dreamt of ecstatic damnation.

Gomar bade a sleepy goodbye and walked south toward the Chariot of Fire. Lord knew what had transpired since he had abandoned Mr. Dennison to the fury of Sister Honora.

When the children and the widows climbed into the tent, Sister Temperance burst forth with a decidedly unsolemn, "My lovelies!"

Hugs, minimal explanations, pinch the wick, darkness, snowfall, sleep. Except for Auguste. He lay in bed, recalling the melody his father had whistled for him at Finoula's. He unwound the tendrils, a double helix of *do re mi fa so la si do,* and reassembled them into elastic embraces, dramatic separations, semi-tonic shifts, birds sharing the same atmospheric column, gliding, bumping, soaring.

He loved this.

Well before dawn, Auguste crept out for a night-piss. The snow had ceased, the clouds had dissolved. He stood just outside the tent in his bedclothes, barefooted, wide awake. A waning moon glowed amidst a sparkling of stars, coloring the virgin snow a cool blue. He wiggled his toes in the snow. He bent and gathered a handful, squeezed until it became icy solid. He licked it, then released it to the ground.

Beckoned by moon-lit, snow-laden boughs, he walked behind the tent, leaving dark footprints in the snow, until he was just inside the woods at the edge of the clearing.

There, he found a single, starlit bootprint, with none other leading to or from. In the heel of the bootprint lay a cow's incisor.

Auguste pinched the tooth out of the snow. He placed it in his right cheek. It tasted like rotten cheese. He removed it, scrubbed it in the snow and then re-inserted it. Better. He pulled the other tooth from his pocket and slid it into his left cheek.

Together again.

He blew soft tones that matched the ones that had been playing in his head ever since he'd spoken to his father. Equations of sound which answered questions that math could not ask. He did this until his own teeth began chattering and then he returned to the tent.

All the while, he'd been observed by a shivering, yellow-eyed figure crouched upon a thick branch above.

Auguste climbed under the quilt, snuggled next to Pansy.

"So you found it," whispered the girl.

"You heard me?"

"I did. Where was it?"

"It was just sitting there."

"It's funny how things can come and go."

"Snow is my favorite," whispered Auguste, and then he welcomed a well-deserved sleep.

Chapter Sixty-Eight

THE NEXT MORNING WAS DECEMBER THIRTY-FIRST. THIS WOULD BE the final full day of the All-Tent Revival, and the merciful heavens seemed to know it. The sun rose white in the cloudless, pale sky. Sleepy heads poked out of tents, snapping icicles that had formed overnight. Snowmelt rained from leafless trees.

Sister Temperance was first to emerge from the Solemnitic tent. She built a fire inside the bread stove then set water over the cook-fire. Breakfast would be boiled eggs and yesterday's bread. She was pleased that everyone had made it home okay, but, other than this, the previous night had been terribly disappointing. After the widows had gone to seek the children, news of Honora's confrontation with the wheelman had spread throughout the camp ("The poor woman seemed out of her mind" "Ah, she's one of those Solemnites"). After so many gawking stares, Sister Temperance had retreated to her cot in the dark, waiting, waiting for the village to fall asleep, waiting for the children and the widows to return.

And the children and the widows had returned and now they were all asleep, safe and solemn.

Pansy was next out of the tent, blinking against the winter sun.

From where she sat in front of the fire, Temperance said, "Good morning, young Sister."

"Blessed morning to you," said Pansy.

"I'll soon be putting the eggs to boil. Might you start the dough for our daily bread?"

"I shall do so with enthusiasm, after my toilet." The girl skipped toward the middengrounds.

Inhabitants of the neighboring tents were blinking at their own sunlight, boiling their own water. Next door, Resina Cotton, wife of Jimrod Cotton, First Minister of the Church of Nimrodian Protectorites, waved hello. Temperance responded with a solemn twitch of her head.

Upon Pansy's return, Temperance intended to query the girl about what, precisely, had transpired inside the COSMIC tent. The widows had been unclear on the subject last night.

But first, their camp was visited by a woman wearing a black dress with a widow's veil. "Psst. Sister Temperance."

"Sister Honora! I wouldn't have recognized you."

"There was some trouble last night."

"At the Pleasure wheel? I may have heard something about that."

"Pay no mind to that tattle."

Pansy skipped back into the scene. "Mother! Who died?"

Honora grimaced under the veil. "None has died. How was your yesterday, daughter?"

Pansy and Sister Temperance exchanged a look. Pansy understood, and said to Honora, "It was wonderful, Mother. Auguste and I met many children and shared with them the promise of solemnity. Otherwise, nothing whatsoever out of the ordinary."

"Good girl. I must be going."

"Please, Mother," said Pansy, "stay a bit longer."

"I'm afraid you won't see much of me today. Very busy. Good

luck. I'll be here first thing tomorrow. The Reverend will meet us with the wagon for our journey home." Honora patted the girl on the head.

"I miss you, Mother," said Pansy. "And I worry that this revival is causing you strain."

Honora's chin—the only part of her face that wasn't hidden by the veil—dimpled. Her voice trembled. "Oh, daughter, you perceive too well. Yes, I am dismayed. I'm trying to calm myself, as the Lord would have me. But, oh, I confronted the wheelman last night, and he defied me, and none would come to my defense."

"I would defend you with all my might," said Pansy.

"I would like that," said Honora, hugging her daughter.

Encouragingly, Temperance said, "Only one more day, Sister."

"Yes." Honora's voice grew righteous. "The most temptatious day of all." She gestured to the waking village. "Look at them."

"They seem...contented?" said Temperance. Seeing from Honora's face that this had been the wrong answer, she hastily added, "Shamelessly so."

"It gets worse every hour," said Honora. "And, bless their souls, as of this morning the council has assigned me to work the Pitch-Round."

Pansy said, "What is a Pitch-Round, Mother?"

"It is the Revival's culmination. It takes place at the Great Stage, at sunset, and it will be attended by thousands of pilgrims. Each church is invited to present an argument in favor of their particular set of beliefs. They call it the world's greatest exhibition of religious talent. I call it a very bad idea."

Pansy thought this very bad idea sounded delightful.

"One after the other," said Honora, "each church will compete for the attention of the masses. I'm told there will be feats of physical prowess, dramatic recitations, and"—she gasped—"song-singing. As a Coordinator of Activities, I'm obliged to see that all this revelry runs smoothly."

Pansy lowered her eyebrows to convey a look of outrage. "The council would submit you to torture! Do they not understand that a talent show contradicts the very concept of Solemnity?"

Honora's chin pointed fondly toward her daughter. "The council understands very well. They believe my 'uniquely critical perspective on the arts' will offer a 'valuable counterpoint' to those who would blindly celebrate non-solemn activities."

Temperance offered, "If any of us could survive such a thing, it would be you, dear Sister."

"Needless to say," said Honora, "I have notified the council that the Church of Solemn will not be sending its emissaries to the spectacle." With a hint of a grunt, she said, "I'm off. Fires to quench. People are complaining of thievery. Foodstuffs, socks, that sort of thing. It seems our burglar has ventured out of Second Solemn."

Pansy said, "Better a burglar than a bear."

Honora's chin smoothed. "I raised an optimist." To Sister Temperance, "Any success at growing our flock?"

"None, Sister."

"I see no reason to try any further. This marketplace has become a disservice to our Lord. I don't want any of you anywhere near the Pitch-Round. Do you hear?"

"Yes, Mother."

"Yes, Sister."

"Same goes for that obscene wheel."

Exit Honora.

By the time the yawning widows finally emerged from the tent, Pansy had already set the dough to proof and Temperance had boiled a dozen eggs.

Euphémie, muss-haired and bleary, walked straight to the Nimrodian Protectorites and returned with a cup of coffee. "Fantastic folks, those Nimrodians."

Auguste remained in the tent over breakfast, re-acquainting himself with his toothwhistles.

Euphémie said, "Sounds like he found his tooth."

Pansy said, "Apparently, he went out to pee last night and there it was, laying in the snow."

Annie tilted her head.

"It wasn't me," said Pansy. "I solemnly swear."

Euphémie said, "Annie and I couldn't help overhearing your conversation with Sister Honora earlier."

"You're aware of the Pitch-Round, then," said Temperance ruefully.

Euphémie said, "And that we are forbidden to attend."

"Honora knows best," said Temperance.

Annie said to Pansy, "Please tell Auguste to come eat."

As Pansy skipped to the tent, Temperance said to the widows, "I'm curious about your adventures last night. You said you found the children in a tent in the middle of the woods, but you said little else. Why would anyone stake a tent so far from the festival?"

"Maybe," said Euphémie, "because she knows how people would feel about her. Sister Honora is losing her mind because some folks will be singing at the Pitch-Round. How do you think she'd react to a woman who talks to ghosts?"

Temperance said, "A ghost-talker! Now I understand. Necromancy is strictly forbidden."

"Even from an All-Tent Revival?" said Euphémie.

"The Revival tolerates none of the demonic arts. Witchery, potions, satanic rituals, curses of all kinds. For the most part, I wholeheartedly agree. This is no place for such stuff." In her timid and adventurous way, Temperance added, "But, if this tent woman was a ghost-talker. Well, it sounds like she may have been practicing Spiritism."

"That's exactly what she called it!" said Annie. "Spiritism."

"I—and Sister Gravity, as well—met a Spiritist in Paris." Temperance's eyelids fluttered with nostalgia. "It was at a café, of course. A kind woman, pious. We only chatted with her; she did not invite us to a *séance*. She explained that she conjures the spirits of the dead. Unusual, but she had an open mind and a Christian heart. Honestly, there are tenters within this village who are a thousand times stranger."

"It's still pretty strange," said Euphémie. "Finoula—that was her name—apparently summoned the ghosts of Sister Gravity and Arthur Lestables."

"Oh my!"

"The ghosts spoke to the kids."

"What fortune!"

"And apparently the ghosts were speaking from inside the belly of the unicorn whale that swallowed Sister Gravity."

Temperance said, "That part's not so outlandish. Shall I remind you of Jonah?"

Euphémie's eyes twinkled. In a bold attempt at English word-play, she said, "Actually, you remind me more of Cinderella."

Neither Annie nor Temperance understood that this was supposed to be a joke, and so they didn't laugh.

After breakfast, Auguste led Pansy to the woods to show her where he'd found the tooth.

"See, here are my footprints."

"Barefoot, eh?" said Pansy. "You really do love snow. It's a shame this lovely sun will turn it all to water."

"Indiana is truly a place of wonders," said Auguste. He pointed. "Look there. What do you see?"

Pansy said, "A half-melted hole in the snow? It bears some resemblance to a footprint, I guess."

"It's a *boot*print, just like's been showing up around Second Solemn."

"Auguste, you do realize that nearly everyone at this festival is wearing boots."

"Some are wearing shoes," clarified Auguste.

"And that's where you found your tooth."

"Yes. In that bootprint."

"In the middle of the night. In the dark."

Auguste said, "Yes. And as you can see, there's no other footprints."

"So you're back to the werebear? The moon isn't even full."

Auguste said, "Of course it isn't. If the moon were full, the werebear would leave *bear* tracks."

"This is all silly. Just like Gomar's fairies."

"Do you remember yesterday, when I told you I'd *seen* the werebear?"

Pansy looked askance at her friend. "What are you talking about?"

"Remember? We were watching Finoula's tent and you said something that reminded me." He sighed in exasperation. "It was just before Harriet and Kermit surprised us. I started telling you that I'd seen it the night before when I went out to pee. But then Harriet and Kermit—"

"Another pee-pee clue," said Pansy. "I see a pattern here."

"Yes, I often pee at night. So often that I don't even have to wake up all the way. I go out and then I come back. It's like rolling over in bed. I know it happens, but I don't really notice it."

"Like sleep-walking."

"Somewhat, yes. Anyway, the night before last, I was peeing and I saw someone creeping around our tent. He was hairy, I think, with a beard. He stared at me with the most awful eyes. Then he ran away."

Pansy said, "So you wake up, but you don't wake up; you urinate right outside our tent—which is disgusting; and then your whistle mysteriously disappears and then reappears."

"Precisely. And in this case, the tooth was found in a bootprint."

"Or maybe the tooth fell out of your pocket one night and then you found it the next."

With a *whoop*, a clump of snow fell from a branch above their heads and landed near the alleged bootprint in question. The impression left by the snowclump was nearly indistinguishable from the bootprint.

"And now there are two bootprints," said Pansy. "I'm sorry, Auguste, but I have to go with the plausible explanation."

"It's not fair," said Auguste, pouting.

"Fair or not," said Pansy, "the werebear is silly and impossible and fantastical. You, however, are rational, and you know this. Let's get back to camp."

As they were exiting the woods, Auguste put the whistles in his cheeks and played a mournful tune. This drew the attention of a passing long-haired man clad only in a cloth diaper. On his head was a crown of thorns that had sprung forth several trickles of blood.

"Hey," said Jesus, "that sounds pretty good."

His Tennessee accent gave him away as a phony.

Auguste tooted a few more notes.

The phony Jesus said, "You've got something in your cheeks, obviously." Smarmy, this Jesus.

Auguste tooted the musical equivalent of, "Yes, I do have some things in my cheeks."

"Very excellent," said the Jesus.

Pansy said, "What are you up to, dressed like that?"

"I'm rehearsing for the Pitch-Round. I've no talent, except for growing a beard and wearing these confounded thorns. I'm more of a prop."

"I would never mistake you for Christ," said Pansy.

The phony Jesus raised one of his bare feet, shook snow off it. "Well, I am walking on water."

Pansy said, "I'd be more convinced if you were speaking Aramaic."

"Actually, Jesus spoke Hebrew," said the phony Jesus.

"Aramaic," said Pansy.

Auguste did not know what language the original Jesus had

spoken, but Pansy had just destroyed his theory that the Revival was being haunted by a werebear, whereas this Jesus had complimented his whistling, and so it was to him that Auguste lent his support. "I'm pretty sure it was Hebrew."

"Whatever," said Pansy.

The phony Jesus said to Auguste, "See you at the Pitch-Round?"

Auguste slid the teeth from his mouth, cupped them in his palm. "I cannot. Our church forbids us from associating with entertainers."

"A shame," said the phony Jesus, "with that whistling of yours."

They bade the phony Jesus a good day and continued to the Solemnitic campsite where Temperance and the widows were cranking up their final day of proselytization.

Auguste handed out bread—the bread remained popular—and idly played his whistlesongs. Soon all the bread was gone. And still, people kept crowding around. They paid no attention to Temperance's invitations to Solemnity; they were there for the little whistler. They'd pause for a few minutes, and then walk away, whistling a tune of their own.

Annie had a thought. "Son, get in the tent. Keep whistling. Pansy, you go, too." To Euphémie and Temperance she said, "As we were. My son will summon them."

With Auguste hidden, the twining melodies that emerged from the tent might as well have been from the lips of a well-rehearsed pair of angels.

The widows and Temperance capitalized at once. "Enter, friends. Listen together, experience the Lord's solemnity."

The tent filled, and remained so for the rest of the afternoon. Pansy would welcome the guests and they would sit or stand or kneel in front of the little boy whose cheeks fluttered asymmetrically and from whose mouth emerged these transcendent sounds. No sermons, just lovely noise. As for the skinny French kid at the source of this music, he closed his eyes and imagined the notes as weightless bricks that he deposited one by one into the shape of a sprawling, turreted castle; a structural manifestation of his questionable understanding of his father's questionable interpretation of Auguste Comte's positivism.

If she noticed Auguste growing tired, or if the tent became too crowded, Pansy would announce an intermission, clear the room and give the boy a few minutes to rest his face.

The pilgrims entered with curiosity. They exited serene and solemn, pleasantly infected by the perpetual settle and ascent of Auguste's tones. After Annie confessed to being the boy's mother, she was confronted by a line of well-wishers.

"You must be honored."

"He's blessed."

Most popular comment: "You're bringing him to Pitch-Round, right?"

At which point Temperance would step in. "Oh, no. We are solemn folk."

Mid-afternoon, their neighbor Resina Cotton made a visit.

"What's making those sounds?"

"My son," said Annie, "Auguste."

"He's taking away our parishioners."

"Sorry," said Annie.

"I don't mind a bit. Jimrod's voice is shot and I'm tired of listening to him. The boy is amazing. He'll be popular in the Pitch-Round."

Temperance said, "He won't be in the Pitch-Round. None of us Solemnites will. It's against our creed."

Resina harrumphed. "It ain't against mine."

Euphémie had been watching all this with a bemused grin. She straightened her face and said to Resina, "A Solemn life is long life." The sentiment nearly came off as genuine.

Resina returned to her post at the tent of the Church of Nimrodian Protectorites.

Chapter Sixty-Nine

THE DAY PROCEEDED INTO A SNOWMELT AFTERNOON, THE SKY sprinkled with low-hanging clouds whose fleet shadows cast brief interruptions against the fine December sun. This being the final full day of the Revival, the pilgrims who'd traveled the greatest distances (the greatest of those being the Church of the Log Cabin's 300-mile hike all the way from Cairo, Illinois) began dismantling their temporary sanctuaries. Pedestrians wandering the Biblical streets had to dodge the occasional wagon creaking and squeaking past with its somber occupants. These occupants frequently included children who complained loudly that they wanted to stay for the Pitch-Round and why must they always miss the best part.

The Solemnites cheerfully ballyhooed for the attention of those few undecided pilgrims who passed their tent. It was a casual affair, and they were all perfectly satisfied when Auguste eventually poked his head out of the tent and complained that his cheeks were sore from whistling. Poor thing. They should have ended this hours ago. Light the fire, slice the fruitcake, enjoy the last sunlight of 1885.

"Say," said Euphémie, "How many did we get?"

Sister Temperance said, "How many?"

"How many new Solemnites?" said Euphémie. "The Pledge of Conversion, or whatever."

Temperance said, "Zero."

Pansy, who was splayed on her back, dropping morsels of fruitcake into her mouth, said, "Zero?"

"Zero," said Temperance.

"Strange," said Pansy, "I don't feel like a failure."

"I rather enjoyed myself," said Auguste.

And who of this crew could suggest otherwise? They'd done everything the people of Solemn had asked of them. Without frivolity, they'd exposed hundreds of pilgrims to the principles of Solemnity. Whether or not anyone actually embraced these principles, well, that was up to the individuals themselves.

Annie looked about. "Where is everybody?"

The entire Village of Godly Illumination had emptied. Dogs sniffed for morsels of food, licked greasy logs in extinguished firepits.

"They're off to the Pitch-Round, all of them," said Temperance.

Yonder, a trumpet sounded, followed by evangelical hoots and hollers.

Pansy said, "It begins."

The shadows lengthened, and so did a pestering sense of incompletion; the empty village, the impending conclusion of their adventure, the jolly good time that was unfolding a quarter mile from where they had obediently quarantined themselves.

Another cheer drifted in.

Euphémie said, "This is silly."

Annie stood up. "Come, children. We're going to the Pitch-Round. Temperance?"

The pious young woman raised herself from her stool, dusted her skirt. "It's only entertaining if we allow ourselves to be entertained."

Chapter Seventy

THE GREAT STAGE WAS AN ELEVATED WHITEWASHED SEMI-CIRCLE large enough to have accommodated a team of trained elephants, of which there were, sadly, none this day. Constructed by Second Solemnites who were not allowed to witness its use, its planks were lain solidly upon a forest of sawed-off tree trunks that suspended it precisely three biblical cubits above the ground, three cubits being five-feet, three-inches, or, the exact height of Annie Lestables.

Fanning out from the stage was a mindbogglingly huge crowd, no less than three thousand people. For those lucky enough to be within spitting distance of the stage, there were several rows of wooden benches, constructed of split pine. Everyone else had to stand. The ground here was sloping, forming a natural amphitheater, a credit to the Second Solemnites' excellent site planning.

Imagine a condensed baseball diamond, with the Great Stage at home plate and the woods forming a natural outfield wall, and everything in-between filled with eager pilgrims.

At the moment, those pilgrims were watching an elderly, slender black man shuffle onstage. He was dressed in a buckskin suit and a beaverskin hat. Once he'd reached the fore of the stage, he tapped his cane and the audience went silent.

Also at this moment, the Solemnitic emissaries—walking stealthily lest Honora see them—emerged from the woods and merged into the rearmost part of the audience, where the crowd was not so thick.

A nearby woman, dressed in a forest-green friar's frock, and with a hemispherical tonsure shaved into the crown of her head, said to Euphémie, "You haven't missed anything. The convocation took forever. Things are just now about to start for real." She added, "You're a tall one."

From their place at the upper bank of the amphitheater, the stage was perfectly visible.

Seeing the black man on stage, Auguste nudged Pansy's ribs. "There's one."

She said, "It only proves the rule."

§   §   §   §

"I am Reverend P. Wallace Dankum. Welcome to the 1885 All-Tent Revival Pitch-Round!"

This being prior to the invention of public address systems, people knew how to project their voices.

"It is my honor to stand before you as the first Negro ever formally invited to the All-Tent Revival."

From the trees behind our heroes, a voice that sounded suspiciously like that of Harriet Stovepipe cried, "I hope you're getting paid for this, brother!"

Dankum did not hear this.

"Why am I invited to stand before all you?" he asked. "My life has been blessed a thousand times, that's why. I'm formerly the property of Colonel Jefferson Sweet Dankum of Statham County Missouri. After the emancipation, I founded of the Church of Voluntary Servitude. That's right. I'm a free man in bondage to the word of Christ. We welcome reformed chattel of all races and kinships."

"Well, I'll be," muttered much of the audience.

Reverend Dankum continued. "This evening, all domina-tions, sects, and variants of Christianity are invited to this stage to present their doctrinal argument. Understand, friends, that some of the speakers may present their case thru song or play-acting or other forms of self-expression. If this sort of thing doesn't fit with you, the Church of Christ is holding a silent baptism down at the riverbank. I guarantee it won't be crowded."

This last was met with both chuckles and howls. The Reverend, known for his corn-pone humor, was also known to toss the occasional jab.

"The Pitch-Round will conclude at ten o'clock. As always, your final presenters will be the Kentucky Spider-Handlers. Their pastor, Old John Hobbins, couldn't be here this year, on account of last year's accident. So his son, Young John Hobbins will do his best to fill in."

Pansy said, "I see my mother!"

There she was, in her longest, greyest dress, amongst a group of white-clad Friends of the Revival who were carrying with some difficulty four shiny brass contraptions. These, they placed directly in front of the stage. The contraptions resembled small, stubby cannons balanced upon wooden tripods. Honora was clearly in charge of the operation, dictating who should go where with what.

Once the contraptions were placed to Honora's satisfaction, the Friends of the Revival rolled out a wooden barrel, to which they attached eight black hoses, which they connected to the stubby brass cannons. Completed, the whole thing resembled a bizarre, mechanical, four-armed octopus.

Reverend Dankum said, "Let's give a hand to our Revival Friends"

Hands were given.

"As you can see, we've got a special deal this year: stage lights!" To someone offstage, he said, "Is it dark enough yet?"

The answer was affirmative.

"Fire 'em up!" said the Reverend.

Honora re-appeared, carrying an acolyte's brass candlelighter. While a Friend of the Revival frantically turned knobs on the octopus, she ignited the lamps one by one. The stage, which had begun to fall into shadow, now glowed with the light of four white-hot suns casting four unworldly shadow-mimics on the trees behind. Honora hurried out of sight.

Dankum shaded his eyes and bellowed, "Let there be light!"

More hands were given. *Oohs* and *aahs* were exhaled.

"Lordy, those things are *warm!* Everybody ready?"

Yes, everybody was ready.

"Let us bow our heads. Don't worry, I'll keep it short." The crowd emitted a murmur of gratitude.

"Lord Almighty, I ask that you grant us the grace to allow for the slim chance that our neighbor's truth is your truth. Amen."

The crowd uttered their *blessed-bes* and *amens* and *thanks-be-to-Gods* and then the entire assembly raised their heads and resumed their whispered conversations.

With another tap of his cane, Reverend Dankum cried, *"Here, at the 1885 All-Tent Revival, we all pray to the same god!"*

The crowd emitted a joyful noise and glowed with a satisfied gleam. This being the gleam of those who took great pride in the message of racial unity as demonstrated by the All-Tent Revival's willingness to allow a darkie on the Great Stage.

The Reverend performed an old-man version of the softshoe. That perked up the crowd even more. "Guidelines are thus. Three minutes for each representative. Faith healings may be administered only to those with obvious physical deformities. And remember, this is an exhibition, not a competition. There is only one winner, and his name is"—the Reverend consulted a note card—"God."

Righteous agreement from the three-thousand.

"And so, let us welcome...from the Church of the Sanguine Lamb, Mister and Missus Davey Shortner...and their dancing lambs."

As the three-thousand celebrated the official beginning of the Pitch-Round, the Reverend exited the stage on his arthritic knees, supported by a petticoated Friend of the Revival.

The Shortners, white-robed, both bald, lifted two lambs onto the stage. They guided the animals, longlegged, bucking with excitement, to the center of the stage, where Mister Shortner waved a carrot in front of their noses. The lambs, like eager dogs, stood upon their hind legs and danced circles. Pansy and Auguste and the widows shared a look that said, "Isn't this just about the most darling thing?"

Missus Shortner unsheathed a sword—inherited from her Confederate brother, deceased July 9, 1863, Battle of Corydon—held it aloft, screamed rebelliously, and beheaded both of the still-dancing lambs in a single righteous arc. Blood splashed the stage, and those in the front rows, and the gaslights, which vaporized the fluid into pungency.

This did not evoke a single gasp, with the notable exception of the four Solemnites, who gasped, gagged, and shuddered. Among those who noted this was the tonsured woman in the friar's frock who had spoken to them earlier. She turned to Euphémie, "Must be your first time. Pitch-Rounds always commence with the decapitation of livestock. Make a splash, you know?"

Their pitch concluded, the Shortners bowed. Before they exited the stage, Missus Shortner hollered, "Come by the tent tomorrow for a sunrise lamb roast!"

The next act was a nineteen-year-old boy from the Church of Supply and Demand. For three minutes, he recited a poorly rehearsed speech about morality-as-derived-from-profiting-a-man's-soul. Zero decapitations.

Next, a wide-shouldered strongman from the Church of Corporeality staggered onstage with an upright piano strapped to his back. Sweating and straining under this incredible weight, he remained stock-still for three minutes of increasing suspense. Then he squatted, unstrapped the piano, and, without a word, staggered off stage, leaving the piano where it sat.

Several Friends of the Revival appeared and hurriedly pushed the piano out of the way to the left side of the stage. There was much slipping in lamb's blood. A piano bench was produced and they placed it in front of the instrument, in case someone might want to play it later.

Overseeing this was Sister Honora. Even from this distance, Pansy could sense her mother's great discomfort.

Chapter Seventy-One

AFTER A FURTHER HOUR OF PERFORMANCES—HIGHLIGHTS INCLUDING phony Jesus losing his diaper halfway thru his attempt to break the record for fastest reenactment of the stations of the cross, followed immediately by a baptism that concluded with an entire barrel of milk being spilled on stage—Reverend Dankum introduced Jimrod and Resina Cotton from the Church of Nimrodian Protectorites. "They all gonna demonstrate the powers of blessed cotton, or some such."

The presentation was only a mild failure, with Jimrod receiving an arrow in the sternum. It barely penetrated to the bone, but Jimrod screamed to holy hell so the crowd loved it, with noticeable enthusiasm coming from the Solemnitic contingent in deep centerfield.

After Jimrod had dislodged the arrow, but before the applause had died down, Resina stepped forth and shouted, "Blessed be the cotton of Nimrod." She cast a mischievous glance at Reverend Dankum. "Now, if you all don't mind, I've a favor. There's a little boy I'd like to insert into the program, if he's amongst us this evening. You may have heard him earlier in the village. The little Solemnite who whistles like an angel."

Apparently, a lot of people had heard him, for a great cheer went up.

"Could we spare three minutes for a little boy?"

More cheering.

Reverend Dankum, who had been preparing to introduce a squad of vegetarians on velocipedes, took a look at his note card, took a look at the crowd, and thought to himself, Aw, fuck it. Aloud, he said, "Brothers and sisters! What say you?"

Feverish *huzzahs* and *amens* and *hallelujahs*.

"Bring him up!" acquiesced Dankum.

Back in centerfield, Temperance was horrified. Three thousand pilgrims were ready to drag the little Solemnite boy onstage, if only they knew where he was.

He was hiding behind his mother's skirt.

Lord only knew whose hide Honora would have if somehow Auguste were recognized by this whistle-mad crowd.

Poor Honora, she'd had a rough go of it these past three days.

Where had she gotten off to, anyway?

Chapter Seventy-Two

HONORA WAS IN THE WOODS, HAVING FLED THE PITCH-ROUND AFTER being confronted backstage by a half-dozen Amish Extremists from nearby Switzerland County who vigorously objected to the installation of artificial stage lighting. Honora had nearly gotten things cooled down—in spite of her inability to speak Swiss-German-Amish—when things flared up again, thanks to the peacemaking efforts of the same kid who a few days earlier had been pestering her to organize a Revival-wide pray-in to worsen the weather. The kid proposed a compromise wherein the assembled masses would pray for God to extend the day by four hours, thereby eliminating the need for artificial lighting. This led to a full on multi-lingual dispute—refereed by Sister Honora—between the weather boy and the Amish extremists. Things were further escalated when a well-meaning Monk of the Order of Orderliness tried to calm things down by introducing Robert's Rules of Order into the debate. His motion to table the discussion until the sun had actually gone down—because, who knows, maybe the sun *won't* go down today—was countered by Sister Honora, who declared, "I move that all of you stop acting like spoiled deviants!"

Neither motion was seconded.

Disgusted and demoralized and seeking to recover some sense of composure, Honora had immediately marched into the forest behind the stage. She'd intended to take a short break from the inglorious celebration of intermingling truths, lean her forehead against a tree, perhaps.

But she just kept walking.

Murmuring a Möbius strip of prayer that petitioned the Lord to grant her the solemnity to wield His power to tame these celebrating heathens, she walked under leafless trees, her boots pressing into the soft ground.

Chapter Seventy-Three

PANSY, UNLIKE TEMPERANCE, WAS NOT THE LEAST HORRIFIED AT THE prospect of Auguste showing off his skills at the Pitch-Round. Although it was counter to Sister Honora's instructions, Pansy knew that her mother would understand once she saw three thousand pilgrims in the thrall of Solemnity.

So she raised her voice, "Right here folks! Auguste Lestables! Church of Solemn. You heard him in a tent, hear him on the Great Stage!"

This ignited a spark...

"By golly, if that ain't him."

"Say!"

"Come on kid!"

"The Little Whistler!"

...which turned into a conflagration...

"LIT-TLE WHIS-TLER! LIT-TLE WHIS-TLER! LIT-TLE WHIS-TLER! LIT-TLE WHIS-TLER! LIT-TLE WHIS-TLER!"

The Solemnites were soon trapped within a bubble of happy, clapping revivalists. Temperance prayed for divine intervention. Annie and Euphémie shrugged.

Pansy brought Auguste close to her, forehead to forehead. "This your calling. You have to answer."

Auguste managed only to reply, "Bif, bif."

Pansy placed a folded sheet of paper in his hand. "This is for you." She kissed his cheek, and then a sea of hands ferried Auguste away from the people he loved.

The sun had set.

Chapter Seventy-Four

AFTER AN INDELICATE RIDE, THE HANDS DEPOSITED AUGUSTE ON THE front lip of the Great Stage. He blinked into the hissing limelights.

The stage had begun to resemble an elevated slaughterhouse; the whitewashed boards were slick with lamb's blood and spilt baptismal milk. It smelled like sin.

The three-thousand became silent.

Reverend Dankum's face peeked over the edge, stage right. *Get a move-on, kid, I got a schedule to follow.*

Auguste bowed his head.

Thinking this was a prayer, the audience obediently followed suit.

Far away, in centerfield, Pansy said to Annie, "Does he look nervous to you?"

Annie said, "He'll be fine, as long as your mother doesn't strangle him."

The helpless boy was staring at the note Pansy had just given him. The handwriting was not hers, not at all. Pansy's script was upright, round, and sloppy; these words leaned at a precise forty-five degree angle, narrow and elegant. It may have been Pansy who'd held the pencil, but her hand had been guided by a ghost, a ghost with an imprecise understanding of French.

> Ma chèr Auguste.
>
> Tu es bonne garçon. Ne t'inquiet pas à mon accorde. À ce moment, tu dois être fort. Écoute ton père. Écoute attentivement. Le son est musical. La musique est partout, et c'est bonne. Reste toi-même, sans peur et sans reproche.
>
> Ta Bonne Sœur Gravity
>
> Post Scriptum : L'oursette est bonne aussi.

Or, *en anglais:*

> My dear Auguste.
>
> You're good boy. Don't worry yourself on my account. Right now, you have to be strong. Listen to your father. Listen carefully. Sound is music. Music is everywhere, and it is good. Remain yourself, fearless and beyond reproach.
>
> Sister Gravity
>
> PS: The she-bear is also good.

The majority of the audience had bowed their heads, and so they didn't see Auguste scrunch his eyebrows together as he revisited the evening in Finoula's tent. Uncanny ambience, snowflakes on canvas, fizzle of candlewax, synchronized respirations, the rumble-drone of blood flowing thru his ears, branches groaning in the wind, and the moment when his father's insubstantial lips had formed an O and ghostly wind had fused all these non-silences into a song both deliberate and kind.

Arthur Lestables' ghost had whistled an autobiography of air, of the swirlings and smashenings and bashenings of the atmosphere itself, of the gravity that ties us to the firmament, the heat that causes our breath to steam on cold wet nights, the magical force that aligned the compass needle to the north; it was a destruction of frontiers, a sewing-together of happenstance, and it was the final confession of Arthur Lestables.

> *Son, I was wrong. Reason can guide, but it cannot lead. It can describe, but it cannot be the thing it describes. It is a measuring stick, nothing more. I am a phantom, son, and nothing more.*
>
> *Things are far more complicated than I wanted them to be. Such is the price of wisdom.*

Auguste placed the note into his right trouser pocket and extracted from his left pocket the tooth-whistles. He raised his head, and, in a voice heard throughout the amphitheater, he said, "Amen."

The audience raised their bowed heads and sent forth a great *hurrah.*

Auguste slid the whistles inside his cheeks.

With three thousand pairs of eyes eagerly trained upon the Little Whistler, none saw the shadowy, yellow-eyed figure that crept out of the woods and slunk into the rearmost portion of the crowd, not ten yards from the Solemnites.

Chapter Seventy-Five

"Honora will be most displeased," said Sister Temperance, watching Auguste on the distant stage.

Annie said, "I haven't seen her since the piano guy."

"She's probably gone to fetch an axe," said Euphémie.

"Hush," said Pansy. "He's starting."

Auguste was strong. He was fearless. He was the son of Arthur Lestables, and of Annie Lestables. From his lips came the opening notes of a song no one had ever heard, and which no one would ever hear again.

The shadowy figure moved swiftly, its yellow eyes locked on Auguste. It pushed aside those in its path. Those whom it touched recoiled from the withered fingers, the stumbling walk, the stench, the absurd syllables that hissed from its blistered lips.

The agitation drew Euphémie's attention. Just over there, someone was plowing people aside in order to get a closer view. She elbowed Annie. "That's not very Christian."

Annie said, "Quiet."

Euphémie said, "Seriously, something weird's happening."

The commotion passed to their left, stirring ripples of disgust.

"See?" said Euphémie.

"What goes on?" said Pansy, who, as with most other people, lacked the advantage of Euphémie's height.

Euphémie said, "A maniac is running toward the stage."

Pansy's face became solemn.

"Probably just a drunk," said Annie.

"Or," said Sister Temperance, "Sister Honora."

Pansy clenched her fists.

Euphémie stood on tiptoes. "Definitely not Honora. More like an unwashed hermit. Animalistic, even."

Pansy cried, "It's the werebear! He's after Auguste! WE MUST STOP HIM!" She plunged in the mass of legs before her.

Temperance cried, "Pansy, no!"

Annie cried, *"Suis-le!"*

Annie and Euphémie and Temperance cast themselves forward, unsure whether they were following Pansy or charging toward a madman.

This was all accompanied by the sound of Auguste blowing thru a pair of cowteeth.

Most of the crowd had no idea.

It was as if the whistles were playing themselves. Auguste had only to open his mouth and breathe. No, it was as if someone else were playing them. No, it was as if each of the whistles were being played by a separate entity.

His right cheek ejected a sequence of notes not found on any musical staff. Meanwhile, his left cheek structured its harmony into a series of notes that surrounded, contained, and sustained those coming from his right cheek.

Sounds became harmonies and harmonies became melodies and melodies became harmonies and all of it was musical.

The creature ran faster, shoved harder, grew more manic. Those who saw it shrieked and backed away. Few did see it, so thoroughly had Auguste captivated the crowd.

Pansy was causing her own, lesser, disturbance as she chased behind the creature, pushing between legs, crying, "Let me pass! There's a werebear!"

Several steps back of Pansy, Annie called for her to slow down.

Pansy yelled back, "Run faster!"

A churning dream took hold behind Auguste's half-closed eyes. Disembodied ideas rising to the surface; ideas formless, buoyed by reason, consumed by whirling hubris; opalescent threads of spray flung in great arcs, collapsing in scribbles upon maddened waves, smoothing the froth into dimpled mirrors; reflected sun stretched into ellipses, dividing into pairs, merging, melting, blinding; a decoherence animated by toothwhistle vibrations.

My father is in my right cheek, thought Auguste, and Sister Gravity is within the left. Reason and wisdom, churning, smoothing, binding, melting the shape of the sun.

I am within the sun and I am within the thread. I am as the fat of the lamb and I am as the wool. And from my mouth is manifest Gomar's allegorical model of the religious universe.

With a twitch of his head, Auguste dismissed both his father and Sister Gravity and sent from his O-shaped lips a searing ball of musical lard constrained by its own fatty skin.

Searing, musical geysers cracked the crust, rose as high as gravity would allow, and then fell as prismatic rain to the tallowy surface from whence they had escaped and of which they were now becoming.

For the majority of the audience who were unaware that a feral madman was bee-lining toward the stage, this new turn of the song was positively euphoric.

Chapter Seventy-Six

SISTER HONORA HAD FLED THE PITCH-ROUND, ABDICATED HER DUTY, and now her boots had carried her to the Village of Godly Illumination, to the threshold of the Solemnitic tent.

The tent was abandoned. They had disobeyed her.

"I believed I could lead strangers from temptation. I couldn't even tame my own flock. Not even my own daughter."

The evening was now deep in shadow. Discarded leaflets shifted back and forth in a gentle wind. A teat-heavy dog approached, squatted next to the tent, and splashed piss on the canvas wall.

Honora lifted a cold stone from the fire pit and chucked it. The dog sidestepped without interrupting its piss.

Another stone, another miss. The dog now flopped to its side and began licking its crotch.

Honora hurled another stone. This one struck its target. The dog yelped and ran away to the litter of pups she had birthed earlier that morning.

Sister Honora left the campsite and started south, toward the Chariot of Fire. Rather than take the cleared road that led directly to the wheel, she entered the woods, desiring to circle around and arrive at the awful machine from the west, unseen.

Chapter Seventy-Seven

THE FERAL MADMAN WAS CLAMBERING OVER THE WOODEN BENCHES AT the front of the stage.

Several yards behind, Pansy was caught in a mass of elderly pilgrims with poor eyesight and frightful balance. As politely as possible, she navigated the canes and confusion, hopping up and down to shout the name of her friend.

"AUGUSTE!! AUGUSTE!!"

Pansy? Not possible. She was in the back with the others. Close your eyes, Auguste, focus on the great ball of lard.

Sounds of human struggle, grunting.

Focus, Auguste.

"THE WEREBEAR!!!"

He ceased his whistling. His right hand slid into his pocket, squeezed Sister Gravity's ghostly note.

Be solemn, he thought. Do not fear the she-bear.

Standing small in the center of the whitewashed, blood-and-milk-wet stage, he could not see his friend in the great darkness that lay beyond the hissing lamps. An angular shape emerged from between two of the lamps and stood itself directly before the stage, a skeleton wrapped in skin and rotted trousers and a tattered wool sweater.

The werebear is a preposterous notion, thought Auguste.

The emaciated creature had twigs in its hair, a prominent Adam's apple, and a patchy growth of beard. Faced with a three-cubit climb, it paused for a moment, drummed its fingers on the lip of the stage.

The werebear is not a werebear, thought Auguste.

The werebear leered at Auguste with murderous yellow eyes. The lips pulled back to reveal a set of yellow teeth. With an inelegant hop, it thrusted itself onto the stage. In doing so, one of its feet struck a limelight and sent it to the ground.

Thoughtful pilgrims immediately snuffed the flames.

Auguste let slip a gasp that was converted by his toothwhistles into a musical question mark. The song was over, its final euphoric waves vanishing into the ether as the crowd whimpered ecstatic moans.

The werebear stood before him, only inches away. It reached forth with its talons, met Auguste's brown eyes with its own.

"*Mon dieu,*" said Auguste, his voice accompanied by a duet of whistles.

"*Mon frère,*" seethed Junior Deplouc, the son of Euphémie and Henri Deplouc, he whose shoulders Arthur Lestables had balanced upon before his neck was snapped by a noose tied by the Vicar of Sanvisa, he whom Auguste had left trapped in the Deplouc mausoleum all those distant months past.

Chapter Seventy-Eight

"You are not here," said Auguste. "You are in France."

"*Parle français, pas cette langue de merde, connard!*"

Auguste switched to French. "You haven't been eating well."

"I dine on vengeance."

"It was you who stole my whistle," said Auguste, who still had the cowteeth stuffed adorably in his cheeks.

"You left me to rot with my father's corpse."

"Why did you return it?" said Auguste. "The tooth."

"It only made small noises. Piece of trash. So I rubbed it on my nuts and dropped it in the snow. I was watching when you put it into your mouth this morning."

The Little Whistler was arguing with a half-crazed French hillbilly in a foreign language; this was a bit much for the audience, especially after the abrupt conclusion to that lovely song. More whistling, by God. Sounds of displeasure floated over the limelights. Reverend Dankum slapped the stage and pointed to his wrist, international sign language for, *Get this thing over with boys.*

Auguste said, "And you wish to murder me."

"To satisfy the memory of my father, yes."

"Would you be satisfied to learn that I believe my father's actions were misguided?"

"Fuck you."

Junior's eyes were awfully yellow.

Auguste said, "Have you been eating enough carrots?"

Junior said, "My father is dead. My mother is a *putain*. I am a piece of *merde*." Foamy saliva oozed over his bottom lip and into the soft hairs that covered his chin. "I chased. I scavenged. I devoured rotted creatures and bitter plants until my stomach swelled so I resembled a pregnant wench. Feverish and delirious, I withstood visions of a world stretched into foulness beyond imagination. I am a wretched animal. And now, before this assembly of idiots, I will strangle you."

Reverend Dankum slapped the stage again. "Get them idjits outta here!" The Friends of the Festival were nowhere to be seen.

A narrow column of wind fought to escape Junior's phlegmy bronchia. His spine undulated and he spat a bright green blob at Auguste's feet. Junior raised his hands toward the younger boy's throat.

Auguste stepped back. "You would kill me in front of your own mother?"

Junior sneered. "And yours, as well."

Chapter Seventy-Nine

FOR MANY YEARS, THE VILLAGE OF SOLEMN HAD COUNTED AMONGST its population a shoemaker of great skill. Brother Discretion had crafted the footwear for every one of the town's eighty-odd citizens. Solid, remarkable footwear of leather and brass and cork and wood and, lately, soled with carved rubber strips imported from Brazil. Every one of these shoes was waterproofed with a concoction of beeswax and goatbutter that Brother Discretion lovingly applied as his last act before placing the shoes on a shelf where they would await their inevitable destruction under the weight of yet another member of this depressing cult.

Solemnity in all things.

The shoes he'd made for Sister Honora were amongst the finest of his creations; ankle-high with buckskin uppers assembled in his own variation on the Adelaide style. He'd been heartbroken to see them leave his shop. His only solace: at least Honora wasn't the type to go traipsing around the woods.

⁂

It had been many, many months since Honora had traipsed around the woods, and she was grateful for Brother Discretion's handiwork as she trod the forest's shadow-safe patches of snow, mud, twigs, and squirrel bones.

In a few more steps, she would veer left to exit the forest into the glade that the Second Solemnites had cleared for the great wheel. But the land began to slope upward, and she knew she had lost her way.

There was smoke in the air. None to see, but to smell, and she could not resist following her nose over just one more small hill before she turned back west.

She ascended the hillock directly to a clearing that led to the base of a larger hill. She recognized this place, even though she hadn't been here in nearly twenty years. Trees had grown, vines had crept, rust had advanced. But the rocks hadn't moved, and the wreckage remained.

Brother Discretion's shoes had carried Sister Honora to the site of the mine explosion that had killed her father.

She had been eleven years old, floating bark boats down a creek when she'd heard the explosion, a crack of thunder that reverberated between the hills, followed by a rain of pulverized stone. She'd rushed to the mine—for that was where the sound had come from. Others had gotten there before her. They wandered dazedly in the proliferating cloud of smoke and dust, seeking some evidence of human life.

Sister Honora—still known by her birth-name, Effie Bell—asked one of these dusty apparitions if anyone had seen her father.

"We've only seen parts of people."

Then she'd spotted the man in the tree. She thought he was dead, but his eyes opened. He coughed, wept, pleaded for mercy. He cursed the man who'd caused the explosion. "The juggling fool." He was speaking of Effie Bell's father.

The ground was warm under her bare feet as she watched the

man die.

The tree was still there, the limb still black with blood.

The smell, and, oh, the smell was exactly the same. Coal smoke and despair. That horrible day. The grief that shook her, this is why the place had been declared Maximum Taboo. It was she who'd insisted on it.

"Ma'am?" said a rustic voice. Honora twisted and saw a boy dressed in hillbilly clothes, bare feet, leaves in his hair. A long-barreled musket leaned upon his shoulder. Dead squirrels hung from a rope strung around his waist.

Honora touched her cheeks to see if she'd been crying. She had not.

"You oughtn't be here, young man."

"I been hunting squirrels. It's such a nice day."

"It's evening now," said Honora.

"You're one of them that don't allow for laughter."

"I am Solemn, yes."

"Well, you ought to get on. There's a bair lives up in these parts."

"The bear's asleep."

"Don't you bet on it. Nice days like this, a bair's likely to think spring has sprang."

"Would you kindly point me the way to the Chariot of Fire?"

"Pardon?"

"Also known as a Pleasure Wheel. The great wooden circle that was recently installed by a man and a boy."

"Oh, that thing." He pointed. "Straight thataway. Would you like for me to accompany you?"

"I'll be fine. I grew up in these woods."

"I'd just hate for something to happen to a nice lady like you."

"You're very kind, but no."

"As you please." The boy did not argue; he was expected home soon. "If you walk good, you'll make it before it gets altogether dark."

Sister Honora considered for a moment the meaning of *walk good*, then she considered the boy's bare feet.

"One moment, young man."

Standing first on one leg and then the other, Sister Honora removed her shoes, which she tossed to the boy. He caught them, pleased with this gift from this strange lady. "You sure? Your feet gonna get cold."

"Such a thoughtful boy," said Honora. "Go feed your family."

He tugged the shoes onto his dirty feet. "I've met a mess o' people, and ain't never one of them gave me a pair of shoes."

Sister Honora was already walking good in the direction of straight thataway.

Chapter Eighty

EIGHT MONTHS PRIOR, AUGUSTE HAD SURVIVED A SKIRMISH WITH Junior Deplouc, not by overpowering him with his fists, but by smacking him in the face with a shovel.

In Auguste's favor that night at the graveyard, Junior had been drunk on strawberry wine, and Auguste, the grave-digger, had been awfully strong for an eleven-year-old.

Over the intervening months, Auguste had reverted to a typical eleven-year-old, strengthwise. Meanwhile, Junior had suffered a far greater decline: sun-charred skin, shuddering ribcage, scabs on his lips, and his fingernails had grown long and yellow, like shards of butterscotch.

For all Auguste knew, Junior had swum across the ocean and walked himself eight hundred American miles to get here. Impossible, of course; no human could ever manage such a thing; but this thing before him, it was barely human.

Junior's skeletal hands clenched around Auguste's throat, fingernails indenting the soft skin. Auguste thrashed and grabbed at Junior's wrists. The two boys toppled and writhed in sheep's blood and cow's milk. Junior grunted like a piglet. Whistle squeaks emerged from Auguste's mouth.

Reverend Dankum hollered, "Knock it off!"

"Let 'em fight it out!" shouted someone in the crowd. General agreement, with vociferous encouragement from the Sons of Dodo.

Reverend Dankum gave up. "Fuck this." He pulled out his note card, ripped it in half, and marched into the night.

Despite whatever miseries he had endured these past months, Junior's grip remained solid. Auguste wrestled and grabbed and kicked at his bony frame but the hands did not loosen, and Auguste grew lightheaded.

Junior elbowed himself up to straddle Auguste's prostrate body. He was sitting now on his stomach, hands and fingers spasmodically clenching his throat.

The Little Whistler gurgled, went limp. First one, then the other toothwhistle slid out of his mouth and clunked on the stage.

Chapter Eighty-One

Pansy had lost her patience with the white-hairs in the front rows. She elbowed a delicate codger out of her way, ran past the limelights, balled her fists, and flew onto the stage, screaming, "To hell! To hell!" A blur of dress and skinny limbs, she flung herself upon the werebear's back and pummeled until her knuckles were bruised.

Junior paid her no heed.

She cried, "Burn, thou beast of Gévaudan!"

Junior paused. He knew that word, *Gévaudan*, and he knew what stories it conjured. This silly little girl believed he was a *loup-garou*, a werewolf. Absurd—and wonderful! Junior would prove to her just what a beast he was.

He slammed Auguste's head against the stage, released his fingers from the boy's throat, and then spun and brandished those same fingers at Pansy, who, on seeing Junior's butterscotch claws, attempted to flee. Before she could do so, Junior raised one of his booted feet and kicked her in the middle of the back. Pansy fell forward several paces until she collided with the piano that the strongman had earlier deposited onstage. Her face struck the keyboard, raising a devilish chord.

• • •

Which of these imps ought Junior to dispatch first? He'd come here specifically for Auguste. But one mustn't forget one's audience. The expanse of American dimwits deserved a proper scare. Whose death would horrify them the most? The little girl's, obviously. Save her for last, then.

Oh, but what's this? A small, airborne woman. Change of plans.

Flung by Euphémie, Annie landed onstage and immediately scrambled to Auguste. Euphémie followed, less dramatically, and marched toward the madman.

"Hello, Mother."

Euphémie froze. There was no conceivable circumstance in which her son ought to be within two thousand miles of this place.

Junior bared his teeth, showing the gap where his father had long ago knocked out one of his canines with a doorframe.

"You should not be here," said Euphémie.

"And yet."

In two strides, Euphémie was upon him, smacking him about the ears while he flailed with his fingernails. Pansy joined in, grabbing one of Junior's feet with the intent of twisting it off his leg as if it were a chicken's head.

A cheer went up. The crowd wanted to this play out to a natural conclusion, schedule be damned, and they were firmly in the camp of anyone fighting on the side of the Little Whistler.

Junior grabbed his mother by the hair and flung her to the stage next to Pansy. He took lurching steps toward Annie and Auguste, dragging Pansy behind. The pestersome girl refused to release his ankle.

With a casual motion, Junior pushed Annie aside, such a small creature was she. He knelt and once again wrapped his hands around Auguste's throat. Pansy redirected her efforts to prying loose those fingers.

Junior maintained his grip, even as Annie began stomping his calves. He could feel the life squirming out of Auguste's neck. It was time, now, to recite the lines of verse he'd carefully rehearsed on all those cold nauseating nights he'd spent in the wet lonely places of America.

Pour la mort de mon père
À cause de ma mère
Je t'enverrai en enfer

He'd expected this to send his combatants howling away in terror. Instead, they acted as if they hadn't even heard. No one had ever listened to Junior Deplouc.

Pansy gave up on dislodging his grip and instead began tearing his fingernails off one-by-one.

Euphémie now joined the melee. Limbs clawed, torsos twisted, fingers squeezed. In the midst of this, Auguste had gone as limp as a rag.

The crowd of three thousand was on their tiptoes. The crazed beast-boy was being beaten simultaneously by an eleven-year-old dervish girl and two ferocious women, one of whom was—gee whiz—awfully tall. And none of this was having any noticeable effect.

Like a slow-moving dust devil, the tangled frenzy migrated stage-left, drawing near to the piano.

From the mass of wrestling bodies, an arm emerged. At one end of that arm was a hand. The hand groped until it clasped a leg of the piano's bench. The other end of the arm was attached to Euphémie, who now rose, wielding the bench with fists whose vessels flowed with pure maternal rage. Seeing what was to come, Annie and Pansy scampered away, their palms and knees making pink splashes of the spilled milk-blood.

Junior's hands were still clenched around Auguste's throat. Listen to me, ignore me; either way, you shall die.

Euphémie glowed in the limelights, a goddess colossus towering over her mad spawn. She raised the piano bench and, with a great cry, flung it.

Chapter Eighty-Two

DENNIS DENNISON AND GOMAR HIMMELBAUM WERE UNHITCHING the draft horses from the wheel engine when Sister Honora walked barefooted out of the woods and into the light that shone from the Pleasure Wheel's sixteen lovely lanterns.

At the sight of The Woman Who Hated Fun, Mr. Dennison dived behind a barrel, and so it was a very nervous Gomar who was left to confront Sister Honora as she strode directly toward him.

"Ma'am, oughtn't you be at the Pitch-Round?"

"I ought to," said Honora, stepping over horse turds without even looking, "except I've recently discovered that I'm not suited for Pitch-Rounds. Or," she added, "for tent revivals."

"I wouldn't think you're suited for those sorts of things, neither," said Gomar.

Honora said, "From your expression, it's clear that you are wondering at my intentions. Do I intend to burn you out, perhaps?"

"Since you've no torch, I'm inclined to think otherwise. But, yes, given your prior interactions with Mr. Dennison, and given your stated feelings about the wheel, I am mightily curious."

"And wary?"

"A sprinkle of that." Gomar greatly desired for Mr. Dennison to unhide himself and kindly ask this righteous woman to be on her way.

"I, too, am curious and wary," said Sister Honora. "Mostly curious."

The woman who had once been called Effie Bell directed her gaze toward the Pleasure Wheel: timbers of pine; great wooden gears; sixteen flickering lanterns.

"Curious how?" said Gomar.

"I wish," said Sister Honora, "to ride it."

Dennis Dennison stood up from behind the barrel. "That'll be one ha'penny."

Chapter Eighty-Three

THE PIANO BENCH STRUCK JUNIOR IN THE FACE. HIS HANDS UNWOUND from Auguste's throat and he thudded to the blood-milk stage.

The three-thousand heartily approved.

Annie crouched next to Auguste, caressed his sweated brow. He hacked, coughed. His color reverted to the normal pinkish hue of a slightly unwashed, somewhat dazed child.

Euphémie stood over her own son, fingers clenching and unclenching. Junior had curled into a fetal ball. His temple was bleeding and one hand moved to cover his broken nose. His victory was gliding away. And he was in a great deal of pain.

Pansy began landing kicks on his rib cage. "Demon!" *oof* "Fiend!" *oof* "Incubus!" *oof*.

Euphémie lifted the girl by the collar and set her away from Junior. "I shall handle it. This abomination is only my son."

Pansy rushed in for one more kick. "Sorry," she said, before retreating.

Euphémie hissed at Junior, "It astonishes me that something so disgusting spent nine months inside my body."

Pus dripped from Junior's right eye. "I know what you did, Mother. I seen you fucking that woman."

Euphémie paused.

Junior said, "On the smoking mountain; the one with the broken metal. *You were rubbing your titties on her face!*"

So he'd been watching them.

Junior pushed himself upright. Blood filled his adolescent moustache and dripped into his teeth. He reached into his pocket, pulled out a small lump of shriveled, dried meat; the insult, the reminder.

"Regard," he spewed. He spun toward Annie. "Regard, Madame Lestables, my gift for you." He tossed it and it bounced off her sternum and landed in a puddle.

Annie looked at it, uncomprehendingly.

"Your husband's silver tongue, severed while he hung, languidly defaced, a gift of bitter taste." This rhyme had come to him spontaneously, quite good, he thought. As with his previous effort, it went unacknowledged.

Junior licked his lips. "*Ma chère* Annie, did you ever wonder *why* my mother's fingers got broke? Remember her fingers? Father found out what she'd been doing with them is why. Madame Vignolles' granddaughter—remember her?—saw the two of you frolicking in the pond—you know the one. And Madame Vignolle told Papa all about it. Poking and floating you were, she said. So he snapped Mother's fingers like bird legs. *Comprenez-vous?* It was *your* perversions that forced my father to break my mother's fingers; it was those broke fingers that inspired your vile husband to drown my father, who, by the way, was a *very* good swimmer; and the murder of my father led to your husband swinging from a tree. And now I'm here. It was *you* that caused all this."

Annie raised her eyes to Euphémie. Euphémie tilted her head, offered a hint of a shrug. *For you, I'd do it all again.*

Annie responded with a look of pure adoration.

To Junior, Euphémie said, "I hate you."

He drew back his arm and punched his mother in the stomach.

Euphémie crumpled backward, gulping. Annie abandoned Auguste and rushed toward her lover; Pansy quickly took Annie's place next to Auguste.

The three-thousand witnesses crowded closer.

Chapter Eighty-Four

Sister Honora was safely installed in the wooden gondola at the bottom of the Pleasure Wheel.

"Close your eyes," said Dennison. He chirped the horses into motion. "It's more pleasurable thataway."

Honora obeyed. The horses snorted chilly air and began their circle. The slack went out of the harnesses, the drive gears synchronized, and the Pleasure Wheel lifted Sister Honora toward the heavens.

Dennison said, "They still closed?"

They were, but Honora didn't bother saying so. Being lifted in this manner, it reminded her of the motion of the *Isère*, except there wasn't an unfathomable ocean below.

Up, now, and over, and she was an autumn leaf, lazing earthward.

Mr. Dennison and Gomar were prepared at any moment for her to call upon God to once again render the wheel asunder, or, at the least, to berate them as joy-mongers. Instead, when she'd completed her first revolution, she said, with her eyes still shut, "Make it go faster."

Dennison clucked the horses to a spritely walk. After another revolution, Honora said, "Faster."

Dennison brought the horses to a trot. He'd given Gomar strict orders to never even think about doing something so reckless; it was a sure way to break one of the horses' necks. The wheel spun, clunking gears, wood squeaking on wood.

Sister Honora began to anticipate when her hair would float or when it would sink to her shoulders, or when, at the apex, the Revival noises would reach from beyond the trees and into her ears.

Her mouth whispered a vague memory from her days as Effie Bell.

Love not pleasure more than God,
It was for thee he suffered pain;
Know thee why he spilt his blood;
Wouldst thee have him bleed in vain?

"Faster!" she demanded. Dennison raised the horses to a canter. The wheel had absolutely no business moving so quickly, and it groaned and clattered as if to make this obvious to anyone with ears.

Another round, head thrown back. Honora could no longer tell up from down, no longer cared to know. Full voice, eyes clamped shut, fireworks in her skull.

In fairest land, all lands excelling,
Seat of pleasures, and of torture;
Venus, here, would choose her dwelling,
Forsaking all her solemn orchards.

Gomar said, "Ought we to slow it down? I think she's having a seizure."

"Nah, kid," said Mr. Dennison. "What she's having is called a personal ecstatic epiphany. Happens more often than you'd expect. I first witnessed the phenomenon at a log-rolling demonstration back in Mont—BOLLOCKS!"

An overly-stressed gear jumped out of its grooves, tried to crawl atop its geminic twin, squeezing and stressing the wood-fiber until it began to steam.

The machine locked up, nearly throwing Sister Honora from her seat, and dislodging fifteen of the sixteen lanterns that hung from the wheel's eight gondolas. The lights fell to the ground and spilled their flame and oil.

"God-dammit!" shouted Mr. Dennison.

Gomar called upward, "You okay, Miss?"

From her perch at the very top of the wheel, Honora replied, "I'm entirely unbroken. But there is a fire." She pointed at the scattered broken lanterns. "And another. Oh, and more."

"On it!" Gomar hurried to tend to the blazes.

Mr. Dennison confirmed that his horses were not injured, then tilted his neck to Honora. "We'll get you down, ma'am, lickety-split."

Honora acknowledged this with a jaunty wave. She began rocking back and forth in her chair. The moon had by now risen, a grey glow behind the soiled clouds. In its meager light, and at this vantage, Honora was able to look upon the checkerboard of grey, empty tents that made up the Village of Godly Illumination. A vacant failure.

She twisted south to face the circles of Solemn. The chapel's windows were aglow. This was December thirty-first; she was missing Reverend Steadfast's year-end sermon on the Inevitable Passing of Time. She did not regret this.

Earlier, she had been singing. She did not regret this either.

Turning north again, the amphitheater and the Great Stage were obscured by the forest, but the misted air glowed orange above the debauchery.

The breeze. The sputter of flame in the single lantern that remained hanging off the left side of her gondola. A break in the clouds, and the waning moon shone. For the first time in ages, Sister Honora allowed herself to experience delight.

Then came a great, monstrous howl, followed by three thousand tiny, horrified screams.

Chapter Eighty-Five

THE SAME MOONLIGHT THAT SHONE ON HONORA SWEPT OVER THE Pitch-Round. With all the madness on the Great Stage, it went largely unnoticed, and then the clouds closed up and it was gone.

It had been enough.

Junior groaned, twitched, spasmed. His nose turned black and shiny, his teeth extended from his gums, his fingernails—broken off earlier by Pansy—clawed out of his fingertips, and black hairs spilled out of his every pore.

Pansy checked a quick glance to Auguste.

They'd been right.

With a deft movement, the creature scooped Auguste out of Pansy's grip and, holding him under the armpits, raised him in the air. The creature swayed like a drunken willow. It sniffed Auguste's lolling head and then it spread its jaws.

Annie Lestables of Sanvisa, France would not stand for this.

"*LAISSE-LE TRANQUILLE!*"

The creature—Junior Deplouc, werebear, world-traveler, whatever it was—raised an ear. A string of saliva slid from its lower jaw and splashed loudly on the wet stage.

"What the fuck is wrong with you," said Annie, "that you would..." She couldn't utter the words.

Eat her boy, thought the brain inside the creature's skull. The mother wants to know why I would eat her boy. The answer is hunger. The answer is always hunger. I am emptiness. I am the void, with teeth. I am the grave that devoured the shovel that dug me. I smell the rage, and the rage listens. It hears my creaking heart, the tiny bubbles bursting within my skull.

A wind rises, a savage, grinding howl, like a millstone dragged over four thousand miles of bones, beaten and beatific and beastly.

A new hunger is awakened.

It is displeased.

It is the she-bear.

She exploded from the woods behind the stage, a thunderbolt of black fur. She crossed the clearing with two graceful bounds. With a third, she landed onstage. For one exceedingly brief moment, she stood on her hind legs, arms raised, jaws wide.

But her calloused black feet found no purchase on the wet surface. She spun a circle, one arm raised skyward, as if she were thrusting forth a handful of flame, the other arm clutched to her breast for balance. A whirling statue of black fur. An ear, an ear, an ear.

Her feet went out and she fell bottom-first and slid into Junior, who still held Auguste.

Three thousand spectators and four citizens of Solemn looked on as the collision of three-eared bear, Junior, and Auguste glided off the edge and tumbled three biblical cubits to the ground below.

The audience finally understood. It was time to panic.

Chapter Eighty-Six

A HALF MILE DISTANT, PERCHED ATOP THE PLEASURE WHEEL, Honora cried, "Something horrible has happened!"

"A trifling!" shouted Mr. Dennison. "We'll have you down in a jiffy. Gomar! Fetch the ladder!"

"But the fires," said Gomar, still trying to quell the mingling conflagrations of the fifteen broken kerosene lanterns. He stomped madly as flames climbed atop one another, swallowing air, flickering shadows.

"Not *me*," cried Honora, "the Pitch-Round! They're screaming!" She pushed herself out of the gondola and began to descend the Pleasure Wheel.

Mr. Dennison shouted, "We've got a ladder, for chrissakes. Gomar! Leave off all that and—oh, fine."

Honora scurried down the wheel's timbers, as agile as if she'd transformed into young Effie Bell. She leapt the final fathom and landed on her bare feet. "My daughter. We must go there, now."

Gomar abandoned his fire-quenching—he had managed little more than to set the cuffs of his trousers smoking—and he said to Honora, "Your daughter is called Pansy, yes?"

"Yes," said Honora, "and she's at the Pitch-Round. I know it."

Gomar sprinted to the horses, which were still attached to the wheel engine. "Come, Mr. D We must ready the wagon."

Panicked revivalists were now streaming out of the forest, sprinting past without stopping.

Dennis Dennison concluded that his career as a wheelman had run its course. Yes, it was time to ready the wagon.

With the horses hitched and the last of the leathers secured, Gomar, Dennison, and Honora leapt aboard the wagon. As Gomar readied to snap the reins, Dennison said, "Hang on a minute."

He jumped off, rushed thru the growing wall of flame, and returned with a leather valise which he heaved into the wagon-bed. He bounded in after and landed in Honora's lap. With a wink, he said, "Pennies, my dear. Nothing profiteth like profit."

Gomar lashed the horses forward.

"To the Great Stage!" bellowed Mr. Dennison with the flair of a man who hadn't time to dwell on temporary setbacks.

"What about your Pleasure Wheel?" said Honora.

Dennison regarded the growing inferno. "I hereby donate it to the Revival council."

Honora said, "It truly is a wondrous device."

The wheel was on fire, now, spinning of its own accord in the winds of its destruction.

Sister Honora moaned softly. The beauty of it.

Chapter Eighty-Seven

THERE WAS NO SENSE TO JUNIOR'S THOUGHTS, JUST A CHURNING NEED to drive them out of his misshapen head. He'd done nothing to provoke the animal, and yet it had attacked him, and now it was trying to devour him. No fair. The bear was hungry, yes, but so was Junior.

He dodged a swipe from the bear's black claws, then he leaned in and grabbed it by its side-ears. He pulled its head to his mouth and closed his teeth over the third ear. It vibrated wildly against his tongue, and Junior flinched backward, pulling away. The ear remained attached to the bear's head, minus several strands of fur that had wedged between Junior's incisors.

The bear rose onto her hind legs. Junior tackled her to the ground and pinned her on her back. She clapped her jaws as Junior's hands darted in like copperheads, slapping her ears until she curled into a ball and covered her head with her front paws.

"He's going to kill it!" cried Pansy.

"No he isn't," said Euphémie. "And our *vicieuse* is not an *it*, she is a *her*."

Junior attacked the bear with a series of punches to the back of her neck. He did not cease this until the bear relaxed onto her side, ribs heaving, eyes wandering, whimpering. Junior danced before her, a manic, vengeful child readying himself to dispatch his tormentor.

Euphémie said, "Annie?"

"Yes?" said Annie.

"*Je t'adore.*" Euphémie leapt off the stage.

Annie cried, "*C'est de la folie!*" She made as if to follow her lover, but before she could do so, Pansy grabbed her tightly and dragged her away from the edge.

As Euphémie landed, Junior turned his back to the whimpering bear and faced his *maman*. Obviously, she was upset about something. Perhaps she, too, suffered from the emptiness.

With a voice calm and frigid, Euphémie said, "Look at yourself."

Junior was mess; crooked nose leaking blood over his mouth and chin; one eye nearly swollen shut; a tuft of hair missing from his head. And this was neglecting the bruises and torn muscles and broken ribs that were hidden beneath his clothes, stretched and torn and splattered with liquids that ought to have been buried under a ton of dirt.

Euphémie was not in any great shape herself, but she was far better off than Junior. Her eyes pegged him like lances. Junior recalled one of his father's favorite phrases: You've got your mother's eyes, and my asshole.

Euphémie said, "You can't even speak."

Had he been able to, he would have said, please don't let them put me in that stone box with my father.

He managed only to croak, "*Maman.*"

Euphémie swatted him across the cheek. He lurched backward.

"You have no *maman*."

"*Maman.*"

Euphémie tilted her head.

"*Je vous en pris, Maman.*"

Euphémie sought within his features some portion that was

not repulsive. He averted his eyes. His shoulders drooped. His lips formed wavering shapes.

Euphémie was familiar with this posture. His entire life, Junior had fallen into it whenever he was confronted by Henri. And it had always been immediately followed by a blow from his father's hand.

She recognized herself within this posture. She, too, had shrunk before Henri a thousand times. After each of the thousand blows that had followed, she'd wondered, Do I shrink from Henri because I know he's going to strike? Or does Henri strike me because he hates that I fear him?

So, after all. My son and I have a kinship.

Kinship or not, Euphémie's face remained firm.

All aspects of Junior, his desires, his fears, his loves, his every human emotion had been obscured by a sooty fog from the moment Euphémie had weened him from her breast. What lay behind that fog, she simply did not wish to see.

The amphitheater had cleared of revivalists. The stage-lights hissed and glowed in the night air. Annie and Pansy watched, mute and motionless.

The she-bear's eyes skipped from Junior to Euphémie. Her three ears jittered like bees' wings. With great effort, she heaved herself from her side and onto her belly, remaining there with all four legs splayed wide.

Junior's eyes grew thick with moisture. One of his hands raised as if lifted by a string. It hovered in the atmosphere, trembling violently. Then it began to drift toward Euphémie. As it approached her face, her gaze flitted to it, and then back to Junior's dewy eyes.

His tremoring hand brushed her cheek.

Euphémie allowed some minor part of her body to shift—a squint of an eye, perhaps, or a soft intake of air—a fractional physical acknowledgment of this impossibly difficult situation. It was gesture that Junior had seen from her a thousand times, but which he had never before noted.

He would respond with an unconscious gesture of his own.

When, in later years, Euphémie would recall this moment, and those that immediately followed, she would invariably approach the subject from a distance; observable fact X led to involuntary act Y, which led to inevitable conclusion Z. All other data was to be discarded. Feelings could hold no place, and would never be welcomed, within this portion of her history.

Any suggestion that anything other than animal instinct had been at play, any suggestion that Euphémie had discovered a flicker of love for Junior in that impossibly difficult moment, or that he could have ever wanted to be loved...such a reality would remain dreadful beyond her capacity to carry on.

Junior Deplouc hugged his mother. Euphémie kept her arms at her sides, denying herself any response. Junior squeezed her so tightly that she winced. Pain, yes, but not physical. A tiny *ooh* escaped her mouth.

It was enough.

The she-bear rose up and quietly plunged her teeth into the back of Junior's neck.

The struggle was brief and conclusive.

Euphémie, with her arms still at her sides, whispered, "*Oh, ma vicieuse.*" Her breath came in tiny, half choked spasms.

With her three miraculous ears, the bear heard Euphémie's stuttered respirations; heard three thousand horrified revelers sprinting pell-mell thru the woods; heard a breeze shuffle the branches of ten-thousand trees; heard as clouds collided and then broke apart; heard as flakes of snow begin their haphazard journey earthward; heard the anxious clatter of hooves.

"Back to your cave," said Euphémie. "And take him with you."

The bear was uncertain.

"Do it," said Euphémie.

The three-eared she-bear sank her teeth into the corpse's shoulder and, walking backward, dragged it into the woods and disappeared into the trees.

Annie appeared, now, breathless, half-mad. She shook Euphémie by the arms "What has become of Auguste?"

Chapter Eighty-Eight

SISTER TEMPERANCE HAD DONE HER BEST. WHEN THE CROWD HAD begun chanting for the Little Whistler, she'd remained solemn. When hundreds of hands had borne Auguste to the Great Stage, she'd remained solemn. She'd remained solemn when the Foul Thing had run past her. When Annie had cried for the Solemnites to follow, she'd solemnly followed. When Auguste's noble tones had nearly melted her into a splash of rain, she'd solemnly pushed her way thru the unhappy pilgrims left in the wake of Pansy and the widows.

She'd kept on even as the Foul Thing had jumped on stage and cut short Auguste's noble tones.

It was only when she'd seen Auguste's horrible, stunned face that her solemnity had faltered. She paused just long enough for the crowd to tighten around her, locking her into a swelling and retracting consecration of terror.

Solemnity had no answer for this.

So she began to fight, striking anyone who stood in her way, and she climbed past the old folks on the wooden benches, and, finally, she slipped into the glare of the limelights and faced the Great Stage.

And then the ferocious mass of fur had come sliding toward her.

She scrambled under the stage just as the mass tumbled to the ground. Directly before her, the bear and the Foul Thing rose and faced each other, snorting and shaking off dirt, and now Temperance saw that a third body had fallen. There, between the beasts lay Auguste, senseless and unmoving.

A cry escaped Temperance's lips. At this, the bear's ears—it had three of them!—rotated toward her. The center ear appeared to wave at her, friendly-like. Then the bear dove at the Foul Thing, sending it to stagger backward, and away from the boy.

She knew what she must do, and she did it.

And so it was that, after the implausible three-eared bear had dragged the implausible corpse into the trees, Temperance and Auguste were met by their friends with great relief as they crawled out from under the stage.

Chapter Eighty-Nine

THE PITCH-ROUND WAS FINISHED, THE 1885 ALL TENT REVIVAL WAS in shambles. All that remained now were our Solemnitic emissaries, bloody, bruised, shivering in the cold.

"Where is my mother?" said Pansy.

The first flakes of snow drifted out of the sky.

A quartet of galloping draft horses approached, followed by a wagon. Gomar's adolescent voice shouted *whoa!* and the horses skidded to stop.

From his place on the seat next to Gomar, Mr. Dennison said, "Hell, Sister, you were right."

Honora raised up from the wagon bed. Her eyes met Pansy's and the little girl sprang into her mother's arms.

Mr. Dennison helped the weary Solemnites into the wagon, where they huddled with Honora in one of the foremost corners. Dennison removed a woolen blanket from the tack box and laid it upon their laps. He offered a jug of wine, which Euphémie accepted wordlessly.

"Everybody okay?"

They nodded.

He climbed into the seat and said, "Take us back to Solemn, Gomar."

"No," said Sister Honora.

"Sorry?"

"We're not going back."

"You're serious?"

Honora nodded, and so did the rest of the Solemnites.

"Very well," said Mr. Dennison. "Northward, Gomar."

The young man snapped reins and the horses eagerly obeyed.

They would talk about this all, someday.

The world had grown quiet. Snowflakes accumulated in their eyelashes.

Pansy whispered to Auguste, "I found your teeth." Under the blanket, she passed him the whistles. Their fingers lingered a moment.

"Mother," said Auguste, "may I play a song?"

"Softly," said Annie,

He made a melancholy tune.

Pansy snuggled deep between Auguste and her mother. Within Honora's body, Effie Bell rose and fell upon a great wooden wheel. Annie laid Euphémie's head in her lap and petted her hair. Temperance gazed ahead, to the swirling snow and the horses' bouncing manes.

"Say," said Mr. Dennison, twisting around on the seat, "you wouldn't be the kid everybody was talking about earlier? The whistler?"

"He is," said Pansy. "What of it?"

"Just a thought," said Mr. Dennison. He turned to the road ahead. "It'll save for tomorrow. Whistle us onward, Monsieur Stables!"

"It's *Lestables*, Mr. Dennison," said Gomar.

"Yes, Gomar, but how *many* tables? How *many*?"

The horses skipped into a canter and led the wagon under the stars and the clouds and the snow and the trees, and they all partook of the thick air of a tragic winter's evening in southern Indiana.

APPENDIX
How To Speak Stables

EUPHÉMIE

French pronunciation: *OOH-FEY-MI*

American pronunciation: *you-FUH-MI*

AUGUSTE

French pronunciation: *OW-GOOS-TUH*

American pronunciation: *AH-GUSSED*

ANNIE

French pronunciation: *AH-NEE*

American pronunciation: *AN-EE*

LESTABLES

In France, Lestables (as in *les tables*, meaning "the tables") would have been pronounced *lay-tah-bluh*. Americans universally mis-translated *les tables* as *le stables* which they pronounced, per the uncertain rules of English as *lay-stay-bulls*. This misunderstanding is somewhat explained by the fact that *Lestables* was an anomaly even in France, where surnames almost never employ the plural. The name should properly have been *Latable*, which looks just as odd in French as it does in English, this being a possible explanation for the shift from one-table to more-than-one-table. In any event, they'll soon change their name to "Stables" at which point the *tables*-related confusion will be replaced by confusion with the gospel/soul/R&B group, the Staples Singers.

A TERMINAL NOTE FROM AUTHOR, C.I. STABLES

I was recently contacted by an individual who claims to have found a substantial trove of Stables Family documents within the belongings of a deceased relative.

For this reason, and others that I prefer not to disclose, my "ghostwriter", Gregory Hill, has been dismissed from this project.

Form No. 168.

THE WESTERN UNION TELEGRAPH COMPANY.
INCORPORATED
23,000 OFFICES IN AMERICA.   CABLE SERVICE TO ALL THE WORLD.

This Company TRANSMITS and DELIVERS messages only on conditions limiting its liability, which have been assented to by the sender of the following message. Errors can be guarded against only by repeating a message back to the sending station for comparison, and the Company will not hold itself liable for errors or delays in transmission or delivery of Unrepeated Messages, beyond the amount of tolls paid thereon, nor in any case where the claim is not presented in writing within sixty days after the message is filed with the Company for transmission.
This is an UNREPEATED MESSAGE, and is delivered by request of the sender, under the conditions named above.
ROBERT C. CLOWRY, President and General Manager.

RECEIVED   Last Chance Line OCT 3 2022   170

    MR HILL
    YOU NO LONGER WORK FOR ME STOP

    CI STABLES COUNTRY STAR LAST CHANCE COLO

                                        DT SF

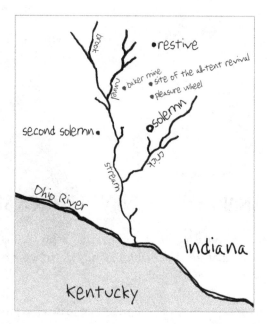

Solemn and its environs

Artist's rendering of Solemn, Indiana

ACKNOWLEDGMENTS

Maureen Hearty (love!), Paul Handley (Kris Kringle kindred!), Mom (*Okay by me in America!*), Rebecca Hill (pink purple polka dots!), Paul Epstein (chef's kiss!), Brett Duesing (holistic everythingness!), Terry Welty (retroactive bonus for helping with the final sentence of Zebra Skin Shirt, and for reading the entirety of that novel aloud under torturous circumstances!), Chris Slough (the diminished scale!), Eric Allen (archivist of my memories!), Marrion Irons (unfuckwithablity!), Mike Molnar (for typing the phrase "Lizard King of Manitoba"!), Mark Stevens (solidarity!), Sarah Megyesy (lesbian fact check!), Debbie Hearty (Prussians!), Lisa Graziano (kindness!), Sylvie Parker (French consultant, title inventor!), Mike Lindstrom (precision!), Cory Casciato (Ether Diver!), Bob Clark (rickshaw!), Hunter Maul (just because!), Jacey Tramutt (more solidarity!), Amy Carbone (V7 to I, baby!), Michael Welty (that one time!), Andy Gross (micro mega music!), all the people who've allowed me to read their unpublished manuscripts (you *exist*, gawd-dammit!), Tony Parella (Tristram kissed 'im!), Chuck Cuthill (blackout, man!), Zach Boddicker (ear key!), Tom Dodds (Western Electric!), Kirstin Stoltz (graphic content!), and Jason Francis McDaniel (for suggesting, in a motel in Jackson, Wyoming, that we start a fake band called the Stables Boys, which we didn't do!).

I forgot some folks.

Gregory Hill lives on the anarchic High Plains of eastern Colorado where he writes novels, makes odd music, and frequently wonders why.

You may learn more at www.gregoryhillauthor.com.

Rebecca Hill and her little brother, December 1979

9 798218 081690